The GLORIOUS East Wind

K.G.E. KONKEL

Random House
Toronto

Published in Canada in 1987 by Random House of Canada Limited.

Canadian Cataloguing in Publication Data

Konkel, K. G. E.
  The glorious east wind

ISBN 0-394-22018-8

I. Title.

PS8571.064G58 1987   C813'.54   C87-094243-3
PR9199.3.K66G58 1987

DESIGN: Brant Cowie/Artplus Limited
COVER ILLUSTRATION: Ken Suzana

Printed in Canada

*To my mother Ann, my father Edward
and especially to my dear wife, Robin.*

This novel contains many places you will no longer find in Hong Kong. They have been torn down to make way for the future. The people who once lived in them have moved elsewhere or gone to their final rest in the mists of England or the tiered slopes of the New Territories.

But such is the way of the world. Things change and so do people. Perhaps it is better that way.

CHAPTER ONE

At the shipping office in Rayong, an elfin man he had never seen before had given him the sealed envelope and instructions, a gray envelope with official red trim wrapped in a postdated money order for five thousand U.S. dollars. When he'd left to make certain the draft was safe at the Bank of Siam, the unlisted cargo was already being loaded in the hold of his ship and a single sealed carton had been placed in his cabin.

Now, the pasty-faced Thai captain sat like a Shan warlord, surveying his domain from atop his lonely perch in the wheelhouse of the ramshackle freighter. It was almost six o'clock in the morning, nearly time, according to instructions, to open the sealed envelope. Behind him the night was still, slowly rolling back like a dark satin sheet on the China Sea. Ahead, a thin ridge of light haloed out: ivory, flaxen, lemon rays of sunlight reaching to touch huge formations of clouds.

As if for reassurance, he tapped the pocket of his faded coveralls, the only uniform he wore at sea. The sound of the rustling envelope broke the silence and the Fukienese first mate looked up from his fixed position over his charts and template.

"Yes, captain, sir?" he asked nervously.

"What are you staring at, you wormy bastard?" the captain bellowed, causing the first mate to cringe. "Get on with it or we'll never make Nagasaki."

The stifling heat of the wheelhouse was too much to bear, and the captain moved outside to the bridge. He couldn't decide which he hated more, the sniveling crew or the confining spaces of his World War Two vintage tramp coaster. He thought of his money at the bank in Rayong and of the whores in Bangkok he could chase around never-ending red-walled rooms once his run was over.

He belched and glanced back quickly to see if the helmsman or the first mate smirked. Bastards, he thought. He knew his stomach troubles were the basis of a string of jokes by the crew.

Neither man looked up. The captain turned back, popped a mint from a mangled roll in his patch pocket and straightened the baseball cap on his head. Once royal blue with the letters KC emblazoned on it in gold Gothic print, the cap had been a gift from a U.S. Air Force supply sergeant at Udon Thani, the B52 bomber base in the poverty-filled northeast pocket of Thailand. For the captain, those had been more opportune and, eventually, more disastrous times. Salt-stained, filthy with grease and faded to an uneven azure by the brutal China Sea sun, the cap left his head only in port. At sea, where he slept rarely and felt safer topside, it remained firmly planted, completely covering his bristling crew cut and shading his deep-set eyes.

"Please, captain, sir?"

The Fukienese mate had approached silently, his voice as respectful as he could make it.

"You're lower than whale shit at the bottom of the ocean," the captain bellowed.

"Yes, sir, captain," the mate agreed, nodding.

"What is it now?"

"You asked to be told when it was six o'clock, sir."

"And?"

"It is six o'clock, captain sir."

"Then say so, damn it."

The captain swept past the cowering mate and headed through a small draped opening at the rear of the wheelhouse, down a narrow galley way and into the cramped cabin that was his home at sea.

It reeked of Japanese whiskey and sweaty Burmese teak floors. The walls were sunflower yellow and peeling from moisture and age. The deck was spotted with odd-shaped remnants of greasy chocolate-colored rugs, which stank of diesel oil.

The captain heard a rustling as he entered the semidark room. He clucked his tongue gently.

"Loo, loo, loo," he whispered.

A curious *caw-chirp* sound greeted him.

"Good morning," he cooed. In the cabin corner a white, sulphur-crested cockatoo on a plum-colored perch winked knowingly. The bird was named Put Put, and it normally screamed and shrieked with the same stubborn persistence as its master. Put Put was the captain's only friend, a remnant, along with a faded photograph on the bulkhead wall and the glass-framed diploma on the opposite bulkhead, of better times, times of pressed whites, shiny Oxfords and aviator glasses.

The photo was of Bhumibol Adulyadej, Rama IX, King of Thailand. The diploma, signed by the monarch, granted a commission of first lieutenant in the Royal Thai Navy. There was no discharge paper alongside. The captain's parting from the fold of the Siamese seafarers had not been the most honorable.

He sat at his desk, turned on the gooseneck lamp and broke the seal of the envelope. After reading the letter twice, he opened the carton that had been placed in his cabin. The instructions in the envelope described what was to be done with the cans of paint and the blood-red flag with the yellow stars that were in the carton. The letter made no mention of the cargo in the hold. He wondered about it only a moment, then caught himself. He was paid to carry out instructions, a dog's body, a "go for." Other go fors would obviously be concerned about the cargo once he reached port. He would do better thinking about the pleasures his money would buy in Bangkok.

He stood up and headed back to the wheelhouse.

The leaden air and sky hinted it would be a hot and stormy day at sea. There would be rain before nightfall.

The first mate was once again bent over his charts. The helmsman, dozy-eyed and barefoot, was slumped half awake against the huge oak wheel. The captain viciously jabbed the helmsman in the ribs and turned to the first mate.

"Piss on those scribblings," he said. "We're changing course."

Within minutes, like a cranky sea turtle, broad-nosed and resisting, the ancient freighter began to turn due north across the emerald South China Sea toward its new destination, the "fragrant harbor," Hong Kong.

An old air conditioner coughed out puffs of cold air from its place by the windows. The dawn light that crept in was vague, icy blue. The room, with its many shadows, was softened by the touch. Outside, along Queens Road, a tram clanged by on its lonely run to Kennedy Town. Somewhere in the building the growl of a hearty Chinese curse echoed off the walls. There was the sound of men's laughter followed by the hollow slamming of doors. Then, silence.

David Andrews turned over in his bed, yawned and slowly roused from his sleep. He sat up and stretched as if to challenge the demons that had once again tormented his dreams, voices that for weeks had mocked and urged him to resign.

He brushed his hand over his face, sighed and looked around the room. The police station known as Western was an old building, and the single quarters were not well kept. The ceilings were high and patched; stained rusty from moisture, they buckled in places where the plaster had fallen in despair. Most of the walls were veined with cracks, the paint peeling.

In the far corner of his room stood a cheap rattan chair. On it lay his police tunic and summer Bermudas, neatly folded, his Sam Browne belt spun tightly in a loop resting atop them, forage cap to one side. Beneath the chair was a pair of Oxfords, low-cut, spit-shone, prepared for the night's duties.

The furniture in the room was drab and functional. Had the barrack sergeant at Western not been over budget and desperate to fill the gaping spaces in the single inspectors' quarters, the pieces would have remained buried forever in the darkest recesses of some government warehouse. There was a commode, two chests of drawers and a writing table that now held letters, paperwork and a photograph of an older couple in a silver filigreed frame. A dun-colored sofa, its hopsack material worn and patched, shared part of the length of one wall with a cracked full-length mirror. On the back of the door was a China Products calendar with the dates crossed off to Sunday, August twentieth.

David got out of bed, wrapped himself in his old cotton dressing gown and shuffled over to the writing table, his feet padding on the cold tile floor. He rustled impatiently through the papers till he found what he was looking for, the note he'd written in the early morning hours, the note that might finally put an end to his torment.

Folded neatly three times, it was in a plain envelope placed near the portrait. He carefully opened it up.

Black on white, his own words now mocked him. Resignation. Just what the bastards would want me to do, he thought. Leave the Force. After he'd fought them tooth and nail, fought to save his reputation and integrity against the innuendoes and lies. And now, weary from the fight, it seemed almost done.

Almost. And, if he signed the document, they would all be proven right.

He thought back to a dreary February morning six months ago. Brendan Williams, his best friend, newly transferred into Narcotics Bureau, had been found dead in the officer's mess at Western. A sloppy death, an apparent suicide, it was awkwardly brushed under the rug for the family's sake and, as David had bitterly reasoned, for the force's image.

He'd never believed the gossip, the rumors that Williams had taken money from a mysterious drug dealer on the Ko Shing, the warehouse district where most of the colony's heroin was manufactured, while he was working the drug squad. But the rumors had floated around the force after his death, lingering to envelop David, so that he, too, was suspect.

The talk, the stares and finally the cold shoulders had slowly worn David down; now the letter of resignation awaited only his signature.

He peered wistfully out the window. Below him, the buildings of Western district slumped like so many misshapen sacks of flour, filling the lowland to the waterline and stretching outward to the far horizon of Central. He could see it all, the tottering tenements, bulky, bland godowns, razor-edged high-rises piercing the sky. And then the harbor: junks tied up along Waterfront Road, bobbing like caps on a calliope, their company flags cracking in the brisk offshore breeze, the rough waters muddy brown in the morning tide.

And the Peak. Victoria. The great green wall towering over the colony, wreathed in soft mist in the morning sun.

He paused in thought. Damn it! He wasn't going to give up yet. There had to be something out there, someone in the stinking rat maze around him who had an answer to Brendan's death. And, with it, his own salvation from this purgatory.

Williams had had a girl friend, a bar girl named Mei Ling. It was an unusual match, the tubby Englishman and the lithesome Chinese, but they'd seemed to enjoy each other's company. David had known Mei well. Quite well, he mused. In fact, he had introduced Williams to her more than a year ago and watched as their friendship had apparently blossomed.

He knew the squads had talked at length to Mei soon after Williams's body was found. It was a foregone conclusion, of course, that they would have raked her over the coals. A police death in such suspicious circumstances, and a man who'd worked for Special Branch and Narcotics to boot. He couldn't blame them for seeking her out. Then, because of his growing unease about the matter, within days of the discovery he'd quietly tried to do the same.

But when he'd gone down to Wanchai to look for Mei soon after the tragedy, she'd vanished.

He'd been to Popeye's, where she'd been working when Brendan died. The barkeep had been noncommittal, if not downright surly. She was no longer in the house employ.

Then he'd gone to Joe-Joes, the Philippino body rub in Tsim Tsi, another place she'd been seen. Again no luck. Mei was nowhere to be found. The girls had said not to worry, that she was okay. It was just that she'd had enough heat and she wanted to be left alone. No amount of coaxing, no amount of flash money could convince them otherwise. Mei would appear again in good time.

After a few months of wandering the streets and checking old police reports without a lead, David's interests had waned, only to be replaced by thoughts of resignation in the face of all the innuendo about both himself and Williams. There seemed nothing else he could do.

Till now. He looked down at his words and anger once again welled up inside him. He'd always had the haunting suspicion that Mei might know something about Williams's death, something that she'd held back, for whatever reason, from the other investigators. He had to find out—if for nothing else than to calm the demons inside him.

He shaved and showered and, ritual complete, dressed. As he did so, he rang down to the bar and spoke to the mess boy. He'd have coffee and toast with marmalade for breakfast and, yes, if anyone asked for him he'd be out for the rest of the day.

The chamber was at the end of a long corridor on the sixth floor of the Bank of China building, a chamber not easily found or entered without permission or purpose. High-ceilinged, finished in muted pastels and furnished with Scandinavian pieces, it was not in keeping with the proletarian austerity of the rest of the building, but its occupant had never intended it to be. Despite the source of the rent check, it was his chamber, not the people's.

Three huge imposing windows overlooked the square, the bustling harbor and the distant hills. A washed-out portrait of Lenin stared with unfeeling eyes at an indefinite East. At the other end of the room hung a van Gogh print and another by Renoir.

To lesser souls, this bourgeois extravagance would have been fatal, but Lee Shiu Shing was too old, too wise, too influential in the Party. His staff was carefully chosen and quite willing to overlook their director's eccentricities and independence of thought.

He had been there since four in the morning, before the sweepers had left the building. The director of the Resource Section of the Bank of China was a busy man.

Situation reports, clippings and papers had been read and lay in a neat pile on the teapoy by the lounge chair. His notations, in bold stroke, were on the comment sheet to one side, ready for his secretary. He glanced over to his desk clock. Six. Somewhere on an old coaster in the China Sea the envelope was being opened at this very moment, its contents being read, his project, with all its complexities, being set into motion.

Keep him out of their little schemes, would they? Well, he thought, he would see about that. And very quickly.

Lee walked to a window, his shoes resounding on the shiny hardwood floor, and gazed out at the city. In the harbor, lighters, like brown tackwood maggots, snuggled alongside the rust-hided tramp steamers, their spindly loading derricks feverishly removing produce. Below him, commuters by the dozens debarked from green trams and red double-decker buses and walked across the square toward the ferry berths. To his right, the limed domes of the Supreme Court and the smooth lawns of the cricket club completed a picture of the Crown colony of Hong Kong.

The copper sky was turning orange. It was going to be a blistering-hot August day. To the north, the distant mauve hills of the Kowloon Peninsula, dim with heat haze, held promise of heavy rain.

Lee rang a buzzer. An aide brought Earl Grey tea and cookies sweet with almond paste. He drank the tea and ate the cookies in silence, then picked up the phone, dialing the numbers with some difficulty. The arthritis that had been a petty and bothersome nuisance in earlier years had become worse.

"Wei? Hello?" He gazed up at the van Gogh. An answer at the other end. "Is that you, my dear friend?" Lee's voice was toneless. "Tonight. Green Island Cement at Kennedy Town. Pier Four. Eleven o'clock."

As a voice chirped on the line, Lee picked up a pen and jotted down some figures.

"The Metropole restaurant, North Point. Fifteen orders of chau mein with side orders of beef, shrimp, chicken and *garoupa*. Thirty bottles of San Miguel, the big green ones. And three bottles of Remy Martin for the captain, for services rendered." He closed his free hand then opened it, absently considering the veins. "Yes, quite right. It's only fitting. The cost? Just place it on my chit. The maître d' knows me very well." His eyes narrowed. "And the surprise? It will be ready for later in the night? When they are asleep?" The chirping once more. "Good. Their dreams till then should be very pleasant." He lingered over the last words; after a moment he slowly put the phone back on its cradle.

A portly European in beige slacks and blue blazer strolled up to the patio of the cricket club. The sprinklers on the lawn laced the air with misted rainbows. The man sat in a wicker chair in the shade. A Chinese waiter in a starched white coat appeared and brought him the morning paper. Day in Hong Kong had begun.

CHAPTER TWO

Near the southwest tip of the tiny island of Miao
Wan, less than ten hours' sailing time from its
new berth at the Green Island Cement Company
at Hong Kong, the mangy freighter doggedly
plowed the seas. Her Liberian flag of convenience had been
replaced. Around the bulkhead and across her prow, freshly
painted, she wore a new name.

David spent the better part of the morning in Wanchai looking for Mei Ling, but with a singular lack of success. Mei had
stopped coming around her usual haunts about two months
ago and no one knew, or would say, where she was now. It
was only by chance that he'd asked Bun, the hunchback news
vendor, about the girl and found out she now worked in
Lulu's, an armpit of a bar off Hennessy Road.

It was just after noon when he arrived. There weren't
many patrons in the place. An Aussie frigate with its brash
crowd of pommie-bashing navvies had left the evening before
and it was too early for the business special.

The room was dark as pitch and stank of stale air. The few
bar girls who worked the floor sat huddled together by the
jukebox drinking their softs and chattering like magpies. They
looked up expectantly when he parted the shabby, beaded curtain that hung over the entrance. Eyes heavy with mascara followed him to the stand-up bar, then lost interest when it was

apparent he wanted something other than creature comforts.

The pockmarked Russian who mixed the drinks had more mouth than business sense and a heated discussion took place about Mei's whereabouts. He'd never heard of the woman; she didn't exist here at Lulu's; and he didn't care if Andrews was police. He had nothing to hide.

But all was smoothed over when Andrews offered Ivan a fifty for his trouble. And Ivan developed the power of instant recall when saw another fifty.

She'd been around, though the police attention had been annoying to some people, so she'd been sent to the houses that serviced the airstrip at Sek Kong in the New Territories. That is, till very recently.

Another twenty and his memory improved even more.

David offered him a pen and paper. After looking furtively around the room, he scribbled a few words.

"It didn't come from me, right?" he whispered anxiously, then turned and was gone.

The address, 16 SeaBreeze Terrace, sounded grand, but the building was nothing more than a tumbledown slum on the waterfront, leaning wearily for salvation against similarly decrepit tenements.

He took the back staircase, following the directions he'd been given. The steps groaned under his weight. A fire door crashed open on the second landing and a ferret-faced addict ran out, pushing Andrews aside as he tumbled into the bowels of the building, feverishly seeking his supplier.

David reached the fifth floor, opened the door and made his way in semidarkness down the hallway.

The stench of urine and steaming rice was overpowering. The walls were cracked, the lath exposed where someone had attempted unsuccessfully to repair the plumbing. Rusty brown pipes gaped through the holes and the floor was littered with dog shit and broken needles. Pieces of tin foil shone in the half-light. The addicts had been busy. The white rice had been flowing.

He found the room at the end of the hall. The wooden number nine was gone and had left a grimy shadow. He knocked and heard sounds from within.

The door opened slightly and Mei Ling's face appeared in the opening. He'd forgotten how beautiful she was.

She started when she saw him. "David," she whispered. There was a moment's pause.

"Hello," he said simply.

She nodded.

"May I come in? I'll only be a minute."

She hesitated.

"Please?"

She opened the door slowly and he walked past her into the tiny flat.

Inside, the heat was stifling; the air felt as thick as soy paste and stank of cabbage, sweat and dirty linen. A woman's undergarments hung from a rope stretched across the room; there were also babies' diapers, which dripped soiled water onto a floor covered with newspapers and table scraps.

In one corner stood a bunk bed with its grimy sheets tossed about, and beside it was a cheap, pastel-pink crib.

She caught his stare. "It's my roommate," she blurted apologetically. "She's got a baby daughter. They've gone out." She looked away.

"It's been a long time, Mei," he said quietly. "Where have you been?"

"Places," she replied abstractly. "They sent me places."

She took a backless chair from a corner and motioned for him to sit down. He took the chair and Mei sat on the edge of the bed.

"The police attention after Brendan was too much for them. It was bad for business," she said matter-of-factly.

"You still work, then," he began, but her hurt look told him not to press. "It's been a long time since we talked."

"What do you want from me, David?" she interrupted him. "I've told them everything I know."

"Why do you think he died, Mei?"

"You ask me?" Her eyes glazed over. "I slept with him, David. That was all."

"And he confided in you."

She laughed a short, ironic laugh. "You're naive, trusting. You always were." Her features turned serious. "Why should he confide in me?"

"I know you, Mei. You had the gift."

She shook her head and looked away, not wanting to meet his eyes. "You're too generous, David."

He looked at her without responding.

After a time, Mei felt compelled to break the silence. "We talked. Of course we talked. But it wasn't anything important. Cheap talk. Lover's talk. You know . . ." She stopped. Her eyes hardened.

"He said nothing then?"

Her voice was a whisper. "It isn't healthy to dwell on the dead like this, David. They should rest in peace." She got up from the bed. "Can I make you tea?" she asked.

David nodded.

She rummaged under the bed till she found an old kettle, then went over to the chipped sink and turned on the tap. The spigot rattled as the brackish fluid sputtered out.

David watched her movements. Tall, lithe, she was a very beautiful woman. Her black pajamas did little to hide her figure. Her hair, her pride and joy, was silky smooth to the touch. He hesitated before speaking once more.

"I'd like to see you again, Mei."

She paused and turned to him. There was genuine surprise in her eyes.

"When?"

"Tuesday?"

Moments passed. Her face was expressionless when finally she spoke.

"All right, David. It has, as you say, been a long time. A very long time. How do you like your tea? Western or Chinese? I'm afraid I've forgotten."

Robert Maguire, director of Special Branch, passed the dish of curried prawns to the squat Malay seated across from him. "Care for some more?" Maguire's manner was as cheery as if he were at an Oxford tea.

Winston Chin brushed the napkin across his lips. "No, no.

I've had enough, Robert." And a touch too much brandy as well, thought Maguire.

Their other luncheon companion, a consort of Winston's with the unlikely Western name of Precious Ibrahim Raman, did not speak often, but nodded at regular intervals. Raman spoke no English and Maguire knew no Tamil. Civility, after all, had its limits. But the man's plate had been emptied after two full helpings, so all was not lost.

Behind them, golfers gracefully drove balls down a narrow fairway framed by bunyan trees and Chinese fir. Golf carts putted around the trim greens. The perfume of blooming bougainvillaea filled the humid summer day. In the distance, traffic raced on Route One to the Sek Kong airstrip.

The meal had been a placid affair. The usual pleasantries had been exchanged, small talk about the weather, the Asia Cup, the fine cuisine, with both parties tactfully skirting the issue of money.

Maguire had been briefed by the governor: Say nothing contentious; hum, haw, defer; in short, be the perfect host to his counterparts in the Malay State Security office. Winston's superior, the sultan of an obscure state in the Cameron High-lands north of Kuala Lumpur, an innocuous and thoroughly distasteful gremlin of a man, was at this moment being properly entertained at the Mirimar Hotel by a lady friend of Maguire's.

A Royal Hong Kong Police security team was covering the dalliance. Winston and Raman's presence was not required outside the room while the sultan rutted like a pig within, so Maguire had offered to take them on a tour of Hong Kong they would never forget.

The Malays had been suitably impressed. Maguire obviously knew all the right places and, more importantly, all the right people in the colony. With the support of some of them, he had bypassed most of his peers in the police force on his way toward the top.

As he selected a warm bun from the basket, cut it open and placed a cold pat of butter on it, he reflected on how much he had been making of those contacts, and they of him, in recent weeks.

His chit at the Fanling Golf and Country Club showed more than his usual number of "official" visits. Maguire knew his guests came to Hong Kong for more than the Chinese cuisine, the tailor shops and the duty-free liquor and U.S. cigarettes. With the British lease on Hong Kong negotiated away, the colony was living on borrowed time. The thrust now was to make an attractive economic package, to keep the mainland Chinese at bay until the day Communist troops replaced the British at the Botanic Road entrance to Government House. And that, in the mind of the new governor, Sir Thomas Driscoll, included attracting investment capital that would benefit past masters and be irresistible to the future rulers of the tiny territory, or at least to make the appearance of doing so.

The word had quietly filtered out. The Hong Kong government offered an enormous business opportunity to selected takers, uncommonly lucrative even by Asian standards. The colony was actively soliciting potential partners for a huge project in Kwantung Province, just north of the border: a super airport for 747s and Concorde flights, to be located within twenty miles of Canton.

The scheme was to be enacted with the People's Republic of China. As the scrambling of prospective suitors—including, in his more sober moments, Winston's randy superior, the sultan—would seem to indicate, the venture was certainly worthy of serious consideration.

But the crowning jewel of them all still loomed misty and unspoken on the business horizon: a rumored transaction investors might kill to have a part of.

A powerful consortium was supposedly divesting itself of assets worth billions of dollars on the open market. The Peninsula Hotel, the Ocean Terminal complex, broad sections of Nathan Road, the famed Kowloon Golden Mile, fully seven tenths of the harbor frontage off Canton Road on the scenic west side of the Tsim Tsi district—in effect, much of the Kowloon Peninsula—were allegedly available for the right price in the bidder's envelope.

It was an invitation to make rickshaw-loads of money if one had the "in." But few people did. The deal was very mysterious and very, very exclusive. Maguire knew that no one had talked, and that, he had been told, was the way it would remain.

Winston coughed. A second time.

"Do you think His Excellency the Sultan will be successful?" The voice was slightly slurred.

Maguire looked up with what appeared to be intense concentration as he spread the melting butter on his bun.

"I beg your pardon?"

Winston cleared his throat and repeated the question.

Maguire leaned forward. "I'm led to believe," he said softly, "the female is surmountable."

Winston burst out laughing.

"And the other?" he whispered like an excited child gleefully sharing a secret. "He has a chance despite the local investors?"

Maguire poured some brandy into his glass, none into Winston's.

Winston glanced at Raman, who looked back benignly as he munched on some dried apricots from a side dish, his glasses reflecting the bright sun.

Winston smiled and nodded, then looked at Maguire. His voice was sober, expectant. "Robert?"

Maguire took a bite of his bun. When he next spoke it was with the slightest trace of condescension. "Our citizens know that by our agreement with the People's Republic of China our lease for the Crown colony of Hong Kong expires in 1997. That knowledge has made them somewhat less than eager to enter into investment schemes in the region."

"I see, Robert." Winston coyly turned his head. "Then there is some concern among your entrepreneurs, both white and Chinese. . . ." The smile left his face. "Do they perhaps not worry about the loss of economic freedom under the new rulers? The loss of, say, their existing property rights?"

Maguire sat back in his chair. He bit into his bun once more. "We have been assured by the Chinese premier there will be no loss, and we accept that assurance as fact. For Hong Kong, the Chinese Communists maintain it will be business as usual, albeit under a new master."

Chin gazed around the room. "You can promise them this?" He spoke in a hushed voice.

"Most assuredly, my dear Winston." Maguire nodded to the north. "They can, and they will." He emphasized the last words. Then he calmly finished his flaky bun, sliced open another, picked a pat of butter from the tray with a deft jab and jammed it on the bread.

"You see, Winston, the Chinese are not fools. Hong Kong is land. This tiny territory is important to China not only because of its prudent location at the mouth of the Pearl, but because of its physical essence. Empires of steel and concrete wrenched out of barren soil give it meaning and worth."

A waiter hovered near the table. Maguire quietly motioned him off, then continued.

"The very soul of Hong Kong and its people is written into the rock faces and etched into the hillsides of the colony. The mainland Chinese cannot allow the struggles of their long-lost brothers against time and nature to seem meaningless upon repatriation.

"Therefore, they will not allow the land values to tumble, else this place will be no more than a granite millstone around their necks. The property we call Hong Kong is of great importance to the Peking authorities, no less than to us 'corrupt capitalists.'" He smiled. "That reality will not be allowed to change, regardless of who rules."

Winston looked bemused. "And yet they will not invest in the airport proposal for Canton. . . ."

"Perhaps they have not been told," Maguire replied impatiently. He winked to soften the effect of his words, then offered Winston more brandy. The Malay tactfully accepted.

They drank, considering the tone of the conversation and perhaps their respective realities. Raman sat between them, smiling nonsensically.

Winston broke the silence. "My sources indicate there might be another financial scheme in the offing. One far more impressive than the one offered to my sultan." His eyes narrowed. "One not generally known."

Maguire's voice was like fingernails rasping on slate. "That, dear chap, is pure conjecture. The sultan would benefit greatly from the most gracious proposal now being offered by His Excellency, the governor, in Kwantung Province. Nothing more and nothing less."

Winston moved forward in his chair. "Are those your true feelings in the matter?" he persisted. "Is there not, in fact, a vast opportunity your governor has kept from my superior? A massive land deal on the Kowloon Peninsula?" There was an edge in his voice.

Maguire's stare was withering. "Winston, my friend, our superiors command and we respond. In my case, the governor has commanded that I act as your host, and I have been delighted to do so." He smiled a wooden smile. "It would be ungracious of me to question beyond so pleasant an assignment, to delve tactlessly into higher matters of state and finance without permission. Don't you agree?" He arched his eyebrows.

"Of course." The Malay nodded impatiently. "But your own feelings? Your professional instincts?" He ponderously pronounced the last words. "There is something more, is there not? Something you are not telling me."

The smile left Maguire's face. His manner was suddenly distant, cold. He knew his impatience showed and, for the moment, he didn't much care. "We are survivors, you and I, Superintendent Chin. Our opinion is rarely sought on certain matters, and we do not volunteer it unsolicited. Neither do we compromise our superiors through idle or misleading chatter. It is through the successful exercise of that discretion, both with our masters and with our equals, that we may continue to enjoy the pleasures of our respective offices." His point made, Maguire's features softened. "Have I made myself sufficiently obtuse?"

For a moment Winston Chin was tempted to accept the challenge and probe further. He paused and let his mind wander past the questions he burned to ask, let it wander until it settled on his family, his mistress and his household of seven to feed and clothe and shelter.

"I do believe I will have some more food, Robert." He motioned timidly to the rice tray. Maguire passed it over. Chin waited a discreet while, then made a small joke, hiding behind the laughter, realizing that it was just what Maguire wished him to do and knowing he could do nothing else.

Maguire laughed politely. Raman joined in between loud slurps of ginger ale, even though he didn't understand a word being said, then he turned to Winston. They chatted amiably in Malay for a moment, both glancing over at a comely young girl seated nearby. The girl looked away angrily.

Winston fiddled with the cutlery. "My friend and I were wondering . . . if perhaps . . . you could arrange . . . a lady friend or two?" He lifted his eyebrows curiously but avoided Maguire's gaze.

Maguire's face was bland, expressionless. "Certainly, Winston. Most certainly. Excuse me for just a moment."

He returned to the table after a few short calls on a safe line. "Arranged," he said. "Another round, gentlemen?" With a flourish, Maguire offered the brandy to Winston, then poured a topper for himself. Raman opened another bottle of ginger ale.

The clock on the mantelpiece trilled the hour. Two in the afternoon. Everything's arranged, Winston, Maguire thought snidely. Two girls, suitably white. One hotel room, suitably furnished. And three hidden cameras, suitably rolling, just in case.

He sipped his brandy slowly. Perhaps these monkeys in Malay State security didn't worry about their reputation, Maguire reasoned to himself, but Hong Kong Special Branch did. The cameras? They were there just in case things didn't go as planned.

CHAPTER THREE

———

The little tramp struggled north by northeast into the Sulphur Channel and the beckoning refuge of Hong Kong harbor. The open waters of the sound were treacherous and the captain stayed on the bridge.

He wore a slickered raincoat that shone like patent leather and, with his now-sodden baseball cap sticking wildly from his head, he screeched commands into the accordioned voice pipe. He was in his realm, and the ship was in excellent hands.

The storm had burst upon them suddenly, a summer shower full of virulent fury and unpredictability, but likely to expend itself quickly.

Ahead of them, rising and falling in the choppy gray-green swells, was an ancient junk, its yellow batwing sail broken loose and fluttering in the headwind. It came crashing and yawing out of the downpour, across the tramp's bow, missing by scant inches. Then, just as swiftly, it disappeared in the deluge, its diesel motor whining until the echo was lost in the wind.

In the captain's cabin, Put Put slept on his perch.

Sweat. David could feel the smothering heat; it was almost ninety, and the monsoon humidity made the steam rise out of the colony's narrow alleys. After midnight, old Sai Ying

Poon, the Western waterfront, became like a Ming ancestral tomb, large and still, dark and foreboding. Rotten-timbered junks lay side by side, creaking and swaying in the dank August breeze that wafted through the narrow channel from North Point.

The sharp smells of bamboo and sea salt, spice and over-ripe vegetable greens mixed with the stench and steam of the tired tenements that crowded one another for precious space and inched from the sea up the rugged face of Victoria Peak. "Bombay bombers," cockroaches the size of a human thumb, and rats a foot long, sleek and slimy, scurried around. Putrid mounds of garbage were piled haphazardly in the street to await the morning *lap sap* sweeper.

David passed through the arching colonnades that graced Des Voeux Road West. He wore the light-green safari suit, olive knee socks and blue hose toppings that marked the RHKP *bomban,* an inspector in the Royal Hong Kong Police.

Newspapers rustled in the hot wind. A thousand tiny black windows peered down at him from behind a thousand metal typhoon grills. He flashed his light into the alleyway at Sutherland Street near the Bank of America: more garbage, beggars' rags and beggars asleep on cardboard mats. The sign at the Luen Wah fish market squeaked. A child coughed. Here and there a few joss sticks were stuck into buckets of gravel. Yellowed bundles of bamboo were stacked like long, knotted toothpicks. He moved past a hoarding, boards broken, warning lanterns extinguished and, behind it, a weary building scaffold, a skeleton of cross-laced bamboo. Mud tracks, heaps of litter, pools of oil-slicked water were everywhere.

In the distance, to the north, separated by the black, hulk-ing mass of Stonecutter's Island with its twinkling telegraph masts and the myriad shapes of merchantmen slumbering in silence, glowed the neon and tinsel, the million lights of Kowloon.

In the close night air Andrews softly whistled easy lilting Highland melodies that trickled strangely through the de-serted Chinese alleys. When he ran out of tunes to whistle he trod silently on, feeling the heat pressing down on him like black molasses.

His patrol took two hours and covered four and a half miles. He had forty men under his command to check, in a routine that never seemed to vary.

David Andrews was a shade over thirty and had been in Hong Kong for five years. He'd been the route, written his promotionals, done uniform work, tactical work, CID. While in the Criminal Investigation Department, he'd done a stint at police headquarters where he'd taken the place of an anemic Liverpudlian forever off with the flu. During his time there he'd been partnered with a local chief inspector named James Peng. Andrews and Peng had gotten along and David had hoped that the move was permanent. But before the ink was dry on the paper, his transfer was in again and he was back in uniform, doing duty rosters and evaluations, wearing down his soles on the beat while his classmates were making those career moves they'd joked about at the police training school.

It wasn't Peng who had recommended the posting; it wasn't his style to go behind a person's back. But David knew it was more than a coincidence that he was returned to Western. Williams had been found dead four days before the move. David had heard a rumor that the order had come from very high within the system, perhaps even from the commissioner's desk.

Tiny droplets of rain splattered onto the brim of his hat. He glanced at his image in a store window, distorted by rainwater dribbling down in intricate patterns, delicate and glistening. And then the sky lit up and finally thundered. Torrents of rain tumbled to the earth. David stood under a store canopy and dragged slowly on a cigarette. It would be a long night. He looked down Des Voeux Road where foul rivers of water gushed into the sewers and heard a wind chime tinkling fragilely in the rising winds.

He thought of Mei Ling and what he would ask of her in their next meeting. He silently finished his cigarette and stepped into the hot, filthy rain. Within moments he was drenched, but once he was soaked it didn't matter anymore. For now, at least, there was work to be done.

Quickly the summer storm began to quench the island, easing the burden of a steamy night that had smothered the narrow crag streets.

In the high ground, above the old Western station, up among the forested foothills and deep valleys that draped the Peak like a regal mantle, the air rushed and swirled in restless troughs and eddies, and rain cascaded down from clouds puffed heavy with water.

Here among the untamed beauty were isolated mansions and estates, consulates, pastel company villas, embassies and millionaires' penthouses, resting precariously in space on giraffe-like pillars.

One home, more simple than most of the others, was situated along the switchback road that jutted off Lady Clementy's Ride, overlooking Hong Kong harbor and the teeming city below. A solitary light shone from a downstairs study where a man worked into the night.

It was well after two, but for John Cleve, Commissioner of the Royal Hong Kong Police, the day's labor which had begun at seven that morning was far from over. Reports were piled on his desk like ledger books at a bankruptcy. Some required careful consideration, others merely a signature, but all needed his perusal.

Damned air conditioning! he thought. It was chilly. Cleve drew his tattered bathrobe closer to him. A cigar stub jutted from his mouth as he tried to focus his strained eyes on the report.

A riff of thunder rumbled outside. His Alsatian pup, Tory, growled at his feet, ears perked. Cleve patted him. The animal was nervous and in need of exercise. Cleve made a mental note to have his driver take the dog out tomorrow. At one time he would have done it himself, but the last three years as commissioner had gradually removed all his freedom. Eat, work and sleep. That's all there was left. Patches of color on his face, the color of coffee stains, betrayed the wear and tear.

Cleve reminded himself that he never used to think so often and so much about his troubles, that he didn't even know he had any. He was efficient and successful; he had worked as commissioner of police—CP—without a thought for anything beyond the force. Now, as he was winding down his tenure and seriously considering retirement, he knew that he had the loyalty of many, the envy of some and the downright dislike of a few to show for it.

Friends? Maybe Dennis Dunn, head of the PTU, the Police Tactical Unit, one of the few department heads who wanted to fill Cleve's shoes but was ready to wait until Cleve chose to vacate them.

Bob Maguire? Once, perhaps, long ago, when Cleve had not been as cautious in the ways of men and Maguire had seemed the shining star, the flyer, the heir apparent to Cleve's position at the head of the RHKP. But that had changed as Cleve grew more knowledgeable in his role and as he began to understand what Maguire did as director of Special Branch. Cleve was trying to rein in Maguire and his SB section. But Maguire was pulling back, turning cold at the sudden and unwelcome intrusion into his murky realm. Cleve was left to wonder at the reason.

He thought back to when they were friends, before Maguire had learned to lust after power. The cruelest hurt of all was the realization that the confidences he'd so often shared in the past with an old friend over a drink at the mess were no longer reciprocated. Cleve missed Maguire. Except for Digger Dunn, Cleve thought sadly, he was very much alone.

He pressed on to finish the priority file he was reading on the internal situation in Mainland China, its potential for unsettling the temper of the colony and the delicate position of Hong Kong as it awaited the ultimate transfer of sovereignty. The report was written by Special Branch and signed, as always, by Maguire.

In his assessment, Maguire had opted for the status quo response: that Hong Kong was safe until 1997 and far beyond it for as long as China was allowed to benefit from any new wealth and prosperity the colony created; that drawing massive doses of investment through Hong Kong—even though some of it would filter to China anyway—prolonged the British presence and guaranteed the territory's stability as an economic entrepôt regardless of any grass-roots turmoil or patriotic fervor that might ravage mainland China in the interim.

Judging from the new governor's public pronouncements, Maguire was backing the right horse. These days, it seemed, when Peking sneezed Hong Kong said, "Bless you," and provided the tissue paper to boot. With the chance for monetary windfall at the end of the rainbow for politicos in Peking, this seemed unlikely to change.

But Cleve could not escape the nagging fear that there was a dark horse to be considered in the mad dash for 1997; that Maguire's theory had one serious flaw. While his director might correctly assess the importance of the business reality of Hong Kong to the mainland, he had not come to grips with the intense emotional one.

John Cleve knew the Chinese wished to retake the tiny territory, to complete their sense of national identity and to right the taking of Hong Kong almost a century earlier, a slight his ancestors had visited on the Chinese and one for which, if he were not cautious, he might be made to pay dearly.

The recent treaty with Peking, signed by Margaret Thatcher and Deng Xiaoping, had all but put the final nail into the political coffin. Bevies of faceless government mandarins on both sides now spoke of the final days of British rule in vague and almost melodious tones, of "equitable liaison," of a "gradual period of economic transition" and of "fifty years of adjustment."

But Cleve was not fooled. The year 1997 was not that far away and the change, if not properly handled, would be sudden and harsh, not mild and accommodating. As any seasoned punter at Happy Valley knew, it was the dark horse in any race that bore watching.

He considered the beast and was uneasy. Over the course of the past months there had been much talk of unrest in China. All was not going smoothly. Increased consumerism had brought with it increased greed and rumors of widespread government corruption.

There had been student disturbances in the major centers and calls for greater democratization. These had been answered with quick suppression, then stony silence, with the unspoken but ever-implicit threat from the more unorthodox in the government that such insurrection was never to be repeated.

Drug addiction, long a taboo topic in China, was on the rise; the popular drugs were opium and heroin, long forbidden under pain of death. Beggars were seen on the streets of China's capital cities; for the first time in memory there were women and children among them.

There was talk of vigorous criminal activity everywhere, cases of armed robbery, rape, even murder disquieting the populace. Hints of Triad cells springing up in the southern provinces made the population uneasy, cells the People's Militia seemed unwilling or unable to stamp out.

Production in the workplace was sagging in all areas. And the Chinese *rinminbee*, the national currency, was facing severe pressure from the world banking community.

The grand experiment of opening wide China's doors to a jaded and fickle world was on perilous ground, and the jackals were ready to pounce on a suddenly timorous leadership within.

Cleve glanced at a precis he'd received this afternoon from Stu Chaukley, his studious head of Commercial Crime. It had been marked urgent and was hand-delivered. After he'd read it, Cleve could understand why.

A high-ranking member of China's Central Committee, Yun Jianging, a civil engineer of some repute from Chengdu, had been accused of negligence and overall incompetence. Serious structural faults had gone unnoticed on the upgrading of a cantilever bridge that traversed a two-hundred-meter-deep gorge on the Dadu River in Sichuan province. A crowded passenger train bound for Xiuchang from Leshan had skidded off a worn trestle and careened into the raging river below. The death toll exceeded two hundred and fifty.

Initially, no inquiry had been ordered. Fault for the disaster was placed squarely in the hands of one Poi Chin, the engineer of the ill-fated train; government investigators alleged he took the hairpin curve to the gorge at breakneck speed, precipitating the crash.

Poi was a blackened cinder in the riverbed and there the matter might have rested but for the guilty conscience of Fan Luk Wing, a laborer who worked on the ten-mile stretch of railway that included the Dadu River basin.

After a few sleepless nights, Fan surrendered himself to the People's Militia post in his village to unburden his soul to the investigators.

He stated that the entire length of rail line from Leshan to Xiuchang was in need of repair. In the new spirit of entrepreneurial initiative and freedom encouraged by Premier Deng, the maintenance contract for this stretch of track had been given to the then fledgling firm of Yun Jianging. It had been Yun who had designed and constructed the great bridge over the Dadu River gorge. His reputation was impeccable.

But, according to Fan the worker, in the five-year period Yun held the contract, no corrective work had been done to the rail bed, although work orders existed. He knew, he had seen them. In fact, as Fan had meekly stated, the section by the gorge, the section including the bridge itself, was the most dangerous of all.

The investigator at the police post, a cynical veteran of several internal purges in the name of progress, was interested; an inquiry was begun and it quickly bore fruit. Paper formalized paper. The railroad line from Leshan to Xiuchang proved to be in horrendous condition: spikes rusting, wood rotting, gravel bed uneven and untended. There were allegations of technical malpractice, and the militia uncovered fraudulent work orders and invoices, as well as monies that had been received for tasks never completed and in many cases never commenced.

It was rumored that many government palms had been greased to ensure silence in the matter; but it appeared that no official inquiry was deemed necessary. The militia was directed to deal with it as a local issue and to bring the minor functionaries involved to trial for corruption and misappropriation of the People's funds.

But it became public. Yun Jianging, a member of the Central Committee, was quietly implicated in the whisper

campaign raging across China about the Dadu disaster. He
was a close friend of Premier Deng Xiaoping, had been for
some fifteen years, and the inevitable question soon was
asked. How much did Deng know, and what was he prepared
to do to make things right, or at least to give the appearance
of being so? For now there was no answer from Deng: only
silence, a brutal, condemning silence.

Cleve knew China. In time the crunch would come. The
shadow talk concerning Yun would become an angry popular
outcry. China would demand justice—or blood. The mood
in the People's Republic was volatile. John Cleve, as commissioner of police, had every reason to be concerned for the
safety and tranquillity of the Crown colony of Hong Kong.

Chaukley's information about the whole affair was
rudimentary. The story had broken in Canton only a few
days ago and had not yet filtered through to Hong Kong's
media circus. Cleve was thankful for such small blessings. He
could already see the locals mindlessly headlining this one;
the radicals would try to ride it to flaming glory amid a trail
of turmoil and burning tires—to further embarrass the
Chinese hierarchy and upset the tenuous accommodation set
up between Hong Kong and the homeland in this period of
transition. But unrest was the last thing this weary little territory needed in its final days under British rule. Of that
Cleve was certain.

He picked his leather-bound diary from amid a pile of files,
opened it to the next day, jotted down Maguire's name and,
beside it, in small, neat handwriting, "See him for further
evaluation of situation in China. Special emphasis. Dadu
River disaster. Could it become critical?" He made a second
note to remind his orderly sergeant to get his dress uniform
ready for his evening meeting with the governor to discuss
the police force budget.

The buzz from Government House was that cutbacks were
imminent, part of the larger political portfolio with which
His Excellency, the Right Honorable Thomas Driscoll, had
been dispatched. A burgeoning population, multiplying
crime statistics, demonstrations, riots threatening because of
a rate of inflation that ate up the Hong Kong dollar like

moon cakes at the mid-autumn festival—all this to deal with, and Driscoll, an emissary of the new liberal spirit in Whitehall, was going to somehow reduce and improve the police force at the same time.

Cleve couldn't guess at the rest of the agenda, but he hadn't failed to note that the governor had made fast friends with some of Hong Kong's leading businessmen, including Sir Robert Burden and his circle of financial lackies. Stinking rich, they were the first to encourage police cutbacks, to hover like vultures at the thought of money to be made, no matter what the political stripe.

Cleve yawned. Perhaps it was time to call it a night. Seven o'clock would come all too soon. Five hours of sleep was not nearly enough any more. The force doctor, Sam Bond, had been after him lately. "Pace yourself," he'd said. "Take care of your body." But there were so many things to be done, and there never seemed to be enough time. Occasionally Cleve felt the sharpness in his chest, the shortness of breath, the telltale signs of his body's rebellion.

He put the reports away, switched off the light and went into the kitchen, the pup obediently following. He got out the cocoa, the milk, sugar, remembering that he'd eaten the last of the marshmallows on Saturday. He felt his expanding stomach. Outside, the rain pelted a merciless tattoo on the windows. Lightning flashed in the sky.

After Cleve finished the drink, he rinsed the mug and made his way down the darkened hallway to the staircase. He paused by the downstairs bedroom and saw that Matt was fast asleep, a foot thrust out from under the blanket. This week he'd promised to sneak a half day off to take the lad up to the New Territories. With Emily married and settled in New Zealand and Guy mining for ore somewhere in the wilds of northern Alberta, there was now only one left in the nest. Soon there would be none. Yes, tomorrow he'd spend time with Matthew. He left Tory nuzzled up to the sleeping youngster and climbed the stairs to his own bedroom, took off his bathrobe and placed it on the chair by the dresser. He looked down at the figure on the bed.

She slept silently, her features untroubled. He pulled down

the blanket, lay beside her and lifted a stray curl from her forehead. "Poor girl," he whispered. He sighed and lay back, waiting for sleep to come. Why, Margaret, why can't you understand that I have to do this, if only for a little longer? Cleve stared at the ceiling. Then, finally, eyes heavy, he dozed off to another fitful sleep.

CHAPTER FOUR

This part of the circuit, Kennedy Town, was so routine the four men in Emergency Unit Land Rover 16 could do it in their sleep—and sometimes did.

The Rover slithered down Belcher Street, its treads leaving telltale grease stains on the road. Then it was on to the Praya, the Kennedy Town waterfront, past crates laden with oyster paste, tangerines, ginseng root, dried prunes and cackling chickens, cargo pallets piled high with black kegs of tar from Canton and wooden hampers overflowing with *bac-choi*, ginger and lotus roots from the communes of the People's Republic for the busy marketplaces of the Crown colony.

David sheltered himself from the rising wind. He was drenched, tired, his rounds nearly complete, his beats in order. He looked up as the EU police vehicle passed him at the junction of the Praya, grimly signed the visiting book as the rain plopped angry blue blotches onto his quickly scrawled signature. Then he started off again, away from the waterfront and up toward Belcher Street. It was month's end and he had a good few hours of paperwork ahead of him.

Across the street, beyond the high, grimy stone pier, three feeble dock lights barely outlined the decrepit old coastal trawler that had moored off the slip that evening. David noted the flag flapping from the staff on her stern.

There were no lights aft in the crew's quarters, or forward in the steering cabin. No sign of life. On the leeward side, safe from the main force of the gale, a door stood ajar, slamming shut now and then with a feeble crash as the ship pitched and yawed in the swells. The night watch was asleep at his station, the crew below decks. The refuse of a wild and raucous party—chicken bones, pasty-dried rice and vomit—lay everywhere.

In the passing EU Land Rover, no one saw the solitary policeman. Their minds were suddenly on something else, a dark figure darting down from the ramp of the ship and into the shadows of the loading dock at the Green Island Cement Company.

The EU sergeant nodded to his driver. *"Fai-di!"* Hurry. No need for other words. On a tedious night like this it was worth a stop-and-search. Maybe it was a *do-yau*, a drug addict.

The driver gunned the motor. The Land Rover responded with shakes and shudders and then tore down the street, turning sharply into the narrow parking area to cut off the suspect's escape route. The Rover slid and knocked over some crates of *bac-choi*, sending the fresh cabbages pouring onto the road.

David turned at the sound. He looked down the street and saw the hunched human figure freeze, illuminated in the Land Rover's light, his clothes soaking wet. Then the man bolted southward, away from the waterfront, away from the ship toward the shelter of the alleyways and tenements that made up old Kennedy Town.

Straight toward David.

Doors slammed. Slickered policemen moved out into the curtain of rain. Arcs of light crisscrossed wildly. Feet clattered on the cobblestones as the police ran after the unknown man.

David was less than a hundred yards away. He saw the figure coming toward him, heard the sound of rapid footsteps brushing pavement, the rush of hurried breathing. He moved into the darkness to trap the suspect. A ridge of lightning split the sky, and filthy rainwater gushed anew from the heavens.

David saw the long jagged scar carved into the Chinese face and he knew he'd never forget the look in those eyes. He readied himself. This one had some explaining to do. Any moment now and he'd have him. Any moment. . . .

The first explosion caught the EU sergeant in the shoulder blades and threw him with the force of twenty-two hundred pounds per square inch onto the wet concrete. As his head struck the pavement, he lost consciousness. He never felt the second explosion, the set charges that tore the heart out of the ship. When he awoke briefly, in pain, he looked to where the Land Rover was—or had been. Now there was only a smoldering hole, crackling steel, rubbery slime. The fiery skeleton of the Rover burned furiously in the rain. Gold, crimson, hot-white sparks licked the sky. A stone's throw away, the oily water too was aflame, gurgling, wretching and smoking around the hulk of the ship.

At Island Control, a woman constable screamed. Her communications telephone dropped with a hollow, plastic clatter from her hand to the tiled floor, then dangled loosely on the twirling cord. From the mouthpiece came a shrill, high-pitched whine.

Four other constables looked up from their phones, momentarily stunned. Without hesitation, the sergeant rushed to the woman's side, calling for the first-aid kit. A small trickle of blood was coming out of the woman's ears. Efficiently, the sergeant tore the yellow computer card from the constable's message pad. While one of the others administered first aid, he handed the form to the duty inspector.

Rubbing sleep from his eyes, the inspector glanced down at the delicate English script:

EMERGENCY UNIT
UNIT> CAR 16   TIME: 03:36 HRS   DATE 21   AUG

LOCATION: KENNEDY TOWN PRAYA O/S GREEN IS-
LAND CEMENT

REMARKS: IN PURSUIT: CHINESE MALE, WANTED
INVESTIGATION

and then some drops of blood on the paper. That was all.

The EU sergeant, writhing on the ground, rain-soaked, felt
his forehead. Warm, wet, sticky, like soy paste. Dark blotches
of red came off on his hand. There was no feeling on his left
side. His ears and head throbbed madly. His nervous system
was in the white shock of pain. He looked across the rubble
to a small bloody mass of pulp and realized it was a hand. He
wondered whose. With the realization it was his, he gurgled
a mouthful of rich, red blood. And died.

Andrews could see the men as they jumped from the deck
of the ship into the murky waters; they were consumed in the
fiery pools of diesel fuel that escaped from the ship's bunkers.
The sky was a pale orange rainbow, smoking gold and tinted
red. Black, belching smoke loomed above the buildings and
sliced through curtains of rain to mingle with storm clouds
skudding overhead.

The wail of ambulance and fire sirens began to fill the
night air. David looked back, searching for the shadowy
figure with the scar on his face. The man was gone.

He ran toward the explosion. Flaming sparks singed his
eyes and clothing, and swirling black ash began to color
everything a deep ebony. He could not breath easily in the
heat. As he came nearer he felt it: the roar, long and deep,
rising from the bowels of the earth as a three-story
waterfront slum, shaken by the original blast, started to collapse on itself. Screaming, shouting people rushed out of the
white-hot steam, bloodied and stunned, carrying what few
possessions they could.

Police began to arrive on foot. David shouted instructions
to them—to tear into the concrete womb of the collapsed
building for the injured and dying.

Now there were fire reels everywhere. White threads of
water from scores of heavy-duty hoses spurted forlornly into
the thick smoke. Firemen moved frantically through a
landscape of earthworm hoses. Three perished when a tongue

of flame wrenched the derelict ship and reached up to touch the stone wall where they had set up their feeble jet of water. Quickly, others took their place.

The night was filled with fear and death, anger and sorrow. And everywhere the odor of chemicals, burning wood, wet cloth. The acrid smell of ancient bricks torn from their foundations and the porcine stench of charred human flesh. Minutes after his arrival, David had handed over command to the divisional superintendent, Jeffrey Lane.

The division didn't have the manpower to deal with the catastrophe, and the Police Tactical Unit was called out from its reserve status. A company of Blue Berets swarmed out of the North Point barracks in a police convoy and streamed through the night rain across the island to Western.

Within a half hour, and without fanfare, John Cleve arrived at the scene in an old divisional Land Rover. In his safari suit under a blue trench coat, with no rank visible save the braid on his cap visor, Cleve looked rumpled and tired.

He made his way through the confusion to the command post. He found Lane at the tail gate of a Rover, a map of the area pinned to a makeshift briefing board. The young divisional superintendent was busy on the hand-held radio, checking his duties to the east of the flash point where a section of men had come upon another tenement verging on collapse. "Yes, Timmy! Take them out of there. Take the people out! Now!" Lane grimly crossed the building off the chart with a red wax pencil: another building evacuated. A sergeant marked the building site on a clipboard.

Lane's clothing was mud-caked and sodden. He saw the commissioner and moved to salute, but Cleve stopped him. "Stand easy, Jeff. There's no need for that now."

Cleve glanced around at the evacuees: dejected, shivering, huddled in the morning drizzle or hiding in dark stairwells. He asked Lane for the radio.

"Island Control. Island Control. This is the CP." Firmly, calling through the static. "Island Control. Do you copy."

A detached voice: "This is Island Control. We copy."

"Island Control. You will contact Civil Aid Services and the Department of Home Affairs." He looked over to Lane, whispered something and, apparently satisfied with the reply, turned back to the radio. "I want temporary accommodation laid out for six hundred people. I also want soup kitchens for all police and civilian personnel. Right now. Do you copy?"

He received a quick affirmative from the "I Control" duty inspector, then handed the radio back to Lane. "Thank you, Jeffrey. Thank you very much." And Lane knew his superior meant every word.

In the rubble of what had once been the waterfront tenement, David, his face covered with a dirty handkerchief to mask the dust and stench of death, wearily lifted chunks of concrete, wood and cracked plaster searching for bodies. All around him, police and civil-aid personnel were working. No one could be alive in there.

He was aware of his own burning exhaustion, felt his muscles ache. He heard shouts, looked over toward what was once the building entrance, saw an older man in a senior-officer's trench coat move quickly from the road to help the shouting constables lift a beam. He marveled at the man's apparent strength and stamina. Someone passed David a mug of water. He nodded his thanks, sipping from its contents, spitting out the dust that caked his lips and mouth as he did so.

Shouts nearby. The frenzied waving of hands as search teams located movement among the ruins of the tenement. David rushed gingerly across the mountain of rubble toward the commotion, tripping and stumbling as he did so. He found himself joined by others.

Soon they were all digging, picking at the filthy bed of concrete, firebrick and soot, gasping and cursing, hoping that they might be saving someone from the crushing weight and the horrible suffocation.

Then: part of a man's chest, still breathing. David plunged deeper into the slime, trying to etch out space for the human to survive. His face streamed sweat, his body screamed from exhaustion. Four or five pairs of hands were helping. Then they had him, a man of indeterminate age, bleeding, cut, torn by the explosion and the sharp-edged bricks that had rained down upon him. But breathing, damn it, breathing!

The call for ambulance attendants. Many pairs of hands tenderly lifting the body onto the white stretcher. Blood dripping from cuts, the man wincing and whimpering with the pain of broken bones and the trauma of being buried. But they carried him tenderly out, and he was alive.

David found himself shaking. He brushed the sweat from his forehead and looked around at the rescue team. The man in the trench coat was standing next to him, dirty with red brick dust and ancient soot which had hidden in the building's creaking joints for decades. The man's face was lined with grease and caked dirt. He seemed terribly world-weary, yet his eyes twinkled with life. David started. It was the commissioner, John Cleve.

"Good work, inspector," Cleve said. "We'll manage here, won't we?"

"Yes, sir," Andrews whispered.

Cleve saw an orderly at the command post waving wildly in his direction. "If you'll excuse me, inspector," he said, brushing the dirt off his clothing, "I have some details to attend to."

"Certainly, sir," Andrews replied, but the CP was already making his way down the rubbled slope.

Cleve stood at the entrance to the crowded command post, his face bathed in the yellow glow of the hurricane lamp. He brushed against the tarpaulin that half draped the entry and a cascade of rain tumbled to the ground behind him.

A constable diffidently beckoned the CP inside and handed him the portable phone.

"Cleve."

"You wish to speak to me, sir." It was Robert Maguire, his voice still groggy with sleep.

"You've been advised of what we have here at Western?"

"Some. My duty officer called and briefed me earlier." Maguire's voice was uninterested. He was slightly irritated at being awakened. It was a matter he felt his subordinates could handle, and he didn't care if his tone of voice showed it.

"Well?" Cleve asked. "What do you think, Robert?"

Maguire's voice took on the semblance of practised authority. "I gather it's at the Communist pier by Green Island Cement."

"Yes."

The director continued to recite the facts as he would a simple equation. "There's a civilian death toll. There are no survivors on the ship. And we've lost some of ours."

"Yes, we have," Cleve replied quietly.

Maguire cleared his throat. "Do we have a name for the ship yet, sir?"

"The bow is still visible, though burning. We can't make out any of the characters, but we might be able to piece together the shape of the vessel. And, of course, because it was Sunday night, the ship still hadn't been registered at the port. I want to talk to you about this, Robert. It's rather important. I think I'd like you here immediately."

Maguire's voice became distant. "There's not much I can do at this stage, Commissioner." He pronounced the title carefully, as if considering it. "It really is a uniform responsibility, at the very most a CIB matter, at this point. . . ."

"I want you here tonight, Robert," Cleve repeated, his voice rising as he caught Maguire's petulance.

"It's not my mandate, sir," Maguire blurted out.

"Yet." Cleve abruptly completed the phrase. He waited for the meaning to sink in. "So let's just anticipate the inevitable and have you here to assist me with the political side of things from the beginning, okay?"

"Sir." Maguire coldly acknowledged the command. The phone clicked dead.

By 05:20 hours, there were only minor explosions caused by gas pockets, and the fire was contained to an area of less than a quarter mile.

Drab green Hong Kong government vehicles pulled up a block away. Dour nurses and Hong Kong Regiment volunteers assisted still-shocked families aboard. Police sergeants stood by each vehicle tailgate with clipboards, taking names and addresses. Temporary accommodation awaited the refugees at the old Harcourt Road army barracks in Central.

Other police began the gruesome task of tabulating the living and the dying. Some of the dead had already been counted. Thirteen red government blankets stretched starkly on the wet pavement along Davis Street, blackened, hands and feet haphazardly sticking out, several identified with toe tags. Some had families kneeling alongside, shrieking and wailing as the last glimmers of hope gave way to dreadful certainty. Others were sadly alone.

Five or six fire trucks stood by. Exhausted fire crews began the back-breaking task of rolling up the miles of cracked rubber hose. Fire service unit commanders assessed damages and causes with their police counterparts.

An old seventy-foot Marine police launch from the harbor sector and a small fiberglass jet boat lay some hundred yards offshore. Two dories moved closer to the pier. Royal Navy divers from HMS *Tamar* began the ghoulish task of dredging for the drowned. The fire services ship *Alexander Grantham*, called in minutes after the initial alarm, lay nearby, her fire cannon canting with the swells.

Little remained of the coaster: a blackened hull, a spar, a shriveled life preserver, a length of bow rapidly taking on water in the morning tide.

A dark limousine, the kind government mandarins favored, turned up Davis Street. It had three occupants. The man in the back seat was European. The sergeant at the roadblock stopped the vehicle, had words with the driver, then called for the inspector. David came over from the Western Divisional Rover where he was writing his preliminary reports. It was near six o'clock and he was bone weary. He would soon be going home; home to the station, to a hot bath and to sleep. Whatever the business with the limousine was, he hoped it would not take too long.

The driver flashed a leather wallet. It was police identification. He nodded to the back seat. The object of his attention, smooth-shaven, immaculately dressed and with only the slightest trace of boredom, glanced out the half-opened window.

"Good morning, inspector. My name is Maguire, Robert Maguire." His voice was a dull monotone. There was a scent of cologne in the air, strong and expensive. Andrews wearily looked down at the man and said nothing.

"Do you not salute your superiors?" Maguire's face flushed with sudden anger.

"Sir."

"That's better. I appreciate you're tired but that doesn't excuse breaches in discipline. You can't command the locals without it, you know. They require a firm hand. In fact, they expect it." Maguire looked David directly in the eye, hoping the gesture was not lost. He prided himself on the steely stare, had perfected it over the years with his Chinese staff. The look had no effect.

Maguire coughed, self-consciously. He peered past David at the devastation. There was no hint of emotion on his face.

"A sloppy one, don't you think, inspector?" he muttered, eyes squinting into the dust and mist that cloaked the site. "Do you know how many dead?" He glanced at David, voice clipped, expressionless.

"No, sir. Not yet, sir."

"Hmph." The snort, impatient as the man. The driver and his escort in the front seat had not moved

"It's a running tally, sir. The total is quite high and we haven't completed our sheets as yet." David offered the information more from a sense of discipline than civility.

"Yes." Curt. It was apparent Maguire had caught David's intent. "The command post? Where is it?" Before David could answer, Maguire moved away from the window, sitting back once more in the plush seat. David was left to speak to the driver.

The window hummed closed and the car moved off toward its destination, kicking up a spray of pebbles. David did not salute the man as he left. He trudged back to his Rover, shaking off a painful knee cramp. He reminded himself he'd have to see a doctor about it before long.

"Do you know that one?"

"Sir?" The pudgy Hakka sergeant in the front seat of the car moved uneasily as he looked in the rear-view mirror. The director was in one of his moods.

"You heard me, Li," Maguire said. "Do you know him?"

"Sir?" The Chinese gulped out an answer. "That's Inspector Andrews, sir. David Andrews. They say he was involved in the Williams mess."

"Oh, yes," Maguire replied thoughtfully, "now I remember. The scandal at Western. Williams was the one taking *li tsi* jammed with hundreds of dollars from the heroin peddlers, wasn't he?" The director went on without waiting for a reply. "Suicide." He snorted. "The coward's way out." He glanced back to the retreating Andrews. "I don't suppose we've got anything on the young inspector?"

"No, sir. Not that I'm aware of. The anti-corruption people are on to it and that's all they'll say."

"Well. I think I'll keep my eye on him, Li. He might prove interesting in the future." Maguire sank back in his seat. "One never knows how these loose ends will turn up in the fabric at a later date, does one?"

The Hakka said nothing, for he knew it was not his place to comment on the director's wishes. He'd been Maguire's personal driver and assistant for more than four years, and wanted to remain so until his retirement.

He felt sorry for the young inspector, Andrews. He'd heard some of the barracks stories about him and his part in the kickbacks that Williams had taken before his death. Still, after twenty-seven years of service, Li Fung was too well versed in the police rumor machine to believe all it spewed out. But the anti-corruption people? Now that was another story. He had friends in the unit, and he knew that their ongoing investigation of David Andrews was very much a fact. And now Maguire and Special Branch would be poking their noses into the mess.

David was back at the station before nine o'clock. His body was beyond feeling, his mind still racing with the day's events. Cuts to his hands were flecked with iodine and his clothing stuck to him like a leprous second skin. He knew he stank but he didn't much care any more.

He'd completed most of his reports at the waterfront. The sergeants had been a great help to him and, in the end, beyond the initial observations his part had been quite minor when compared to the work of the divisional superintendent and the others who'd arrived later.

Now there was but one summary to write, the one he'd saved for last. David made his way down the deserted corridor to his office. The musty smell of paper greeted him as he opened the door. The room was small, rectangular; it had no window. He switched on the light and a naked bulb glared back at him from atop an old metal desk awash in paperwork. He searched for the lampshade, found and replaced it over the bulb. It stayed askew, teetering to one side, casting his shadow over a wall filled with old legal ordinances.

He took the ancient Underwood from the typing table, placed it squarely on the center of his desk, then sat down and began to pick at the letters uncertainly, trusting two fingers to do the work of ten. The ribbon was ragged, the letters vague and the quality of his typing marginal, so it took some time. When he had finished and read over the report, he took the page from the typewriter and clipped it to his hand-scribbled notes on the explosion.

Carrying these documents, he went to the superintendent's office. It was dark and quiet inside. David placed the report on the super's in tray, glancing down at the typed page as he did so. He thought back. Yes, that was the man he suspected. The man with the scar on his face. Whoever he might be, and whatever his reason for being there, he was the man David Andrews wanted.

CHAPTER FIVE

————————

The day turned out vague and blustery. The activity around the vast Arsenal Yard compound seemed strangely muted. A pale, bone-weary Cleve mounted the steps of Caine House, the row of coral-colored buildings that housed the executive wing of the Royal Hong Kong Police, and its Special Branch. He acknowledged salutes with uncustomary brusqueness, aware of the stares of astonishment as subordinates realized that the grimy, mud-splattered apparition before them was truly their commissioner.

He rode the elevator to the fifth floor, got off and made his way to his offices. His secretary, Mrs. Callicutt, did not blink at his appearance; in twenty years of service, she had seen it all.

"Shall I hold calls, sir?" she asked matter-of-factly, her dour face peering at him from behind tinted spectacles. Her tiny head and wrinkled neck had earned her the nickname "Turtle," which she did not like. It was the cause of the slight smile Cleve always wore when he spoke to her.

"No." He could not afford the luxury of sleep today. "Make it business as usual. Get me the deputy police commissioner for Hong Kong island. Tell him I want him at—" he glanced at his watch "—at nine o'clock. Also call for Superintendent Peng of General Investigations. I want to talk to him as soon as I'm done with the DPC. Oh, and Irene, order me a pot of coffee, black, and a tray of coconut buns. I'm starving."

He entered his office, took a change of clothing from his wardrobe and went into the small anteroom, which served as his emergency quarters. There he stripped out of his safari suit and shoes, washed himself thoroughly and shaved. For the first time since the call from the duty officer about the explosion, he became aware of the painful ache in his shoulder. He stretched his arm and flexed his fingers a few times. It would be a long day.

He changed into the starched uniform, making a mental note of things that could be postponed, and went back to his office. Mrs. Callicutt came in with a tray. He poured himself a mug of coffee and picked out a bun.

"Preliminaries on the disaster, sir." She placed an orange folder on his table. "The latest from SB/Ops and HKI/CID. In triplicate," she added primly.

"Thank you, Mrs. Callicutt." The Turtle was thorough as ever.

She nodded slightly, then left. As the door closed, Cleve sipped his coffee, then bit into one of the pastries. It was spicy-sweet, just the way he liked it.

He began to leaf through the documents slowly, absorbing the information. Then, as things clicked into place, he reached forward, drew a felt pen from an old mess mug atop his desk and began to write.

Eleven bodies had been recovered from the ship thus far. Through the cover of the New China News Agency, Chinese officials had already begun discreetly pressuring the Hong Kong government for immediate return of the remains. They were being kept at the morgue in Kennedy Town until the final cause of death was determined.

The police bomb disposal officer had found bomb fragments on the jetty near the wrecked Land Rover. A diver had found more of them embedded in the hull of the ship. The fragments showed that the bombs were of American manufacture.

Cleve tapped his pen on the tabletop in puzzlement. The Nationalist Chinese might have done the deed, but it would

have been very difficult since SB had cleaned them out a few
months back. Twenty Kuo Min Tang agents now being "entertained" at the Victoria Remand Center were the only
major group operating in the colony. The Russians? Cleve
chuckled. They'd always had abysmal luck in Hong Kong.
And the Yanks? They'd swiftly proclaimed their innocence in
hard-handed correspondence through their liaison at the
U.S. Consulate. And for once Cleve was inclined to agree.
There was no motive for them to jeopardize Sino-American
relations, not when they wanted the wheat contract confirmed in the fall. It was a veritable maze he was entering.

By the time Peng was ushered in, Cleve had met with the
deputy commissioner and had his telephone orders from the
governor. He sat at his desk, the drapes drawn. A reading
lamp bathed the room in a soft amber glow.

"Don't make yourself too comfortable, Peng. I won't take
too long."

The tall superintendent sat forward in a high-backed chair
facing Cleve. Peng had seen the harried look on the face of
the deputy commissioner as he'd left Cleve's office. He knew
this was important.

Cleve looked up and Peng smiled. He liked Cleve, his
method of policing and his integrity. Peng was Cleve's man;
Peng's department, General Investigations Office, was
Cleve's Praetorian Guard.

Cleve lifted the orange file, then dropped it back on his
desk.

"Superintendent, you've heard about the disaster last night
in Western."

Peng nodded. General Investigations, GIO, was the dog's
body of the police force. From fraud to homicide, from missing persons to protection of VIPs, the GIO superintendent
usually, sooner or later, heard it all.

"I've just spoken to the DPC/HKI," Cleve said. "He as-
sures me that the whole thing could have resulted from
natural causes. Frankly, that's a crock."

Peng nodded in agreement. Like Cleve, he was a
policeman born and bred; his family had worn the blue cloth
and served the Crown for generations. His father, a man of

some substance, had been a chief inspector in prewar Shanghai. His grandfather was a sergeant under the legendary Captain Quincy, superintendent of police at Chi Nan Fu, Shantung Province, at the turn of the century. Policing was in his blood.

A large man, soft-spoken, self-effacing in conversation, Jimmy Peng was known as a flyer, a man with a future. His reputation was a tribute to his expertise and, as he ruefully admitted, to that wonderful concoction all seasoned policemen seemed to possess: sheer luck.

It was luck that had placed him in front of a burning shack in Shaukiwan eight years ago, almost to the day. Luck that got him through the flames to the crying baby, which he rescued before the propane heater blew. And luck that got him his Colonial Police Medal for bravery. But it was skill that had put him in General Investigations after a stint in Special Branch, and skill that had recently seen him promoted to superintendent over twenty-three other likely candidates. The consummate skill of the professional. Skill that now told him, too, that "natural causes" was indeed a crock.

Cleve went on. "I don't have much to tell you yet. The ballistics people aren't finished at the scene. But I'm concerned. I have a gut feeling this one's going to be a political hot potato." The commissioner got up and walked to the large window. He opened the drapes and looked off into the distance, out over the harbor.

"Jim, I've read the field reports. Someone set an explosion on that ship. I want to know what it was doing here, its origins and its name." He turned to the younger man, his voice still soft. "Come here."

At a table by the side wall, under a large marine map of the colony, books and blue-jacketed reports were piled in neat columns.

"We're not going to be given much time to get to the bottom of this. These are yours." Cleve handed Peng a blue folio. "Inside are copies of all the documents I have. I want you to note this one especially." Cleve took out a radio-room printout.

The transmissions were from the police unit at Kennedy

Town, Emergency Unit Land Rover 16. Peng read down the page to its abrupt end.

"The unit was a victim of the explosion," Cleve explained. "The radio message doesn't tell us much of anything yet except that immediately before the blast the Rover crew chased this fellow. And, if he isn't one of the dead we've unearthed, they lost him. Which means, dear fellow," he stated wryly, "that he's somewhere around." He stared directly at Peng. "Look into it, along with the rest. I want you to work on this case exclusively. And I want a preliminary report on my desk by tomorrow evening." Cleve tapped the folio. "I've got to know, Jimmy. The governor will probably demand it. I do." He paused, as if holding his breath. "That's all, superintendent. You're free to go."

Peng made his way to the door.

"And Jimmy."

"Sir?"

"Good luck."

Cleve absently reached for another coconut bun.

It was late afternoon before Cleve had time to make the call.

The phone rang seven times—perversely, he thought.

She answered.

"Maggie?"

"Yes." Her voice was already tense, knowing what to expect. And when she was right, why did he resent it so?

"Maggie, I can't make it home tonight." He spoke too quickly. "There's a conference with the governor, and this ship thing is getting pretty serious." Silence. "It's bound to be picked up by the radicals in the streets. It's a lit torch, Maggie." Resigned silence, accusing. Cleve pressed on. "I'll have my driver come by to pick up the reports I'll need."

He could hear her sigh and knew what she was thinking. It was happening again.

"Maggie. I'm sorry, dear. I know it's been hard lately. But there's not much I can do about this one. Really . . ."

"It's okay, John. It can't be helped." The words were washed out, tired.

There was a lull.

Then, "You must be tired, John. Did you get any sleep last night?" There was a sudden, unaccustomed tenderness in her tone.

"Yes, yes. I got a few hours' kip here in the office."

"Good. That's good," she replied, uncomfortable with the familiarity. Her voice changed. The distance returned.

Cleve rummaged in his drawer for a match. With his other hand he felt under the papers on his desk for a cigar. He heard her steady, even breathing on the phone. They'd nearly run out of things to say.

"John? What time can I expect you home?"

He didn't know. He told her so and he wished she weren't so accusing about the whole thing. It wasn't as if he were whoring around or getting drunk in Wanchai bars. He tried to hide his irritation from her. For twenty-eight years she had been married to a man who worked sixty hours a week and spent his infrequent days off in court, days Maggie spent rearing children alone. It was bound to take its toll. She'd been like a single parent to their first two, and it had almost cost them their marriage. Now there was only Matthew, and John wondered sometimes if his son thought of him as a father or a stranger, a newspaper clipping turned flesh and blood who occasionally asked after the boy's well-being.

"You know you promised Matthew a day's outing in the New Territories?" It was as if she had read his mind.

"Yes, yes." He cursed himself for forgetting. "It'll be okay before the end of the week. Should be. I'll have some free time by then." His voice was not too convincing.

Then, almost as an afterthought, she said, "Take care of yourself, John."

He said nothing.

She interrupted the embarrassed silence, her voice a whisper. "You know I really love you, don't you?"

She hung up before he could answer.

It was drizzling as Jim Peng swung his old Sunbeam onto Arsenal Street, narrowly avoiding a swaying double decker bound for Kowloon via the cross-harbor tunnel. He turned left past the indifferent gate sentry and into Arsenal Yard, then came to a jarring stop at his reserved space under the car portico.

The main hall of May House, the modern twenty-one-story police operational center, was empty. There was a hint of cheap disinfectant in the deserted corridors. Peng winced. It reminded him of morgues and the things that lay on cold, hard slabs inside them.

He identified himself to the desk receptionist and took the lift to his darkened office on the twelfth floor. There he switched on the desk lamp, plucked some files from the in tray and placed his briefcase in the center of his desk. Glancing at his wristwatch, he paged through to the commissary. Gimpy Chin was still there and, with a bit of arm twisting, the old cook would rustle up some coffee, club sandwiches with extra mayonnaise and lots of pickles.

Settling into his leather swivel chair, Peng picked up a felt-tip pen and opened the files one by one.

Five hours later, tie askew, composure lost, he was no further ahead: doodles, diagrams, sketches on notepads, mounds of crumpled paper scattered in and around the rattan wastebasket. It was a timer device, according to the police bomb disposal officer, one expertly rigged to the ship's hull, to totally destroy it. And a man had been seen running away from the scene moments before the explosion. Why? They could probably learn the answer only from the running man, and to date no one knew who he was.

Peng glanced at the draft of his Telex to the divisions and bureaus. There were no replies clipped to it yet. He hadn't really expected any. It would challenge credibility to hope someone had so good an informant at this early stage. He glanced ruefully at the warrant-card photographs of the deceased policemen, frozen in the mock-serious expressions of youth.

Who would blow up a ship at the Communist dock in Hong Kong harbor? And most importantly—why?

Peng twirled his chair around so he could look out the windows, toward the east and the playpen of Wanchai. It was raining, and the pulsing neon glow from cheap bars and dance parlors seemed more tawdry than ever. Down below, over in Caine House, he could see the lights of the fourth and fifth floors burning in the night. Maguire, the sly bastard, probably had his own people following Peng's investigative teams at this very moment and taking credit for the results. He wouldn't put it past the man. Not that it would do him any good. Maybe the head of Special Branch could do better with the case than GIO could; Maguire certainly had more contacts. But in this instance Peng sincerely doubted it. There was just no information.

And then the mail-room clerk scampered in, flustered and apologetic. There was a file to add to today's mail. A letter that had been overlooked.

Peng was too weary to be angry. With a wave, he dismissed the man and opened the manila envelope. Inside was a handwritten note from the superintendent at Western. It was an addendum to his original brief concerning the explosion of the ship. Attached to it was the report from David Andrews.

The night was quiet for David. He was easy on his charges, completing rounds early and proceeding immediately to the "mob-fix" at Davis Street, which guarded the disaster scene. He sat in the Land Rover, the eerie stillness broken only by an occasional tired cough or struck match. He resolved to spend his night shift there, and could see the murky shadows of the perimeter guards in the distance. Perhaps some of his men were also having a *bong-sau*, a break. He worried little; they deserved it.

Looking around him, David sighed with relief. Things were peaceful for the moment. The waves lapped gently on the stone breakwater and the pier. The sky was puffy white, the clouds breaking up. The rain was light and the radio reports from the colony were normal: a Public Light Bus with a driver and five passengers was robbed on the Castle Peak Road as it entered Yuen Long by two males armed with triangular files. Raids by plainclothes teams from Kowloon City Division netted two wizened coolies, one syringe with traces of suspected dangerous drugs, and one porcelain spoon with same. A gambling warrant on Cheung Chau Island returned zealous constables $29.50, a set of Chinese playing cards and six embarrassed Hoklo fishermen. A gang fight erupted near a cooked-food stall on Johnston Road, Wanchai, over the protection of the Red Apple Music Parlor. Three men were arrested at the scene and were subsequently charged with being members of a Triad society and with wounding with intent. A man died later that night at Kwong Wah Hospital as a result of the altercation. He had refused to make a statement to police.

A floating opium divan was discovered on Ap Li Chau, but no arrests were made: its occupants jumped into the sea and an eager guard dog bit one of the constables in the buttocks. In Chaiwan Squatter Area Number Three, a young woman was raped and murdered by an unknown assailant. Thirteen illegal immigrants jumped into the black waters of Mirs Bay from Mainland China aiming for the freedom of Hong Kong. By morning, nine of them would have escaped through the shadowy dragnet set up by patrolling Communist launches. In the next week, three bloated, waterlogged bodies would wash ashore along the various beaches of the New Territories. It would be another two months before the thirteenth body surfaced.

At Ng Uk Tsuen, off the Sha Tau Kok Road, less than a mile from the Chinese border, a young man in a neat white lab coat was slowly and dispassionately adding ether and hydrochloric acid to a large flask of morphine dissolved in alcohol. The result was a fine grade of heroin, number four, ninety-three percent pure, which would command a high price on the overseas markets of Vancouver and Amsterdam.

Vehicle searches along the Li Chi Kok Road resulted in one summons for a defective exhaust system. A courting couple, who had discovered the remains of a maggot-infested male suicide hanging from a rope in an abandoned bunker on the slopes of Mount Davis, forgot all about making love. Life in the British protectorate of Hong Kong had indeed returned to normal. Almost.

A sticky Tuesday morning. The man stirred once more. Air conditioning chilled the cavernous room. Neon hummed incessantly and the harsh glow stung his eyes. His mouth was dry. He stretched his lanky frame uncomfortably and pulled the rough gray blanket over his head. The sturdy government cot creaked. Settling, he knocked over the wicker-covered tea thermos and it fell to the floor with a muffled clatter. Again the shrill buzz.

Kot Kwai Wing (in English he was called Adam) groaned, waking into what felt like a term in solitary. Thirty-one years old, ten years on the force, a senior inspector. He'd just come back from a six-month training course in England with a repertoire of rugby songs, which he sung to himself in a reedy tenor, and a bit more insecurity about his future significance to the RHKP. He'd taken a lot of ribbing from his British instructors—"Nothing solid in senior inspector, old chap. Besides, Hong Kong?"—but his colleagues had noted more than once that he was not easily waylaid.

The light on the switchboard of the left-hand control panel of the operations level flashed cherry red, and with it came again the monotonous buzz. Kot stumbled out of his bed, down the wide, tiled staircase that separated the command module from the panels, to the offending noise, rubbing sleep from his eyes and stifling a yawn as he went. A bored watchkeeper in a twentieth-century dungeon, the night watch at Colony police-military headquarters—Pol/Mil, as it was called.

It had been a busy night. His Army counterpart, who, in theory at least, shared the responsibilities of this office from a duplicate panel to the right of the police desk, was sleeping soundly in one of the back rooms of the labyrinth. Not that he was needed, Kot mused. The calls and responsibilities, as usual, were all for the police. The military was just there for show.

He pressed the toggle switch down and lifted the desk phone from its cradle. The red light flicked off. With his other hand, he pulled the pen from his safari tunic and rummaged through the pile of girlie magazines on top of the major-occurance register until he found a communications pad.

"Police headquarters, Inspector Kot speaking." A faint crackling. A distinctly Australian voice on the line, impatient.

"Deputy Commissioner Hong Kong Island here, Mr. Kot. Would you be good enough to activate the emergency callback provisions?"

"Now, sir?" Adam replied, impressed early on the job with the danger of ambiguity.

"Yes, now, damn it!" rasped the voice. "Not tomorrow, not next year. Now! This damn ship explosion is getting serious. The CP wants everyone on the priority one list alerted and at their post." The phone clicked. End of conversation.

Kot logged the call. He got the passkey out of his pocket, opened the outer door of the safe and took out a long, dove-gray government envelope. The two sheets of white foolscap inside had "Staff-In-Confidence" stamped in red at the top and bottom, in both English and Cantonese. He read the instructions.

Within minutes, certain carefully selected phones throughout the colony were ringing, and senior officers of the force were hurrying through the predawn darkness to their offices, attachments and duties to prepare themselves and their units for further assignment on what all realized might be a very eventful day.

CHAPTER SIX

———

Flecks of morning sun were already touching the Nine Pins and the lighthouse keeper at Waglan Island breathed a sigh of relief as the rain clouds broke up, wispy white, over the China Sea. Fingers of light inched through the Tat Hong Channel and played on the emerald waters. The morning ferry from Macau was still struggling through high seas at Kap Sui Mun Gap, along the north shore of Lantau Island, but the clouds had stopped swirling and a gentle stillness gave a hint of the possibility of better weather. The Asian sun had rediscovered the city on the Pearl River Estuary, and with hot, heavy hands was slowly and steadily embracing Hong Kong.

The roar of the Police Tactical Unit convoy funneled through the narrow Lion Rock Tunnel. Brown, oily Asian heat mixed with putrid diesel fumes. And then, as each vehicle left the tunnel at the east end, there was the shock and exhilaration of that first sighting of the city spreading below them to the south, fortresslike, the maze of concrete, glass, steel and bamboo: narrow, winding streets echoing with chattering humanity; bamboo washpoles dripping rainbows; the broad continental avenues of Kowloon.

Ahead of them there was the Lung Cheung cloverleaf. To the left, the teeming, black-numbered matchboxes of Wong Tai Sin Resettlement Estate and the inhuman, fetid anthills of the Wong Tau Hom and San Po Kong districts. Far off, shimmering in the ocher-flecked heat haze of a China morning, the cement finger of Kaitak runway.

The vehicles of the tactical unit swung down onto Waterloo Road, down toward the cross-harbor tunnel, which led to Hong Kong Island. In the vehicles, behind the wire meshing, the men sat in two rows, each facing inward, uncomfortably close, swaying in unison. They had received only a cursory briefing from their commander, but it had been enough to set the adrenaline flowing. The explosion of the unknown ship at the pier had roused the radical Communist cadres of Hong Kong to mass protest in Statue Square. The potential for violence was great. Thirty-four minutes had passed since they had been called out and they didn't have much time.

As the last unit raced past the open barriers of the checkered gate and into the gaping tunnel entrance, a brown uniformed toll-authority officer scribbled the fleet numbers onto a check sheet. He glanced up at the clock: twenty-nine minutes past six. The Hong Kong government would be billed at a later date. There was no hurry.

Drops of rain trickled down the rigid face of Sir Timothy Jackson, baronet and chief manager of the Hong Kong Shanghai Banking Corporation at the turn of the nineteenth century, the last heady days of British Imperial greatness. Now Sir Timothy stood captive, waistcoated, stern and proper in Statue Square, immortalized in bronze.

Statue Square. Two hundred yards long and one hundred yards wide, a gigantic chessboard of plants and pavement. The players had assembled: Hong Kong's discontented, its newsmen and its police.

"Zulu Charlie, this is DS Central. . . . Zulu Charlie, this is DS Central. . ."

"DS Central, send."

"DS Central to Zulu Charlie. Message is from DS Central to DPC/HKI. Have spoken to senior demonstration organizer, one Chinese male, Mak Kim Fan. Demonstration will proceed without authorized permit from present location in Statue Square, along Garden Road, to target, Government

House. Commencement time is 08:30 hours. Organizers
have agreed to abide by police traffic direction and instructions regarding peaceful furtherance of demo at consular site.
Reason for demonstration is as expected, to protest alleged
British involvement in destruction of the ship at the Communist pier. Mak has stated he will read list of all allegations
in front of consular grounds and that the demo will be peaceful. He will not produce a copy of his speech for my perusal.
Present mood of crowd is good but I have every reason to
believe this will not continue. No weapons or implements of
violence sighted. No women or children seen. Roger so far?"

The click of the mike button, some interference. A metallic
voice: "Roger, so far." In the cool atmosphere of Island
Pol/Mil and in the wider, airier spaces of the Colony
Pol/Mil bunker, Special Branch officers nodded sagely. Only
one thing could happen: the crowd would be allowed to go
ahead, whatever the consequences.

"DS Central. . .prepare to deal with demonstration."

Garden Road curved elegantly past the Hilton Hotel and up
a gentle rise. It led to the mid-levels and the Peak, the solid
European neighborhoods of shady trees, chauffeured Mer-
cedes-Benzes, white flannel suits and occasional Chinese
mistresses as temptestuous as the summer storm clouds over
the China Sea.

Government House stood in the midst of this genteel
splendor, at the junction of Lower Albert Road and Garden
Road. Discreetly hidden by trees and sweeping parkland, it
was the residence of His Excellency, the governor of Hong
Kong.

DS Central had three columns gathered hurriedly from
morning roll calls at stations across the island, twenty-four
men in uniform without weapons save their regulation short
baton, and twenty-four unarmed policewomen. They had es-
corted the demonstrators to where they lingered, chanting,
three thousand strong, just in sight of the mansion. The
police walked in pairs on the edge of the crowd. Countless
banners were now unfurled and fluttered tamely in the limp
breeze. Bold red Chinese strokes on white background:

"Hong Kong British Are Murderers" and "Remember Your Comrades" and "Revenge Your Comrades Savagely Slain by British Paper Tigers" and "Driscoll—Cease These Atrocities Against Our Brothers" and "Blood Debt Must Be Repaid in Blood."

The crowd was young, mostly unemployed, mostly male but was still good-natured. At Government House, a double row of Mills barriers was locked in place along the two-hundred-foot frontage, and some sixty additional police stood on the road to greet the marchers. Off to one side, hidden by bushes, a platoon of Blue Berets from the PTU waited calmly. Storm shutters were up on all three floors of the building. On the roof, shielded from view by the buttresses, two crouching SB members took photographs.

In the roadway, Mak Kim Fan grimly took his place in front of the exuberant audience. News photographers clustered around to capture the image of his time-worn face. Microphones were thrust under his nose.

Mak began. He spoke nervously. His eyes darted about, blinking furiously as beads of sweat trickled across his brow and down his long neck. His voice broke; the battery-powered megaphone he was using to address the crowd was not properly adjusted. What he said was lost to all but the first few rows of his listeners. Hecklers interrupted him. They wanted action. "Move on, elder brother, move on!"

The sun beat down. The people pressed in, one on the other, and Mak's words began to rain down on them.

Mak was gathering confidence. Face red, sweating profusely, from his left shirt pocket he took out a book and opened it. "Comrades!" he shouted. "In this treacherous act let us seek solace and guidance from the thoughts of our departed chairman!" He began to read and, like a litany, coursing and swelling, the crowd joined in and the thousands read as one: "Dare to struggle, dare to win. . ." When he reached the end of the passage, Mak Kim Fan felt power. The chant started slowly from the back of the crowd, first a ripple, then a wave, finally a torrent. "Dare to struggle, dare to win. Dare to struggle, dare to win. *Dare to struggle, dare to win!*" And the songs of a revolutionary China, which had been sublimated for too long, "The East is Red" and "Sailing the Seas depends on the Helmsman."

Now the mountains called Nine Dragons were not forbidding walls blocking off Mother China and separating it from these, her children, but delicate passageways within the same stately mansion. The singers were arrogant and vengeful. The pain of the destroyed vessel was theirs. Sweat and heat and tension were pressed into a volatile mixture, which now had only one outlet. Proud, martial, three thousand voices reverberated boldly through the heart of the tiny British colony.

A false stillness settled as the last bar was sung. It was a little after ten o'clock.

The first rock arched serenely from somewhere in the middle of the crowd and landed with a dull thud on the patio courtyard of the colonial governor. Silence. A long, sullen silence. A shout. Then more shouts. Suddenly, from the heart of the throng, yelling, screaming, cursing. "Fuck your mothers! *Hum Gar Chan!* Fuck your ancestors!" Spitting. Hectoring. *"Du Lai Lo Mo Chau Hai!"*

"Dare to struggle! Dare to win!" The crowd pushed steadily toward the gates. More stones and rough pieces of bamboo tossed through the steaming air. "Move, yellow-skinned running dogs!" A woman constable stumbled, fell, blood flowing from an ugly scarlet gash on her forehead and staining her tan uniform. The crowd streamed through the fragile Mills barriers. A second woman constable was struck and fell, shaking, on her knees. The superintendent ordered the women withdrawn. The PTU platoon reinforced the line that had buckled under the pressure of the crowds. The constables linked arms, tiger-claw fashion, pushed, groaned, sweated to hold the line.

"Remember the Ship! Remember the Dead! Fuck the Imperialist British! Fuck the governor, the dog Driscoll!"

The constables grabbed their batons and held them diagonally to push the crowd back. The superintendent gave an order and the constables swooped and lunged at fists and claws, sixty men holding back three thousand. The crowd was elbows, hands, nails, teeth and fists. Police batons lashed out.

All along Garden Road, riot platoons hurried into forma-
tion. Each platoon had four sections. The first carried black
riot shields; the second carried tear gas; the third had shotguns and the last was the lock-up with handcuffs and revolvers. The order to move out was given.

The first metal canisters were fired into the crowd: blue-
gray smoke, gas. Eyes watered, became swollen, red; people
shed tears in the pepper fog. It was strangely silent. The sun
was a pale red orb seen faintly through rising chemical mists.
The rotating blue dome light of the Number Three platoon
Land Rover vainly pierced the haze. Weakly the cry came
from the police sound system in English and Cantonese:
"Disperse peacefully or we use further force. . . .Disperse
peacefully or we use further force. . . . Disperse peacefully or
we use. . .or we use. . .or we. . ." The tape was caught, the
sound drowned out.

For a sixteen-year-old youth in the mob—poorly
employed, ill-educated, the product of the resettlement estates and the crime they spawned, the tear gas crystallized his
hatred of the white devil and the colonial system.

For a seventy-eight-year-old grandfather, caught in the
outer circle of the crowd, a passerby crippled by the Japanese
in the Canton bombings and a refugee in 1956 from the
Great China he never understood or wanted, the demonstration was another trial in a life filled with them.

For a PTU sergeant, bleeding from a head wound and
screaming in pain from a dislocated shoulder, it was the first
time his own people had turned against him. His family's
disowning of their police son had new meaning.

Then there was the second wave of the maddened crowd
when the smoke settled. Young toughs splashed a police orderly with acid; his shoulder and back were burned like a
blazing red prune. The man who tried to run at the
prisoner's compound to free his friends was shot in the legs
with Remington birdshot at seven paces. Three unarmed
policemen were found lying in the rubble, razor-cut like jigsaw puzzles. The police, anguish in their eyes as they saw
their bleeding comrades and the taunting crowd, knew there
was nothing they could do.

And the mob, finally beaten, retreated to the alleys and the hovels of Wanchai and Central, to regroup and fan their hatred. Oriental riots, Oriental tortures, but occidental rules of fair play.

This year would be remembered as the Year of the Troubles. There had been frost on the peak of Tai Mo Shan last winter. The legend was true.

In a quiet corner of a large room on the sixth floor of the Bank of China building, Lee Shiu Shing got up from his desk and walked to his new painting, freshly hung, a print of Picasso's *Guernica*. It was a picture of mindless carnage for a now-meaningless political purpose, a poignant statement of frustration and futility. Lee had chosen the picture for its fiery beauty, and today it was a reminder of the reality of life. He patiently straightened the frame.

Lee moved to the window and looked down at the rubble-strewn square. Puffs of tear gas lingered among the China fern. A few rioters, in ragged lines, faced the bubble-helmeted police. Rocks, debris, bamboo missiles filled the air. Police shields reflected the white-hot sun. Bodies lay about, darkening red stains on some.

"Governor Driscoll, you may not be pleased," Lee muttered to himself. "That is most unfortunate. You should not have been so quick to exclude me." He smiled. Everything was proceeding according to plan; his message to those who should hear it, including His Excellency the Governor, would be quite clear.

He went back to his desk, to the Chinese daily open at the Hang Seng stock-exchange page. He looked down the columns to one listing, Burden Silver, one of Sir Robert Burden's most important companies. Some said the company was the bulwark of his vast empire. Trading volume was up today, substantially, and the bottom had dropped out of the asking price. A pity.

Lee Shiu Shing glanced at the clock on the wall. It wouldn't be long now. He took a pen and, with one stroke, crossed out the company name. Robert Burden, Thomas Driscoll. Two down, one to go. He shook his head. Soon the last one, too, would come to regret his greed, and pay the price.

While most of his associates were in the gazetted officers' mess at the top of May House drinking black coffee laced with brandy, Robert Maguire sat ruminating behind his desk on the fourth floor of Caine House. He was drinking Perrier with a twist of lemon.

Maguire's office was huge, with a few pieces of teak government furniture. Maguire liked his spartan surroundings. Walls pale cream, barren but for the obligatory portrait of Her Majesty; desk equally bare, except for a photo of his wife and two children—both of them looked like their father—and a single rose in a black lacquered vase. Clear desk, clear mind, Maguire like to say. And, to his overworked staff: Remember it's all in a good cause. Special Branch—a pygmy among the shadowed giants of East and West. A referee; at times, the radar system of a squeamish, hesitant colonial government.

The report on the morning's rioting was already in reasonable shape. The commissioner had scheduled a conference for that evening, and Maguire was ready. Photographs, dossiers, assessments by all his sections. And with each file, on olive drab paper, a curt summation of its contents from the appropriate section head. He could trust his people to be on top of the situation, to pinpoint with surgical precision the next outbreak. So he could afford to waffle. For now.

Maguire was also confident in his knowledge of China. As he had already explained to the commissioner, the Dadu Railway incident was certainly a potential source of large-scale unrest on the mainland. His informant indicated that increasing pressure was being put on the Chinese leader, Deng, to punish his old friend Yun. But the premier was resisting the challenge to his authority and, with his built-in influence in the Central Committee, he seemed quite capable of doing so. There was talk of an internal inquiry with sweeping powers, but if it were like other "sweeping internal inquiries" in China, there was no need for concern. Flowery statements without substance, a few cosmetic changes without import—such were the ways of monolithic governments. Deng had scheduled a public pronouncement for Friday; the situation would hold till then.

Yet Robert Maguire was experiencing a sensation new to him: he wanted to know why the ship had exploded, but the answer wouldn't come.

A respectful rattle at the door. His sergeant peered in. "Sir, outside line." Maguire looked up and recalled with irritation a scheduled luncheon date. "If it's the Malays. . . ." He left the rest menacingly unsaid.

The sergeant shook his head. "No, sir." He hesitated, then said nervously, "I think you'd better take it." He was gone before Maguire could answer him.

A few minutes later, seated restlessly in the back seat of the air-conditioned black government Cedric, headlights on, cutting through the dull August haze of urban Kowloon, Robert Maguire was bound for the most unusual meeting of his distinguished career.

CHAPTER SEVEN

———

David felt the August sun baking his back as he wandered along the sand, Mei Ling by his side. The beach at Cheung Chau was almost deserted. There were a few soldiers' wives on cheap Somerset blankets, some young Chinese women and their boyfriends playing with a beach ball, an old *lap-sap* picker looking pathetic in a bright-yellow Urban-Services T-shirt as he swept away rubbish with a broad bamboo broom. A faint breeze blew in from the Lamma Channel.

The surf trickled playfully at David's feet, cool, soothing. He felt the knotty strain in his neck slowly ease in the sun. He looked over to Mei Ling: hair blowing carelessly in the wind; fine, high cheekbones sprinkled with freckles, and large, expressive, almond-shaped eyes.

On the horizon, by the goosenecked northern tip of the beach at Tung Wan, a police launch hove into view, making for the inner harbour.

The vessel rushed closer, furiously slicing the waters. David could make out the drab-gray bridge, open and window-trimmed on three sides like a corvette, tapered to a slim black hull, with a gun emplacement on the bow. He saw the armed men walking on the craft and whistled involuntarily.

"What are they doing?"

"I don't know, Mei," he replied. "Might be dropping some people off to help the Island post, but I doubt it.

My guess is they're just trolling the waters, showing the flag."

Yet he knew it was no routine marine patrol.

With two men at the fifty-calibre gun, and the glistening of sun on several sets of binoculars, the crew of that vessel meant serious business. Was there something on Cheung Chau? Drugs? Guns? Snake boats of illegals? No, apparently not. For the launch passed the government jetty without docking. It just cruised menacingly around the harbor in a manner clearly visible to all. And clearly intended to be.

Something told David this was no isolated incident, that other police units in other places in the colony were doing likewise, making a very obvious presence wherever they could. Something told him that in the events since early Monday morning and the ship disaster at Western, "Force-mob Standby," the last stage before the total mobilization of the RHKP to deal with the threat of civil disorder, was coming into effect.

"David?" Mei pressed, a hint of concern in her voice, "is there more trouble coming?"

He watched the craft, now canting southward at quarter speed toward the bottom end of the island. He said nothing, for he didn't have an answer.

They came to a crest of land, with a clear view of the western approaches and, in the distance, the massive bulk of Lantau. The police launch slowly disappeared from sight around the southern tip of Cheung Chau.

In the early afternoon, when it was nearly too hot to breathe and heat waves sizzled from the white sand, they left the beach and strolled leisurely to the cool shaded settlement of Chi Ma Hang.

The town was set back from the shoreline behind a cemented ridge. It was a maze of alleys, side paths and stony tracks, the joyous confusion of a Chinese rural village. Rows of square, sturdy two-story buildings stood ramshackle but neat, pastel gold, lime, orange and coffee-colored. The wrought-iron windows were set high, airy open fronts under cramped little second-story lofts in centuries-old Hakka fashion. Cheap radios blared tinny Cantonese love songs;

televisions showed stilted Mandarin operas. Rickety bicycles whizzed by or lay, abandoned, across the path. In a playground under the drooping banyan trees, a few fishermen crouched on their haunches over a game of Chinese chess while an elder sat, oblivious, puffing contentedly on an ancient reed waterpipe.

The tiny eatery at the end of the main path was marked only by a weather-worn etching of what looked like a benevolent sea serpent hung above the entrance.

Inside was a high-ceilinged room with ten or twelve plain round tables and backless stools. A few silver spittoons had been placed strategically in the corners; two overhead fans clattered, moving the air in slow motion.

At a table in the rear a group of Tanka fishermen played mah-jong amid much clattering, back-slapping and good-natured cursing and merriment. On a shelf a black-and-white television was turned on. It showed the demonstrators on their march from Statue Square, "To the mansion of His Excellency the Governor, full of passion and hate," a news reporter explained. The road was laced with concertina wire, reinforcement for the Mills barriers. With regulation black-oak batons dangling from their right hips, policemen were flanking the throng, directing its flow.

No one in the restaurant paid much attention to the television. David caught sight of his reflection in a mirror and was almost surprised to find himself here, removed from danger. He shook his head. It was as if he'd been looking for himself on the screen. Then he saw Mei Ling's face, the anxious look in her eyes. He touched her hand, caught her half-hearted smile.

"It'll be all right. Don't worry," he whispered.

But as he moved to hold her hand more tightly, he felt her shiver. He asked if she wanted to go home. She declined. "Just the air from the fans. I caught a chill."

David glanced around the room, at the patchwork of advertisements, the twenty kinds of cigarettes, the brandies and liqueurs, a collage of confusion covering the walls. He caught the eye of the *foki*, who was leaning against the cash register picking his fingernails. They were ready to order.

Mei Ling chose the meal but she was hesitant, her manner distracted and upset. As they waited for their food, David told her tales of his boyhood in Kilmarnock. About his mother, Tess, the good woman who held his family together with gusto and steaming portions of porridge. His sister, Celia, who became a school teacher in Dundee and married an emigré biologist from Norway who loved hiking in the Grampians. Sandra, the eldest child in the family, was a writer in Edinburgh.

And his father, Duncan, had served his country as an inspector in British West Africa. His greatest dream was to see his son follow in his footsteps—and to prove himself.

And finally there was the brave little terrier, Jessie, who lived a stubborn and hardy life at eleven, ensconced under the kitchen table of the ancestral home, where she snored with great abandon into the night and yapped softly and with great indignation at the postman as he made his daily rounds on Bannock Street, where they lived.

Mei Ling relaxed. The concern left her features and as he spoke she listened with great interest and for this David was glad. It was then he decided to broach the topic.

"Can we talk about Brendan?"

She looked away. "If you wish," she answered finally.

"You didn't see him the night he died?"

"No." She met his probing stare. Her eyes were cold. "He telephoned early that evening to cancel our date. It was about seven-thirty. He called from a pay phone in a bar somewhere. I remember hearing the background music. He said he was busy, that he was doing something important."

"Did he tell you what he had to do?"

She shrugged. "No. But then, did he ever?" She paused. "It was in the way he spoke," she said. "There was something on his mind, something bothering him. I never found out what it was."

She looked at him curiously. "Why does it involve you still, David? He's dead. Nothing can change that."

The tone in her voice surprised him. It was dispassionate. Cold.

He responded in kind. "There isn't anything else you

remember about that night? Anything that could explain his death?"

Suddenly it seemed too much for her. "What are you after, David?" she asked. "Don't you think I've suffered enough because of this? Can't you leave well enough alone?"

She paused. When she continued, her manner was gentler, her anger spent. "I told the investigators everything I knew. There isn't any more. My part in his life was simple. Brendan lived. Brendan died. We were friends, some said lovers. That's all."

David sighed. "I'm sorry." he said. "I didn't mean for it to be like this. Truly."

"It's over, David. Past. And nothing can change the past." Her eyes searched his, then softened.

The *foki* brought the food to their table.

After the meal they walked to the north end of the village, to the temple called Yu Hau Kung, the Palace of the Jade Vacuity. A long, low building of white stone, its outside was richly embroidered in Chinese calligraphy and delicate artwork. Layered green shingles shaded the entrance, and cold stone dogs guarded the building. Seated by the entrance on a creaky, backless chair was a toothless grandfather. Thin, wizened, his skin like parchment, he stared vacantly from the shadows to the harbor where a few junks bobbed in the blistering afternoon sun. The pungent smell of burning joss filled the air.

The temple honored Pei Ti, the spirit of the north, the disciple of right, goodness and decency in the Chambers of the Heavenly Host. It was Pei Ti, bare-footed, with his hair flowing, in a long black robe and silver breastplate, who raised his black standard amid glowing clouds of fire and challenged the Forces of Evil and Disorder in the name of Righteousness. Pei Ti fought against Mo Wang, the Demon King, and hurled him into the fiery mouth of hell at Peng Tu, the gate of the infernal regions.

David and Mei started through the high arched portico toward the temple sanctuary.

Suddenly, the old man held up his hand, speaking rapidly to Mei Ling in low, harsh tones.

"What does he say?" David asked her.

"Nothing, nothing." She pulled him away.

The old man went on speaking in a gutteral Cantonese; then he spat.

"We have to go," Mei Ling whispered, then started to run. David caught up to her.

"Mei Ling, calm down. What's wrong?"

She shook her head. She was catching her breath.

"Come on. What did he say?"

"That—that. . ." She tried to shrug and laugh. "Only that the time for Pei Ti is at hand, and that it is you, the white devils, who are the demon gods."

"That was all?"

She nodded, but David guessed the truth. He cupped her chin in his hand. "And I know what else he said to you: that you are a white-dog lover, a disgrace to your people. Bear him no mind, Mei Ling, he's touched."

She stiffened and her eyes went hard. "It's not so simple, David. There are many who feel as he does, who feel I have no business being seen with you."

"The times have changed," he said. "These things don't matter."

"No, David," she said sadly, "I think you know better. I am Chinese and you are British. These are realities; they matter very much." She held up her hand to his. "Look. The colors are different, as sun and moon. And so, it seems, are we."

"Do you believe that?"

"No." She shook her head in confusion. "I wish it were not so. But. . . ." She hesitated. "David, with the ship explosion and with the rioting, things are changing very quickly in Hong Kong. I think far more quickly than you're aware of."

She looked off into the pristine harbor with its lolling junks. On the horizon off Lantau, huge cloud tufts filled the sky. Finally she turned back to him.

"David," she asked, "hold me."

And for a long time, and with the greatest tenderness, he did.

CHAPTER EIGHT

———

Tai Po Gau was a noisy fishing hamlet in the New Territories, on the south shore of Tolo Harbor, nestled serene and timeless on the road to Shatin. Hovels balanced tremulously on uneven bamboo poles, awaiting the typhoon tides from Tolo. Long, silvery rows of fish netting were strung out to dry, baked white-hot in the August sun. At low tide, a long, pebbled beach ran along the causeway, leading into oozing, rich brown mud flats, where the odd pearl, oyster and creeping flamingo-red crayfish were retrieved. When the waters were high, junks and sampans scuttled about.

Maguire motioned to his driver to park the Cedric. He got out and walked to his rendezvous, a copse of trees, cool, dark and green. Sitting down on a smooth, oblong piece of granite, he waited.

Hoklo children, screaming with laughter, jumped nude from the rotting plank of an old grounded junk into the murky inlet waters. A two-horsepower sampan wheezed and coughed through the anchorage; there was the clanking of kitchen pots somewhere in the distance. A sudden gust of wind wafted across Maguire's face. He looked at his watch. Any second now.

A crackle of dry twigs. A tall figure coming toward him out of the shadows.

"Ah, Mr. Maguire. So glad you could make it." A practiced

smoothness of tone. "I don't believe we've had the pleasure of meeting before, but I can assure you I've admired your work for some time."

Lee Shiu Shing brushed a low branch from his face and stopped a few feet away. Gray business suit, well-tailored. Slim, sensitive features, hair fashionably long. Nature had been kind to him: he did not look his alleged seventy-six years. The Special Branch file needed updating.

The Chinese accepted his scrutiny patiently. Then he spoke, shrewdly, catching the concern. "No need to look so worried, Mr. Maguire. We are alone." The Elysée for political studies, the dossier had stated. The slight French accent, even now.

Maguire pointed to an ill-concealed figure on the slope behind them.

Lee was amused. His voice showed it.

"Come, come, Maguire. Your men are here also." His companion nodded in the direction of a white Ford Galaxie and two Hawaiian-shirted men, suddenly very busy taking photographs of the flora. Maguire swore silently. The damned ghost car. And so amateurishly obvious.

Lee turned back to face Maguire and placed a hand in his coat pocket. Maguire tensed. But the man only took out a gold-embossed cigarette package. He smiled and offered one. "Dutch, my friend. I never did like Red Victory." Maguire glanced at the package, a skating Dutch boy on the cover and the time in Amsterdam slotted in. The Chinese flicked a gold lighter.

Lee Shiu Shing held the highest executive post of the Chinese resource section, whose headquarters occupied six floors of the Bank of China building in Statue Square. Its import-and-export division did a legitimate trade in controlling the flow of capital investment to the mainland. And, in this endeavor, Lee was very astute, as members of the Hong Kong and Far East stock exchanges were quick to point out over brandies at the Marco Polo Club.

Maguire inhaled deeply and blew a soft, fragrant cloud of tobacco smoke into the air. "Shall we get down to business?"

Lee reached forward and touched Maguire's arm. "As I

indicated to you in answer to your concerns on the phone, what I am about to tell you may seem far-fetched, but I beg you to consider it as a resolution to your present difficulties." Maguire started to ask a question but Lee hushed him. "I know what you are thinking. Believe me, I am beyond charades. I have been in this game for many years, as you know, and I tire easily now of the. . ." He paused, smiled. "Cloak and dagger, isn't it? It has been a long time, a very long time."

"Since 1931."

Lee turned, an appreciative gleam in his eye. "You know much about us, don't you?" Maguire looked slightly away. "Well." Lee tightened his grip on Maguire's arm. "That should not shock me. I suppose I should be flattered that I am worthy of your continued attention."

Lee smiled when he caught Maguire's hesitation. "No, no. Don't deny it, my friend. I respect your service a great deal. Technically you are excellent in your craft. And that is what we are, is it not? Craftsmen? Operating in a musty purgatory between heaven and hell. Having many masters, and yet truly none but ourselves. Yes." He chuckled. "We are a dying breed, you and I."

The sounds of children in the distance died away. It was silent. The land was slowly seduced by heat.

Lee and his subordinates had been very helpful to Special Branch in the past. Most recently in the late fall a few years ago, in a major roundup of Kuo Min Tang operatives. And in the case of the two KGB agents operating from a Soviet freighter berthed in the Whampoa dockyard in Kowloon. Lee had even put them on to some Triad business that carried over to the mainland.

But the information from the elder Chinese had always been discreetly funneled through Government House. Lee himself had been shrouded in the fog of diplomatic channels. This was the first time the director of Special Branch and the head of Chinese intelligence in Hong Kong had actually met.

Lee was smooth, charming. "You know, Maguire, my father would have been very surprised to see me here like this. I was not always spiritually the man you see before you.

No, not I." His voice turned chilly. "Father was a Shanghai businessman. A Republican. Misguided. A man who lived for the dollar and made money his god."

Maguire regarded his counterpart dispassionately. Lee Shiu Shing's fortune had been intertwined with that of the Chinese Communist Party from its very inception. His rise to prominence had been a long, carefully plotted one, and the foundations of his present power were firmly rooted.

"It began for me, Maguire, as you said, in 1931. I returned from schooling overseas full of ideals, ready to change the world. Brash. Perhaps too naive and certainly too opinionated for my own good." Lee's voice trailed off. "It was the fourth congress of the Chinese Communist Party. Yes, the fourth. I was a youth observer and my first task was to organize the labor movement in Shanghai. Shanghai, of all places! Why, my father would have died of shame had he known!"

"And it was there you met Kang." The look on Lee's face, the flash of distrust, and Maguire instantly regretted his words. One didn't trespass on such intimacies and friendships lightly. There was a long, agonizing silence.

"Yes," Lee said finally. "It was there I met Kang." His features softened, his manner seemed almost reverent. "He was a great source of inspiration to me, Maguire. A great source of inspiration. It was Kang Shung who made the Social Affairs Department a respected agency during the war against the Imperial Japanese. With this you must agree."

Maguire nodded. Lee spoke the truth. The *She Hui Pu,* or Social Affairs Department, was the Party's central organ for intelligence-gathering and had developed an enviable reputation in China during the war years. A reputation in no small measure attributable to Lee's mentor, Kang.

But Kang Shung had not crafted the agency's activities alone. And both Lee and Maguire knew it. "You give yourself too little credit, Lee. It was you who developed the field-intelligence net, not Kang." Lee smiled politely. "And you who first successfully made the dangerous courier run from Hopei Province to the Allied Administration in New Delhi." There was a twinkle in Lee's eye as Maguire spoke.

"You can count yourself fortunate that Generalissimo Chiang was never made aware of your informant, Maguire. Could you imagine what he would have done had he known? The lives of his beloved Nationalist troops dependent on intelligence gathered by Communists? Yet who is to say now? We have a saying, my friend: In the winter storm, the jackal and the lamb may find themselves sharing a cave." Lee paused. "Which do you think I am, Maguire? The jackal?" The Irishman, in spite of his reserve, found himself openly laughing. They began to walk.

The man was good—of that there was no doubt. In 1960 Lee Shiu Shing was sent to the Hague as the senior China News correspondent. Thereafter, things "seemed" to happen in the Dutch capital. An American scientist—diplomatic gossip had it he worked for the CIA in Iran—was found floating in a garbage-filled Dutch canal, his body heavily weighted. An Indonesian, ostensibly dealing in import-export with Eastern Europe while in the employ of the Chinese, overstepped the bounds of his office and became too friendly with the Russians. He, too, was silenced. The Dutch state police, the Maurits Chauseé, sensed they were dealing with an expert. But before they could act, in mid-1965, Lee Shiu Shing was quietly recalled to Peking.

His next posting was closer to home, Hong Kong, and he became assistant to the head of the resource section—the position Lee now held. In China the tempestuous Red Guard movement challenged the intellectual dexterity of the Old Guard with greater frequency. And then it happened.

The Year of the Tiger, 1967. The great struggle of wills began. Lee was made director of the resource section in Hong Kong. Perhaps coincidently, well-organized riots shattered the fragile facade of English gentility in the British colony. In the rising heat, Hong Kong went up in a firestorm of rioting, bombings and full-scale destruction. Special Branch had received detailed communications from a Dutch agent of the shipping firm Rotterdamse Lloyd and was only too well acquainted with Lee. And yet there was nothing concrete, nothing solid, no reason to lay the blame on him.

Then, slowly, the events on the mainland stabilized and the

heated summer passions gave way to cooler heads. A subtle change occurred. Trickling communications seeped from the sixth floor of the Bank of China building, inklings that the mainland was prepared to denounce the actions of what were now considered ideologically impure hotheads and opportunistic street gangs.

The British, to their credit, accurately interpreted these minute signs, and the end of 1967 brought with it an end to the rioting; an uneasy truce set in and the economic and political climate of Asia changed once more. Mainland China shyly opened its doors to the world. Lee Shiu Shing again began to show his face in public.

Proud, erect, a man not to be taken lightly, he was soon held in great esteem by local governments and banking communities. Lee became eminently respectable, an elder uncle whose advice was eagerly sought and carefully considered. On occasion he deigned to attend soirées and cocktail parties selected for their gentility and good taste. Other than that, he avoided the public eye doggedly.

Rumor had it that he had grown accustomed to the comfortable life and the pleasures it bore. He appeared to have no part in the mad scurrying going on everywhere in the colony as the clock to repatriation ticked down. But Maguire doubted it. If there was maneuvering going on, Lee was part of it. The man was just that good. A formidable adversary, if ever there was one.

"So what is it, Lee?" Maguire asked pointedly. "Why do you want me here? Or should I even ask? Certainly it isn't to speak of the bank rate."

Lee laughed easily. "No, most assuredly, it isn't something as fickle as that."

The director of SB stopped and faced the older man impatiently. "Then what is it you want?"

The two Special Branch detectives by the ghost car were already smoking their second Viceroys. Their roll of film had run out long ago. Besides, at this distance, Maguire and the "subject" had moved out of view.

So who cared? It wasn't their fault if the boss couldn't even follow his own stage directions.

They saw Lee's shadow team standing, in the open now, about the same distance away from the players. They waved tentatively, self-consciously at the three. One of the figures waved back. And they wondered out loud what it was like doing this for the other side.

Cleve had the first reports on his desk shortly after the last shell was spent, the last rioter dispersed. His worst fears were confirmed. The situation was approaching a crisis. He feverishly jotted down notes for the evening's meeting of department heads. His day with Matthew would have to wait. He called Margaret, but got no answer, so he asked Mrs. Callicutt to relay the message for him when she could find time. And to bring him some coffee and coconut buns.

Then he plowed into the mountainous files already on his desk, gray-white smoke curling furiously to the ceiling from the cigar clenched in his mouth.

Peng's reports were to the point. To date: no leads and, beyond Andrews's chance run-in with the scar-faced man, very little good evidence. The governor, who seemed to be sending memos down with every passing car, was more fulsome. Driscoll could "predict with certainty further disturbances in the colony if the Force did not act with restraint." Cleve threw the memo in the air, and it floated for a moment before settling into the ashtray. Could the governor, he wondered, predict with certainty what Peking would do?

The phone rang. It was Chaukley from Commercial Crime with an update of the economic situation.

"The Hang Seng stock exchange is mixed, sir. Nothing drastic either way as yet. No runs on the market."

"Good, good." Cleve brushed cigar ash off desk.

"Except," Chaukley continued, "on one of Robert Burden's principal companies, Burden Silver."

"Yes?" Cleve's voice raised in interest.

"This morning the bottom fell out. They've stopped trading to sort it out."

"Any reason?" Cleve stubbed the cigar into the ashtray.

"Very odd, sir. There've been unconfirmed reports of a

cave-in this morning at a Burden mine on Luzon. No word of casualties. Could be hundreds."

"Reaction?"

"The Burden people on the floor of the exchange are denying it, of course. Some say the mine is still operative. Others think Burden can absorb the indemnity claims. But you know how the market is these days. A rumor is all it takes to start them scurrying around."

"Like Chicken Little?" Cleve interrupted.

"Sir?"

"Nothing, Chaukley. Continue."

A pause. The sound of papers shuffling.

"I think it's fair to say the disaster has hurt them on the market."

"But that wouldn't be enough to cause a run, would it?"

"A small one, perhaps. Nothing like this. But that's the weird thing. It seems that within minutes of the disaster on Luzon, Burden's rubber plantations in Sumatra were hit with a wildcat walkout. No reason given and no indication at all of a quick return."

"Your thoughts?"

"The investors aren't fools, sir. They see these two things happening so close together and know it isn't a coincidence. Somebody in the marketplace doesn't like Sir Robert and seems intent on showing him that in a big way."

Cleve picked up a pencil and began tapping it on the desk top. He considered the possibilities. "And how is my good friend Sir Robert taking these minor inconveniences?"

"It couldn't happen at a worse time for the Burden chain of companies. He's just getting over last year's financial bloodbath. They say he lost millions on that airline in the outback of New Guinea. And of course, there was his losing venture in Brunei. Only two of his ten wells even turned a profit. I think, sir, it's fair to say today's debacle stretches Sir Robert to near the breaking point."

Cleve stopped tapping his pencil. "Thank you, Chaukley." Cleve moved to hang up.

"Oh, sir?"

"Yes, Stu."

"On China, sir. My man tells me the railroad scandal broke to their public today. There's heat on Deng, tremendous heat."

"Wonderful," muttered Cleve, "flipping wonderful." He put the pencil down and thought a moment. "You seem to have plugged into a hot lead."

"I try, sir."

"Any idea what the Chinese premier might do?"

"My man says he's assigning Kang Shung of the Security Branch to head an internal inquiry into malpractice by the railway-engineering firm that did the Dadu project. They should report publicly by Friday."

"Wonderful," Cleve repeated in a dull monotone. With internal pressure no doubt increasing on him to do something about the explosion of the ship, this public airing of the crisis in China was the last thing the Chinese premier needed. If only he knew something about that ship, what it was doing in Hong Kong, why it was at the Communist pier—even if he knew its name. . . . Cleve could see the scenario developing, and he didn't like its tones. He picked up the pencil and started doodling on a scratch pad.

"The word on Kang?"

"One of the old Guard. He'll do his best to protect the status quo."

"Will it work?" He penciled a giant ellipse.

"As well as anything these days," Chaukley allowed.

Cleve crossed the ellipse with a dramatic stroke.

"Keep me posted." He absently tossed the pencil to one side of his desk.

"Sir."

He hung up and reached into his drawer for a file marked "Kowloon Project," a file he'd opened when Her Majesty's most recent representative had arrived in the colony. Among the good cheer and promises Driscoll had brought with him was a rumor of a conciliatory gesture from Whitehall to Peking in the form of a parcel of land. No one had officially acknowledged to Cleve that the deal even existed, not in the public view, and not in the closed corridors of power. And, in the purest logic of the diplomatic world, because no one spoke of it, it did not exist. But Cleve knew otherwise. It was there, all right. To be traded away as surely as he was a coal miner's son.

He looked down at the map. There it was, bordered in red marker, on Kowloon side, in the very heart of Tsim Tsa Tsui, the thriving hub of the peninsula. Two hundred thirty-six acres of land abutting on the harbor, some of the choicest property in Asia, perhaps in the world.

Cleve took out some glossy photographs of the skyline that surrounded the parcel of land. The New World Center; the Peninsula Hotel; the Ocean Terminal; much of the Golden Mile along Nathan Road.

The buildings were worth billions. Yet even in this wealthy place, it was the land that held the true worth. For each building was tied to a lease; and each lease, so it seemed, was held, ultimately, by one company. It was the land China coveted, and it was the land Whitehall wished to give away.

But if Whitehall wished to give it away, they first had to own it—and, in so doing, they would make the present owners even richer men. From the information he'd quietly collected over the past year, Cleve had found a tangle of land titles, holding companies and trusts. He had begun to guess who those owners might be, to see how they operated on the fringes of legitimacy. And to see the day when His Excellency might have to heed the advice, if not formal censure, of the commissioner of police. Explosions in Burden's mine, Cleve thought. Interesting.

A knock on the door.

It was Mrs. Callicutt. Dunn of the PTU, already bellowing his greetings from behind her, was here to report on police casualties in the riot.

CHAPTER NINE

——————

He said what, Maguire?" The governor's voice cracked sharply through the large sitting room.

The director of Special Branch uncrossed his legs and sat forward in the armchair. Through no fault of his own, this audience with His Excellency the governor—Maguire's men referred to him as "H.E."—was becoming very awkward, if not downright unpleasant. He cleared his throat.

"He said, sir, that the land deal was now open to renegotiation."

Thomas Croydon Driscoll stepped into the light. He was a tall, spare man, ruddy-faced, white-haired, lean and confident in the way only Whitehall made one. He moved with the practised grace of the moneyed classes.

"And what did you think he implied by that?"

Maguire hesitated. "I don't know, sir," he answered very carefully. "Lee wasn't too clear on the matter."

The governor looked out the window. "Maguire," he cautioned, "you do know what he means by 'the land deal.'"

"Yes, sir," the director offered. "The arrangements being worked out between the Hong Kong government, the People's Republic of China and an intermediary for the Kowloon land."

"Quite, quite," Driscoll interrupted impatiently. "Well, I should think his impetuosity is rather glaring, wouldn't you?"

His eyes bore into Maguire's; there was no hiding the fury and anger in them.

Robert Maguire wisely said nothing. A grandfather clock bonged the half hour from its place in the corner of the room. Far off, beyond the lace-curtained windows, the director could make out the sound of a police siren. Then another. The snapping of firecrackers? Or was it guns?

The governor sighed deeply. Slowly. When next he spoke to Maguire his voice was calmer, more reasoned.

"Anything further, Maguire?"

"Yes, sir," Maguire answered, "Lee said that there were more obvious ways to make his concerns felt. That today's events should indicate the tone and tenure of his displeasure."

A scowl came to Driscoll's face. "Do you take it he meant the riot?"

"Sir," Maguire offered apologetically in a half-whisper, "from our conversation earlier today, the connection is inescapable. The riot is certainly Lee's doing, and its motivation is not the ship disaster but rather the land."

Thomas Driscoll was silent for a long time, as if weighing alternatives. Finally he spoke. "We shall see, then, won't we, Maguire? I have no intention of quaking in my boots at the mere whim of a greedy Chinaman. Have I made myself clear?"

"I take it then, sir, the land deal stands as it is?" Maguire offered hopefully by way of clarification. But he realized as he did so that he had gone too far.

Driscoll glared at the director of Special Branch. "Maguire, you will take it any bloody way that I tell you, do you understand?"

"Sir," Maguire replied red-faced.

"And Maguire," the governor continued in a menacing voice, "I wouldn't get too adventurous with this if I were you. I have old friends in the colonial secretariat—dear friends. Correct me if I'm wrong, Maguire. I think you're approaching the age where you're eligible for a substantial pension—if there are no complications. Is that not so?"

Maguire said nothing.

"Good." The governor smiled approvingly. "I'm glad we understand one another."

Maguire nodded meekly. With an impatient wave, Driscoll dismissed him and strode out of the room.

The clouds, high and fluffed, were tinged with vermilion in the late afternoon sky by the time the *Man Tat* creaked morosely into its berth at the Wilmer Street ferry pier. Junks bound for the typhoon shelter puttered by, their bat sails limp in the crosswind; hydrofoils crisscrossed in the western distance on the supper-hour shuttle to Macau like elegant low-flying geese.

David trundled along the rotting gangplank, Mei Ling at his side. He'd been trying to cheer her up since their flight from the temple earlier that afternoon, yet she had barely managed a smile. He offered to take her home. She fended him off, saying she was tired and needed to rest for the next day's work, so David flagged a taxi on Connaught Road West. He tried to talk to Mei but she was already climbing into the back seat of the old Mercedes diesel.

He waved politely as the taxi pulled off, then strolled westward. The station was only two blocks away, and it was a lovely, hazy Tuesday evening. Harbor water splashed softly onto the dock pylons and the hulls of moored junks, children scampering around their decks. Dogs yelped happily at passing strangers. The hot breeze caressed his face.

He thought back to what Mei had said earlier in the day about Brendan's passing. He considered her innocence in the matter. She had nothing to gain by his death, and she knew nothing of the circumstances surrounding it.

He paused. Perhaps she was right. Perhaps he was tilting at windmills after all. Perhaps it was wrong to disturb the dead in an attempt to calm his own troubled spirit.

A lone hawk came from Kowloon, riding the fragile currents of air in proud, sweeping arcs, uttering a high, yearning cry as it moved. The sun was settling slowly over the peaks of Lantau, rich crimson, tinker orange.

He began to hum a Highland tune, a low, lilting air. The

letter of resignation sitting unsigned in his quarters was suddenly the furthest thing from his mind. Tonight, Hong Kong was a good place to be.

Yes, for tonight, at least, Hong Kong was home.

Mei Ling sat in the taxi and glanced with distaste across the black, iron-grilled road partition to the reeking slums of Wanchai. The signs of the bar district reached skyward in gawdy oranges, reds and dragon yellows. The driver's window was open, and Mei Ling inhaled the salty stench from the nearby land-reclamation project. The Japanese dash fan turned in feeble semi-circles, its metal blades weakly slicing the foul air.

Mei touched the jade brooch in her hair, her last gift from Brendan. It was lily-shaped, large and opulent.

The driver looked back at her through the chipped rear-view mirror. Not bad, he mused, not bad at all.

Abruptly she leaned forward and spoke to him in harsh Cantonese, redirecting the cab to an address in Causeway Bay.

He shrugged. "Sure, miss, no trouble. It's your money." He'd already figured her for a high-class working girl.

She sat back in the seat, her eyes closed, one hand across her face.

"You okay, miss?"

She looked at him through the rear-view mirror. "Yes. . . it's all right. Just the heat."

"Don't I know it?" He started to tell a small joke, but she wasn't paying attention. Don't waste time on this one, he thought, she isn't worth it. He concentrated on his driving.

A few minutes later they arrived at the turnoff to Causeway Bay, a street lined with apartments, stores, restaurants, even a McDonald's. People poured from a thousand and one camera shops, tailor shops and electronic showrooms. Tourists swarmed in and out of the hotels—the Plaza, the Excelsior. Chinese scurried to the latest Charles Bronson movie at the Isis or a ten-year-old Disney rerun at the East Town.

The cabby turned in at the entrance to the Pearl City

mansion. A large Nissan tour bus had just pulled into the last parking spot in the driveway. About forty jabbering Germans stumbled from the bus, squinting as their eyes grew accustomed to the Asian air. Four or five liveried Indian coachmen, turbanned, in deep purple tunics, white jodhpurs and gleaming black riding boots, ran to greet them, all proper smiles of servitude and outstretched palms.

Then there was space for the cab. Mei Ling got out, paid her fare. The cabby extended his hand for the tip—but there was none. He slammed the door shut, cursing loudly in Cantonese, got back in and pulled back into the bumper-to-bumper traffic.

Mei Ling stopped in the palm-shrouded doorway. Beside her was the tinted sliding door. Controlled torrents of arctic air came from the foyer as elegant couples glided in and out.

Two smartly dressed Philippine businessmen stood a few feet away. One poked the other in the ribs. They looked over, eyeing the trade, and she glanced back expressionless.

Suddenly she turned away from the building, darted across the road and entered a narrow portico between two music showrooms. From the open-fronted shops, noise poured out of three cassette players: reedy Mandarin, a People's Opera and a too-fast, tinny Sinatra.

Mei Ling moved through the bleak foyer, past the two tiny elevators and up the narrow side staircase. Her wooden clogs clattered hollow on the hard stone and, as she climbed, the smell of fried rice, cabbage soup, human sweat and age followed her.

On the fourth floor she saw him, sitting like a leather-skinned toad in the rattan armchair, potbellied, nicotine-stained fingers and bleary eyes. The Chiu Chau who controlled her life.

"Hurry up! You're keeping the customers waiting tonight, and there's an American ship in."

She spat at him and he smiled slowly.

"Where have you been?"

"It's none of your business."

"But it is, you little whore, it is."

He saw her face flinch and knew he had the advantage.

"You don't like the word, do you? Trying to look respectable. Well, you don't fool anyone."

She flushed. "Be quiet, you pimp."

He slapped her with the back of his hand, not very hard, not enough to spoil the merchandise.

"Bitch! You'd still be a penniless farm slut if it weren't for us! A pimp? You dare call me a pimp? Well, what of you, my little Hakka maiden? You're a cheap sailor's whore, and not even a good one. Now, tell me, where were you?"

"With the police, if you must know. They still wonder about Williams."

He leaned forward in the chair, his face shining with sweat. She saw the grease on his forehead, the huge blackheads in his nose.

"This police death has caused the master trouble. There have been countless raids and unwanted attention as they sought you out and badgered us about your whereabouts. Yip Lam has not been pleased. For this inconvenience, you owe us greatly." He hissed. "It will be many nights before you rest alone. Many nights."

She walked past the smirking man to the beckoning frosted door. A whore. She pushed open the portals to the bordello. The obese woman behind the reception desk was waving a plastic fan in front of heavily made-up eyes. She cursed Mei Ling heartily as Mei walked down the narrow corridor to her room. She entered and lay down on the filthy bed. The room was nothing more than a little cubicle, mirrored and painted in loud, vulgar colors, with all the intimacy of a public lavatory. She could hear the groans and shrill laughter, the drunken snorts of customers, the brittle cajoling of the other girls.

She undressed slowly and put on a sheer pink slip. The air was close. It was a still and sultry night, not unlike the night she had left her family home in a village in the New Territories for the last time. She had felt no remorse; she'd been full of the fickle anger of youth and armed with a naive determination. Careful not to awaken anyone, she had taken with her only a torn brown hamper, stuffed with all her worldly possessions, precious and meager though they might be.

She had begun the walk southward to her destiny, to the
jeweled dragon of Nathan Road, to live with a black-sheep
relative of whom the family spoke little, a cousin who, in the
sadness of Chinese existence, turned out to be a *do-yau*—a
drug addict.

She had wanted a life of freedom and luxury, and had
wound up in a tin shack on Causeway Bay, overlooking the
jade and diamond beauty of the foreigners' hotels. She lived
in a shanty made of corrugated metal, rusting Coca-Cola
signs and rotting teakwood.

At first she had worked hard, finding her freedom ex-
hilarating, window-shopping at whim, seeing for herself the
joyful opulence of the Jade City. But her tastes were rich, and
soon looking was not enough. She wanted to possess these
things of beauty, to feel them, to touch. To see the look in
men's eyes, that covetous half-mad look that told her she was
wanted. What a fool she had been! What an empty-headed
fool!

Her cousin spent most of his time on the waterfront in a
drug-induced stupor; once in a while he would be caught by
the police and sent to prison. Then he returned no more.
Perhaps he had finally succumbed to the *bac-fan*, the white
rice, heroin. Mei Ling did not miss him.

The little hut on the hillside became her own, a rusted
castle nestled high on a crested slope between two rocky out-
crops, overlooking the twinkling lights of the city she desired
with all her heart.

At night, in the crisp stillness, her black *sam-foo* buttoned
up to her throat, she would sit silently on a rocky ledge, her
knees tucked in, her face nestled in her hands. Childlike, feet
weary from working for twelve hours at the perfume counter,
she would sit there staring and dreaming, looking down at
the warm green glow of the shining city, surrounded by garbage and rot. In the early morning hours, head drowsy with
sleep, she would meander the few feet back down the stony
slope to her bamboo bed on the dusty floor. She would rest
as the city pulsed below.

Men were attracted to her then. It was inevitable, and she
was naive, a lovely Asian beauty.

And then one day she was strolling aimlessly, cool and casual, on Blake Pier, looking out at the anchored cruise ships and reading the exotic place names: Rotterdam, Napolia and Durban. Then she met him, a young, debonaire Chinese called Johnny.

He was everything she had dreamed of, and he courted her with the same gentility as the men in her fantasies. Before the month was out she had moved into his plush Cleveland Street mansion.

She was caressed, pampered, given all the clothing she desired. She loved the Mercedes he drove and his many extravagances: the nights in the illegal casinos frittering away money until dawn; the trips to Macau and Tokyo and Taipei in the first-class luxury of the Cathay Pacific L1011.

And then, when she had lost her soul to him, it happened. She asked innocently if she might return to the New Territories to see her parents. He wanted her to go with him on a business trip to Tokyo. She was his show piece, a bauble. She refused. Foolishly. She argued. He threatened. She reached out to strike him, and he responded in kind. His name was Johnny Yip, and his father was Yip Lam, a powerful Triad figure who rode roughshod over half the Hong Kong underworld with his spoiled son canting along at his side. And Johnny had broken her like a skittish mare.

Her fate was decided after the beating. She was still too beautiful to cast aside entirely, and the investment in her was, after all, too great. She was sent to one of the brothel madams, who would break her in.

Mei Ling faced an endless succession of men, glaring, greedy, insolent, impotent. Her spirit was bowed; she could not find refuge even in insanity. She couldn't go home; not now, perhaps never.

The year passed quickly. Her night hours were filled with forced passion, her day time jealously guarded by custodians at the apartment doors. She was protected like valuable property, a lucrative investment. Like the others, she was well-fed and looked after; her whims were catered to. After a while, the rebellious spirit in her died.

The Feast of the Clear and Bright in the Chinese calendar, the spring Ching Ming festival, came and went. It ushered in the summer sun which shimmered on the sands of Lantau and Big Wave Bay. The time rushed by. The Fall Moon festival became a memory. And she worked on, conditioned now, her spirit broken. She was now allowed to go out alone without the mama san or a male protector. But no matter; her journeys were mechanical. No longer did she gaze in starry admiration at the dresses and jewelry in gaudy window displays. No more were her eyes entranced by jade and ruby; jewels were hers for the asking. She had paid the price many times over.

She worked in a variety of brothels, dance halls and bars, all owned by the same man. Now and again she saw Johnny, but she looked at him with different eyes than before. Hurt, abused, tormented eyes. She hated him, but she could not summon the spirit to do anything about it. And he looked at her with a mocking smile that said, "You are mine, my lovely. You are mine."

Mei Ling left her room and moved into the arena. The earthy smells of sex and beer and sweat wafted through the air. The blood-red lights exaggerated the rude couplings around her. For this whore in Wanchai, the night had just begun.

Maguire picked up the receiver and dialed. He felt strange making the call. He was not accustomed to chances, and his first meeting with Lee had been as close to the seventh circle as he normally would have traveled. But Driscoll had pushed him to this point, and there was no turning back.

There was something not quite right about the governor and his land deal, something sordid and tawdry. It wasn't the increasing hint of corruption that particularly bothered Maguire. Tea money, whatever form it took, did much to grease the wheels that made the colony function. No, it was Driscoll himself that annoyed the director. The man could have been more discreet, more amenable to compromise with Lee. If he had been, Maguire was certain, this whole unpleasant mess with the ship explosion could have been avoided. And it was this unwillingness to bend that had brought them to this sorry state.

He'd gone along with Driscoll in the beginning when the meetings were arranged and the proposals between Peking, the British and the holders of the valuable Kowloon properties were first broached.

Don't tell Cleve, Driscoll had whispered initially. It's none of the CP's business. Don't let on about what you know, Robert. I trust you. You're a confidante of this house.

And Maguire, like a naive fool, hadn't said a word. Not a word. Not to Cleve or any one else who snooped around. Not that John Cleve was a particularly good friend of his, any more, or a competent commissioner of police, for that matter.

Entertaining bigwigs for the Canton airport project, that's what Maguire did. Nothing more. And since his reputation was well known throughout the Hang Seng stock exchange, everyone seemed reasonably satisfied to let him get on with it unchallenged.

Maguire had kept his mouth shut—until now. He did not like the way the governor had treated him in their meeting a few hours ago. Shabbily, without grace or dignity. Well, two could play at this game. Maguire felt more than up for a match.

The phone was answered by an underling. Maguire politely introduced himself and was surprised at how quickly he was transferred.

"Lee?"

"Yes."

"It's Maguire. Robert Maguire. I'd like to discuss a matter of mutual interest with you."

The voice was expectantly cheerful. "Oh, good. I expect you have the governor's reply?"

Maguire hesitated. "I'm afraid it isn't what you wanted."

Stony silence. He heard the slow, calculated breathing. "I see. He does not wish to reconsider?"

Thinking back to the stormy meeting, Maguire replied tactfully, "No, I'm afraid he is firm."

"You realize that complicates things."

Maguire allowed that it did. "You mean there will be more disturbances? More bloodshed?"

"Precisely."

Maguire glanced at his hands. Funny how they looked dirty. Maybe it was the light. He shuffled in his seat and looked at his reflection in the mirror. "I felt that would be your reaction and so did the governor," he said calmly.

"And yet he would not bend?"

"No."

Silence.

"You know of my intent in the riot, Maguire?"

"Yes," Maguire said carefully, "I suppose I do. The ship was Communist Chinese. The dead were your people. You had no choice; it was a professional necessity."

After a long pause, Lee answered. "Not totally a necessity, Robert. Not nearly as much as you would think, though there was a great deal of personal as well as professional satisfaction in what I had done." Lee's voice had taken on a strange, almost confiding, tone.

"Sometimes you must bend the rules to get what you want," Maguire said simply.

"And what do you think that is, Maguire?"

"I don't know, Lee. Land, perhaps. Money. More than what you have been offered. Maybe, like all of us, you want more." Silence. A long silence. "Don't you?"

"Very astute, Robert," Lee answered finally, "I always knew you were an intelligent man."

"Thank you, Lee. I always try to exercise my initiative." Maguire caught himself smiling at his reflection in the mirror. He stopped.

It was Lee who spoke next. "And where would your initiative lead you in these circumstances?"

"Are you bribing me?" There was playfulness in Maguire's voice.

"No, far from it," Lee answered soberly. "I'm just curious as to why you would call me so readily as the bearer of bad news. It is not logical unless you are amenable to a transaction of sorts." Lee paused. "Face it, Maguire. You, too, want more. But of what? Position? Power? Wealth? Come, tell me. You will never have another chance."

Now it was Maguire's turn to be still. Again he turned to the mirror, ran his fingers absently through his hair, noticed the gray. His face looked weary. Pinch marks showed around his eyes from straining all these years in the Asian sun, from straining to make a go of it here, from running on the treadmill. He thought of Driscoll, so prim, so proper, so imperiously perfect.

He sighed. "All right, I'll tell you what I want, Lee." Maguire's voice was bitter. "An edge. Every man needs an edge. I'm no different."

"Ambitious, Robert?" Lee chided softly.

"Aren't we all?" Maguire answered coldly.

"An edge on whom, my friend? Cleve? The governor?"

"No, not them. Let's just say the future and my part in it." Maguire's voice grew hard. "You see, Lee, I think you know more about the explosion than you've let on. You have to, or you couldn't have been so quick to capitalize on its effects to pressure Driscoll."

Lee seemed to consider the statement. Then he spoke. "Perhaps. But, my young friend, you disregard too readily the masses and their will."

Maguire laughed. "The masses? Ha. We both know how to manipulate them. We both have, Lee."

"And what does that knowledge lead you to propose, Maguire? Do you wish a margin of the Kowloon land profits? It can be arranged. My government would never know. Nor would yours."

"No," Maguire replied truthfully. "I don't like the altitude you lads move in. It's too airy and laced with danger. Although in some ways the offer is enticing, I have to decline. My tastes are more simple, my needs more immediate. I have but two requests. The first is basic: a sum of money. Five million Hong Kong dollars, in a secret account in the Seychelles Islands."

"And why should I give it to you?"

"Because," Maguire said forcefully, "it behooves you to. Remember, Lee, I've added two and two and come up with four. I've got the goods on you now, no matter what happens to the colony. I don't think you would be wise to forget it."

"I could kill you in the blink of an eyelid."

"And the letter is already in a post-office strong box with instructions for it to be forwarded to your superiors on my death. I don't imagine they would be too happy to hear of the little parcel you want under the table as your part in the land deal. That sort of corruption is rather déclassé in Peking these days, wouldn't you say?"

"How do you know I won't kill you anyway?" Lee noted, almost academically.

"The letter, Lee. The letter," Maguire purred. "It makes for interesting reading. Especially since I had you taped at Tai Po Gau. The tapes came through very well. Made excellent transcripts. As clear as the photos we took. Though I admit you do take a better profile. And when that data is compared to the tape I have of you now. . . ." Maguire let the implication lie. "And properly edited?" he continued smugly. "How would your superiors feel about these things? They're a bit jumpy, I would think, wouldn't you? I should imagine they'd hang just about anyone out to dry, if only to deflect the heat from them. . . ."

"Clever, Maguire, very clever, I must say," Lee whispered. "Now your second request?"

"A simpler one. Professional, if you will. That edge to my career. The one thing that would give me the greatest personal satisfaction. I need to know the name of the ship and who set the explosion."

"And you think I can tell you?"

"Yes."

"You don't ask for much," Lee commented dryly.

"I try to keep my tastes plebian."

"Why do you wish to know? It is done, and in the long run it is a relatively minor thing. Nothing will change the future of this colony. The explosion may only quicken it."

"The CP is getting old. He may soon retire. Perhaps the successful resolution of this matter will be considered important enough to make me a legitimate candidate for the vacant post."

"In that case," Lee allowed, "I would like to help you, but I don't really care."

"I beg your pardon?" Maguire said. "Eleven people die. A ship explodes at the Communist pier, at the hands of unknown parties and you don't really care. I would think at the very least you would want revenge. After all, it is your ship."

"Is it?" Lee answered simply.

"I beg your pardon?"

"Is it my ship?"

Robert Maguire considered the strange reply. "Then if not yours—whose?"

"Ah," Lee said coolly, "now there I can help you and resolve your dilemma. But before we continue, the bills. Do you want them in hundreds or thousands?"

A smile slowly came to Maguire's face. It was a warm smile. It was a smile of success.

CHAPTER TEN

———

Outside the commissioner's office, at 22:30 hours in the May House courtyard, was a hurriedly drawn-up line of Land Rovers and black government sedans. Doors slammed, feet pattered on concrete steps, quick, brushed salutes were exchanged.

On the fourth floor, two uniformed constables stood near a closed door muttering about the Macau dog races. The in-conference bulb shone harshly above the entrance.

Inside, a group of men sat around a heavy table, uncomfortable and insolent from lack of sleep. Some wore wrinkled safari suits, others hastily donned summer uniforms, salt stains ringing the armpits. Others stood in the shadowed corners chatting hoarsely with each other.

Stale tobacco clouds drifted lazily upward. The room had four large windows; at one end hung an oil painting of the Queen, at the other a portrait of the commander-in-chief of the Royal Hong Kong Police, Princess Alexandra.

For all the intentions of its original architects, the chamber had the cloistered, clammy feel that permeated all parts of the colony in the dead heat of summer. The air conditioners, struggling furiously, whined bitterly and emitted a chilly blast that seemed to match the mood of the men in the room. The tension was palpable.

A mess sergeant stormed in carrying a huge silver tray with

three large wicker thermoses, each steaming at the neck. He was followed by two *fokis* with similar trays and, waddling madly to keep up, a squat amah balancing a serving board on which were heaped an odd assortment of cups, some plastic, some glass, a few the white, chipped porcelain with an anemic-green "HK" of the government emblazoned on their sides. The mess sergeant placed his tray on a large brown teapoy set against the long wall and motioned to his charges to do likewise. The men went to get coffee. John Cleve, who had quietly come in from his adjoining office, sat at the head of the table, rested his massive hands on the plush green velour and shrewdly appraised the officers under his command.

"Right, gentlemen. To business."

The talk ceased abruptly; the only sound came from the air conditioners which growled by the windows like senile chow dogs.

Cleve nodded to Maguire, and the director of Special Branch began. His voice had a falsely honeyed tone that had all the warmth of cold North Sea amber.

"In playing out our various scenarios, we have come to the conclusion that the riot this morning at the governor's mansion, and any events that may flow from it are, in all probability, spontaneous. After careful thought and much consideration, Special Branch can no longer support the prevalent theory that either the Communist Party in Peking or its following within the left-wing labor movement in the colony have anything to gain by the ship's destruction and the attendant emotional overflow it may seem to have caused."

Maguire glanced up from his prepared text. He was wearing a buff safari suit; the creases along his shirt sleeves were razor-sharp. His pale gray eyes betrayed nothing. There were hints of a smile on his smooth features, as if he found something amusing. His last statement to the assembled officers had the desired effect.

Questions. Angry questions.

No, Maguire didn't think Peking had incited the disturbance.

Yes, in recent days the moderates in Peking's inner

sanctum had come under increasing pressure from young hotheads, both left-wing and right.

Yes, with the talk of corruption in high places, the situation in China was admittedly very tense—but not tense enough to bring about the incident at Government House, and others that were sure to follow in the next few days, and not tense enough to capitalize on them. No, he repeated with a casual nod of the head, no, it wasn't nearly that bad. Then he told them that the riot was tied to the explosions only insofar as local Communist sympathizers reacted to local grievances. Nothing else.

From the front of the conference table there was a roar. "Damn it, Bob!" It was Digger Dunn. "You can't really believe it wasn't the mainland Chinese! It plays right into the hands of the radicals in Peking!" Heads turned toward the speaker. It was apparent that Dunn expressed the views of most. Maguire braced himself.

Dennis Dunn was a large man but he knew it and he usually carried himself with grace and good humor. Now he glowered in his seat, his face reddening.

Maguire stared at him, unperturbed. "I really don't think it's so simple."

"Not so simple?" Dunn's face was livid. "My dear man, it doesn't take a university baccalaureate to see the equation! Make the existence of 'enslaved' Hong Kong a cause for liberating the masses from a 'bourgeois,' fumbling leadership in Peking. It's brilliant in its simplicity! It's relatively bloodless and efficient—a few canisters of high explosive placed on an old tramp steamer and the left-wing unions in Hong Kong can be mobilized in only a few hours to give you ready-made anarchy."

"A very interesting theory, Dennis," Maguire replied with barely concealed boredom, "but I don't think it washes."

"No?" Dunn looked around the table. "Let's face it, gentlemen. Whoever blew up that ship did so to force the governments of Hong Kong and Peking into quick action, knowing full well the chaos it would create. Show that the British are ineffective in maintaining control over this little territory, and you destroy the lucrative economic relationship

Hong Kong has with moderate-ruled China. You may kill the goose that laid the golden egg in the process—but he will be purged in death and cleanse you in his bloodbath." Dunn paused for breath. "Show the regime in Peking to be a bumbling tool of the capitalists, that's what the name of this charade is! And the cost is so little. A beat-up hulk of a ship and eleven 'enlightened' sons of the proletariat—and the bastards don't give a damn about them anyway. That's what it's all about, Maguire. Power. And you can't deny it."

"See here, Dennis!" Maguire said, his voice edged with impatience, "I think we can all agree there is a potential for unrest in the colony. What is at issue is its source."

"You honestly don't think it's Peking that's stirring up the trade unions?"

"No." Maguire shook his head slowly. "No, I do not."

Dunn turned to Cleve. "Sir, I cannot for a moment believe the mainland Chinese are not manipulating this exercise to the hilt. I won't let my men have their lives endangered just to play out a role for some politico in Peking. We must attack trade-union headquarters throughout the colony and break their backs before they intensify their activities against us. It is totally wrong to let the unions force our hand, and by their actions—and innuendo—the direction of the investigation. Either we move to regain control of the streets, or the streets are lost to us forever. And, with the streets, our credibility as a police force."

There were loud and boisterous cries of, "Well done!" throughout the room. Men thumped the tabletop.

Maguire met Dunn's stare and held it. He had always thought of Dunn as a big Scots drunkard and buffoon, a typical dumb copper full of bombast and bravado, more suited to pounding a backwater beat in Glasgow than rising to a position of responsibility with the colonial police. Maguire looked around the table. He knew if he could silence Dunn, he'd silence his chief opposition. All eyes were on him.

"Mr. Dunn." He measured his speech carefully. "I don't think it would be proper to act with haste. We have our informants. The unions will be disciplined internally. And, if the situation necessitates further action, I will certainly make the proper recommendations. The unions will be controlled by the Chinese themselves, rest assured. Your men should be competent enough to maintain order in the streets. Trust mine to exercise their function in a similar—if not better—fashion."

He knew he'd hit home with these last words, but he couldn't resist plunging the dagger deeper. "Mr. Dunn, I have come to a remarkable conclusion." Maguire sensed the tension and savored it. "I don't think you understand the subtlety of the Oriental mind."

"And you?" gasped the enraged Scot, his face ruddy with anger. "And you do?"

"Yes, chief superintendent." Maguire sat back in his chair. "Yes, I do."

"Bullshit!" With one word Dunn spat out his feelings about Maguire, the man and his theories. The two men sat glaring at each other.

"Gentlemen!" Cleve started to rise. He looked first to Dunn, then to Maguire. Then around the table. Silence. An embarrassed, self-conscious silence. "Are there any further questions of the director?"

An eager young man asked from the corner, "Who stands to gain locally by the disturbances?" Maguire answered with a soothing smile. A fine question, a good one. But he could give only the vaguest of answers, understandably, because the matter was under SB investigation and necessarily sensitive.

Then, from a dour Chinese superintendent sitting like a rice buddha along the wall, "Was there anyone internationally who stood to make political advantage?" Again Maguire begged off. Too much talk would threaten the integrity of his inquiry. But not to worry, the matter was in good hands.

Then, from one of the senior officers: why the ship explosion?

Maguire looked away at the other end of the table, as though he had not heard the question. But it was repeated, in a louder, more insistent voice.

Maguire could not avoid answering. He would not

comment, he replied icily, until he had reviewed the matter with the commissioner. Till then, the material was accessible only on a need-to-know basis.

"We can't wait forever, Maguire," flared Dunn. "It's something we have a right to know about now, before there's more serious trouble."

"There won't be," Maguire replied coldly.

"You mean to say that, after the mess we've had in the past two days—the bomb, the march, the riot—you honestly believe there won't be increased violence in the Crown colony?" Dunn's tone was almost mocking.

"Increased violence?" Maguire answered the question with almost casual disdain. "It's possible. Anything is possible. But my sources indicate that complications are unlikely."

"And you believe them?" asked Dunn, fury in his eyes.

Maguire responded quietly. "Yes, I do. Special Branch stakes its reputation on it."

With that simple phrase, Maguire had them right where he wanted them. It must be left to Special Branch—and there was nothing more to say.

Cleve knew it, too. He'd known it from the beginning, much as a part of him despised the knowledge. It was a fact of life in Hong Kong. He could understand Dunn's anguish and frustration; still felt that way himself. But he knew such emotions were a luxury, one he could no longer afford in his present position. Things weren't as simple and straightforward as he'd like them to be any more. Hong Kong Special Branch was an entity uniquely crafted to the realities of the tiny colony. Sometimes what it said might irritate; sometimes what it advocated might be painful. But invariably, in the resolution, if not the theory, its proposals made sense. And it was sense that Cleve desperately needed, not blind loyalty or unrequited schoolboy bravery.

As the policemen left the room, Maguire stayed behind in the shadows of the drawn drapery. Cleve walked slowly to the far side of the room.

"You have something, don't you, Bob?"

"Yes, sir, I do."

Cleve looked up. "Why wasn't I told?"

The stare made the director uncomfortable, but he replied in a careful voice. "I didn't want to bother you until I was sure." Silently he went back to his place at the table, reached down and opened his attaché case. He took out a pink folder, gave its contents a cursory glance. "I think you'd better see this, sir."

Cleve hesitated, then sat down and opened the folder. It contained an informant report, only a few pages. The signature of the SB operative who'd spun the player for information was unusual—it was Maguire's.

As Cleve read, he rubbed his temples. What could he say? It seemed so implausible—but then so did many things in the Orient. Should he believe the report? It was too perfect, too concocted, and yet he knew the line between reality and fantasy was sometimes a vague and ill-defined one at best, especially in political intelligence.

This man had once been a friend. What had changed? He and Maguire? Or the world? The information in the folder meant that Maguire's shadow would one day loom large to fill his position. Cleve dreaded the thought.

Finally he spoke. "I don't buy it." He motioned to the folder in front of him. "It's just too pat. Unless you have corroboration?"

The director sensed his indecision and moved in quickly. "I'm afraid that's what my informant said, sir. And, based on information from other sources at our disposal, we believe him."

Cleve shot him a look. "Sources? What sources? You mean you have something to back up that telephone conversation?" He knew that Special Branch was like a giant cross-indexing machine; that was its purpose. Every item it received was checked and rechecked by thousands of separate cells, each one not knowing what the others did. "Projects" were made up of separate parts, each part meaningless on its own. Then they were brought together—and Maguire was given the luxury of the total picture.

"Yes, sir," replied Maguire, "I do."

"Maguire," Cleve said, "you're telling me the ship that exploded is not and never was a Communist vessel. And your primary source is Lee Shiu Shing, the head of Chinese intelligence here in Hong Kong!"

Maguire smiled grimly. "Yes, sir. Here is the corroboration: on August 10, a vessel matching the description of our ship, but without the markings we found after the explosion, left the coastal port of Rayong, Thailand. The vessel was called the *Kampong Tekek* and had a Liberian registry out of Malaysia. She was a Japanese gunboat during the last war and, in more recent times, a sea bitch known to ply the area and sell her services to the highest bidder."

Maguire placed a blurry black-and-white blowup on the table. In a corner was a red chop mark: "23/05/86 #786386 USDEC to RHKP Narcotics Branch" and Maguire's scrawled initials. The United States Drug Enforcement Commission, USDEC, kept photo files of every non-Communist vessel in the South China Sea. The photograph had somehow wandered to the narcotics bureau files, and from there to SB, no questions asked.

The vessel itself could have been any one of a hundred creaky mongrel coasters. The photograph had been taken from a distance on a clear Pacific day. Nothing distinctive. High prow, wooden bridge. Cargo loaded helter-skelter around the decks. A few goats and chickens, some in crates, some loose. Some men, crew or passengers, all dressed alike in cut-offs, T-shirts and sandals. This was not the stuff over which wars were fought.

Maguire handed Cleve a second sheet. "This is the blueprint reconstruction of our ship, as the marine department engineers say she looked."

Cleve looked down at the fine pen-sketch measurements, waiver lines, minute details. Then the photograph. The silhouettes were identical. He turned to Maguire.

The director anticipated his question. "You would say they're the same as scores of other vessels plying their trade in the South China Sea. The importance lies not in their appearance, but in their cargo. On this particular voyage from Rayong, our source discovered there were three peculiar things about this ship. First, it took on a number of Chinese, young men whose dress and demeanor were at odds with those of other peasants in the area. They were more like 'villains.'" Maguire could not hide his distaste for the police terminology he used.

"Second, our ship took on a cargo of fifty-kilo bags from the stock of the Punkaponkap-Jade Hill Trading Company. But nothing on the original ship's manifest, which we obtained via the Thai police in Ban Phatthaya, indicated what was in the bags.

"And finally, we have evidence that the captain met a man named Boonlikit in Rayong, and that he was the potential recipient of a postdated money order for five thousand U.S. dollars, which Boonlikit had deposited two weeks ago at the Bank of Siam in Rayong, pending the captain's completion of his task.

"The vessel headed east en route to its official destination, the Kamakami dockyard in Nagasaki." Maguire unfolded a Marine Services map of the South China Sea with certain details marked in red grease pencil: winds, sea conditions, cloud cover, moon. From Rayong a broken line was traced, moving southeast through the Gulf of Thailand and thence around the coast of Vietnam, then north-northeast toward the Strait of Luzon. The line ended abruptly in a circle. He pointed emphatically to it.

"Approximately here, two hundred miles east of the island of Hainan, the ship changed course and veered sharply due north. We estimate the change to have occurred at about six o'clock Sunday morning, the twentieth of August. We believe the cargo was fourteen hundred kilos of raw opium and three hundred kilos of 999 morphine block from Chiang Mai, up near the triangle."

"Source of this information?"

"Much of it is from Lee; the rest is from the American special narcotics organization in Thailand and Superintendent Webster, Hong Kong liaison officer in Bangkok."

"Francis Webster? From the narcotics bureau?"

"Yes, sir. It seems that Boonlikit, our Chinese messenger, was arrested by the Thai border police yesterday afternoon. He'd lain low for awhile and then tried to return to his home in Malaysia. He almost made it. According to Francis, the

Thai police received an anonymous tip to pick up a Chinese male in a third-class carriage in the train from Chumphon to Malaysia. No reason given. They acted. Boonlikit was taken to the nearest police station. After a few hours, he told them about the contract with the captain, the money in the bank and the cargo. And he told them the name painted on the hull. But he couldn't tell them who financed the deal, who paid for the ship, what the Chinese were doing on board or where, specifically, the ship was destined."

"Why not?"

"He's dead."

"What?"

"Shot through the head with a high-powered rifle. It appears they used a scope sight when he was sitting near a second-story window."

A bullet to plug a leak, Cleve thought, scowling. "Who let him near a window? Did they catch the killer?"

Maguire's silence answered the questions.

"So what did Francis get? Transcripts? How can we be sure they weren't doctored?"

"They weren't transcripts, sir." He handed Cleve a copy of a confidential British government cable. "Webster was there for the interrogation—as much as there was one. He was choppered in by the Thais as soon as they suspected Boonlikit was dealing in drugs."

Cleve glanced at the buff-colored piece of paper.

"Back to square one. What of the vessel?"

"From Rayong, the craft we know as the *Kampong Tekek* disappears from the face of the earth. Then on Sunday afternoon, just a few hours before the explosion, the secret Royal Navy watchpost at Tai O peninsula logged a Communist vessel. If we figure the *Kampong* moved at a speed of approximately nine knots, heading due north from her last course change off Hainan, she could have made landfall off Lantau at roughly the same time as our exploding ship. A great way to enter colony waters carrying drugs without interference—as a Communist vessel."

"Fascinating." The word escaped Cleve's clenched lips involuntarily.

"Significantly, Peking has to this moment released nothing of the ship's demise for internal press consumption. Beyond the accepted utterances of astonisment and 'pro-forma' pity in the international arena, the regime in Peking has acted in a remarkably subdued manner. It has to. The balance of power in Peking is just too delicate. If the story ever broke on the mainland, rioting for the 'righteous cause' could easily get out of hand and play into the hands of the radicals. And that is the last thing the Peking mandarins want, or need, to have happen."

Maguire continued, "Lee has given us a perfect lead to the destroyer of the vessel, a way to save face and see justice done, at minimal cost to all."

"Facts now, Maguire. You know I need more than intuition and gossip, however well-founded, to commit the lives of the men on this force." Cleve's stare was piercing; he felt the scent of the hunt. "Why do you believe Lee?"

"Because his information was given to me independently of all our own sources, and it dovetails perfectly with what we know now. And I think my own sources are airtight. The record of the vessel, the interrogation of Boonlikit and, finally, the ship's name—the *Glorious East Wind*. . ." Maguire paused. "He even knows of the scar-faced man chased by the Rover. This one." Maguire took out a photocopy of the radio-room computer card and placed it before the commissioner.

Cleve looked up.

"Who does he say the man was?"

"Just a *ma-jai*—a follower."

"I sensed that," Cleve said impatiently. "But whose follower?"

"Yip Lam."

"Impossible."

Maguire disagreed. "It's perfectly logical, and so simple I don't know how we could have missed it. We all know of the intense drug rivalry between the Chuen Triad lodge, led by Yip, and a new unknown syndicate. They're fighting for control of the heroin trade in Hong Kong. And it's a fact that the street supply of domestic number-three grade is down. The factories have been straining to meet the requirement for overseas trade.

"Yip wrenched temporary control of the trade from the unknown syndicate. Then the syndicate bought all those drugs on the ship. It was their attempt to secretly tip the balance in their favor. Yip found out about the drugs—from whom, Lee was not able to say—and sent his man to sabotage the vessel. An act," Maguire added matter-of-factly, "he was obviously quite competent at."

The commissioner sighed and took up a pen in his hand. He tore some paper off a notepad and started to doodle on the page. After a few silent moments, he put the pen down and looked up at Maguire.

"You have Yip's portfolio, I presume?" From his attaché case, Maguire took a bulky file wrapped tightly in red binding.

Cleve took the brief and set it on the table. He smoothed over the jacket cover, considered it a moment, wrinkled his brow as if to collect his thoughts, then opened the file.

Indices, case diaries, photographs, the odd conviction in the early seventies, before Yip Lam had made his mark in the trade and hired the efficient stable of Oxford-trained barristers to protect his interests. An avalanche of photographs— Chinese press, European tabloids, preventive services, immigration, Special Branch, narcotics bureau, Triad society bureau, general investigations.

Yip Lam's activities had not changed much in the past fifteen years. He was the *Dai-Lo*, head of a vice network that had bled the honor from an underpaid, overworked colonial police in a series of shocking scandals. He had long controlled all the illegal betting at the Jockey Club, and he would silence any hint of competition—by murder, if necessary.

Yip's betting centers in Hong Kong were a monopoly, discreet and efficient. His brothels had survived the moral purges of the past two years because they were genteel and discreet. As well, Yip Lam had installed a bell-pager service for each girl. The pager raised the price for the client, but guaranteed anonymity and comfort.

But drugs were Yip's forte. Drugs made him what he was, and drugs made Cleve curse his name. Yip Lam was the murderer of thousands of Chinese, and had recently extended his operation to Holland and America, so poor souls there could also be held in the brutal bondage of number-three-grade rice.

The file told Cleve little he didn't already know. Golden Triangle heroin couriers were sent to Bangkok, and thence to Amsterdam. There were many small drug seizures, all connected to Yip, but none could be proven. Here and there was a success, such as in 1979 when Preventive Services had seized one hundred seventy kilos of drugs stored in the caves on Bluff Island. But again, they did not have enough proof for the courts. The seizures had scarcely made a dent in Yip's trade.

Cleve turned to Maguire. "You know, Bob, I feel I know this man like a brother." Maguire smiled stiffly, and Cleve felt a chill—at the thought of Yip Lam's intense will for survival? Or his own director's? He placed the file to one side. Time was precious now.

"I need more than this, Bob. Did Lee tell you who owned the *Glorious East Wind?* Who the syndicate is?"

Maguire faltered slightly, fumbling for words. "Well, he said. . . . I assumed stopping Yip and getting assurances for nonintervention from Peking were enough for the present."

Cleve sat in silence for a moment before responding. "We know one of the parties responsible for our present predicament, at least I'm presuming we do. We have a motive and a culprit. Triad society bureau can go and scoop Yip Lam. I'll call Steven Tak about it immediately. This one—" he tapped the radio-room card with his finger "—this one we can ferret out when we've spoken to Yip."

"What about Peng?" Maguire asked pointedly.

"I'll start him on the other side of the equation. I want you to brief him on all the new information we have. Then he can go find out who wants to overturn Yip's applecart."

Maguire smiled his cool smile. "That's not going to be easy."

"I know that." Cleve looked back, stone-faced. "That's why Peng's such a good copper, because he can tackle what isn't easy."

Maguire turned and started to pack up quickly. The commissioner began making lists. Number one: Steven Tak and the Triad society bureau would follow Yip Lam. Number two: Peng would track down an unnamed syndicate. Number three said simply: Driscoll.

Cleve sat back for a moment and pondered his lingering disbelief in Maguire and his informant. The director was almost out the door.

"Bob?"

"Yes, sir?"

"I'd appreciate a copy of that Special Branch dossier on Lee." Maguire stared back as if he hadn't understood. "Within the hour, Bob, okay?"

Cleve listed point number four: Maguire + Lee Shiu Shing. Beside them he placed a huge question mark.

CHAPTER ELEVEN

H e waited impatiently on the sidewalk, hands on
hips, a trim, hatchet-faced figure in cream-
colored shirt and creased green shorts. His
shoes were black where the mud hadn't splattered them and his legs were pale and not very muscular, the
legs of someone who sat behind a desk and ordered rather
than did. David's Rover stopped beside him.

"Are you Andrews?" he asked shrilly above the coughing
motor.

David moved to answer but was curtly waved off.

"The name's Proctor, Anthony Proctor," the stranger said
by way of identification. He was of indeterminate age and
British, a Yorkshireman. David didn't like him. He sensed the
feeling was mutual.

"You're late, Andrews. Come with me." Proctor turned
away. His clipped tone indicated that David had best obey,
and quickly.

Andrews followed the man up the rubble-covered
sidewalk. The factories loomed above him; blank stares from
their blacked-out and broken windows made him feel uneasy.
There were three or four police Cortinas and a few Rovers
parked carelessly around the dead-end street. A white ambulance, its doors open, blue prism light flashing, was backed
up to a squat, three-story building.

They walked behind the building and over a garbage-strewn

field, their shoes oozing in mud. An orange Day-Glo strip marked their path. High-powered police lighting illuminated the field, making it look like a battlefield from the Great War. It was not a pleasant place to be.

A small doorway and hall at the back of the building were dark and narrow and seemed to go on forever. Voices were raised somewhere above him, gruff, businesslike, the voices of people who'd rather be anywhere else but here this night.

The stench hit David halfway up and he had to hold back the urge to vomit. The smell from the top of the staircase was overpowering. He swallowed back bile.

They reached the landing. The constable at the door stepped to one side and let them in, thankful for the opportunity to move away from the odor. The room reeked of dampness and decomposing flesh. It was small, a storage area filled with boxes marked "Super Space Station" and "Tuffy" and "Toto Doggies." Orderly piles of balsa wood and crate-framing wood were on the far side. A rumpled bedsheet on several pieces of flattened cardboard, a cloth suitcase, opened, with its contents strewn around and a mound of dirty clothes tossed to one side defined the bedroom. The occupant of this room had been transient or poor, or both.

A dirty light bulb glowed down from empty rafters. Rusty pipes crisscrossed the ceiling, dripping moisture. A knotted length of rope twirled aimlessly down from a crossbeam. It was cut about three feet down. A chair stood upright under the rope and a rough purple blanket lay spread over a lumpy form on the floor near the chair. The stench came from under the blanket.

There were three people already in the room—four, really, if one counted "it." But David tried hard not to. A young man, furiously chewing gum, was taking measurements from the chair to the body, triangulating them from the fixed point offered by the rope hanging from the ceiling. An older man in a sweat-stained T-shirt that barely hid a massive beer belly was taking photographs with ghoulish enthusiasm. The third had buck teeth and gold-rimmed glasses that kept slipping down his button nose; he stood in the corner writing notes for the team. David noted the cotton batting in their noses, the bottle of Vaseline in the hip pocket of the writer. Anything to mask the smell. No one looked up as he entered the room. They had better things to do, and the faster they were finished, the faster they could leave.

Proctor strode over to the blanket, bent down and motioned to David to come over. He lifted one end of the blanket. "Do you know this man?"

David gritted his teeth and bent over the corpse. The body was upturned. The face, if one could still call it that, was puffy and yellow with discoloration. Blood had settled a deep purple at the base of the skull and bulged the skin to bursting. The death mask mocked him. The tongue stuck out, a rich ox-blood color framed obscenely in magenta lips. The jaundiced eyes peered piglike from the decaying flesh. A length of rope, knotted at the Adam's apple, gave the corpse its final formal attire. It had been roughly cut and matched the grade of rope hanging from the ceiling. There had been no need for artificial respiration.

The scar. The color was gone, but the ridgelike scar was there, too. Scarface. David nodded absently. Yes, this was the one, the man at the waterfront.

"Read him the facts, sergeant."

The man with gold-rimmed glasses read from his shabby notebook.

"The deceased is Chan Man Sui, also known as Simon Chan, aged forty-four. Used to be a waiter at the Shang Tsi Garden restaurant. He has a record for drugs. A member of the Triad societies, apparently inactive. No known connections with organized crime. No signs of struggle or theft. Apparently a suicide, sir." He completed his reading and looked up at David as if for approval. "Just waiting for the coroner's assistant," he felt compelled to add. "Once he signs the papers, the body goes to the morgue."

"Who found him?" David asked.

There was no answer. David might as well have been talking to the wall. Anthony Proctor walked away. The sergeant looked back pan-faced.

"Who found him?" he repeated stubbornly.

Proctor sauntered back to the blanket. "We got a phone call."

"That's it?"

"Yes, that's it," he replied sarcastically. "What do we need? An engraved invitation?" He continued almost grudgingly. "The caller said he was a night watchman here. He rented the place to this fellow—" a nod at the blanket "—for a few days at eight dollars a day so he could visit his family in China. Thought he would have the place protected in his absence. And he came back and found this." He saw Andrews' look of approbation. "They checked the watchman out, and someone's interviewing him right now, for the record. He's seventy and clean, a retired policeman, no rank, no trouble with the anti-corruption people. Not bent like some of them were." He looked at David. "It's a simple suicide, nothing more, nothing less. His being by the waterfront a few nights ago was a coincidence, Andrews. Let's just leave it at that, a coincidence."

The flow of their conversation had changed, become personal. Proctor brushed closer to him and spoke in a hiss. "He looks to be how old, Andrews? A few days, don't you think?" He hovered over the corpse. "They say it's hard to tell in this heat. A body can be dead a few hours and look like it's weeks old. But you know about this better than I, don't you, Andrews?"

The stench in the room was suddenly overpowering. David felt faint. He saw the image of young Williams, the pale, lifeless face, the vacant eyes staring up at him in horror. He pushed past the sneering Yorkshireman.

"Does the room stink too much for you, Andrews? I'm surprised."

David stopped, turned and gave the man a withering glance. "Fuck off, you piss-assed little git." Then he stormed out of the room.

Outside in the darkened lot he felt the air brushing his brow. He knew if he had stayed any longer he would have struck Proctor. He stood a while, collecting his thoughts. He stank of death, his life stank of it. Everything he touched seemed to ooze with it.

After a few minutes, he sensed he wasn't alone and glanced up. It was James Peng, an old friend, an unexpected one, one of the few he could still count on.

"How are you, Davie?" Peng asked.

"Sir?"

"They still riding you?" David didn't answer. "Was it him?" Peng continued glancing up at the room.

David nodded. "Yes, it's him. But then, your man up there will tell you all you need to know."

Peng shook his head. "He's not mine, Davie, not that one. Thank God."

David looked up.

"That's Tony Proctor from SB," Peng told him. "I'd take no notice of him. He's a fool. He loves the gory story because he can trample all over it without getting his own fingers dirty." Peng motioned David down the path toward the parked vehicles.

"Proctor's not accountable. None of them are." Peng's voice made clear his distaste for Special Branch.

"It's my case now, David. I called you here to view the body. I wanted confirmation. Proctor's just along for the ride, a courtesy to his superiors. I'm sorry he got to you before I did." Peng's concern seemed genuine, and David had no reason to disbelieve him.

In front of the building, Peng gestured to an unmarked Cortina. A detective was lounging against the hood, but straightened quickly when he saw them.

"This Simon Chan. Is he of any use to you?" David asked.

Peng answered him clinically. "Right now, no. He might open an avenue, but the man himself was a nobody, a big fat zero."

David stopped. "Then why is Maguire interested in this if it's only a small thing?"

"Because, Davie, he's the type who wants everything, from beginning to end. Even when the reasons aren't apparent to the rest of us. It helps him in his glory-seeking."

David thought about Peng's comment. "Sir?"

"Let's just say it's an instinct I've got, shall we? That and a few salient facts." Peng's voice had an edge of anger. "First, that man up there. Simon Chan. He's no more of a suicide than I'm a Shanghai streetwalker. The evidence is all wrong. The chair was upright, not toppled by the fall or the deceased's weight. The knot in the neck was too taut. Simon Chan—if that's his name—could never have tied it and lived, let alone strung himself up to die."

"And Maguire?" David asked.

"Maguire's being Maguire. He'll keep this suicide close to his vest, as will I. As we all will, eh, Davie?" The rise in his voice shook Andrews. "Until we find something to connect the explosion to this poor sod's death. If, in fact, there is any connection at all."

"You don't find it curious that this fellow is found dead a few days after I place him at the waterfront explosion?"

"Curious? Yes. Intriguing? Perhaps. But crucial? Not nearly yet. Not until I get hard evidence to prove it so." There was rare mirth in Peng's eyes. He took Andrews by the shoulder.

"Davie," he said, "would you like to work this case? With me?" He barely masked his enthusiasm. "You're a natural for it. You've done CID in the past. You were at the scene, so you're familiar with all the details. And besides, we've worked together well before, haven't we?"

David paused and considered the offer. He respected this man, always had. He'd not been hard done by at CID. Had a natural flair for it, it seemed. But then the specter hit him like a tidal wave.

Peng shrewdly caught it. "It's Williams, isn't it?"

Silence.

Peng's tone was that of a stern taskmaster: rough, demanding, full of implied challenge. "Knock off the bullshit, Davie. What's done is done. No one blamed you for it. The man was unbalanced. It was just one of those things."

David looked away.

"So you're going to walk in shadows the rest of your life? You're running from it, Davie."

"Perhaps. . . ." David turned and stared directly at his accuser.

Peng folded his arms over his chest and tilted his head to

one side. "Davie. Listen to me. People like Proctor don't forget. They never do. But you can't hide from them. It feeds their twisted little minds. That's just what they want from you." He paused. "Have you ever done anything wrong in the force?"

Andrews bristled. "No way. Not ever."

"Then will you work on this case? For me? For your own self-esteem?"

David looked into the darkness, the hint of a grimace on his features as all the pain and hurt and confusion came together. Then he nodded, slowly, and with more determination.

"I take it that means yes?"

David looked over at him, his manner at once calm and purposeful. "Damned right, superintendent. You've got yourself a partner."

"Good." Peng rested his arm on David's shoulder. The gesture of trust was not lost on the younger man. A smile came to his face. For the first time, he noticed that his Rover and driver were gone.

"I suppose you've already received my super's approval?"

A simple shrug. "What Peng wants, Peng usually gets."

"Sir?"

"I have the commissioner's."

"So you would have ordered me to work with you?"

"Yes, I could have. But wouldn't. I prefer to have you make the choice."

"Thanks. I appreciate it."

Peng's face turned serious. "Don't thank me. You'll earn your keep, by more than you realize." He gestured to the parked sedan, the driver suddenly alert. "Come on, the night's still young and we have lots to do. To start with, you need some decent clothes."

The two men stepped into the Cortina. The driver closed the passenger door and got into the front seat. He looked expectantly into the rear-view mirror for directions. "Hong Kong Island, sir?"

A nod from Peng. The car slid into gear. Soon it was lost in the steamy China night.

CHAPTER TWELVE

―――――――

The parking lot at the reservoir was deserted, as Lee had known it would be. The road to Taitam was little traveled at the best of times, and at this late hour he did not expect any traffic.

He opened his window a trifle and felt the stagnant heat of the Asian summer. The air was laden with fetid dampness, the earth sour to its red clay roots. The scent of rotting, decaying vegetation was everywhere.

A car came around the bend, a Mercedes limousine with tinted windows. A few yards behind it, Lee could make out a second car, stationary. The Mercedes cut its lights and stopped in the center of the parking lot facing him.

Lee leaned forward and touched his driver on the shoulder. They drove to the limousine and parked alongside.

Lee opened his window. The passenger in the back seat of the Mercedes did likewise. Lee could see he was alone.

The other man sat hunched forward, clasping his frail hands on the head of a cane that was shaped like a phoenix.

Lee spoke first. "I met them just as I warned you I would." He paused. "And I told them."

"Of what?" the other asked.

"Of Yip Lam," Lee stated simply.

The man was silent, then he snorted in contempt. "So they will follow Yip Lam, and find a dead end. The biggest surprise will be for that bastard Yip. It will serve him right for being so greedy with the drugs, for trying to keep it a monopoly, for resisting our initiatives. Dead end," he repeated.

"No," Lee replied. "If I know John Cleve as well as I think I do, it will be thorough. They will investigate both sides."

The passenger in the Mercedes looked into the distance. He quietly tapped his cane on the floor, his head nodding in time. Lee could hear him humming. It was an old Nationalist marching song.

"You are not worried?" Lee asked.

The man stopped his humming and turned to face Lee.

"Thoroughness has its limits," he replied. "If I were you, I would be far more concerned about my own part in the financing of the cargoes these past few months." His tone grew stronger, more aggressive.

"There are no written records. They would only find out if you told them. And we were partners in the financing," Lee said harshly.

The noncommittal shrug.

"So you would expose me?"

The man chuckled. "No. I think you know better. For now, we need each other. But it is always nice to remember." He smiled coldly. "You blew up the ship, didn't you, Lee?"

Lee paused as if considering how best to answer, then abruptly said, "I want in on the Kowloon project."

The man looked at him with curiosity in his eyes. He shook his head. "What are you talking about, Lee? You are in. China and the British representatives and, of course, my firm. We are all in on the deal."

"I want in."

The man hesitated. "But you are in," he repeated in a soothing voice. "We have acted fairly with all the governments, yours and the British. Everyone seems pleased. If your superiors are concerned about an edge, there is none. We, the landholders, Whitehall and the Hong Kong government—the intermediaries—and China, the recipient. We all received the amounts noted on the documents of transaction."

"And the extra monies?"

"Sorry? I didn't quite catch what you said." The man's smile was frozen. He didn't like this conversation and started tapping with his cane once more.

"The kickbacks." Lee stared into the other's eyes.

The tapping of the cane stopped. The smile left his face. "I don't know what you are talking about," he replied in a monotone.

"I think you do," Lee said calmly. "I've already spoken to your associate, Robert Burden. It's amazing how a morning of labor unrest can alter a man's sense of clarity, especially a man like Sir Robert. He was really quite amenable toward my inclusion in matters once I placed all the options before him."

"Options?" the old man asked. "What options?"

"Well, I would imagine circumstances would differ for each party. In Burden's case, his companies just can't weather the strain of my continued interest. In yours, there is a matter of a particular period of history." Lee saw the flitter of cognition in the old man's eyes. He let the words hang.

"Be careful, Lee."

Lee handed the man a letter. "I have been."

The older man's expression turned sour as he read. "I wouldn't waste my time tearing it up, if I were you," Lee cautioned. "Sir Robert was quite serious. There are, of course, other copies."

"Of course."

"I especially like the line that says, 'I strongly suggest that Lee now be included in the subcontracts.' Subcontracts? Is that the term you used for the tea money, my friend?" Lee's voice was coy.

The old man's face reddened. He stomped his cane angrily, a tattoo of rage and frustration. "I won't allow it!" he sputtered. "You have no power over us! The deals are done!"

"Won't allow it? I don't think you have a choice," Lee replied sarcastically. "It would seem to me you have gone out of your way to exclude a countryman from your good fortune."

"Countryman?" the other man screeched. "Countryman?

You use the term generously. I would rather die than be considered one of you."

Lee's face was livid with anger. "You never said that when you needed my connections to clear the drugs. Then you were only too happy to use my good offices."

"I would rather die." Once more the muttered words, the tapping cane.

"As time goes on and as the police hunt begins into your past, you will wish you already had."

"You threaten my exposure?" The man was breathing heavily. His hands were trembling. There was hate in his eyes.

"Yes, I suppose I do," Lee replied simply, "I suppose I do."

"Do you really think they will believe you?" the man hissed. "You have no proof."

"Oh, I think I know where to find some if I really try." Lee's voice was calm, almost detached.

A resigned silence, then a rustling in the back seat. "The British!" the man said feverishly. "What of my other partners? They'll never accept your inclusion with us."

"British?" Lee's voice betrayed his contempt. "By the time I'm finished with them, they'll scamper whichever way I want. And you?" He shook his head in mock sadness. "You will be left with nothing."

The tapping cane stopped. Lee heard the sigh.

"The Kowloon waterfront deal can be revoked quite easily," Lee said. "My government does not care one way or the other. There are so many plots of land available, so many enticing packages. It will be ours in the end anyway." He shrugged.

"And if I, for my part, were to allow you in?" the man asked cautiously.

"I will keep the police away from you."

"How?"

"Leave that to me," Lee said. "They will believe what I tell them."

"And?" the man pressed.

"You want more?" Lee's voice rose.

The shrug. "A man should try for what he can."

"What I have offered should be enough. Fear what you must. Consider what you will. Just remember that for some, the past is never forgotten." He paused. "I will give you time to reflect, but I expect an answer from you quickly. A simple yes on a piece of paper. I will know where it came from. We can discuss percentages later."

The reluctant nod of understanding. Lee waved it off as the window of the Mercedes closed and the vehicle moved away.

"You don't like me, do you, Irishman?" the voice whispered roughly in a grating East European accent Maguire had grown to despise.

Maguire said nothing. He sat silently in his pew; he did not look back at the man kneeling behind him.

"No, I thought not," Veidjur continued. "What bothers you most, eh? The fact that I drink schnapps? Or my sexual habits? Or the fact that you have to pay me if you want my services?" The man was embittered. His breath was close now, at Maguire's neck. Veidjur smelled of garlic and fouled underwear. Maguire felt distinctly uncomfortable in his presence.

"Well, Irish?" Veidjur challenged him. "I am here once more, at your command." The softening, the resignation that always followed the outburst.

Veidjur coughed. The gurgling sound echoed through the empty cathedral to the darkened reaches of the choir loft. The spray tickled Maguire's neck. He flinched. "Not here, Veidjur, not here," he whispered urgently. "We'll go to the vestibule to talk." He motioned with a nod of his head to the rear of the church.

"As you wish, Irish." The hiss, like steam escaping from a pressure cooker.

Maguire waited. Heard the clop, clop, clop of footsteps fading. He looked back, saw the receding figure, then glanced around. The church was empty.

Veidjur stood in the dappled candlelight that flickered in from the side altars. His clothes hung on his large frame limp and formless, like prairie wash before a storm. A baggy, double-breasted gray suit badly in need of pressing; a stained white shirt with long collar tabs; a vulgar maroon and pea-green tie. Marcus Veidjur had not changed much over the years.

He looked at the director with rheumy blue eyes. His skin was like wrinkled cheesecloth. Uneven strands of blond hair, like dried wisps of straw, shot outward from a pale freckled forehead. A crooked smile showed stained teeth. It was hard to believe that this huge misshapen ox of a man was at all competent in his field. But he was.

It had not been easy at first to find out whom he worked for. He had a photographic memory, a guileful disposition and an ability to find the lowest common denominator among his opponents, then surprise them by sinking to even lower depths. He had started as a salesman for a small Hungarian watch firm, a master salesman, as he emphatically expressed it. His passports could have been Yugoslav or Bulgarian or Czech, and sometimes were. He was originally from a fishing village along the shallow east Baltic coast, a dust fleck of a town on a map whose hues and colors changed like the ebb and flow of Danzig tides.

A few years ago he had stolen the specifications for a new microcomputer the Yugoslavs were planning to introduce at the Canton Trade Fair. He sold the specs to a neutral Asian country that was quite happy to pirate copyrighted merchandise. Marcus got paid and went out on the town.

He hadn't counted on the room at the Hilton being bugged. Hadn't expected the film footage to be so graphic. It wouldn't have been so bad had it been women, but. . . . And that's how Maguire had trapped him. That and the tapes of the business luncheon where Marcus, over pieces of braised duckling, had told the Asians about the new computer.

Maguire had been cautious, but he learned that when Veidjur's appetites could be curbed, he was one of the best at his craft.

And so Maguire had manipulated Veidjur ever since. They understood each other as only users could. And Maguire had the goods on Veidjur. They sat in his safe along with the films of the crazy Malays and the errant Frenchmen and countless others. For two years and some odd days, Maguire had played the puppet master with this bedraggled refugee from the Cold War, and with surprising success.

"So what is it you want, Irishman?" Veidjur asked. The garlic smell was overpowering.

"The following, Marcus. . . ."

"Call me Kingpin," the European interrupted, his voice echoing with curious pride. "After all, that is what your reports refer to me as, isn't it? Kingpin?" He savored both the flattering code name and the hint that he had a source in Maguire's office.

Maguire continued as if he hadn't heard. "I need to know about China. What's happening now? How has the explosion affected what's being done in the Great Hall? How will it affect us?" His voice was an urgent whisper, as if he were reciting his sins. "And . . . ." He hesitated. "How much more can you find me on Lee?"

The man peered at him, then looked away. Maguire could see his jaw tighten.

A dark form passed, which turned out to be the verger on his rounds. Maguire opened a pamphlet on St. John, patron saint of the cathedral, while Veidjur peered off as if in a trance. They were alone once more as the figure melded into shadow.

"Well?" Maguire insisted.

Nothing.

He grabbed the man's hand. "You really don't have much of an option, you know, Kingpin." The cold grin.

"I've already compromised my informants as much as I dare." The voice was anxious, lacking fire. "The man is tight as a drum, Maguire." The look begged compassion, but found none in the Irishman's eyes.

"You'll find more, though?" The hard stare.

Moments passed. Veidjur spoke, businesslike once more.

"The money."

"Our usual rate."

"Ten percent more."

Maguire did not answer.

"Inflation." Veidjur said it with a sarcastic smile, and Maguire knew the man deserved no pity.

"Granted. The means?" Maguire's question was his way of giving Veidjur the respect he knew the mission deserved.

"As always. Frankfurter *Zeitung*."

"Washington *Post*," Maguire countered. He would give Marcus only so much respect and freedom to maneuver.

"As you wish. It is simple either way." The gleam in his eyes showed that Veidjur was in his realm. "Phillips, on Ice House Street. Third copy." Veidjur glanced at his watch, a Patek Phillipe. "Ten tomorrow morning. Prompt."

Maguire nodded. It was done.

"And my money?"

"Don't worry, Kingpin. You'll have it." The firm tone of businessmen closing a deal.

As he left the church, Marcus Veidjur made the sign of the cross with holy water. Maguire waited a few minutes. Then he, too, left the cathedral. It was not a place where he felt comfortable any more.

CHAPTER THIRTEEN

————————

His name was Lo Chu and he was a huge man, built like a bullfrog, with ripples of fat that caused him no small discomfort when he moved. This he did with slow and acquired grace. He wore flowing black robes and drove somber Cadillac Seville limousines, which lurked outside the choicest restaurants and hotels, waiting his beck and call.

Ready for a meeting at ten o'clock, he sat on the patio of the hotel, looking over Repulse Bay and the humid China morning. He could see the faint purple and green cliffs and valleys of Lantau Island. He knew Lantau well, had walked the hills, spent time in a retreat in the Buddhist monastery with other believers. It was a truly beautiful place, like the ancient China of his ancestors. A land lost in time.

He sipped his tea slowly and noticed that the patio was almost empty. Locals rarely came here, and for the past few days the usual patrons, the expatriate community, had stayed home, afraid of more violence. Lo had heard of assorted bomb threats, and of evacuations of schools and public buildings throughout the colony; there were posters plastered on walls screaming for justice against "the White Devil Foreigner." Lo had seen several police patrols stalking back lanes and side alleys as pei dogs, fungous and scabby, yapped and pranced at their feet. But overt acts of violence? At night, it was true, when tension laced the air. But the days were quiet, for the making of money and, if Kwan Dai willed, a solution to the crisis. Lo had seen much in his seventy-odd years on this earth—feast and famine, trial and tribulation—a little rattling of sabers would not deter him from his customary brunch. Still, he wouldn't bet on a quick resolution to this dispute.

A man approached Lo's table. He was dressed in a lightweight cream-colored business suit and wore a striped tie, a police tie. He might have been forty years of age; Lo wasn't sure any more, because he'd stopped counting.

He'd known Steven Tak since he was an infant, had held him on his knee and lulled him to sleep too many times to recall when Lo had stayed at the family retreat at Kwei Lein before the revolution.

Tak's hair was cropped close, his face wrinkled. He had the cynical look of a career custodian of the public's darkest fears and nightmares. But he had the same gentleness in his eyes that his mother had before she died.

Lo motioned to a wicker chair. Tak sat down opposite him and was offered tea and some croissants and toast. Tak wordlessly accepted.

"How is your father, Steven?" Lo spread marmalade on a slice of toast and bit into it vigorously.

"Fine, Lo Chu." He nodded slightly in deference to the man's age. "He sends—"

"Young man, young man," the elder interrupted. "You are just like your mother was, too polite for your own good. Call me uncle." He softened his voice. "You are among friends."

"Very well then," Steven said with the trace of a smile. "Uncle."

"Good. Good." Lo gave a quiet chuckle. "Come on, eat. The toast will not be enough. Have some eggs," he said over Tak's half-hearted protests.

Lo called the waiter. Senior Superintendent Tak was hungry. Was there anything the hotel could prepare quickly? There was the edge of command in the last words. Lo was not a man to be trifled with. The waiter understood this well. He had served Lo for many years. And he always treaded cautiously. Lo Chu was a very powerful man.

Could the hotel suggest eggs Benedict, strip-fried bacon, toast with the best British marmalade and imported Brazilian coffee? Yes? Good, and as quickly as Lo wished.

As the harried waiter rushed off, the two men sat in silence and looked at the beach, which curved in a long crescent. The sand was banana yellow in the morning sunlight, the heat unmerciful.

Lo said, "The word is that you wish to see Mr. Yip."

Tak watched a huge container vessel bound for the terminal at Kwai Chung, on the Castle Peak peninsula, then asked, "Does Mr. Yip know of my interest?"

Lo munched on toast, sipped a little tea, gave a false smile. "I think he does. He doesn't quite know why you want him, but he does know."

Tak sat forward in his chair. "And will he surrender himself with his lawyer?"

"To you?" The blunt stare. "He doesn't feel he's done anything wrong."

The waiter arrived with Tak's food, placed it before the policeman, then scurried out of hearing distance. Tak spread marmalade on his toast, poured some milk in his coffee and added two spoons of sugar.

Lo Chu's tone became confiding. "Steven." His features softened. "Steven, Mr. Yip is a proud man—an honorable one, even if you choose not to believe it. He is of no use to you, certainly not in relation to this present affair."

"Let us be the ones to decide that, Uncle."

Lo touched his hand. The elder's fingers were gnarled like the roots of an ancient tree, but the skin of his hands was surprisingly smooth. Liver spots flecked the surface.

"I knew your father for many years. In his youth, he was a strong, fine person." Lo's voice became wistful. "He should never have become a policeman. But he knew no better. That is why I warn you, young Steven. Things are not what they seem."

Tak responded coldly to the gentle admonition. "Let me be the judge of that, Uncle. It is my prerogative."

Lo Chu had sorrow in his voice as he spoke. "If that is your decision, Steven, you must live with it. And its consequences." He took his hand away. "Mr. Yip is not coming to your offices. Not this time. Not for what you wish to see him about." Lo's expression was distant. He had been this route before, in other times and other places, and knew in the end it was a situation where no one was victorious.

Tak did not finish his meal. There was no reason to remain with his host. He thanked Lo Chu for his hospitality and promised to pass on his warmest greetings to his father, as he always had in the past. Then he left the patio of the Repulse Bay Hotel and began the drive back to Victoria.

With a quick radio call, his alternate plan would be set into motion. As he drove, he took the Panasonic pocket recorder from his jacket and replayed the tape. The meeting with Lo Chu, "friend" of the Triad boss Yip Lam, would be fully logged, the tapes carefully stored to protect them and to guard Steven's integrity.

As director of the Police Triad Society Bureau, Steven Tak had had many similar meetings over the years, made many accommodations to avoid unnecessary bloodshed. It was easy to gossip with the old man about Yip Lam, for the lucid edge of Lo Chu's wit invariably had its basis in truth and fairness. But Lo should not have denied Tak this request, knowing, as he must, the terrible consequences for Lo and for the innocent people of Hong Kong. Still Steven Tak's heart was heavy, for he knew he would never see him again. And that caused him no small sadness.

Tak was conscientious, but he was also dutiful in the manner of a proper Chinese son. The emptiness he felt with the parting from an old family friend would remain his own private loss, a secret his father would never know.

A thick layer of smog hung over the island. The morning was muggy and hot, brutally so. Carbon monoxide choked the urban streets. Not one tree grew in the urban core. David Andrews wondered if any ever had. He slouched in the passenger seat of the little Cortina, eyes stinging from lack of sleep.

Hong Kong had the densest traffic in the world—and the densest drivers. And every day seemed to reconfirm this as

the little Chan Fats of the territory took their rust-bucket,
brake-worn Nissans, Escorts and Austins to tempt fate and
the vagaries of the pre-noon rush hour which, in typical
Hong Kong fashion, never seemed to end till afternoon tea.
Andrews looked around. Be it greed or necessity, many
people appeared determined to go on with their lives
whatever the rumblings of unrest about the grand old
colony.

"You're awfully quiet, Davie. You okay?" The driver of the
Cortina looked over with mock concern.

Andrews stifled another yawn and replied with a nod.
"How much longer?" he asked.

Peng glanced at his Seiko. "Plenty of time, sport. Don't
worry. Care for a cigarette?"

Andrews took it wordlessly, lit and inhaled. His eyes smart-
ed.

"Damn." Peng cursed, braking violently to avoid a
tangerine-colored double-decker bus shunting from side to
side like a beetle crab. Andrews took a long drag. Royal
Crowns. He hated Royal Crowns. He glanced out the window. Warehouses, nightclubs, tenements, storefront garages,
cranes and construction hoardings—old Wanchai mingling
with the new. And always the construction. Pounding, scrap-
ing, tearing down to make way, to make the money that
made more money.

The traffic lightened. The Cortina moved deftly past Victoria Park into the Bayview district, up Kings Road, away
from the waterfront, then around toward the eastern part of
the island.

Their investigation itself had almost been conceived stillborn. The key lay in a yellowed index card at Narcotics
Bureau records, overlooked but for an apparently lucky afterthought.

Peng had started with one working assumption—that Yip
had destroyed the *Glorious East Wind*, or whatever it had
been called originally, to protect his control of the drug
trade, and that control had been challenged by a group of
businessmen. The CP wanted to know who they were, and
quickly. Ambitious objectives at the best of times, but Cleve's

voice, strained and curt, did little to dispel his feelings on the matter. "Find them, Peng. . . . Find them, whatever the cost, and find them soon."

So they'd plodded through the files, operational diaries and surveillance reports, looking for the link, the clue. Four syndicates in various stages of preparation. But none of the existing groups appeared to be involved.

And then, in the lift en route to a Central tea house in the sour nicotine and caffeine sharpened early hours of the day, Peng wondered out loud how he'd forgotten. True, it was only a straw. But clutching at straws was a policeman's lot and salvation. He'd stopped the lift between floors and, before an astonished Andrews could react, pushed the button to go back to the fifteenth floor. Confronting a grumbling old detective constable, he'd demanded and received access to the incident and contact files.

As he did so, Peng explained his theory to his young partner. In the wooly orange hours of the Asian dawn, it began to make sense; together they'd attacked the mounds of paper with renewed vengeance.

First, the incident report. They should have seen the signs last October, in Sham Shui Po. Everyone in the force had heard about the dispute within the Triad; it had reached the CP's morning report and been discussed at one of the weekly Friday meetings of the superintendents. A follow-up file had been started in the Triad Society Bureau and with good reason—the word was on the street, and the bureau had to keep tabs on it. But that was all the information they had, a new group to worry about. No name, no leader, no objectives—at least none that were known.

The report had been straightforward enough. On Friday, October 3, at approximately 23:45 hours, a group of six males armed with knives, choppers and triangular files got out of a beige-colored *pak-pai*, an unlicensed taxi. The police had some of the license-plate numbers for the car, a Diatsu, which they had parked on Yee Kuk Street, Sham Shui Po, Kowloon. The six had run into an alley, right past fifteen diners at a cooked-food stall.

A few moments later a series of piercing screams cut the

night air, then twenty or so drug addicts rushed out of the
laneway, followed by the six men, one of whom was carrying
a large plastic bag filled with what witnesses stated was a
white powder just like laundry soap. (The police report sur-
mised that it was good-quality heroin.) Five of the men
managed to make it back to the waiting car. The sixth
stumbled and fell, injured. Three policemen had responded
to a call and were in time to arrest the man.

Only one of the witnesses, a form-six student, had been of
even remote assistance. He'd recalled the face of the *pak-pai*
driver—gaunt, wearing glasses. Half the population of Hong
Kong, it seemed, wore glasses. But he'd remembered something else. The man had a very bad case of acne, and drove
the others away westward and then north in a vehicle whose
license number began "K6." Follow-up inquiries had led
nowhere; the police knew that the plate, already illegal, could
easily be replaced.

The three policemen on the scene had been bright. The
senior man had found three hoodlums in the alley amid the
rancid garbage and rotting fish. He had also seized a number
of syringes and traces of dangerous drugs. If nothing else,
the three hoods could be charged with possession of narcotics.

All three had criminal records and Triad file numbers,
which tied them to Yip's syndicate. They'd been badly cut by
the six males but remained sullen and silent. One said something about "Four Eyes"—probably a reference to one of
their attackers. All subsequent charges were for drugs, but it
scarcely mattered: they did their punishment silently.
Revenge would be theirs in their own time.

The injured assailant was a man called Lai Man Yi. There
had been no witnesses to the assault, at least none that would
admit to seeing it, so the police could do nothing but lock
the man up for Triad membership. The courts had been uncommonly good and he'd received three months in Stanley
Prison. He had spent his time in isolation: Yip's tentacles extended even into the prison. Lai had been released in
February.

Peng considered the facts. If Lai was on a contract squad,

he had to know his master, or at least his sponsor. The information he had before him wasn't much, but it was something. The threat of turning Lai loose for Yip's pleasure, however hollow, would be worth it just to see the expression on his face.

Peng was going to find this man. And the contact files, devised recently as a means of keeping tabs on known criminals and criminal types, might help. With Andrews at his side, he'd plodded through index card after index card.

In twenty minutes they had narrowed down the field. Then they found it: a card dated April 7, about an incident on Yuet Yuen Street in North Point. The investigating officer was a detective inspector named Sather. The circumstance was a drug raid carried out at 03:00 hours with, as usual, no result. They'd found forty twenty-dollar notes, but the addicts had scattered and the evidence was flushed away. The police had nothing to hold Lai on, so they'd let him go after a cursory questioning. And Sather had completed an index card.

Peng reached for the phone, checked the tattered white government directory and dialed the number. It was 05:00 hours.

A few rings and then a sleepy voice answered, "Wai?"—a woman. He asked for Sather.

"Who the hell is this?" The voice was hung over, irritable.

Peng identified himself, and Sather began to wake up. He remembered Lai very well; they'd started a small file on him at the division. A real rascal, always caught with the money after a drug raid, but never with the goods. He was about five feet five, in his early twenties. Hakka. A malignant-looking growth on his neck. His nickname was "Elephant Man," because he was so ugly; there was a whimsical Chinese irony even in crime. His haunts were the same as always: the North Point ferry area. The detective inspector didn't think he was independent or small time; he was well-funded, always well-dressed. Even in casual attire he had a touch of class about him. He had a good supply of drugs, and from what street sources told police, not to mention what the government labs were able to deduce, it was prime stuff.

Sather's street people didn't know too much about Lai's syndicate, but informants were beginning to open up. Some said it was a well-run operation, a very well-run operation. The top man was someone with a funny-sounding first name, maybe a Eurasian.

Peng thanked him and, with a chuckle in his voice, told him he could get back to the business at hand. There was a female giggle in the distance as he hung up.

And now Peng and Andrews were entering Elephant Man's turf, North Point. Peng followed the streetcar tracks eastward, avoiding the people and pushcarts that shot in front of him with alarming frequency. Peng actually seemed to be enjoying the obstacle course of cars, rickshaws and people. Hong Kong traffic.

Slowly, imperceptibly, Andrews dozed off into a heavy sleep.

CHAPTER FOURTEEN

—————

The sign on the office door read Steven Tak, Senior Superintendent, Triad Society Bureau. The walls of the office were covered with banners seized from Triad groups, the largest one from Chuen, thirty-one letters arranged in mystical symmetry on a white background; the others—from Yee On, Wo Sing Wo, 14K—were the small red flags of Chuen rivals and cohorts. All were enemies to the police.

It was hard for the young Chinese seated in front of the desk to connect this immense operation to the scholarly-looking gentleman sitting across from him. Yet he knew that Steven Tak was unnerved by nothing, a bear for detail, said to remember everything.

Tak himself would point out, with a crooked smile, that the underworld's hatred for him had been earned by painstaking effort on his part; that the contract out on his life was only the base market assessment of his true value and that he wanted the price to rise before he would concur in arranging his own demise. It was also rumored, though more guardedly, that Tak had very high and personal contacts in the old Triad lodges, contacts who fed him the information he needed to keep on top of things. What was never fully explained was the reason for their generosity. But in Hong Kong the logical was not necessarily true or valid, and so the questions remained mute and unanswered.

Tak sat at his desk, facing the young police inspector. "You wonder why you are here, don't you?"

Adam Kot, smiling self-consciously, agreed that he did.

"Perfectly understandable." Tak's voice was high, his words clipped, as if each made its own point. With an impatient forefinger he brushed back the bifocals that threatened to slip off the edge of his nose. "By the way." He looked quizzically at Kot. "Your hair's a trifle long, don't you think?"

Kot's face turned red and he was about to blurt out a half-hearted apology but Tak calmed him. "For the moment I would have been more pleased if it had been a bit longer."

Adam Kot's impulse to apologize collided with excitement. Something interesting was going on. Whatever it was, it was better than answering telephones at Colony Pol/Mil.

The superintendent folded back a crisp, clean cuff and glanced at his watch. "It's now 10:17. We have very little time." Briskly he continued: "You seem to be educated and knowledgeable—if somewhat naive." Kot turned redder. "Your record of service shows you have taken a degree in political science." Tak turned to a folder. "And have just returned from an advanced course at the British Police College at Hendon—" he glanced obliquely from the file "—where you did rather well."

Adam smiled, pleased. "Yes, sir. I try to do my best."

"Yes, I'm sure you do." Tak closed the file suddenly, as if closing the door on Kot. "Now, tell me all you know about the inner hierarchy of the Triad Lodge run by Yip Lam as it exists today in Hong Kong."

"Well. . . ."

The silence that followed seemed to prove the point Tak wished to make. He spoke kindly. "You know as much as most policemen these days know—as much as they should know." Tak was referring to his predecessor, now cooling his heels for five years at Stanley Prison for abusing his privileged position. The inference was not lost on Kot. Tak handed him a thick ringed binder. "Read this prospectus. Ask questions where necessary."

Kot opened the binder, stamped boldly, Top Secret—For Official Use Only. He began to read.

1945, Triad 14K formed in Canton. 1956, Triad gangs move into densely populated areas, settlement centers in Hong Kong for refugees fleeing from mainland. 1956, disturbances in resettlement blocks, North Kowloon, incited by 14K and Wo Sing Wo gangs. 1956–1959, police action against Triads accelerated—over 10,000 Triad officials and members arrested; 600 deported. 1960, intensification of Triad activity. 1967, membership in Triad lodges growing at alarming rate. Estimate 90,000 Triad members in Hong Kong, of which 62,000 are active. 1972–1975 major crackdowns on gangs, with little effect. 1975, Saigon falls, influx of Indo-Chinese refugees. New and virulent strain of Triad activity from refugee camps. 1983, membership breaks 100,000. Four murders involving elder Triad bosses. Central control appears lost. Active membership in all lodges increases 22% in ten years. Vietnamese gangs fighting Chinese for refugee camp gold. Chuen Triad Lodge battles 14K for supremacy of bar girls in Wanchai. Five officials of 14K found murdered in Rennies Mill, no arrests. Chuen Triad rumored to be supreme.

Then came the information on Yip Lam.

Adam Kot had heard stories of the Triads all his life. Like fairy tales of the gentle glories of Peking and the warrior gods of old, of musty teak and opium-reeking divans, long-fingered mandarins in fir-treed gardens and silk watercolors of trading junks cutting the phosphorous around the Nine Pins, they were a part of Chinese legend and folklore. But this—the information in the file—was not what he had expected.

"You wonder perhaps why there is no summary here?" Kot, startled by Tak's voice, realized that he had been staring through the superintendent for some moments. Tak's gaze was piercing. "It is quite simple. The story is still being written, and—" Tak appeared to inspect the back of his hands, then his fingernails. "Hopefully, you will be its author, I its conclusion."

Tak was silent. Kot shifted in his chair. "Are you a Christian, Kot?"

The slight nod.

"Well, I am a Buddhist. But we are both wise enough to know the strength of allegory. The power that poetry and pretense have to move men's spirits."

The men in the Triad bureau referred to this as "the other side of the superintendent."

Tak went on:

"Vestiges of glory. The trappings of greatness. It makes the otherwise weak and penniless feel purpose and worth. Romance, tradition, a touch of mythology, common enough motivations, don't you think?" His voice was reflective. "The Triad. Paper fan. Bamboo sandal. Brotherhood of blood. The righting of the wrongs of centuries. . . ."

Abruptly Tak's voice changed, became hard. "The facts. We have figures here, tentative and probably low, of at least eleven extortions and three drug transactions involving large quantities of heroin orchestrated by these vermin. My people tell me there are now thirty Triad lodges in Hong Kong, so you can see we have our hands full at the best of times.

"Of these so-called lodges, I am concerned with a few only: Wo Sing Wo, Chin, Chuen, Leung and 14K. They have between them about fifteen thousand members and, contrary to the official line, we do fear them. And one of them—Yip Lam's Chuen—I suddenly fear and loathe above all the others."

"Yes, sir."

"The last few weeks have seen a marked increase in activity by Yip Lam's boys. Twenty-five persons beaten with iron poles; four stabbed with triangular files, two killed with homemade cleavers. And all for one apparent reason."

Tak handed the inspector the contents of a white envelope. "Read this."

When Kot looked up, there was a thin line of perspiration on his upper lip.

"Read it again," said Tak.

Kot read the terse note a second time, then returned it to his superior. Tak put it back in the envelope and took out his silver lighter. The rich, ruddy flame touched the paper at one end. It quickly caught fire, yellow, red. When the paper was half-consumed, Tak placed it in the ashtray. They watched the smoke-tinged document turn to black char. Tiny wisps of burned paper floated out of the ashtray onto the desk. Tak brushed them to the floor.

"Is it understood?"

Adam nodded, his face pale.

"I want that man, Kot. I want him badly and I want him alive. And you, my friend, are going to get him for me. Now be gone. We have not much time."

Adam left, and Tak placed his hand on the white phone on the corner of his desk and dialed a single number. There were two monotone buzzes; then a tired Welsh voice answered.

"He's on his way, sir. With any luck he will find our man." Tak paused, then spoke briskly. "Of course, sir. May our god help us, sir. May your god help us."

Cleve walked briskly into the room, came to attention and waited. The figure stayed in the shadows.

"You wish to see me, sir?"

The governor turned, his voice a rich baritone, his tone imperious. "This will be short, commissioner. I sense you have enough to occupy your time."

"Sir."

Thomas Driscoll stepped into the light. His face was somber, his manner almost severe.

"A drink, commissioner?"

"No. Thank you, sir."

There was no warmth in Driscoll's voice. Cleve, for his part, was unaffected by the chill. He hadn't expected this to be the most pleasant of meetings.

"Well, I'll have one if you don't mind." Driscoll tugged the old-fashioned bell-rope, a predecessor's poorly considered attempt at grandeur. There was a faint tinkle in another part of the manse.

An aging manservant appeared at a half-trot, stopped and bowed.

"The usual, Felix." The governor spoke in the bored voice of one accustomed to much luxury.

The two men stood apart while the Philippino carefully prepared the drink. Cleve did not break the awkward silence. The gesture would be lost on the man.

With something in his hand to occupy himself, Driscoll began. He wanted to know what had happened since his last memo. Cleve answered politely. He started to explain about Yip and the syndicate, then caught himself. By his disinterested expression it was apparent it was not what the governor wanted to hear.

Driscoll took a sip of gin, considered the flavor, then spoke. "Can I ask you a simple question, commissioner? One that rises above the mundane details of what you are doing, to the more important direction of your investigation. What is it? Where are we headed and are we going to attain that end?" He gazed directly at Cleve, eyes cold and unfeeling.

"I think we are making progress."

The governor raised his hand to halt him. "Progress." He rolled the word on his tongue. "Progress?" He walked a few paces then turned abruptly. "A wonderful expression, Cleve. Progress. I've heard it often, this word. Seen it in many reports over the years. Progress. What does it mean, commissioner, this progress? Does it mean that when I stand on my balcony here in the morning having a simple breakfast with my wife I have to look down upon a veritable insurrection at my doorstep?" The governor's hand shot out dramatically toward the curtained windows. Through them, Cleve could see the tiny American flag on the U.S. Consulate some quarter of a mile distant.

Driscoll strode to his desk, grabbed some press clippings and held them up menacingly. "Does it mean I face a vituperative press, screaming for my hide? Is that progress, commissioner? Is it?"

Thomas Driscoll found his voice rising sharply. He caught himself. He realized that this little lapse into theatrics had had no effect on his audience. John Cleve continued to stare stolidly at him like a rather bemused parent watching the cresting of a child's fit of pique.

There was no love lost between the new governor and his commissioner of police. Initially Driscoll had tried to be civil, but only for a time. Soon civility had been replaced by distance, then distance by silence. And now this: confrontation.

True, the commissioner and he were obviously not of the same breeding. But Driscoll was peeved to realize that all his years of diplomatic training had not prepared him for Cleve's character, the bluntness of manner and forthrightness of purpose.

Confrontational politics, it seemed, was the commissioner's style: sending out the riot troops to bludgeon the locals, rather than mollify them. After all, what harm would they have done if they had been left alone to prance around the courtyard with their brightly festooned signs and gibberish rhetoric? Precious little, he supposed.

No. It wasn't till Cleve had sent in his storm troopers that the problems had started. And now they would be stuck with unpleasant antagonism for the remainder of this "crisis," a crisis that was interfering with his other plans.

The governor shook his head.

Thomas Driscoll, a career diplomat negotiating a major diplomatic coup, had been stymied by a bunch of rice burners in heat and a bull-necked bear of a policeman who put integrity above efficiency.

Driscoll tried a new approach. His voice was calmer, confiding, a tone he thought might placate this man. "Cleve. . . John. . . ." He stumbled over the familiarity. "Perhaps you don't realize the stakes here?"

"I think I do." Cleve eyed the furnishings around him. "It's concerning the land deal, isn't it?"

The governor bristled. The chill returned.

"Yes, it is. Of course it is, commissioner." Driscoll caught himself before he lost his patience. He spoke in falsely honeyed tones. "The special economic zone. You know of it, Cleve." He sipped some of the gin. "It's in the précis we sent over. Straightforward." He downed the drink, went to the bar and began to mix himself another.

"Yes. Straightforward. The investors are interested. The People's Republic of China wish our assistance to develop the airport near Canton commercially. It's as simple as that. There's land, people, raw materials. All they need is money."

Cleve thought of Maguire and Special Branch entertaining and protecting all those flatulent little millionaires for the cause. He said nothing.

Driscoll felt compelled to fill the silence. "And with that in mind, I believe very strongly that the situation here in the past few hours has come to a crucial stage." He sensed his voice rise again, but caught it. "You don't know the full complexity of the deal, Cleve. You think it's simply a matter of signing documents, exchanging notes, transferring items. There are other considerations you have no idea of. . . ." The governor stopped. The ice in the glass tinkled. Driscoll looked away vaguely.

"I will not allow anything to interfere with the land deal, Cleve. Is that understood? The problem on the streets because of that ship must be settled, and quickly. Talk of progress is just not good enough. I want results—and soon."

"Sir."

Driscoll smiled, a wooden, empty smile.

"Are you certain I can't fix you a drink? It's good gin, private stock."

Cleve again declined.

"I've indicated to you what I expect, commissioner. Nothing more, nothing less. Arrest the culprits who destroyed the vessel. Make it a public event, the maximum media coverage to get our point across. Clean up this unpleasantness with the minimum inconvenience." Driscoll's smile was wry and unnerving. "I'm certain something can be arranged." He nodded. "Commissioner." The audience was over.

Cleve left the room.

Driscoll considered himself in the full-length mirror. He wore a long sleeved powder-blue button-down shirt with gold pin stripes, and with it he wore a proper school tie. His trousers were lightweight cotton. Finely tailored, they emphasized his lanky frame. He considered the gold stripes on his shirt once more. His Shanghai tailor had felt it an odd combination when Driscoll had requested it, had thought, with due respect, that powder blue with gold might look gaudy. But when the shirt was complete, the tailor was forced to admit that the governor had exquisite taste, good sense of shade and definition.

The governor liked gold, liked its feel and color and the image of solidness it created. Sometimes he thought that was why he liked Hong Kong.

Thomas Driscoll was a shrewd man. Born into an old knighted family, he'd been educated at Oxford and weaned on the best the Old World had to offer. Progressive and ambitious, he'd entered the diplomatic corps rather than retire on graduation, as he could have, to the ancestral estate in the rolling fields near York Cathedral.

It had proved a wise move. His family wealth, though at one time substantial, had been foolishly frittered away by his father on bad investments and squandered dreams. In his late forties, Driscoll found himself left with a title and no substance.

But he had a talent for negotiation and a sociable demeanor, and he'd risen quickly in Her Majesty's Service, first in Geneva, serving his apprenticeship in an obscure United Nations body. Then to Sri Lanka, as high commissioner. And then, for a long and successful tenure, as ambassador to Italy.

Driscoll knew he could never return to the hollowed-out shell of a country that was England, to give guided tours of the manse to gold-toothed and red-necked tourists. So when the vacancy in the governor's seat in Hong Kong had cropped up, he'd pounced on it, calling in old-boy favors from chums at Whitehall until the position was his.

Thomas Driscoll was many things, but he was no fool. And that is what angered him most about Cleve's actions. It was not an opportune time for Cleve's sort of rally-round-the-flag nonsense, or for his obstinance and frightening insight. Driscoll had done too much legwork to see it lost now. And he had another problem. He had patiently helped initiate the land deal with the consortium and the Communist Chinese; used the services of the British agent from Whitehall to close it without fanfare. And he'd made the requisite moves to

ensure a little sugar for most of the principals, to their obvious satisfaction.

All save Lee. That had been his decision, and his alone. He
did not like the Chinaman; he thought Lee was too pushy,
too arrogant, too demanding. Hong Kong was returning to
China, it was true. But until it did, the governor ruled the
territory and made the decisions about its future—and
whatever benefits might derive from that future—and not, as
he'd often said to himself, some slant-eyed socialist with
Gucci loafers and pretensions to grandeur.

The money Driscoll had winkled out of the transactions
for the interested parties as icing on the cake was money they
had, through risk-taking and initiative, collectively earned.
Lee was making a ruckus because he had been excluded;
Driscoll thought it was just not on.

Driscoll looked out the window to the horizon. Smudge
spots marred the Kowloon skyline; he heard the faint sound
of gunfire to the east of him, in the area of Wanchai. A frown
came to his face.

He thought of Lee's smug, aloof expression and grimaced.
"So you wish to speak to me, Chinaman. You leave a strange
calling card." He became aware that he was thinking aloud,
and the realization confused him. He'd always prided himself
on his self-control.

Quickly he finished his drink and placed the empty glass
on a teapoy. Time to prepare for affairs of state. The day
would be a busy one.

But something bothered the governor about his commissioner of police, something unspoken, which had seeped into
their conversation and taken root in his subconscious, to
gnaw at his customary feeling of well-being.

How much did Cleve really know of the Kowloon land
deal? How close was he to discovering its true complexities?
Driscoll was certain his comment about the airport in Canton hadn't fooled the commissioner for one minute; Cleve
was too much the old fox to be taken in by it.

Driscoll realized he would have to protect what he had
done before Cleve discovered it and ruined them all.

He tugged the bell-rope to summon his servant. He knew

just the one to assist him in his dilemma, the secretive man from Whitehall named Proctor. Anthony Proctor.

He tugged the rope again. Damn! Where was that fellow? He would have his hide!

It was only when he turned around that he discovered Felix, with his sheepish grin, had been standing there all along, and that everything would be looked after, as it always was.

CHAPTER FIFTEEN

———

It took Dicky Smithers, the ex-RAF warrant officer who ran the Special Branch photography section like a private fiefdom, less than ten minutes to prepare the wet sheets. He'd found the microdot right where it was supposed to be, on page two, in the masthead of the Washington *Post*. Without it there was no "i" in "Washington."

Maguire sat alone in his office in Caine House behind locked doors. He was taking no visitors. In front of him was a brown-jacketed copy of the book he and Veidjur used as the control document for the messages that passed between them. To one side was the contact sheet, a photograph of countless sets of numbers, row on row.

The book was Dante's *Inferno*. Next to the contact sheet Maguire placed a handwritten chart, with the numbers one to five vertically and the same horizontally. In the grid were the letters of the alphabet in order from left to right.

Dante's text was opened at page 267, for the day of the year—yesterday—he'd met Veidjur at the Cathedral. Maguire carefully read the passage:

Through me the road to the City of Desolation
Through me the road to sorrows diuturnal,
Through me the Road among the lost creation.

Justice moved my Great Maker, God Eternal
Wrought me, the power, and the unsearchably
High Wisdom, and the primal love supernal.

Nothing ere I was made was made to be
Save things eterne and I eterne abide,
Lay down all hope, you that go in by me.

A wry smile crossed Maguire's face. Trust Veidjur to be melodramatic. The pickup had been that morning at ten o'clock; the tenth word in the poem was "through." He copied the word, then encoded it from the chart. The letter T equalled four across and four down, forty-four; H was two across, three down: twenty-three. And so on. He completed the series of numbers up to the set of five, which was all the code required. Then he took the numbers from the contact sheet, placed them above the control numbers and subtracted, reversing Veidjur's process of encoding. Slowly the message took place.

Lanchow and Karamai, street riots.
Chungking, factory closures.
Lop Nor, the nuclear research station, a revolt
    suppressed.
Harbin, a militia unit revolt, suppressed.

What Veidjur was reporting was utterly fascinating. A Kangnan-class destroyer had undergone a mutiny ten miles off the Gulf of Chihli before the moderates regained the bridge; a shootout had claimed ten lives. Two Hung Wan hydrofoils were torched at their docks at Tsingtao to prevent a takeover by radical elements. A number of Shanghai-class patrol craft reportedly turned radical and patrolled the coast off Lien Yung Kang, sniping at targets ashore. At air bases in Shangshi, Wuhan and Kunming, armed guards were placed aroung MIG 23s so they couldn't be stolen by young radical ensigns. Purges were reported among the officer cadre along the Amur River and Tienshan, threatening the Sino-Russian border. Veidjur's reports did not indicate whether the officers emerged triumphant. In Harbin, an army brigade rebelled from the central control of the Ministry of Defense and set up its own People's Proletarian Militia under the makeshift flag of the radicals from Shanghai.

But as Maguire continued deciphering, his initial enthusiasm turned first to dismay and then to furious anger. Veidjur had given him nothing on Lee. And, worse, he had coded in closing, "King's Point. 2:00 P.M. Want more money."

That damned impertinent Slav! Maguire thought. I need to remind him where his loyalties should be—and quickly.

Maguire stormed to the bookshelf by his desk and moved an anthology of Somerset Maugham to one side. Behind it was a small combination safe. Maguire opened it, then felt around for the microtapes and cassettes of Veidjur's escapades. They would be the perfect "reminders." But there was nothing there. They were gone. And those of the Malays and the others were also gone. The safe was empty.

He broke into a cold sweat. Only he and Smithers knew of the safe's existence, and Maguire had Smithers where he wanted him.

He buzzed his secretary. She came into the room quickly, cowed by the harshness in his voice. No, no one had been in the office in the past few hours except Maguire, she was certain. Then she paused before leaving the office and said, "A man called concerning your meeting at North Point, this afternoon." The young woman, her face flushed, read her notes. "It is scheduled for two o'clock at the Metropole Restaurant. He says you will learn what happened to his watches." Maguire glowered. Veidjur had just overstepped his bounds—he was never to call Special Branch directly, that was strict policy.

Maguire stopped the woman before she could escape out the door.

"Did the European identify himself on the phone?" Maguire wanted to see how cheeky Veidjur had become.

The secretary gave him a curious stare. "No, sir. He didn't give his name. But he wasn't European, sir. He was Chinese."

The director's face paled. "Get me my car."

"And the backup team?"

"Yes. Put them on with me."

The woman left before Maguire had finished speaking. He went to his desk and, from the right-hand drawer, took out his .38 snub nose. He checked the weapon, found it clean and loaded it with five rounds. He placed the spares in a speed loader, which went into his right-hand pocket. He put on his shoulder holster, tucked the gun inside and left.

The telephone was located at Fanling and it was a mad race to get there on time.

Adam Kot flashed by the baked brown mountains and slimy rice paddies where women worked the fields, sloshing knee-deep in thick, muddy water. The road was lined with wizened, rickety trees, and everywhere the white heat oozed out of a lead-blasted sky.

Adam Kot drove with nervous energy, managing numerous hairpin turns with just enough grace to avoid an accident. He had chosen to drive his own car, a sleek Mitsubishi, over the gutless government sedan he'd been offered—and with just cause: an appointment had been made and it had to be kept. It was now eleven o'clock. He had half an hour left. Another sharp curve; brake; gear down. He just managed to avoid a Kowloon Motor bus.

He passed an army convoy careening south toward the urban core from their base on the Luen Wo Road.

He stepped on the gas pedal in fevered haste. Time was running out. The New Territories rushed by him in a maddening blur. To his left, the looming purple shadow of Tai Mo Shan. At its feet, the multi-tiered graves of Wo Hop Shek cemetery. Ahead, fringed in black prickle bush and stunted shrubbery, spread like a patchwork of tans and greens, the rice fields leading to Mother China.

And then, suddenly, he arrived at the place for his contact, the phone booth at the Fanling railway station.

Kot opened the squeeky phone-booth door and slipped in. It was hot inside. When the phone rang, Kot calmly picked up the receiver and stared absently at the ceiling. Peeling paint—green, cream, orange. What were the original colors of these booths, anyway? He felt the adrenaline pumping through him.

A rough voice at the other end breathed heavily. "Wei?"

"Hello." Kot was shocked by the evenness of his own voice. There was silence on the line. He recalled his instructions. Say nothing at first.

"Is this 5-633238?" Kot wrote down the numbers on the back of a cigarette pack. It was a simple but effective code, using grid references from security maps. The caller could be found in Hong Kong, on the street corner 633238.

Adam tucked the pack of Rothmans away. "Yes, you have the correct number. Is this Mr. Godber?" The muffled confirmation. "You are selling greyhounds?"

"Yes, I have one. To breed for Macau." Their target was a greyhound; their contact was the greyhound dealer.

Kot responded laconically. "My master has an interest in him." He remembered Tak's warning. He wants out from the cold and he wants out bad. Let him make the admission and we'll have it all.

"Oh?" The pregnant pause.

"My master wants to buy him." There, it was said. The greyhound was no longer just to be "observed," to be "paced," to be "weighted" against the other "dogs," but to be bought body and soul.

There was hesitation at the other end. The faint sound of traffic in the distance; the gong of a passing streetcar. Kot stared into space.

I'm losing him, thought Kot. With so much at stake, I'm losing him. He'll just fade into the woodwork and we'll have nothing to show after all these years of planting the seed, of nurturing the contact and allowing it to grow so it could be plucked when the time was ripe. He's dying on me. I'm losing him.

Adam knew he should say something; there was no time for games now.

He chose his words with care, realizing that a slip of the tongue meant death for his contact. His voice was harsh, but with an undercurrent of control.

"Listen, my friend. This is vital to us and you know it." As he talked, Adam thought about his contact. He knew the man wanted to leave the colony. The sign had been there: a mango peel left impaled in the joss tray on the inner wall of the Tien Hau Temple at North Point. This phone call was intended to lay the groundwork for his escape from the world of the damned.

Kot could sense the man's confusion and fear. It was time to offer the man sanctuary. "Understand. We can help you, but you must give us the Greyhound."

There was an expiration of air on the line. "It's impossible. They'll kill me before I can."

And then the man said exactly what Kot had dreaded. "It's no good. I'm leaving without this. I don't need you. I. . .I can disappear. I have money." The caller was indecisive, confused.

Humble him; it must be done. "You don't need us? Come come. Yes, you do, my friend. Alone, where would you go? Macau? They'll find you there and skewer you. Overseas? We won't let you." He heard the gasp of disbelief and pressed on.

"Look, all we ask is the Greyhound's location. Nothing more. We'll provide you with cover and protection."

"But you want me there when you find him, don't you?"

Silence.

"Well, don't you?"

"Yes."

"How do I know you can protect me?"

"Do you have a choice?"

Adam heard the clanging of another streetcar, but nothing more from the other end. A fly buzzed in the telephone booth. Then his contact spoke. "Tonight, eleven o'clock, Nullah Road in Mongkok; the Sai Woo restaurant. He'll be there to receive tributes from his society. You will have Yip Lam, your Greyhound."

The phone clicked. The line was dead.

CHAPTER SIXTEEN

———————

The panda car, a blue-and-white Escort estate wagon with an Emergency Unit crew manning it, screeched to a halt on the pebbled driveway outside the house. The black vinyl upholstery was hot and Cleve thankfully left the front seat. He ordered the sergeant to wait; he'd only be inside a few minutes. Before he'd gone twenty paces, the tea thermos was out from under the emergency riot gear and the men were gulping ice water. He couldn't blame them on a dog day like this.

Cleve had taken the wagon instead of his official vehicle. He found this means of travel as efficient as any, and certainly less obvious. One of the many in the force inventory, the whippet-quick little Escort fit his requirements to a T. Police vehicles were everywhere these last few days; one more or less wouldn't be unusual or attract undue attention. And the last thing the CP wanted to do was to draw attention to his absence from May House, for whatever reason.

There was little he could do right now at headquarters. He'd set the wheels in motion with the Triad Society Bureau, and sent the lad up to the New Territories to make the devil's pact, to deal for Yip Lam, the Greyhound. He'd received an inconclusive update from Peng in his frenzied search for the mysterious business cartel; they were still wading through files. Young Andrews was showing promise and things were working according to plan, though heaven only knew where it would all lead. Still, he had faith in Jim Peng. There were few others he trusted.

And Maguire? Who knew what Special Branch was up to these days. Keeping abreast of Lee and the Communists should keep the snoopers occupied. The rest of the force was too busy for the questionable luxuries of delegation, and that suited Cleve just fine. As commissioner of police, he had enough on his plate without looking for trouble.

The early afternoon promised a lull in the work, and he was taking advantage of it. He could be in constant radio contact with Pol/Mil, and he was only a fifteen-minute drive away, down the slalom-run roads off the Peak face into Central and PHQ.

The driveway was hot. The sun beat down from a sky rapidly becoming crowded with storm clouds, sickly green and puffy with rain. The house was set back in a grove of trees on Lady Clementy's Ride, and framed by decades of tropical undergrowth. Two stories, unpretentious, tan stucco with rust-red roof shutters, it had been home for successive generations of commissioners of police. It was his as long as he was commissioner. Stability was an ephemeral thing, at best, in Hong Kong.

He reached the door and realized sheepishly that he'd forgotten his keys. He rang the bell and, as he waited, he noticed the paint was peeling. It was unlikely the government would fork over money for touch ups.

The door opened. He felt the rush of cool air, the familiar, slightly musky smell of home. Margaret stood there in the shadows, tall and willowy, as if she had expected him. She didn't look forty-six. There was no emotion on her face as he moved to kiss her, but she turned away so that his lips brushed her cheek. There was a distance, a stiffness to her movements. He felt his spirits drop. Nothing had changed for her. A peck on the cheek. Was that what was left of their marriage?

"Hello, John," she said vaguely.

He stepped in, took off his forage cap and removed his Sam Browne, coiling it like a snake before placing it with the cap on the hall table.

Cleve made his way through the silent house and Margaret followed. At the end of the hall a pale blue light coming off the patio bathed the kitchen. He could see the City below, hidden in pillows of smog and sauna steam. He went into the living room, which was in semi-darkness. Slowly his eyes grew accustomed to it; he sat down on his favorite chair and raised his legs onto the foot cushion. Cleve eased his head back, closing his eyes, wallowing in the cool nothingness. Margaret sat herself opposite him on the sofa and silently lit a cigarette.

"How have you been?" Her voice was toneless.

"Fine. Fine." His eyes were closed. He didn't even look back.

"Can I get you something to eat? A sandwich? There's coffee on the brew. . ." She made an attempt at civility.

"Yes, a snack. That would be good, Maggie." He could feel the exhaustion and tension of the past few days oozing out of him like sweat. He felt rubbery tired and his head pounded. Time to unwind—that's what he needed. But it was a luxury he couldn't afford.

"I'm sorry about yesterday. About Matt. . .I called but. . ."

She started to mumble that she forgave him but her features suddenly changed. There was an anger in her, pent-up, hurt anger.

"Sorry, John? You're always sorry. I'm sick of hearing you say you're sorry. You were sorry when Guy broke his arm and when Emily had to be rushed to the hospital with pneumonia." Her voice was searing. "You were sorry. You were always sorry! But you were never there, John. You were never there! What kind of father are you, John Cleve? Two of your children grown up and gone and they didn't even know you.

"You were always out somewhere for the Force! For the good of the Force! You worried more about your precious men than you did for your own children. Their father? By birthright, that was all. You were no more their father than Chiu the bloody gardener! And they saw him a damn sight more than you.

"Sorry?" She spat out the last word and looked at him with contempt.

Cleve said nothing.

"You're going to tell me about the riots and the problems of being commissioner of police." She poured forth her pain. "Face it, husband, you're not a one-man police force. There are others you can delegate the responsibility to, other people only too willing to do the dirty work. And there are always others to be made sacrificial lambs. But don't you keep doing it by yourself—because if you do, that's about all you'll have left to fall back on."

She stubbed the cigarette in the ashtray and sat there.

He'd been stung deeply and the hurt showed through as he spoke. "Maggie. You think it's easy keeping these hours? Pushing myself on and on? Sweating blood to make it work? You think I enjoy it? You think I liked being away from you and the children?" Cleve was sitting forward now, his voice rising with conviction. "It was something I've had to do, Maggie. Something I've had to do. All these years of work-ing. It was in me. I'm a policeman, Margaret. You knew that when you married me. All the hours and pain and shit. A policeman. Would you have loved me if I were any other way?"

She didn't answer. They faced each other, but no words passed between them for some time.

Margaret rose to go to the kitchen. He followed and sat himself by the breakfast nook while she made him a ham sandwich and poured a glass of orange juice. He gulped it down and poured himself another.

"Where's Matthew?"

She looked at him sharply. "Gone to some friends. I'm surprised you asked."

"I try, Maggie, I really do."

She stopped what she was doing and turned to him. Her voice softened. She seemed almost apologetic. "I believe you, John. I believe you. But I wonder sometimes if that's enough anymore. . . ."

Her anger had gone. She sat down opposite him as he ate his sandwich.

Their remaining time together was passed in a mutually agreed silence; it was an argument they'd played out a thousand times before, one they were not likely ever to resolve. It had always ended in this manner. A few minutes passed.

It was time.

He got up. "Look, old girl. I've got to be going. I'll call. Okay?"

They walked to the door. He got his gear and dressed, straightening his hat in the mirror. He could see her watching him, a curious expression of fear and concern etched on her face.

Cleve opened the door and made to leave, but as he stepped into the sunlight he turned. "Aren't you even going to kiss me goodbye?"

Then Margaret came to him to be held in his arms. "Take care, John," she whispered. "Whatever else happens to us, take care." And Cleve could see there were tears in her eyes.

They held each other for a moment. And then he was gone.

Sam Chun Street was a tiny side lane in the Mongkok District of Kowloon, an alleyway of sweat-stained concrete under the blistering sun, near Nathan Road.

Shortly after one o'clock, flames still danced in the heat of the fire-bombed police Bedford, its skeleton broken. The street was littered with bricks, bamboo, torn pieces of lumber, shreds of clothing and spent tear-gas canisters. The rubble of urban combat. Fire hoses splashed tepid water onto the gutted stores nearby. Mills barriers sealed off the end of the street.

Near the blazing Bedford was a small chalked outline, and on the other side of the Mills barriers a crowd waited. Sullen, silent, grouping to avenge the Hakka boy, if not today then certainly tomorrow.

The identification bureau was still photographing the scene and taking measurements from the body to the vehicle from all possible angles. In the corner of the lane farthest from Nathan Road, a chief inspector of Mongkok CID was waiting. He was a patient man, but even his veneer of calm was wearing thin. "Hurry up," he muttered under his breath as he glanced warily at the hostile crowd and then back to the photo crew.

He knew he could not rush the identification team any more than he could change what had happened. He glanced at the statements on the clipboard in his hand. The story was straightforward enough: at about 12:15 hours, Police Tactical Unit Delta Company was traveling along Sam Chun Street en route to a riot call on Prince Edward Road. Delta-3 from number-one platoon was the last one through the laneway. It had stalled behind a crowd of pedestrians that wandered across Nathan Road and blocked its path. There were twelve police in Delta-3, a sergeant and eleven constables. Suddenly a boy had run out of the crowd toward them brandishing a Molotov cocktail. The platoon sergeant ordered him to halt, but had been forced to shoot as the boy merely grinned and let fly with the bottle. The flames had engulfed the vehicle, severely burning four policemen, two critically, and injuring five more.

The inspector was as sensible as he was patient. He knew the sergeant had had no alternative, yet he also knew it would be very difficult to explain to anyone who hadn't been there. He glanced at the crowd impatiently pressing against the barriers; then at the photo team, indifferent to the entire matter. Hurry, he thought, hurry.

The message reached the commissioner while he was en route to headquarters. The communication was short and to the point, and Cleve blanched on hearing it. Too many of his men had been injured and, worse still, there was a child casualty. John Cleve knew the ante had increased dramatically; the rioters had a cause all Hong Kong could identify with. A policeman's shot had killed a thirteen-year-old boy.

Cleve learned later that day that the mother of the dead youth was a policeman's widow. The father, a constable in the Royal Hong Kong Police, had died while foiling a robbery three years earlier. He had been posthumously decorated by the newly appointed commissioner of police, John Cleve.

CHAPTER SEVENTEEN

A streetcar thundered by, mere inches from his door. Andrews, startled, bolted upright in the car mumbling about Peng's driving habits.

"Davie, Davie. You have such little faith. What are you worried about? He missed us, didn't he?"

James Peng swung the coupe sharply down a narrow side street strewn with hampers, crates and boxes; slick with rotting vegetables, it was crowded with gaudily dressed bar girls, blazered schoolchildren and rough-sinewed laborers. Browns, yellows, reds, pastels. Pots and pans and plastic toys. Baby bibs and granny glasses. Paper flowers and Swissair gym bags. Ancient John Dewitt trams struggled through the center of the narrow street like weary tramp steamers floundering in the China Sea. Finally, after much maneuvering, Peng double-parked the vehicle. They had to go to Java Road, near the ferry pier.

When they got out, the heat hit them like an oppressive sauna blanket. Puffs of formless gray clouds moved in from the Mount Parker gap. The storm broke with typical summer suddenness.

They made their way in the rain past the bazaar stalls, greens and fish bones slippery underfoot, the cobblestones rusty-brown with age. Here and there, paper umbrellas were raised like hooded mushrooms in the silver sheets of rain. Some people skittered into stairwells, ink-blotched hands holding already sodden newspapers over their heads. Most continued their buying and selling.

Peng and Andrews slunk behind the vendor's stalls, ducking here and there to avoid the bamboo posts, winding snakelike toward their prey. The almond-eyed stares and snickers of children told them they had been seen. *"Ging-chat!"* the tittering whispers said, "Police!" Who else would come down to the armpit of the colony?

"There! Look!" Peng's voice was a whisper. "At the end of the street." The coolie stood in a crowd of hawkers, idling against the wall of the bakery, a little behind most of the people. His hair was cut short, like a rooster's comb. He spat onto the curbstones, his brown eyes narrow slits, and glanced casually up and down the street. It was the *Tai-soi*—lookout.

"Do you think he's seen us?"

"No—come on." They moved quickly, soundlessly between the stalls and ancient buildings, now and then pausing in a stairwell. The vendors paid no attention to the *Che-Sing Kwai Lo,* "stupid foreign devils." They had learned long ago that curiosity would only spoil sales. Only the children watched them with passing interest.

"There he goes," Peng murmured.

Their suspect was walking off slowly. It didn't appear that he had seen them. They followed his bobbing head down a side street; rattan crates were strewn about, stained in blood from the corner butcher. James could smell urine and dirty rainwater.

The coolie moved faster, stumbling into people, rudely pushing them. "He needs his fix," Peng whispered. "That's the reason he's so careless."

As they approached the wharf at the North Point ferry pier, the crowds thickened. Schoolchildren, businessmen, housewives, all walking to the ferry. The two policemen joined the crush.

Their man turned south, away from the water, up another side street. He looked back. They froze, feigning interest in a news vendor's wares. He moved off and was lost from view.

"Are you sure this is the one?" Andrews asked, gasping for

breath and inwardly cursing himself for those extra beers at the police club.

"It's him," Peng replied harshly. "Have faith. This is the one."

They were beside Hong Kong harbor. There was a hint of breeze in the humid air. A rusty ferry came in view, chopping its way from Kwun Tong with a load of laborers.

They turned down another street. The coolie was again visible, his loud yellow shirt almost shrieking in the steamy day. And then he disappeared.

The two detectives ran, top-heavy, like rugby players in a scrum. They turned up the lane, slipping, breathing heavily. At the end of the lane they reached a T-junction. Peng guessed, pointed to the left, and they turned, bumping into the high walls on both sides, knocking bulging crates to the concrete.

At the end of the alley, they saw the ragamuffin coolies. Thin, bony, with swollen veins like a devil's etchings on scarecrow limbs. A candle flickered softly. They saw a spoon, a syringe dripping fluid, a young man injecting, victims lining up meekly for the lifeblood of their addiction, the cheap brown liquid that had bought their souls long ago. Seven living cadavers.

And the one injecting, the beefy one with the livid telltale growth on his neck, was the one they wanted. Lai Man Yi, Elephant Man.

At that instant one of the coolies looked up and the spell was broken. His eyes terrified, his mouth opening like a wild dog's, his face dark with shock and fear, he screamed, *"Ging-chat!* Police!"

A furious scramble in all directions.

But there was only one exit from the lane, and the hulking policemen blocked it. The addicts struggled like caged rats to break free: clawing, pushing, upsetting carts and cartons.

A kick in the groin. A chop to the face. Andrews and Peng fought them back into the alley. Andrews was bitten on the hand. He drew his revolver, clubbed the man across the temple once, twice. A cold, sticky trickle of blood splattered across his knuckles. A loud thud as bone cracked. The *do-yau* let go and fell, a useless heap.

Two men rushed Peng, who ducked the first blow and caught the man in the solar plexus. A grunt. Spittle spewed forth from his attacker's mouth. The second man tore at Peng's right arm with a knife. Peng swung him around and ground him into the wall with his forearm until he gurgled blood and slumped silent, formless like a sack of dried rice. Two older coolies, terrified and in a drug-inspired daze, cowered along the wall, muttering like frightened children.

Andrews looked up. Peng shouted, "Look out!" David crouched instinctively, and a *tai-soi* went flying over him, a baling hook waving in his right hand. He landed on the cobblestones, dazed and shocked. Andrews cracked the man's skull with the butt of his revolver.

Then he saw the one they wanted, syringe in one hand. He was young and well fed, clearly not an addict. He was their link. A bit paunchier than in the photographs they'd seen, but uglier than sin. Lai, their man—the Elephant Man—had to be taken alive.

Peng smiled coldly. "I want you." Andrews understood the need for silence. Both men had their guns drawn. The youngster still had his syringe. There was little time to waste.

Lai dropped his syringe and a knife was in his hand. He lunged toward them.

Peng's gun spurted a red-yellow flame. Elephant Man shook as the bullet tore into his side and the blood gushed. He grimaced but kept coming, the knife blade waving.

Calmly, without hesitation, Peng shot him again, this time in the arm. Elephant Man screamed and dropped the knife. He was having difficulty standing up. His right arm was a blood-soaked pulp and his legs were shaking. His eyes were huge, brimming with tears.

Peng said in a dry, even voice, "Where is your boss?"

A whisper, feeble but unrepentant. "I'd rather die."

The man was a boy now, his voice tremulous and frightened. A boy who had a mother somewhere in Kwantung Province. A boy who had once dreamed of purple-tailed dragons, gold-armored warriors and velvet-skinned women. He closed his eyes. Tears rolled down his cheeks. He started to swoon. The blood was mingling, rich red, with bits of brick and bamboo filings on the ground.

Peng moved in and took him, almost gently, by the shoulders. "This hurts, doesn't it, little one?" he whispered like a father to an errant son. "Here. Let me look at it." He held the arm and caressed it, then took the ascot from his neck as if to bandage the injury. Elephant Man peered at him through leaden eyes, perplexed. He heard the Chinese policeman's soft voice. "Sit down, now, sit down." The words were soothing.

Then Peng tightened the tourniquet slowly, tighter and tighter.

Elephant Man's eyes widened as he realized that he wasn't being bandaged—he was being tortured. He wanted to curse, to fight back, but he was too weak and the blood kept oozing. His life was flowing from him.

Andrews looked over with unspoken concern. A dead man was no good at all. He said nothing.

Peng looked coolly down at Elephant Man. "Now tell me the name of your master . . . or you die." He tightened the tourniquet with his left hand as his right cupped the man's face. Bone showed crudely through the soaked cloth. Peng slapped him roughly. "Your master. Tell us!" Saliva flecked with blood drooled out of Elephant Man's mouth and ran over the clean, finely manicured fingers of his interrogator. "Tell us!"

Elephant Man tried to form words, his lips dry as he gasped for air.

Peng shouted, then said softly, cajoling, in Cantonese, "Where?"

Elephant Man whispered, "At Blue Cloud." The voice trailed off into the distance.

Peng released his grip. The body slumped down on the pavement. A hollow crunch of bone, like a carcass of discarded meat. A cockroach slithered up his arm into the wound.

Andrews heard sounds of traffic, then the sudden, urgent klaxon of police sirens. He glanced over his shoulder. A curious crowd had gathered at the end of the lane, hushed, subdued, sensing the departure of a spirit. He looked at his partner. Peng's hand was shaking. They both stared down at Elephant Man whose chest was moving only slightly now. The mystery lay in the words uttered from the swollen lips of a dying man. Blue Cloud.

The sound of loud, heavy-heeled feet came up from behind. Black leather; flashing metal. Blue lights shone eerily off midday shadows and packing crates. Harshly shouted orders. Suddenly the two policemen faced a somber picket of black muzzles, AR15s and Remingtons, a police emergency unit team.

The sergeant recognized Peng, nodded acknowledgement. He knew better than to ask Peng what had happened. He briskly ordered his men to move the body. They lifted it like a game trophy, by the arms and legs, and began to carry it to the waiting lorry. Peng stopped them, then asked the sergeant to search the body; trinkets and valuables were placed alongside it, the earthly remains of Lai Man Yi.

Andrews and Peng bent over. Efficiently, dispassionately, they rummaged through the items looking for something, anything that would be a lead, a tracer. There wasn't much. A set of keys, nondescript. A faded brown photo of a mother and infant, severe and posed. A tranquil shot in the Botanic Gardens. Or was it Victoria Park? A dirty handkerchief and a linty orange comb. A cheap pen. A pile of red Hong Kong Shanghai hundreds, neatly folded in an elastic band, a slip of paper scrunched into a ball and a book of matches.

Andrews fumbled with the paper, then looked down at the script, stained, indecipherable. He glanced at Peng, who shrugged his shoulders in resignation. He mumbled a low curse. Just their luck. Well, perhaps the government chemist might make something of it. Unlikely, though. Folding the paper, he placed it in his breast pocket. He scrounged through the other items, fingers deftly separating them, playing with the dead man's effects.

Andrews motioned to his partner that it was time to leave. Blue Cloud. Now that was something else again. What could it mean?

As Peng stood up his knees cracked in the humidity. He spoke a few words to the sergeant, the one who had searched the corpse. The body was to be taken to Kennedy Town morgue. Accompanying paperwork would follow later.

The sergeant asked what he should do with the pile of things.

Peng thought for a moment as he popped a cigarette in his mouth and asked Andrews for a light. His partner rummaged through his safari top. He had none. No one else had any either. Peng returned to the meager pile of belongings and picked out a soft blue pack, which said, "Visit the Metropole Restaurant, North Point" on its front. Elephant Man would have no need of it now. Peng took a match from the folder, struck it and the flame flickered delicately in the heat.

As Peng began to close the match cover, his eyes caught something scribbled in childish English script. A five, a seven . . . a two. Then some illegible digits. A code? Perhaps. More likely a telephone number. Then he saw, in faded pencil in the corner, a Chinese character: *Shia*

CHAPTER EIGHTEEN

Maguire had purposely taken a nondescript Toyota from the car pool and arranged for his best backup team to follow him, but not, he cautioned them severely, to step in unless he required it. The two Chinese sergeants would obey; they knew better than to do otherwise.

His breath tasted foul. His stomach wrenched. He pulled off Kings Road onto a lot at Kam Hong Street and took two antacid tablets from a vial he'd placed in the glove compartment, chewing them distastefully. He tossed the bottle onto the seat next to him.

He glanced into his rear-view mirror. Just in sight was the ghost car, idling away by the minibus stand. He started his motor up again, drove a hundred yards and turned into a tiny laneway by the spice trader, amid the odors of pineapple and prawns and goat bladders spread to dry. As he pulled to the side, he narrowly avoided a rickshaw bearing crates of oysters, its driver groaning as he came to a sudden stop.

The boxes on the rickshaw seat teetered precariously forward, then the wheeled chariot, its bright-red and green paint peeling, its rubber-capped wheels long worn to their hollow wooden bases, jostled on.

Maguire got out of the car and set off quickly. He did not look over his shoulder; he didn't have to. The ghost team was right behind him. He'd parked a few blocks from his destination. The walk would give him time to calm his nerves and gather his thoughts. The street still steamed from the recent downpour. His holster, rough cowgrain, stuck to his torso like a wet rag. He gasped for air as he moved.

Ahead of him, looming amid the oceans of humanity like an Oriental Gibraltar, stood his goal, a magnificent edifice. The Metropole restaurant was gaudy and flamboyant. It was several stories high and glittered with velvet, rose, gilt; there were swirling ballustrades and massive pillars. A large fiery wedding wreath covered most of the facade, announcing to all the world the marriage of Chan Ming Man and Han Siu Je.

As he entered the main doorway, Maguire was met with a rush of ice-cold air. The foyer looked like a Hollywood set, complete with winding ivory staircase, burgundy rugs, stone vases filled with orchids, swirling sea serpents and China-gold loons on bronze fixtures. The walls were covered with paintings of curling dragons and swirling clouds of petite Chinese maidens. Large, black-enameled serving bowls sat piled full of crab's feet, roast pork and pomegranates.

The maître d' led Maguire to Room Six, on the second floor near the rear of the building. The room was isolated, the entrance recessed and covered by a thick velvet curtain. There was no door. Maguire heard the tinkling of glass, a muffled cough. He looked at the maître d' and silently asked with his fingers how many were inside. The maître d' looked at him quizzically, then, comprehending, opened his mouth to speak.

Maguire quickly hushed him with a touch of his hand. The man nodded vigorously, to show that he understood, then raised one finger. He handed the maître d' a five-dollar note for his trouble; the man deftly palmed the money and was gone. There was no one in the hallway or landing.

Maguire gestured to his cover team. They crept up the stairs, hands resting on the butts of their guns, until they were beside him, one on either side of the entrance.

He gingerly parted the green curtain. A man was seated in a high-backed armchair, half in darkness, gently sipping a rich amber brandy while he smoked a cigarette.

"You look surprised, Maguire—whom did you suspect?"

Lee Shiu Shing smiled broadly. "Here. Please be seated. We have much to discuss." He gestured to the adjacent chair, then sensed Maguire's caution. "Do not be concerned. You will not be harmed. Realize we have had ample opportunity to do this from the time you entered the laneway near Kam Hong Street."

"The rickshaw driver. . ." Maguire's tone was one of resigned admiration.

"The driver, among others. We are still *craftsmen*, after all, aren't we, Maguire?" Then, with a disdainful flick of his wrist, he continued. "We will call your two flunkies off. They are superfluous to our discussion."

Maguire glanced at the sergeants in the hall. They were flanked by several waiters, all smiles and friendly nods who also had slight bulges in their waistcoats.

He turned back to his host and began to protest.

"A simple precaution, Maguire. You would do it also." He shrugged his shoulder. "Come, sit down. We truly have much to discuss—beginning with our mutual love of watches."

Maguire sank into the soft velvet chair across from Lee. The room was large, with a high ceiling trimmed in gold leaf. There were velveteen chairs, sofas and teapoys set here and there in casual elegance; intricately woven rugs and tapestries were hung on the walls.

He regarded his adversary cautiously, for he knew he was completely at the man's mercy. Lee placed a half-finished cigarette in the ashtray. "You wish a drink?" He waved toward a nearby teapoy. "Gordon's Gin? Courvoisier? Mac-Claren's? Perhaps some Canadian Club?"

"Thank you. A touch of Courvoisier, if you will."

Lee poured the sweet cognac. "Do you wish ice?"

"Certainly not."

The smile. "I thought not. Americans are strange that way. 'On the rocks,' I believe they call it. Personally, I concur with you British. The drink was meant to be enjoyed uncluttered, without hint of foreign substance." He placed the decanter on the silver tray behind him. Maguire stood and took the soft crystal brandy glass. Lee cast him a look, direct and hard.

As Maguire sat, Lee said, "I propose a toast, a simple one between friends. To the British, to the Chinese—and to us."

Maguire hesitated, then raised his glass slightly. "To us." He felt the mellow tingle of the warm cognac. He knew his face was flushed from exhaustion and hunger.

Lee Shiu Shing quietly considered his guest. He measured his words as he spoke. "I have some things of yours. Perhaps I should talk about them first. Then you can decide if you want them back."

Maguire was silent.

Lee sat forward and set his glass down. Maguire noticed the man's rings, a delicate jade on the fourth finger, a bold amethyst on the third.

"You wonder about Veidjur, don't you, Maguire?" Lee sighed. "Marcus Veidjur." He straightened the jade ring. "A rather productive individual, isn't he, Robert? Amazing how he was able to accumulate all that information so easily, wasn't it?" He caught the horror and confusion in Maguire's face. "Oh, yes, my friend—" he laughed softly "—Veidjur has been a most compliant little man over the past few years."

Maguire felt as cold as ice. "You're bluffing, Lee."

The smile left the elder's face. "Oh, am I, Irishman? Am I? Veidjur has been feeding you what I tell him to. Has been since you turned him three years ago." Maguire stared back stolidly. "How else do you think you would have known about the nuclear incident at Lup Nor? And you knew about the student riots in Mukden, and the problems with our Russian comrades at the Amur River last winter, where several of the Ivans were ambushed and shot by our glorious People's Militia. Come, come, Maguire, we are not children, you and I."

"But the information proved true, Lee." Maguire fumbled. "We had confirmation from other sources, from the Yanks, from our people in Moscow, in every case."

There was genuine sadness and pity in Lee's voice when he spoke. "Yes, in that you are right. But has it not crossed your mind that someone might have been feeding Veidjur nonetheless? Using him as a conduit to give you what we wanted you to know? What we wanted your government to act on?"

"There is no way we would allow that to happen." Maguire shook his head. "Our entire system is designed to prevent that sort of breakdown, set up to ensure that the truth and only the truth survives out of all the various data sources."

"But what if we had Veidjur and we gave you only the truth until you believed him implicitly? How would you know who he was working for? How would you know you were being used? Where the truth ended and the lies began?"

Maguire became silent as the terrible reality of his predicament sunk in.

"You know by now we have the tapes?"

"Yes."

"Of Veidjur and the Malays and the French and who knows how many others?" Lee pressed on.

Maguire said nothing.

"Blackmail has no meaning without the threat of disclosure, Maguire. I think it true to say we have removed the threat for many of your subjects. As you may have guessed, this also includes me. Box 805 at the post office. I have the contents." He took a silken chain from his coat pocket and toyed with it. "And the key."

The director of Special Branch stared at Lee with glassy eyes. There was no point in disputing reality. The leak in the bureau, wherever it was, had been crippling. He was at Lee's mercy—and so was Special Branch.

The maître d' arrived and quietly exchanged a few whispered words with Lee. The man looked blithely at Maguire. "Do you prefer your chicken rare?" Lee asked. "Some Europeans grow weak at the sight of blood."

Maguire answered haltingly that it didn't matter, he'd be pleased regardless. The maître d' bowed and left.

"I'm glad we finally understand each other, Robert—I may call you Robert, may I not?"

Maguire helplessly agreed. "Robert will be fine."

"Good, good," Lee went on. "We still have much to discuss, don't you think? Now that we've done away with the cloak-and-dagger silliness."

"Discuss?" Maguire hesitated.

"Certainly, Robert." Lee took out a gold-embossed cigarette package; he offered it to Maguire, who politely refused. The old man lit one and inhaled, blowing out a heady puff of smoke with evident pleasure. "Damn fine cigarette, this Dutch brand."

Maguire sank back in his wing chair, wordlessly watching.

"You are tired, Robert?" Lee's voice was soothing. "Yes, I believe you are. It's been a strain, has it not?"

Still nothing.

"Your silence bespeaks a thousand words, Robert. You are still unsure of me."

"I believe," Maguire answered at last, "that the actions of our force acknowledge your helpfulness."

"Yes. But perhaps rather too. . ." Lee searched for a word, then smiled. "Forcefully."

"Nonetheless, investigations of Yip Lam are proceeding—"

"And of me, also, I believe," Lee interrupted. "Your commissioner is comprehensive, is he not?"

"It is only a formality."

"Maguire, Maguire," Lee said, as if chiding an errant child. "When will you ever learn? The ante is high. The ante is higher than Hong Kong and its present commissioner of police can match. There is not just my delicate role, but the governor's plans in this matter—in which Mr. Cleve has also taken an interest."

"The governor's plans?" Maguire whispered. Lee caught his surprised look.

"Come now, Robert. Do you really think the governor is at all concerned with the integrity of your police and your precious Special Branch in this fossil of a colony? Those in the major scheme of things don't give you a second thought."

Maguire had no choice. At one time they might have bartered. They could eliminate this suspect; expose the bombing as the handiwork of the Nationalist Kuo Min Tang and the Communist press would forgive and forget. But the riots, the killing of the Hakka boy this afternoon; these had irrevocably altered the balance.

"Hang the Colonial Police!" Those four words were written in dripping red, draped on scrolls in every loft, laneway and alley in the colony. Who knew how far the cancer had gnawed into the very heart of Special Branch? If Lee had the tapes, one could only begin to guess what else he knew. And if the CP ever found out about this monumental leak, it would be the end of Maguire's career, that was certain. He cringed at the thought.

A restaurant *foki* came into the room carrying trays with rice, steamed prawns, chicken, tea. The din from the room next door signaled the wedding party had begun. The *foki* handed Lee a note. Lee looked at it and a slow smile crossed his face. He handed him a handsome tip, then waved him off.

Lee crumpled the paper and tossed it in the ashtray. The message was a simple one: "Yes. The Woodcutter."

Lee took a puff of his cigarette. "Listen, Maguire," he began. "By telling you about Yip I have done you a favor, yes?" He waited until Maguire cautiously nodded. "And I am prepared now to do you another, a personal favor." He tapped methodically on the table with his lighter, then paused. "I am prepared to forgive you your impetuosity. The money you demanded of me is a small issue. I was young once myself."

Maguire smelled a trap. Cautiously he replied, "We ask only that you control your operatives and give us time to get Yip Lam. After that, I should assume all debts are canceled."

"Operatives?" Lee exploded. "You don't seem to grasp the seriousness of the situation. We don't control this riot, Maguire, any more than you do. Once, yes." He nodded. "Yes, once we did. But not now. John Cleve has seen to that."

The two sat facing each other, Maguire's mind in turmoil. Damn that bastard Cleve, taking on Driscoll and Peking! Why hadn't he been told? Prepared?

Little clouds of moisture escaped from the giant Gilman air conditioner, which whirled and puffed in the far corner of the room.

"You have said you wish us to capture a man named Yip Lam, whom you say is responsible for the explosion on the *Glorious East Wind.*"

Lee nodded. "That would please us."

"And you have also suggested that it would go far in removing the threat of external intervention from Peking."

The Chinese man nodded once more.

"What else do you want?"

"Ah, Maguire," Lee chided, "you certainly have found yourself in a muddle. But then, perhaps, so have I. And we two, we both want the same thing, don't we? Peace. It is perhaps your commissioner who sees thing differently."

After pausing for a moment, Lee suddenly added, "If you were commissioner, Robert Maguire, how would you see things?"

Another pause as Maguire considered where Lee was taking their conversation.

"This is a question you take seriously, of course," Lee continued. "The business of success, it's all a game. And you are playing it well. But then, even a good actor needs good lines, as they say. I've done well for you, no?"

"What do you want, Lee?"

The man smiled. "Just a personal favor—for me, for our two countries—in the form of a little discretion involving the removal of an unimportant file from an old government-records office. And rest assured, I know you possess this file. Remove it, and I can make you a promise. I should think that, in the nature of things, you might come to consider that promise as if made—" Lee paused "—by the governor himself."

Lee turned to Maguire. "Come. Let us eat and drink. I'm certain we can arrange something very much to our mutual satisfaction."

Peng returned from the lobby phone just as David began to eat his French fries. They were in a restaurant called Peter's Kitchen, a little niche in the wall on Western Street in old Sai Ying Poon. Peter had been a successful chef in Paris before he came home to Hong Kong; he was an old friend of the police. There were fewer and fewer of those by the hour.

The pager call had come only moments ago. Not many had come in since they'd spread the word onto the street that they were looking for news; the few calls they had received had been feeble dead ends.

Andrews took a bite of his club sandwich and followed it with a mouthful of Coke. "You trust that scumbag?" His expression wasn't at all reassuring, and Peng looked offended.

"He's been good to us in the past, Davie. And besides—" Peng winked "—he makes good monogrammed shirts."

David chuckled, took another bite of his sandwich, chewed slowly, then added some mayonnaise to what remained.

Mohan was a blousy, boisterous, Bombay-born merchant who ran a flea-ridden tailor shop on a side street in Hung Hom. He was a decent enough tailor by police standards—which weren't very good. He was given to exaggeration and overstatement. "A rum and Coke, a dirty joke and a shirt made to measure—if not fit to wear—within forty-eight hours," was Mohan's motto. Andrews knew that for every fifty pieces of totally useless garbage Mohan sent down the pipeline, there was sure to be at least one good piece of information. That made Mohan an excellent fink. He always supplied the bare minimum; the police had to ferret out the details. Andrews knew without asking that such would be the case.

"Well?" He looked at his partner.

Peng's face was placid, expressionless. "Well what?'

"Well, aren't you going to tell me what he said?"

A cunning smile. "I thought you'd never ask." Peng leaned forward and continued in a hushed voice, their humorous byplay suddenly forgotten.

"He knows nothing about Blue Cloud or 'Shia.' But he says the man we want is Chinese and his name is Hans. He says also that Hans met with a follower in Macau a few days ago. Mohan doesn't know the reason, but he knows the location—the Hotel Lisboa, Room 303."

Andrews thought for a moment. "Interesting." He continued to eat.

Peng had hoped for a little more enthusiasm. "Is that all you have to say?"

"No," David answered. "What was his price?"

"Three thousand Hong Kong."

"Did you pay it?"

"Did I have a choice?"

David shrugged his shoulders as he reached for a pickle. "No," he muttered. He bit into the pickle. "No, I guess you didn't."

They finished their food in silence; one waiter took away the dishes and another came with coffee, rich and black and steaming hot. They drank it quickly and asked for their check.

Their list of informants was dwindling fast and time was running out. Another piece was fitting into the puzzle: a Chinese named Hans and a meeting in Macau.

CHAPTER NINETEEN

The old man turned the key and stepped inside. The room was dark and smelled musty. The drapes were open and framed a city restless and uneasy under a vast sky filled with pewter clouds. Streetlights twinkled like flittering fireflies.

The clock in the corner chimed ten o'clock. After a few moments, the man detected someone else breathing. Someone was over by the desk, in the director's chair.

"Sir," the man whispered timidly as he tiptoed in, cleaning pail in hand. "Sir, it's Ah Lai, the room boy." His voice trailed off; he was frightened by the echo.

The chair creaked as Maguire turned to face the intruder.

"Sir," the old man ventured, "I thought you had gone home."

The director sat slouched in the chair. His clothing was disheveled, his eyes bloodshot. "Is everything all right, sir?" Ah Lai asked.

"I've had things that needed attending to. . . ." Maguire spoke in a slurred voice. "Things. . . ." His voice trailed off.

Ah Lai nodded sympathetically. He bowed a few times, in an attempt to give face and to give self-esteem, and then began cleaning.

Old Lai, as he was called by the young policemen, had been the principal cleaner at Special Branch for more than fifteen years; he had been Maguire's personal room boy for the past four. He was privy to most secrets in the bureau and, as he loudly told the others in the servants' lunchroom, in the deepest bowels of May House, the guardian of the dung heap; by his own estimation, he was the most important man at headquarters. He started dusting the filing cabinets, which contained classified Kuo Min Tang quarterlies and KGB assessments. Behind him, the director belched.

Ah Lai moved to the bookshelves, his tubby body straining his frayed T-shirt and boxer shorts. Lai was happy in his work and content with his position. He wanted little from life: an occasional bottle of San Mig, a Lucky Strike, a few bills to throw at the races.

"How long have we known each other, Lai?"

The old man started. "Sir? Four years, sir," he replied.

Maguire smiled, a glassy-eyed, vacant smile, which troubled Lai. This was not the Robert Maguire he knew and feared.

"What are you going to do when it's all over, then, Lai?"

Lai looked at the director with querulous eyes, uncertain as to how he was expected to reply.

Maguire prodded, "When the lease is over. When your distant cousins from the North pay their house call. Claim their reward."

"Do, sir?" Lai shuffled his feet, fumbling for words. Finally he smiled, open-faced, like a child, as a realization came to him. "Why, what I've always done. Clean. Shine. Polish. Look after whomever hires me."

He began dusting the clock, careful not to disturb the delicate mechanism that governed the chimes. "Besides, sir," he offered, "I pose no threat to them as long as I have food in my belly and a roof over my head. My wants are easily met." He glanced down at his cleaning cloth, which was now caked in a fine filmy powder, and folded it so a clean surface presented itself to him. He brushed the chamois over the polished wood of the grandfather clock, gently, so as not to damage the sheen.

"I guess the truth be known, sir, they need me more than I need them."

Maguire considered the answer a moment. "A rather innocent approach, don't you think, Lai?"

"Oh, no, sir," he replied vigorously. "No, sir. Not at all."

The old man stopped and walked over to where Maguire sat.

"You see—" he nodded out the window, his voice a confiding whisper. "It'll go on, sir. This place. It'll go on long after you and I are just specks of dust.

"But not to worry." He shook his head knowingly. "In any event, there will always be the likes of you. And there will always be the likes of me." An ironic smile came to his face. "So we will be around always. The both of us, master and servant, though maybe by another name. And if that's so," he concluded triumphantly, "there's no need to worry our guts out, is there?"

"I'm happy for you, Lai. Happy you've found your place in the scheme of things. . . ." Maguire sighed and turned away from the window.

"Oh, but it's no big deal, sir. I'm sure you could do it, too. It's just a matter of knowing where your best interests lie and then looking after them, isn't it?" Lai had stopped dusting. "I mean, sir, we all have to protect ourselves in the long run, don't we?"

Maguire said nothing. He seemed to be considering Lai's words as the old man moved to another corner of the office, out of hearing.

Maguire picked up the phone and dialed a three-digit number. An in-house number. From where he cleaned, Lai made out the words "records" and "war files" and no more. But he knew the director was doing exactly what he was supposed to, just as his superior had said he might. Ah Lai was secretly pleased.

Maguire placed the phone back in its cradle and turned back toward the window. "It's a grand place," he whispered to himself. "A grand place." And for the briefest moment Lai thought he caught a tear in the director's eyes.

"Is there anything else, sir? Anything more I can do to be of assistance?'

Robert Maguire did not answer, and Lai did not press. His work was done. He stayed in the shadows, watching the foreigner. And then he was gone.

David was waiting for the people at the laser section at the identification bureau to telephone him. The chief technician, a New Zealander of German descent named Fritz Zeigler, had said that with luck the obscured numbers on the matchbook cover would be identified within half an hour. He would call David back.

It was after ten o'clock and drizzling lightly under low cloud as Peng and David wound their way across the Quarry Bay area of the island. Near Bayview Magistracy, they pulled over so Peng could buy some gum. David took the opportunity to call his station to check for messages. There were none. As he stood under the awning, watching the rain splattering the streets, he decided to make one last attempt to ask Mei about Brendan's death. He thought she was holding something back from him, and he was determined to find out what it was.

The ride to Causeway Bay was short, less than fifteen minutes in the steamy night. The streets were slick and almost devoid of traffic. The smell of burning tires still lingered in the air. Garbage littered the sidewalks and abandoned vehicles, some recently vandalized by mobs, cluttered Kings Road, the main thoroughfare. They heard occasional shouts, the shatter of breaking glass from side lanes. There were only a few pedestrians out, timidly wandering around in groups, casting wary glances at one another.

He hadn't told Peng his reasons for wanting to see Mei; he'd said it was a minor part of an old investigation. Peng had been surprisingly accommodating, and David promised it wouldn't take long. Peng, slouched in the car as he sucked the scent out of yet another Royal Crown, appeared unconcerned. "Take as long as you like," he'd offered. "We have five minutes."

Andrews climbed the stairs to the fourth floor two at a time. The fat Chiu Chau was there as always, slumped, snoring in an armchair to one side of the frosted door.

He started as David moved to open the door. "You can't go in there!" He made a feeble attempt to stop Andrews, but froze at the sight of police identification.

"Get me Mei Ling," David orderd.

The Chiu Chau feigned ignorance. "Mei Ling," he answered coyly. "We have no girl by that name here."

Andrews grabbed the man by the hair and pushed his face backward roughly until he shrieked in pain. "Get her now," David said, "before I go in this place and close it down."

The Chiu Chau nodded and begged for release. David let him go and he scurried inside. When the frosted door opened again, it was Mei Ling. She was wearing a cheap cotton wraparound and was smoking a cigarette. Her face was pale without makeup. She nodded only slightly by way of greeting.

"What do you want of me?" she asked coldly.

David hesitated, but Mei had already anticipated his question. "If it's more about Brendan, you're wasting your time." She blew a puff of smoke into the air. Her eyes were hard and unfeeling. "I'm sick of it, David. Sick of it."

"Sick of what, Mei?" he ventured. "Of my wanting to find out what caused Brendan's death?" He shook his head in amazement. "Don't you want to know, too, Mei? After all, you loved him."

She stared strangely at Andrews. Her features softened and the harshness left her voice. "He paid me, David," she answered finally. "He paid me handsomely for the privilege of love. That was all. Money, David. Money."

David did not try to hide his disgust. "You lied to Brendan all along, then, didn't you? All you wanted him for from the very beginning was a rice ticket. A way out. You never cared for him at all. You fucking whore." He turned away.

She gazed at him with great sadness. "At least I know who I am. But you? Who are you, Inspector David Andrews? Are you chasing after honor and justice in this colony? Well, honor doesn't exist here among the addicts and whores and moneychangers.

"And justice?" She laughed sarcastically. "In a place where people sleep penniless and freezing in the streets while others change the color of their living rooms as often as they change their underwear? It's an illusion you're living in, David. A cheap illusion."

"I have responsibilities you can't begin to realize," he began.

"The same as Brendan surely felt," she answered, before

he could finish. "And if you're not careful, you'll die like him. And when you're gone, they'll put you in an old oak casket and place the Union Jack on it and ship you home. For your god, Queen and country." She paused. "They don't care about you, David. They don't give a damn."

"And you do?"

A car horn sounded in the street below. It was Peng.

"So you have nothing to tell me about Brendan?" he asked stiffly.

She looked up at David. Tears glistened in her eyes. She slowly shook her head. "No. He's dead. I have nothing more to tell you."

He turned and walked briskly down the stairs.

CHAPTER TWENTY

———

On Nullah Road, an old amah shuffled by, dour-faced, wearing black pajamas and carrying a hamper of ginger root in her gnarled hands. In a stairwell, a *chi fa* lottery bookie took fifty-cent bets from optimistic souls with money to spare. Children wearing dirty white shirts, hand-me-down shorts and bright orange sandals played catch-the-dragon until exhaustion overtook them and they crawled off to sleep.

Nullah road, womblike, sheltered its own. Though there might be serious cracks in the gentle facade of peace else-where in the colony, they did not reach here. This was the old China. Not the China of Central District of Tsim Tsa Tsui, or even Quarry Bay, but a timeless China where no westerner went anymore, like a sepia-colored post card of Shanghai or Canton or Kwei Lein as they must have been.

At one end of the street was a *dai pai dong*, a cooked-food stall. Red, yellow and orange gaslights were strung on bam-boo poles like festival ornaments. The smell of curried prawns spiced the air; chopsticks clattered wildly as people scooped white rice from the blue-rimmed *fan boi*, rice bowls. The jostling amber-tinged faces of the night people, the coolies, newspaper venders, factory workers, resting cabbies and bus drivers. Near a cauldron of boiling soup, a toothless old cook chattered amiably with some *wallah wallah* boatmen.

A curfew existed in Kowloon: by midnight, it was lights
out and everyone indoors. The curfew had, in fact, been in
effect for the past two days. But it was a curfew in name only.
The neighboring police were apparently too hard-pressed to
enforce it, and the people around Nullah Road were too indifferent to obey it.

There had been rumors about trouble in Wong Tai Sin and
Shek Kip Mei and Tsuen Wan, in the New Territories, and on
Hong Kong Island where the curfew was, according to the
boatmen, strictly enforced. But here, the curfew elicited no
interest.

Still, there had been a few left-wing flyers pasted on walls
and hoardings. People pulled them down before they could
be seized by patrolling police. They had brilliant red characters and flourishing script: "British Pigs Are Paper Tigers"
and "Cleve Dare You Come Out" and "Bow Your Head
Cleve for the Treacherous Deaths on the Ship" and "Cleve
We Will Revenge Our Blood Loss" and "British Pigs Murder
Thirteen-Year-Old Children." The posters spoke of revenge;
over cups of lukewarm tea, long, earnest discussions took
place.

The economy of Hong Kong was good. Pockets were full;
people were fed. The government, though bumbling and in-
competent, was tolerable and relatively inoffensive. On Nullah Road, as in many places where people gathered on this
hot Hong Kong night, there was not the depth of unrest
there had been in 1967. Perhaps the people, too, were becoming fat. But for most of them, life would go on. They did
not want revenge.

The *dai pai dong* of Fook Sai was a popular place. Like
other cooked-food stalls, it was a solid-roofed hut with open
sides. Some customers sat in the stall on benches; most sat on
collapsible chairs at round tables on the sidewalk.

They ate Fook's prawns, beef and pork, *bac-choi*, rice and
noodles. And the house speciality, shark's fin soup. The shark
was brought down from the ancestral fish farm at Shau Kung
Wai, along Deep Bay, in the shadow of Lau Fau Shan in the
New Territories.

Fook Sai, the little Chiu Chau peasant from Fukien

Province, had labored mightily to make the stall a success. He stood behind the bubbling cauldrons, his gold teeth glistening, his hair slicked down over his bony forehead, sweat trickling down his face, horn-rimmed glasses perched on his button nose. He felt it was all worth it. His food was good and his reputation was excellent. He was justifiably proud.

It had not been easy. Fook had worked long, tedious hours to beat the competition. He'd cut costs, missed holidays, made endless sacrifices. And it was still necessary to employ useless relatives—albeit at lesser wages—to make ends meet and keep his in-laws happy. But it had been worth it. Soon he would be able to afford a vacation back to China. His success had come from hard work and perseverence, but there had been a cost: the *yum cha*, tea money he'd paid for protection.

Ten percent of his gross went to protect this lucrative position from interlopers and to assuage the police, for he did not possess a license. Ten percent also went to protect him from violence and bloodshed and the loss of everything he had worked for.

Fook was fortunate, for he paid tea money to only one man. That one man was so powerful that he humbled all challengers, even the police, with intelligence, finesse and, when the circumstances required, relentless brute force.

Fook looked beyond the crowded patio, saw the pink Rolls-Royce and beside it the Korean chauffeur. Fook then looked up, behind the Rolls, at the Astoria building. He knew the owner of the car was in the Sai Woo restaurant, on the second floor of the rundown seven-story building. Built soon after the Second World War by a shrewd Shanghainese intent on making money quickly, if not honorably, the Astoria had survived first as a cut-rate hotel, then as a brothel, and when even the whores had tired of its brown-sludge water showers and lice infested bedding, it had become home for Vietnamese boat people. From some windows, laundry flapped from bent bamboo poles. Outside, frying pans hung anxiously at the bequest of necromancers, deflected from the dwellers the many evil spirits that floated about the China night.

The Sai Woo, a shoddy tea room, recently opened and

nearly always vacant, was yet another feeble attempt to ring as many coppers as possible from the poverty-stricken building for as little cost.

Fook could see a dim light flickering in the loft of the Sai Woo. He glanced at his watch. Eleven o'clock. He knew the tributes would begin soon. The rite was as ancient as the making of one's rice bowl. And tonight Yip Lam was presiding.

Fook wrung the grease out of his towel and looked up at the night sky. The wind was humming; there was moisture in it. More rain. He must drum up business while the weather held. He flicked the dirty towel over his shoulder, then looked about him at the lights and smells of a Chinese street kitchen. Make the money now. Yes, back to work.

Some taxis pulled up with hungry people in them, and the crowd was coming out of the Rex Theater down the street, a throng intent on chicken, prawns and *chau fan*. They all wanted to eat before the curfew.

A gruff voice drew Fook's attention and he saw a heavy-set, youngish man in bright mechanic's coveralls, smeared with grease. "Two orders of Singapore noodles. Two orders of coffee with a little sugar. And hurry it."

Fook nodded and disappeared into the kitchen. He returned quickly with the food, then went back to work.

The man in the coveralls walked back to his partner, carrying the food on a tray. His partner, an older man, sat next to a lorry on a large spare tire. The man in the coveralls handed him a cup of coffee and a paper plate heaped with chau mein. "Here, sarge," the young man said.

"Don't call me that," the "sarge" snapped, looking around to see if anyone had overheard.

The youngster, chastened and red-faced, sat on the tire rim and started eating.

They were right right across from the Rolls, about twenty yards from the Sai Woo. Grimy and greasy, the two men looked like mechanics working on the large Hornchurch Freight lorry which had, it seemed, broken down. They sat so they could observe all movement in and out of the stairway to the restaurant.

The constable swallowed some coffee, too quickly, and coughed.

"Go slow, sonny," the sergeant said. "The force is paying for your food and your time. Besides—" he motioned to the Sai Woo "—they'll probably be there half the night."

Both men looked at the tiny window with its iron grate. The light was dim. The sergeant lowered his gaze. The Korean was standing by the Rolls. This one, the Greyhound, was rich, filthy, stinking rich—and ostentatious as only a self-made millionaire could be.

There was a crackling sound from under the front axle of the vehicle. The sergeant cursed, then lowered himself onto a dolly. Slowly he rolled under the engine, but not before scowling at his amused companion.

A large drop of grease landed on his forehead. It was damp and hot and he had to move his head sideways to avoid bumping it on the lorry's heavy-duty shock absorbers. As he neared it, the crackling grew louder. He cursed, then reached for the tiny radio pack attached to the axle.

"Base to Watcher," said a faint voice cutting though the static. "Base to Watcher, over."

The sergeant raised his hand up, growling as his elbow scraped the cobblestones.

"Watcher to Base. . ." he paused, feeling no need of getting them angry or upset. "No sign of movement."

Faintly: "Anything in the doorway?"

He inched the trolley over so he could see the road. Nothing. He informed Base of the fact. "Yes, sir, we'll be ready if our contact shows." He smirked, looking up at the undercarriage of this mechanical monstrosity, praying to all the Taoist gods he knew for patience. Ready? Of course they'd be ready. Why the hell were they there anyway?

Adam Kot had listened to the sergeant's report carefully. He replaced his receiver and made a notation in his operational diary.

All the teams around Nullah Road were in place. The operation was well planned and the area was surrounded.

23:05 hours. Where was his informant? Had he turned coward? Watcher should see him first; they were the closest.

Kot was sitting in a darkened Austin; he couldn't see anything. He felt his blood running cold. Damn! Where was
Wong, the Greyhound dealer?

At another street corner, just to the north, Steven Tak sat
in the back seat of his car surrounded by five hand-picked
men. We have him now, Tak thought. Five teams in the inner
cordon, four men to a team; an outer cordon of thirty men
should something go wrong.

Watcher had the most important task, the initial identification. Had the informant snuck past them? It wasn't possible,
Tak thought. They had been there since before ten o'clock,
seen the various underlings go in the door, checked off each
on the recognition chart. They were all there—Yip Lam and
his whole bunch.

But it was not enough that Yip Lam was present; they had
to catch him in the act of conducting Triad ceremonies. It
was this activity, under Hong Kong law, that gave them the
power of deportation; and Yip Lam was, after all, Taiwanese
by choice, if not birth. Even Yip's many lawyers couldn't
fight his extradition under the Societies Ordinance—as they
had successfully contested Yip's many other charges in the
past. If they could find him in the act of receiving tributes,
they had him—in custody without bail, bereft of any legal
tricks, with straightforward extradition staring him in the
eyes.

Extradition. It wasn't much really, but with the threat that
they would confiscate his holdings and with the real trump
card that they knew he'd destroyed the *East Wind*, perhaps,
they might get him to crack. It was for that reason the
"Dealer" was crucial to the entire operation. Without him
there was no Yip Lam, and without Yip there was nothing.

Steven Tak had done his homework. This would be a solid
case. Yip had been followed all this time by a police informant who'd seeped information he'd obtained to weaken
Yip's organization, to keep a lid on him, to use what they
had to destroy other criminal groups. But never before had
they had something like this on Yip Lam himself, something
rich and big and juicy. Something to topple the whole stinking rat pack. Yip had had his chance earlier to come to the

bureau with his lawyer and talk civilly. Yip had chosen not to; he was fair game.

"The Dealer is coming, sir. . ."

The sergeant at Watcher was once again beneath the lorry. For the umpteenth time he was checking the muffler while his mate knelt at the rear of the vehicle and banged on a stubborn hubcap cover; a dull, toneless noise, just enough to cover the sound of the police radio.

There was movement in the alcove. The sergeant saw sandaled feet, then gawky legs, formless shirt and then the face. He tried to match it to the photographs he had memorized. Yes, this was "the dealer." The sergeant remembered the photograph. It had been taken eight years ago, of a young man, overly serious as he stood in starched servitude, high-button collar and crisp, smart police uniform, to receive an award at Government House, an award from Her Majesty's government in gracious acknowledgement for services courageously rendered, for bravery. Yes, this was their Dealer, their contact.

The sergeant crawled awkwardly over the cobblestones, ducking engine parts, till he was lying just behind the front wheel. Somehow, in the faint buzzing static of the turned-down radio, he heard the words, "Go to the Dealer." The plan was on.

Adam Kot moved. His eyes stung in the glare of the food-stall lights. He felt the little body pack digging into his ribs; he could hear the soft crackle of the set and the occasional garbled whispers of the other teams. His shirt stuck to his body.

Down the street, he could see the pink Rolls and its driver, forty yards, then thirty yards. He could see shadows in the doorway. His hands fumbled in his pockets. He placed a cigarette in his mouth, cupped his hands to light it, drew in the smoke.

He could see the sergeant's shadow by the front wheel of the lorry. Opposite, another team of three. At the far end of the street two cars idled, their four-way indicators on. One vehicle flickered its right-turn indicator. They were ready for any escape attempt.

Ten yards from the doorway Kot could see the silver bracelet on the Dealer's wrist.

"All right, Adam. We're ready for you to move." It was the soft voice of Tak on the receiver.

Eight yards.

Five.

Kot stopped, took out his handkerchief, dropped it. The cloth floated aimlessly to the dirty sidewalk. The Dealer was watching.

Seconds passed. Then, finally, the Dealer responded: he dropped a bright green cloth. The contact was complete.

Kot butted his cigarette with his heel and glanced back at his men, who were moving toward the Rolls-Royce and its unsuspecting driver. Another team was meandering up the gutter lane, toward the Sai Woo.

The Dealer had earned his ransom.

Kot could hear the cheerful voices coming from the Sai Woo; he could see the tailored loafers and pressed trousers as their suspects came down from the second floor. The Dealer had been true to his word: he had produced the Greyhound. In a few seconds, it would be over. The Greyhound would be theirs.

Behind him, Kot heard the sound of an engine. Then, suddenly, the squeal of tires and a loud shout, a thud and the crash of breaking glass.

Kot ducked instinctively and turned just in time to see the twin beams of light bearing down on him. He stood there, mesmerized, as the car raced toward him.

Fifteen yards. Ten. He could see the faces behind the windscreen. There was no doubt about it. They wanted to kill him.

Five yards. Three.

And then, with just a moment to spare, he tumbled and rolled to one side.

He heard the woosh of cold air as the car passed by, felt the sharp, wrenching pain in his knees, ankles and left shoulder as he crashed to the hard, brick road. And then Adam Kot passed out from shock and pain.

Tak, still in the back of the car, saw Kot fall on the road, saw the surveillance teams rush by from all directions, all pretense of subterfuge gone as they, too, became aware that something terribly wrong was happening to their plan of action.

Frustrated and angry, he sat on the edge of his seat, urging his driver on. He saw a little Cedric screech to a stop outside the restaurant, heard the doors slam, saw the four young men, armed with triangular files and sharpened bamboo poles, jump out and scramble up the staircase toward the Sai Woo.

He saw the chauffeur of the Rolls tumble to the wayside, twitching and screaming, as he was attacked.

Saw the Greyhound Dealer, the faithful one, crumple to the road, the blood gushing freely from his head and chest as he too was assaulted.

Then the four youths went inside, and Tak could see them no more. The Cedric, though, was accelerating rapidly, trying to escape. Tak's Austin, driven by an experienced detective, swerved sharply to the right and braked. The little Cedric didn't even slow down and crashed broadside into Tak's car.

A gust of air became a thunderous roar. Crumple of metal. Shatter of cascading glass. Unearthly sounds. Tak's body jolted forward; the door handle dug into his ribs and his head pounded into the dashboard, only to be whiplashed right back to the headrest. Excruciating pain shot through his chest. His lungs fought for air, and the fresh, salty-sweet taste of warm fluid—blood—was in his mouth.

When the first shock passed, Tak looked up, his eyes stinging. On the windscreen he could see a fresh blood smear, dark, velvet around the sunburst pattern of jigsaw glass shards. Things moved through the night, bright, fluttering as he hovered near the verge of a blackout.

He felt weak and drowsy as he glanced over to where the Cedric should have been, its steel melded to his crumpled Austin.

It wasn't there. Somehow, the little Cedric had survived the crash. Tak looked around, trying to spot it.

There it was; smoke belching from its exhaust, steam billowing from a burst radiator, its right side completely smashed. Its left front tire was flat, the steering gone. A wheel rim scraped the bricks of the curb. Sparks flew. And then, just as suddenly as it had appeared, the Cedric was gone, vanished down one of the thousands of tiny laneways that made Mongkok a maze; lost into the shimmering China night.

For a shocked moment, all was oppressively still.

Tak heard footsteps, shouts, a frenzied call for an ambulance. He could see the figures rushing to the wrecked car. There were uniform police now too, many of them, and the bright, white coats of ambulance attendants scampering up the steps to the Sai Woo and over to the cooked-food stall.

Steven Tak knew he had been beaten, knew the Greyhound was dead. He felt a wave of nausea as the pain jolted electric through his body.

Then the door to his car was wrenched open and he heard the voice of Pat Yiu, his faithful station sergeant. His craggy eyes were filled with concern. "Are you all right, sir?"

Gentle hands lifted him onto a stretcher. The night sky was red and blue, the air oppressively hot. Tak felt cold sweat running down his forehead, felt the pain stabbing down his back. And he shivered. Like a Fanling winter's morning it was. Cold.

"Catch the bastards. Catch them," he whispered through painfully swollen lips, and then the pain overcame him and he passed out.

The old sergeant hushed the well-meaning whispers. What good would it do to tell him? Why shatter his hopes with the truth? Not now. Maybe later. But not now.

The two men beneath the lorry, the sergeant and his young companion, had been only a step behind the Cedric. They had seen Kot's signal and immediately started across the street, revolvers drawn, hearts pumping madly.

They found the chauffeur bleeding. A light bulb, filled with acid, had been thrown in his face. Then they saw the Dealer. He had been killed with vicious slashes from the rusty, razor-tipped bamboo stick, which turned his face into free-flowing, bloody pulp before he, too, died in empty betrayal.

They didn't stop. They were right behind the four attackers as they raced up the darkened stairs to the restaurant.

They heard the sounds of struggle, shouts, breaking glass, piercing screams. Then. . .silence.

They dashed up the stairs and went in.

Yip Lam was there, somewhere, in the mangled bone and flesh. He had to be. And he was, though it would take a police coroner several hours to confirm it, working from old dental comparisons. Yip had been gold-plated at Stanley Prison four years ago while a humble guest of Her Majesty.

The other two bodies had once been high officials of the Triad society. The police had been trying to catch them for years. The detectives looked around the tiny room, looked at the masses of dead flesh that had once been the proud leadership of a feared Triad lodge. Yip Lam and his cronies had been struck from the face of the earth.

There was a mass of crumpled paper in the corner of the room, smoldering furiously. Hot gusts of wind tickled the flames. A uniformed constable stepped out the flames and picked up the charred paper. Government chemists would later decipher figures and dollar signs, quite substantial amounts of money, but with no explanations. They could have been accounts, payoffs, laundered bills. No one would ever know what they meant.

The assassins had been thorough. They must have had a reason for killing Yip Lam, perhaps for revenge or greed. Or maybe they wanted him silenced before the police could get to him. The detectives looked around, confused, angered, frustrated. They could find no clues.

Downstairs, uniformed units dispatched from Kowloon Control had cordoned off the area. Outside the Sai Woo, teams of detectives searched for the assassins. But the killers had eluded them, disappeared without a trace.

The duty inspector at control ordered all police units to stop any vehicles breaking the curfew. Riot police, tumbling out of grimy Bedford lorries, were sent on foot through the streets to arrest and detain any suspicious-looking males.

The chances of success were slim; in the end, they found nothing.

A superintendent from Kowloon CID arrived within eight minutes to take command of the operation. Shortly after, forensic teams were on the scene with pathologists and photography units. Detectives scoured Nullah Road for evidence. Ambulances moved the dead and wounded.

The superintendent considered his options. It did not take an expert to see this was more than just tribal warfare over bar girls, brothels, *dai dongs* or *bac-fan*. Yip could have been eliminated in any one of a hundred places or times. But this was a ritual killing, done with dramatic effect, for a purpose. What that purpose was remained open to conjecture. Whoever had killed the Triad leader had acted with a preconceived plan. The operation was just too smooth, too tight, to be anything else.

And why kill him with so many police around? The killers were not naive. They had to have detected police units in the area. It must have been something of the greatest urgency. Perhaps, the super mused, it was to keep the police from capturing Yip alive. Perhaps they had orders to kill Yip to prevent him from telling the police something. But what? What did Yip know that was so important that it caused his death here in this mean-spirited street? And who had been so great as to dare challenge him?

Cold blue floodlights lit the area. Nervous coolies, raw-boned laborers, acned schoolboys, chattered away with the solemn-faced detectives.

"No, he was taller." The gesture of hand.

"Yes, it was a Cedric. I'm certain on my mother's grave."

"Color? I'm not sure. It was dark, blue, maybe black. But rusty. A *pak-pai*, pirate taxi."

"No, there weren't more than four, and a driver."

"The one I saw was. . .of course he was male!. . ."

"How tall?" A motion of the hand waving wildly in midair. "Five foot six? No he was shorter than me. What do you mean, five feet four. . . ."

After twenty minutes, the first statements were ready for the superintendent. They were sketchy, at best. Most of the witnesses at the cooked-food stall had run at the first sign of trouble, or hid amid the tables and crockery.

No one remembered much, if anything, of the Cedric's license plate. Some thought it began with KS, some thought HG, and all disagreed about the numbers—except the last number. Almost everyone agreed that the last number was an eight. And most people thought the car was dark—blue or black or green.

The witnesses agreed that the youths were Chinese, with nondescript clothing, jeans, jean jackets and T-shirts. The one that appeared to be the leader was taller than the rest, perhaps five foot ten, and wearing a bright pink shirt. He had heavy dark-rimmed glasses, and he shouted commands to the others in Chiu Chau dialect.

Later in the night, a group of plainclothes detectives discovered a crawl space in the wall of the restaurant's loft, behind the altar to the god Kwan Dai. It was framed with freshly broken plaster and was only a few feet high, but it stretched to gloomy infinity.

A volunteer crouched down and disappeared into the murky dark. He discovered a narrow passageway some twenty feet long, and a warren of tunnels that went through four buildings for more than three hundred feet, before petering out at a small back staircase that led down to the rat-infested rear lane. This, then, was the final escape route of their prey, where the assassins had disappeared into the night, never to return.

In the tunnel they found a cleaver handle. Later, it would yield prints. Further on they found a handkerchief with traces of blood and a clump of hair. Old Yip had died, but not without a struggle.

Also that night, a CID team examining Tak's demolished Austin found a front light rim, for a Cedric. In it was a vehicle serial number.

The pieces of the puzzle were slowly fitting together.

CHAPTER TWENTY-ONE

J ohn Cleve slouched back in the old rattan chair, a clay cup of coffee in his hand. He gazed across the massive room at the large, cream-colored map of the colony.

It was divided into sections—Hong Kong Island, Kowloon, the New Territories—bisected by yellow grid lines and cross-laced with numbers and figures. Every street corner was referenced in code; each public building, school, post office and service depot was marked in purple. Red circles showed areas of unrest, blue triangles were police units in action and the blue squares represented units on standby.

Cleve, an old China hand, sensed something was in the air but he couldn't put his finger on it. Things were happening too fast, coming at him from all directions.

He paused to consider his strengths. Twenty police divisions in the colony. Each had at least a company of riot police, some had two and three. In all, there were forty companies of police in varying stages of training readiness. Eight Tactical Unit companies were in peak condition. He also had some marine units, though he'd like them to stay at sea, patrolling the islands. And he had the specialist branches: Criminal Investigations, Triad Bureau, Special Crime Squad. He wanted to keep them as they were. Two army regiments posted to the colony provided some backup support. In addition, Cleve could call on the permanent garrison, the Hong

Kong Regiment known as the Volunteers, and the ever-faithful Ghurkas. With these, Cleve should be able to control the streets, provided things didn't snowball too swiftly.

On paper, at least, he had a formidable force. In reality, that was far from true. Protracted disturbances would leave his men tired, edgy and overworked. Support from the public would be marginal at best. No, it promised to be a long, hard grind. Of this John Cleve was certain.

At the main switchboards, two youthful superintendents, telephones in hand, took incoming calls from district command centers answering the little red lights that now flickered like Christmas trees on the board before them.

Near the action board, chief inspectors sipped iced teas and chatted with each other, clipboards in hand, ready to update casualty figures, fires, break-ins and assaults as they were reported. *Loi ging*—women police—moved the red circles and blue triangles and squares around the games board as the results came in during the early morning hours.

Traffic PCs trooped by with courier pouches containing detailed maps for divisional supers, new situation reports that could not be broadcast in full and, as always, analyses and statistics. For the more important documents there were teams of three—sergeant, radio operator and driver—riding the high-torqued Emergency Unit Mark 12 Land Rovers to and from divisions.

There were more than sixty people in the room, the nerve center of police headquarters. Phones rang. Telexes clicked, voices whispered and talked in Cantonese and clipped English and broad Liverpudlian.

The room had an air of expectancy. As time passed, the military presence also became more evident. The token number of young lieutenants who'd manned offices in the earlier hours of the evening were replaced as the night wore on by captains and higher ranking officers wearing dappled, gray-green fatigues.

Cleve was joined by a solemn-faced colonel from the general staff named Hughes-Halpern, H.H. for short, who was content to let Cleve make the decisions. And that, in the commissioner's way of viewing things, suited him just fine. John Cleve sat unperturbed, sipping lukewarm coffee with a hint of chicory, as he liked it.

Cleve put the cup down. It had left a ring staining an old SB situation report. His desk was littered with files, dispatches and clipboard cuttings. He looked at the occurrence logbook for Hong Kong Island in the past half hour:

1:05 a.m.   Island Control reports a fire on 3 *wallah wallahs*. Fenwick Pier. Possible arson. Fire brigade on scene. HKI Emergency Unit attend. No arrests. All in order.

1:08 a.m.   Wanchai. Island Pol/Mil reports crowd of 800 on Gloucester Road. Weapons—stones, spikes, bottles, sticks. 2 stores looted. 11 injured. 19 arrests. Wanchai riot company called out. Crowd milling about. Des Voeux Road closed. Johnston Road closed. Traffic Hong Kong Island on scene. CID Wanchai and SB teams called out from reserve. Reports continuing.

1:13 a.m.   I Control reports crowd gathering in Happy Valley. Numbers estimated 300-500. Wanchai number 2 riot company called out. CID teams on scene. 5 injured. 6 arrests. Reason for demo—killing of boy in Kowloon.

1:21 a.m.   Island Pol/Mil reports crowd forming Central District. 3000. Central riot company called out. Reason for unrest unknown. Report continuing.

1:23 a.m.   I Control reports crowd milling round Shaukiwan Police station. EU Light Strike force on scene. 3 injuries. 1 policeman cut by glass. Reports continuing.
             Bayview riot company on standby. . . .crowd size 2500.

1:29 a.m.   I Pol/Mil reports crowd of 2000 gathering at Chaiwan resettlement estate. Reason unknown. Reports continuing.
             Alpha company PTU proceeding to scene.

And so it was for Kowloon on a larger scale: arrests, injuries, policemen among them, crowds milling in the street in spite of the curfew. In Tsuen Wan and Yuen Long, in the New Territories, buses were burned in the depots. In the village of Uk Pik, a car was driven into a vegetable stall. On the island of Cheung Chau, at the entrance to the ancient temple of Pei Ti, an effigy of John Cleve was found burning furiously in the starry night. There was no other sign of life.

Cleve didn't need his specialists to tell him that a pattern was developing on Hong Kong Island. Small fires were followed by selective riots; nothing major as yet, but each disturbance was larger than the previous one, with each calling for a greater police response. And the pattern held true for Kowloon and New Territories. Cleve looked up at the tactical board. For each red circle, a blue triangle. There was something in the wind.

Billboards and posters brought in by CID Intelligence protested the death of the sailors on the ship and the death of the youth in Kowloon. The artwork appeared professional, copied on a press, a well-planned onslaught. And most of the posters mentioned him personally: "Cleve the British Pig Dog," "Cleve the Murderer," "Cleve the Assassin."

There was little mention of the police force or the government. For Cleve there was something here that had been missing from all the other outbreaks he had seen in his turbulent years of Hong Kong policing. This was no blanket outpouring of the "righteous anger of the masses." Rather, it was a concerted attack on him, the Commissioner of Police.

At about two in the morning, Cleve received the confirmation he had sought but dreaded. Yip Lam, his one link to the mysterious *East Wind*, was indeed dead, a cold corpse lying on a marble slab at the Kennedy Town mortuary.

His men had a partial description of one of their suspects: male Chinese, mid-twenties, tall, gaunt, about five foot ten, wearing glasses, with heavy acne. A young Chinese killer who spoke Chiu Chau and dressed flamboyantly, defiantly, in a bright pink shirt.

In addition to their prime suspect, they also had copious
data on the automobile. It was a Japanese Cedric, a four
door; model year—between 1971 and 1977. The license
number began "KS," the final digit was "8." It was a *pak-pai*,
an unlicensed taxi, dark blue or perhaps purple, with extensive rust work on its fenders. The serial number from the
light rim was being traced. It had not proved original, but
transport records had managed to narrow the field to three
service garages, all Hong Kong side, which could have supplied the replacement part.

The car, Cleve knew from bitter experience, was much
easier to trace than the man. There were one hundred and
twelve vehicles of a similar year and color on the roads of the
Crown colony. Most could be eliminated because of the plate
number. Of the remaining thirteen, only five were unlicensed
taxis. Two could ticked off the list, since they rested in Tai
Hang police pound, forfeited to the Crown after successful
charges against their operators. One was presently in Macau.

And then there were two.

One was a cannibalized wreck on the Wanchai landfill, a
scavenger's delight awaiting the police Land Rover tow.

And then there was only one. A 1974 purple four-door
Cedric, license plate KS1808, registered to a Tse Tsi Fai, aged
twenty-five, who resided at 17 Ying Kwong Mansion, 2-6
Yee Wo Street, Wanchai.

A young police inspector from Accident Investigation–
Traffic/Hong Kong Island was sent to the address on the
pretext of informing the owner that the vehicle had been involved in an accident on Kowloon side. The apartment was
completely surrounded by heavily armed EU teams.

But the door to number 17 was opened by a frightened
old amah.

Who was the master of the house? A Mr. Lam. Was he in?
No. And who was this Tse Tsi Fai? Her son. And where was
he now? In the New Territories visiting his Uncle Poon.
Where in the New Territories? There was suspicion in the
woman's eyes. You see, mother, someone has stolen his car.
We just want to tell him we have it. The eyes softened. Try
Hut 24, up the Castle Peak Road near 26 milestone, just

outside Kam Tin Walled Village. The uncle is Poon Wan Shun. It's right near Shek Kong, just west. A yellow stone house. They thanked the old woman who muttered her goodbyes and peered nervously up and down the deserted hallway as they left. It was not good to be seen talking to the police these days.

Plainclothes detectives from Yuen Long CID raided Poon's farm within minutes. But beyond disturbing cackling geese and annoyed roosters, in addition to spilling a mah jongg table upon forcing the oak door, they found only five frightened Hakka farmers and their wives. One readily admitted to being Poon, the suspect's uncle, but he had not seen Tse in weeks. And the car? The old Cedric. Did Poon know where it was? No, he had not seen it since he'd last seen Tse. The detectives left with what they had when they arrived: nothing.

At the same time, detectives at the Hong Kong Central Registry were searching through row upon row of filing cabinets. For everyone who lived in Hong Kong there was a registration card with their name and photograph on it. One copy was kept on their person at all times; one copy was for government records. Soon they had what they were looking for. A photograph of Tse Tsi Fai.

From the Ministry of Transport came more information, a change of address application. Tse had moved to Chaiwan, on the windy eastern seaboard of the island, and lived at Chaiwan Resettlement Block D, in room 191.

While Identification Bureau began preparing photo composites of Tse for dispersal to divisions, units rushed to the gloomy four-story apartment block in the mud flats below the Chaiwan Police Station. The whole process of locating their suspect had taken less than one and a half hours. It was not yet 3:00 a.m.

The hall on the ground level of Block D was long, dark and gloomy. Its concrete ceilings were high, with water seeping through cracks and dripping onto greasy puddles. All about were dog feces, blanched urine stains and faded Chinese graffiti. Here and there were discarded joss trays, smoldering sweetly to indifferent dieties.

And then, room 191. The police knocked twice before forcing the door, shotguns at the ready, safety catches off. High-powered flashlights played warily off dingy walls. Inside were a few pieces of furniture and an old China Products calendar. But Tse wasn't there. A cat, scurrying at their legs, whispered down the hall on padded feet.

They searched the place but found nothing. Even the tea cups had layered brown residue in them. Small black shadows crawled around the corners of the cubicle: roaches scampering for food. Some were on the walls. In Hong Kong summer, it didn't take long for them to claim a room as their own.

A PC looked in a drawer by the bedside table and found a syringe, some cotton and a porcelain spoon. Their man was a *do-yau*—a drug addict. Something more to add to the growing file.

After knocking on doors up and down the hallway, the police found one neighbor who knew Tse, and knew what he did with his "taxi." Apparently he drove children to school from the Central police married quarters on Caine Road, and had been doing it for two years. The neighbor also said Tse used to be a police interpreter, but didn't know why he'd left the force.

"It was a pity about his eyesight," the neighbor mused. "He would have been a good constable, except for that."

The RHKP were slowly tying together a damning composite of their suspect, a fox in their own lair.

John Cleve had the rest of the file information within minutes and quickly glanced at the data. First notation: 1982. Last one: late 1983. Tse Tsi Fai: born 17 September 1960. Residence: Yee Wo Street, Wanchai. Education: Form 5. Dialects spoken: Chiu Chau, Cantonese, English. Superiors' comments: Good interpreter . . . a hard worker. Ambitious . . . wants to be a policeman . . . shows potential, good police material . . . might be exempt if can get corrective glasses.

And then, slowly, subtly, the entries changed. Tse had fallen prey to the Dragon: ". . . suffers from personal problems . . . absent from work . . . absent without cause . . . errors in court documents . . . insubordination."

And finally, the damning paragraph: On 16 October 1983 at Aberdeen Police Station, S. Thompson, Detective Inspector, and members of special duty squad, Western division, arrested Tse Tsi Fai. Occupation: police interpreter. Residence: #17 Ying Kwong Mansion 2-6 Yee Wo Street, Wanchai, HKI. Charge: possession of dangerous drugs; five packets of suspected heroin. Stolen from Drug PC at 6:10 hrs report date.

This was followed by the submission of a senior officer subsequently assigned to investigate the matter and determine the appropriate punishment, which was severe: Tse Tsi Fai to be discharged from government service and struck off strength without any benefits said position might accrue.

In red ink at the bottom of the folio were the findings of the criminal court: On 23 October 1983, Magistrate, Western courts, sentenced accused, Tse Tsi Fai, to three months Chi Ma Wan Security Prison, Lantau. Party also to seek methadone treatment.

Records from HM Prisons Department summed it up: Tse Tsi Fai, transferred to Stanley Prison, February 1984. Charged: assault occasioning actual bodily harm in the club beating of another prisoner for alleged homosexual overtures. Sentenced four years. Because of extenuating circumstances, given two years. Released for good behavior, late 1985.

So this was their man, a disgruntled drug addict. No telling whose influence he'd fallen under at Stanley—which Triad boss had paid him the most in heroin for his knowledge of police procedures or which had channeled his hatred of the police into action and made him head of the hit squad that killed Yip Lam. Tse was loose somewhere in the colony; so was the man who had recruited him.

Cleve looked up. A group of staff officers had gathered by the western side of the map. One red circle, two red circles, three, then four. All in a small area. A breakout of trouble at Shek Kip Mei. The Kowloon East switchboard suddenly came alive.

The latest situation report arrived. Cleve hurriedly conferred with his senior advisors. Choi Hing and Ping Shek Estates across from the airport had reported five arsons, all fire bombings of stores. A crowd of nine hundred youths had gathered at #4 Resettlement Block. Another crowd of eight hundred, possibly a thousand, was sweeping in from #6 Block.

Kowloon Control had sent the reserve company from Hung Hom as well as a back-up, three Light Strike Forces from Kowloon West. Cleve nodded grimly and looked again at the map. Two blue triangles had moved; there were two fewer squares in reserve with only a few units left on standby. These brush fires had to be stopped before they consumed the colony.

CHAPTER TWENTY-TWO

———

The two-tone green Cortina, its Semperit tires slithering up Magazine Gap Road, mounted the asphalt serpentine to Victoria Peak. The road was slick with freshly fallen rain, but there was no traffic and the trim little car hugged the curves easily.

Peng and Andrews were grim, eyes bloodshot and red-rimmed from exhaustion. It was dark and clammy and they both wanted to sleep more than anything else in the world.

The car moved smoothly into a sharp turn at the junction of Magazine Gap and Peak Road and then accelerated along Peak Road on the Mount Kellett side towards Jardines Corner. The Peak above was shrouded in clouds and hot mist; thick swirling bellows of moisture hid it from view.

They were soon in the mist themselves where they slowed down and made their way gingerly through the cloud banks. A realm of silky silence protected these heights from the grimness of the city below. Rivulets of rain tumbled down the Asian granite. In the blackness, red clay opened in gaping wounds. The night air was filled with a heady dampness. Gleaming, innocent gilas crept up and down broadleaf plants. Moisture settled on their car in generous drops. All about there was the spicy tang of bracken, the sickly-sweet scent of hibiscus and the rank perfume of rotting vegetable plants.

After a few minutes of patient gearing and cornering, they

reached a place where the fog thinned, the road leveled off and they entered another world—spacious, elegant, timeless. They had arrived at the Peak.

The tattered piece of paper they had found among Elephant Man's possessions had proven worthless—ink blotches without reason. And that was precisely what the government technician had stated.

But the matchbox cover? Now that was something else again. The obscured digits had taken time but, with careful study, all had been deciphered. A phone number, unlisted, one of four traced to the same address: 7 Harlech Road.

They had telephoned, and it was the owner, Henry Szeto, who had named the time. And a very strange time it was indeed.

A sharp turn partially upwards to Harlech Road and, there on a searing precipice, the car jolted to a sudden halt. The doors slammed hollow. Their footsteps were crisp as fireworks on the fine redstone path which led from the roadside to the gateway where, lurking behind a huge black iron gate, two leering gargoyles crouched, immobile. Tendrils of fog trickled through an imposing ten-foot-high picket fence.

On one of the massive pillars was a weather tarnished bronze palque. On it, etched in Gothic script, were the words, "Blue Cloud." And below, in Chinese and English characters, was an inscription:

THERE IS IN THE UNIVERSE AN AURA
WHICH PERMEATES ALL THINGS
AND MAKES THEM WHAT THEY ARE.
IN MAN IT IS CALLED SPIRIT
AND THERE IS NO WHERE WHERE IT IS NOT. . .

wen Tien-hsiang

Peng pressed a buzzer he found to one side of the plaque. No sound. He pressed again. Still nothing. There was a rustle in the heavy air and a figure emerged out of nowhere; slight, stooped, the Chinese servant wore a high-necked coat and formless brown pajamas. A black toque kept most of the face from view.

He shuffled slowly down the walk, almost oblivious to their presence. When he was nearly upon them they could see that he was very old, his jaundiced skin strung taut on high cheekbones. Lazy eyelids barely hid his eyes, which housed huge, livid cataracts.

Peng spoke in Punti. "Is your master in?"

The man looked directly at them. He said nothing.

Peng repeated the question. The man's rasping breathing became more evident. A hoarse, gurgling sound rose from his chest. He had tuberculosis.

Peng tried Swatow. Chiu Chau. Shanghainese. Mandarin. The old man simply canted his head to the side, his heavily lidded eyes betraying nothing.

Andrews had just made an impatient move to open the gate when a voice boomed on an intercom, "Ah Bau, it's all right. Let them pass."

The old man, his hearing suddenly and miraculously restored, moved to unlatch the padlock and open the gate.

They entered the grounds proper. The fog wafted around them as the high Manchu gates clanged ominously behind.

Andrews saw it first. In a clump of trees, a Sanyo Securicor camera followed their every movement. He looked at Peng who nodded slightly.

They followed the aged servant along a deep, circuitous, ocher stone path. The fog enveloped them like a wooly traveler's cloak. Here and there stood bushes of fragrant frangipani; soft pink and gentle saffron, groves of fuchsia and delicate pine; temples of hardy rain-soaked redwood, temples to Lei Kung, the god of thunder, to Lo Hsuan, the stellar sovereign of fire virtue, to the Dragon King and the Monkey Prince; statues of wood and jade and sharp, blue stone. In front of each were feeble, flickering tips of lightly-scented joss sticks, to keep the gods company.

They entered a level clearing where above them stood a worn sandalwood archway guarded by two ferocious stone lions. In front of them was a high-swept footbridge; behind them was the hill they had come down, cresting toward the tumultuous Peak, toward Tai Ping Shan, the Mountain of Great Peace.

They crossed the bridge. Below, in a lotus-covered pond, little ripples played timidly in the amethyst colored water. Goldfish cut through the gentle phosphorus. Ahead loomed the object of their quest: the Mansion of the Blue Cloud. Standing on a solitary aerie, it rose, a sparkling gem of blue cobalt that faded to beryl. It was rooted only slightly to the granite and rich black earth of the Peak. Its coffered roof arched vainly into the scudding clouds in the sky. Built in the Portuguese *compradore* style of Macau, its many windows, French Renaissance cut, were closed, blinds shut, darkened. On this night, no lights shone from within.

It was rumored that the mansion had twenty-nine rooms, though few people had entered it. A beautiful Chinese garden graced the grounds. Hidden behind mammoth walls at the foot of a precipitous rock face, the garden had many temples, peach and orange groves and an exquisite goldfish pond under a delicate black-lacquered footbridge. The house and garden had been created by a Taiwanese architect in his eighties who, it was said, once worked for the fickle and powerful T'Su Shi, empress dowager of Kuang Hsu, the last Chinese House before the collapse of the dynasty and the rise of the republic of Doctor Sun Yat Tsen. The estate, a wary sentinel for the Sulphur Channel, thousands of feet below, stood majestic and secluded, in chill splendor like its owner and master.

That man, the mighty *tai pan*—Henry Szeto—was possibly the most fascinating citizen of Hong Kong, the most fascinating city in the world.

He had entered Hong Kong from the great formless body of China shortly after the Second World War, an impoverished woodcutter with a satchel full of tools, wood-blistered hands, an eye for beauty and a dream that he patiently parlayed in twenty short years into a multimillion-dollar business.

Szeto had started his trade modestly, out of a rusty shack on Canton Road. He crossed the harbor twice a week to scavenge driftwood from Chaiwan Beach and returned, the jagged flotsam weighing down his battered rickshaw, to the dim, oil-lit tin shack that was his workshop and home. There, in the late hours, he carved formless salt-stained wood into tiny figurines and statuettes, the gods and goddesses of his ancestors.

Then, weary and eye sore from work, he would take the cart, laden to the brim with his fineries, down the winding post-war streets of Hong Kong, cajoling equally poor storekeepers into placing an item of his in their barren shop windows. He went to meet the giant ocean liners and bartered shrewdly with the overweight tourists from Queens and the dour British matrons from Hyde Park, leaving his work in the glittering hotels where the foreign devils stayed, where it was sold by greedy middlemen.

His gaunt figure became a familiar one. The quality of his work made him a trusted craftsman. His reputation, spread by word of mouth and excellence of deed, grew and grew.

In a few years he had saved enough to open a small shop on Ladder Street—where centuries before the pirate Koxinga had strode down canted lanes with loot pillaged from burning Dutch and Portuguese frigates, loot stored for a time in the dripping caves of Bias Bay and bartered for taels of gold.

His clients were wealthy and appreciative. Word of his skill spread and he opened a second shop in Wanchai. There, too, his fortune was good and his already burgeoning coffers swelled.

Soon, with more money, he was able to produce lacquered works of art and he hired the best artisans to work with him—older, more patient men, with gnarled fingers and pinched faces and long-suffering eyes. Men who did not shun work and who crouched serenely for hours on bamboo stools in the ill-lit rooms, chiseling life and substance into stubborn, graceless wood.

Szeto's reputation grew. Buyers came from the Peak, from Stanley and Fanling, from Jardines Lookout and Hebe Haven to furnish their airy flats on fat expense accounts. People also came from overseas, from Stockholm, Johannesburg, San Diego, Vancouver, Auckland and London.

For Henry Szeto, money soon begat money in a cold, calculating fashion. His life was a black-lacquered, money-counting abacus to fortune.

He owned an office complex on Ice House Street and several other apartment buildings throughout the colony. There was a resort planned for the island of Lantau. He held a major share in a casino in Santa Domingo, stocks in an air charter based in London and controlling interest in a Liberian-registered cruise line operating out of Montevideo.

His charitable donations had increased dramatically with the hint of a knighthood. He granted land and money to create and furnish new wards at the Ng Uk Tsuen TB Clinic. The Little Sisters of the Poor in Tsuen Wan received money to build a school for underprivileged children. He was chairman of the board of directors for three homes for orphans, two in the New Territories and one in Hung Hom, and he gave generously to numerous other charitable agencies, including an annual and substantial grant to the RHKP widows' and orphans' fund.

His close friends included the mighty Macau gambling king and international business entrepreneur, Yuen Hon, and Sir Timothy Fan, the most powerful Chinese businessman in the Crown colony, men to whom even the governor paid quiet respect and subservience.

Szeto shunned the English. He seemed more at ease with his own. His lawyers and corporate presidents handled his business affairs well. He paid them handsomely to do so.

He grew comfortably old in the clique and camaraderie of self-made men, moving within the close and close-mouthed circle of intimates. He invested funds warily and with discretion, and so became even wealthier.

Henry Szeto, the intinerate, black-pajamaed carpenter from China, made his mark on Tai Ping Shan, the Mountain of Great Peace. He had walked through a pass in the nine dragons of China to make this tiny colony his home.

Yet of his life before Hong Kong nothing was known. Henry Szeto, a millionaire many times over, had no past. And he chose to keep it that way.

For his aesthetic hands were not altogether clean. In late 1985, the Police Commercial Crime Squad come across a scheme of Szeto's to purchase three huge Chinese restaurants in the Netherlands—in Amsterdam, Delft and the Hague— with an unknown confederate. The funds came from undetermined sources not tied to any of Szeto's known companies. Then, just before the squad was ready to request an audit of his books, the plan seemed to die stillborn. The other man was never identified.

There were rumblings within Hong Kong's infamous underworld of Szeto's connection to powerful and ruthless gangsters, always unnamed; the informants were strangely silent after the initial information was given.

Henry Szeto was not nearly as perfect as he was made out to appear.

Wordlessly, Peng and Andrews entered a large hall. A mirrored ceiling bathed them in soft, muted light. From the center of the ceiling hung a huge, glittering chandelier. Its glass petals tinkled melodically in a faint breeze. On the walls hung woodcuts framed in expensive teak. On one was a scroll with the Chinese characters wealth, health and honor in bold, black ink set on a fiery-red background. The floor was a mosiac of light red and gold chips of marble intricately defining the shape of a phoenix, the venerable symbol of the household. A sweeping staircase led upstairs to the bed chambers.

Ah Bau motioned them down a passage. They passed blue and white Ming vases, rich wall hangings, sepia photographs of Lin Ka Fung, the Sung Wong Toi Rock and the Viceroy of Canton.

Suddenly, before a massive oak door, Ah Bau stopped. He rapped on the brass dragon's-head knocker once, twice, a third time.

Then he opened the door, and they entered a huge, dimly lit chamber. At the far end of the room, a tiny man, dwarfed by the somber immensity around him, sat behind a desk, outlined by a single, honey-colored reading lamp. He wore a burgundy velvet smoking jacket and gold silk pajamas. His gentle face was partially hidden behind a thick pair of bifocals, which he adjusted occasionally as they slid down his pug nose.

He sat hunched over an alligator-bound volume containing a collection of stamps. Every so often he would rustle impatiently, a sigh would escape his lips and he would adjust his glasses. Then he picked up his tweezers and gazed with unreserved intensity at the multi-colored rectangles before him. He was not to be hurried.

When he was done, he put the tweezers down and leaned forward on his elbows. He peered at them quizzically from behind the bifocals. Then, Henry Szeto smiled; a warm, friendly smile, refreshingly open and bereft of pretension. He seemed, for all the world, like a benign and bemused Hakka farmer.

A gracious host, he asked his guests to sit, and offered drinks. They politely declined the latter. Szeto excused himself with a conspiratorial wink; he said he was old and needed to keep the blood circulating. There was mirth in his voice.

They seated themselves on chairs of lacquered redwood bordered with inlaid mother of pearl. Ah Bau left the room, returning with a rich, red wine in an expensive Delphin decanter.

Szeto pulled a fine, Taipei-brocaded comforter over his legs. He took the delicate decanter in his gnarled hands, filled his glass to the brim and downed it in a single gulp. His face colored to a wonderfully rich glow. His eyes closed for a moment, then opened again.

"Now," he whispered, "to business. What can I do for you, gentlemen? Surely there must be more important things to concern yourselves with than the health of an old panda like me."

Andrews and Peng said nothing.

"Yes." Szeto waited, listening to the silence the way a musician might listen to a slightly out-of-tune instrument. "I hardly think you would bother me with something minor, especially now." He tilted his head to one side, impatient for an answer.

Andrews said, "Szeto, we do have one request, a small one only. Something you could do to greatly assist us." Szeto stared back, curious.

Andrews ruffled through the flap pocket of his tunic, took

out a weather-beaten leather case and from it withdrew a dog-eared photograph, passport-sized, the kind used by police identification bureaus throughout the world. He handed it to Szeto, who took it wordlessly. Andrews waited for a response, a reaction, a glimmer of recognition.

There was none.

"Have you ever seen this man?"

Szeto peered intently at the photograph, gave it careful measured thought. He fingered the edge of the print, tracing the rectangular outline. Without a word, he handed it back, then shook his head.

The room was very still. David finally spoke again. "As yet we are not at liberty to say, sir," he said carefully, "but we believe you may have had contact with this person. May even know him."

Szeto smiled. "I'm assuming that this individual, whomever he may be," he paused, "is of sufficient importance to merit the attention of two senior police officials." He looked first at David, then at Peng. Neither interrupted.

"After all," Szeto went on, "I am but an old woodcutter. But, as you look around you, it should become apparent that this man in the photograph has little in common with me, and I even less with him. Don't you agree?"

Silence.

"Well, I can see that you do not."

The smile had gone from Szeto's face. It was replaced by a look of utter contempt—for what, David could not at first determine.

"May I ask what he is being investigated for?"

"I'm afraid not," Peng replied simply.

"And do you have him in your custody?" Szeto continued, undeterred. "Is he assisting you in your investigation?"

A long pause, which neither Peng nor Andrews chose to fill.

"Where is he?"

The wind moaned in the branches outside.

"Gentlemen?" Szeto challenged them in an imperious voice.

"I'm afraid," Peng replied with some degree of truth, "that at this precise moment, we do not know."

Szeto sat back in his chair and closed his eyes, then sighed and turned to Peng.

"Well, then, superintendent—that is your rank, isn't it, young man?—I strongly suggest you find him. Perhaps he might tell you what you wish to know. I have never met or dealt with this fellow. Have I made myself clear?"

David would never forget the old man's hatred and contempt for their efforts. The room itself now seemed ice cold, hostile.

Henry Szeto refilled his glass from the decanter, his liver-spotted hands shaking. The chamber was hushed. A hollow wind whispered along the eaves. The fog swirled outside, entrancing, inviting. Their shadows grew and danced on the distant walls, fed by the light of the desk lamp.

Szeto spoke again, quietly, calmly. "So, I can assume then, gentlemen, that I am not under investigation; that no warrant exists for my arrest. Because, if there is a warrant," he said in a voice that did little to hide the menace, "you can rest assured that my attorneys will deal with the matter quite efficiently. And," he paused to let the words sink in, "I will have your careers.

"That is not a threat, gentlemen." A distant smile, the kind one used on servants who were being fired. "Let us just call it a promise."

Szeto bowed his head slightly toward his guests. There was once more warmth in his voice. "Are you positive I cannot offer you some of the hospitality of this house? A drink? A meal, perhaps? I have some excellent prawns from Lau Fo Shan. My cook has been with me for years, and he makes them butter-soft and tender."

Silence.

"Well then, some other time. Yes, another time." Henry Szeto stared at the fog with world-weary eyes. He was once more a harmless old man. From near the arm of his chair, he grasped a walking cane. With difficulty he clasped it by the neck, caressed the figure of a phoenix that adorned it.

His servant appeared out of the lingering shadows of the library. He might have been there all along.

"Ah Bau. You will please show my friends out."

The interview was over.

They were ushered from the chamber and back down the darkened corridor, Ah Bau's peasant slippers moving softly, trippingly on the gleaming marble floor. From the direction of the library they heard the faint sound of the cane beating its lonely tattoo.

At the main foyer, Ah Bau, with some effort, opened the huge door. The chill reached in to touch them with its caress.

Peng turned to Ah Bau and spoke roughly in the Punti accent of the peasant. "We can find our own way out from here." But Ah Bau's unfeeling stare indicated they would not be given any freedom on the grounds.

The old man still had not spoken a word when they reached the gate. The iron sockets creaked, the massive barriers parted just enough to let them through.

Suddenly, Peng turned back. He pulled a package of matches from his pocket and shoved it in Ah Bau's face. The servant's drooping eyelids flickered, slowly, patiently.

On the matchbox was drawn a symbol.

Ah Bau mouthed the word "Shia." Peng and Andrews waited. The old Chinese canted his head to one side, then looked back at them. "No," he whispered. "I do not know this character, do not know this man. I have never heard the name."

Peng peered into the brush. The camera had caught nothing.

Andrews abruptly grabbed the old man's wrist and squeezed. He motioned to Peng, who leaned toward Ah Bau and spoke in his ear. "Shia," Peng repeated, over and over.

Ah Bau bent forward, jerked his head up and screamed at Peng.

Andrews loosened his grip.

"He says Szeto's sick, dying," Peng explained. "He says we should leave them in peace."

The two policemen trudged wearily in the darkness to their car. "Do you think he bought it, Jim?"

Peng shrugged his shoulders and looked back at the mansion as if to confirm something. "I don't know, David. But I sense Ah Bau told us quite a bit more than he meant to."

David looked at him quizzically.

"He told us the character referred to a person, didn't he? We didn't tell him. In fact, till he said that, I hadn't even thought it might be a person."

"I think our friend Szeto is involved in something and, if he is, he'll talk to someone on the phone soon enough. And then we'll know too, won't we?" He looked over at his partner.

"He's certainly edgy about something, and it isn't his constipation." Peng chuckled, his breath misting in the damp. He tossed the keys to Andrews. "Here, you drive. It's my turn to be amused."

Their faint laughter rang in the emptiness of the early hour. As they got in the car, Andrews glanced at the dashboard clock. It was nearing four in the morning and they had much more to do. Peng curled up in the passenger seat and David switched on the ignition. The motor kicked over testily, caught, and they headed back down the mountainous route.

The Peak Road was still, haven once more to its gods and ghosts.

CHAPTER TWENTY-THREE

———————

He snores. Hot, cotton-candy night. Every movement forced; sweaty, greasy. The bed creaks. The room, dark but for the cheap, red light fringing the entry, creeping in from the hallway onto the shadows; long, mocking, sleazy. A circular bed, fluffy purple, puffed headboard, flouncy, quilted blankets tumbled askew and mirrors on all walls.

Mei rolled over onto her side; the ritualistic love rites she performed for money were complete. The grunts and groans, pawing and panting were replaced by an empty, mocking silence, broken only by the throaty phlegm-filled snores of the man beside her.

He was asleep. Good. The liquor had done its work.

She washed his seed from between her thighs, revolted by his passion. He was sloppy—uncaring and sloppy. She sat at the mirror and began to brush her hair, glancing over her shoulder at the figure on the bed as she did so. A youngster really, that's all he was, an ugly, pimple-faced youngster.

He had been comic at first, stumbling around the room in his filthy jockey shorts, fumbling at her bra straps. He truly needed his glasses. He had been angry when she'd innocently asked him why he never wore them to bed. He didn't have to scream at her for asking.

So, frightened by his outburst, she had said no more. In that manner he had taken her, without preliminaries, with no attempt at affection or kindness. The glasses now lay on the side table next to his clothes, a testament to his deepest fears and lifelong anguish.

The knife was at her throat before she knew it, and his free hand was over her mouth to muffle her screams. The smell of whiskey and sweat and rancid rice breath overwhelmed her. She looked up at his image looming above her in the mirror and her eyes filled with terror.

The youth was suddenly very sober, very aware and very frightening. His naked chest heaved from the excitement of the moment. His eyes were sharp, clear, like those of a wolverine stalking its prey. And she saw his arms, thin, sinewy, tracked with the death scars of the *do-yau*—the heroin addict. She had known this one was capable of anything.

"Hush, little bitch. Be still," he hissed, "and you won't be hurt." He tightened his grasp over Mei's face till she felt she might pass out. The knife edge glistened.

"I have some things to ask you. Do you understand?"

She nodded feverishly. Anything, anything not to face the knife.

"If I remove my hand, you may speak, but only when I ask you a question," he whispered menacingly in her ear. "Make a false move, make an unexpected sound and you'll be left a whore fit only for the blind. Is that clear?" He stroked the blade teasingly across her face. Mei shivered in terror and nodded again.

"Good," the youth said. "Good. I'm glad you're beginning to appreciate my finer attributes."

He slowly eased his hand from her mouth but kept the knife by Mei's throat. His breathing was rushed. Sweat trickled freely down his lean body. He did not seem concerned about interruptions. It was as if he knew there wouldn't be any.

"Did Williams ever tell you what he was after just before he died?"

"What?" she began. "Brendan?"

"Yes, you slut," he rasped impatiently, "the maggot Williams."

She was silent. The youth waited a few seconds, then repeated his question.

"What was he after in those last few days?" he demanded. "Surely he must have told you something."

Mei's eyes filled with terror. She did not have an answer. She did not know. "I'm sorry," she began, but it was too late. He slapped her heavily across the face. She winced in pain. He hit her a second time. The jade brooch flew out of her hair and smashed against the far wall. Blood began to trickle from her mouth.

She was shaking uncontrollably. A low cry forced its way from the back of her throat, a cry of abject fear.

He pulled her hair, jerking her head back till tears glistened in her eyes.

"And this bastard Andrews?" he pressed. "What is he seeking?"

"I don't know," she sobbed. "Please. Believe me. I don't know."

"In all the time you've been with him since Williams's death, he hasn't told you what he wants?"

She shook her head. "No," she blurted out. "He's said nothing."

He did not hide his disbelief. "What were you then? A good lay and nothing more? Surely he speaks of his work?"

"No," she cried hysterically, repeating the word as if it were a charm to relieve her of this terror. "No."

"That's too bad, then, isn't it?" the man said. "It would have been so easy to spare you."

He moved his hand over her eyes. She did not resist. There was no point in struggling. She knew what was to come.

He slashed the knife across her face several times. The cold steel tore into her skin, leaving gaping wounds from which blood poured freely. A harsh blackness engulfed Mei, and she passed out. She slumped limply to the ground, a pool of rich red blood growing around her head like a halo.

Then he stabbed her in the chest, deeply, and with great hatred so that the knife was soaked.

He stood over the body and snorted in disgust, his duty done. This one was as good as dead. The European would be pleased. He had earned his reward, five hundred Hong Kong dollars.

"Was I any good, whore?" he whispered anxiously as he peered down at the body. "Was I as good as the white devils?" And then, carefully, he wiped the blood stains from his knife.

Mei lay unconscious for some time. Then, gradually—almost in slow motion—she could feel herself regaining consciousness. She sensed the blood, warm and sticky on her face, and also the deep wound, burning like a white heat in her chest. She gasped weakly for air, tasted blood, spat it out, felt her lungs fill with it once more. She crawled over to the wall and lay up against it. Her hand brushed against something. It was Brendan's jade brooch, broken open and shattered. And inside it a tiny rolled-up spool of film. Was this what the bastard had been after?

Peng sipped tea in a shabby bun shop. After a few hours of fruitless work, contacting people with nothing left to say, going over reports that said nothing new, he'd left Andrews at Western. Against the young man's protestations, he'd suggested David get a few hours sleep while he'd gone off alone to mull over the work to date.

Peng was stiff from being driven down too many narrow, cobblestone streets, with too little rest and not enough useful information coming his way. The tea was weak and tepid. He scowled at the owner as though he could make him mend his ways with a look alone. What an idiot I am, he thought. Save the world. A one-man crusade for justice. That was it. What did Cleve always say? "Safe as houses." Not around here, he thought, smiling.

Outside, after a moment's thought, he decided to stretch his legs and walk the block over to Nathan Road. The early-morning streets were hot and sullen. Rubbish was everywhere, along with the faint animal-like scent of conflict. Many stores were shuttered and businesses closed, yet the people scampered about, beginning their daily activities.

Long neon signs hung over the street, demanding attention. He shouldered his way through the human traffic for several hundred yards, was just beginning to think of walking back to the car when he saw it, his sign, the symbol on the matchbox. He stopped, then nearly laughed out loud. It wasn't the character *Shia*, which meant armor.

With the addition of a few simple strokes, it had taken on a new meaning altogether, becoming *shin-yut*, September.

He turned on his heels and headed back the way he'd come.

I'm getting too old for this work, he thought. Beginning to see things. *Shin-yut*—September—I'll be seeing elephants next.

But the characters *shin yut* didn't go away. He couldn't laugh them away. As he walked off Nathan Road and up toward the car, the word tickled his memory. September. He knew something about September, but what was it?

Within the hour, Peng was back at headquarters reexamining sealed files scattered about his work table. The files had come from the central records storage room where the few remaining items having to do with the war were kept. It had only been a few weeks ago that this particular batch of files, contained in a chocolate-brown folio and simply marked "Japanese occupation—Sham Shui Po Camp 1941-1945," had crossed his desk in the on-going stocktaking of old war papers.

It had taken Peng four solid days to read through the reports. Scattered throughout were the vague black and white photographs of scarecrow bodies silhouetted against the ever-present concertina wire of the camps. There were also pages and pages of statements in Chinese, Japanese, French, Dutch—now faded and worn, with appropriate translations into the Queen's English attached where it had been deemed appropriate. Here and there, among the documents, were blurred minute sheets from the original investigation teams; stapled to these, foolscap with the scribbled critiques and intrusions of countless anonymous readers.

Peng found the heading marked "Prisoner's Interviews" and took out its contents. For nearly twenty minutes he flipped through the uneven yellowed pages, fingers tracing the margins, looking for the clue he knew would lead him to September. Somewhere there was a Chinese character, a code name for an agent, one of the few not properly identified at war's end, one that had always intrigued his peers and predecessors on the force.

Then he remembered. St. Jamestown. A Canadian soldier from St. Jamestown, Quebec.

He pored through the sheets until he found the debriefing of Corporal Peter Burdzinski, Royal Rifles of Canada, born in St. Jamestown, Quebec. The interview had taken place in September, 1945, at the British Army Hospital, Stanley Barracks, Hong Kong, just prior to Burdzinski's repatriation.

> By the morning hours of Christmas Day 1941, even the most naive among us on the island knew the jig was up. The governor, Sir Mark Young, broadcast a Christmas message I'll never forget. He asked us to fight on and "Hold fast for King

and Empire in this our finest hour." Silly words, those, especially when we'd been doing without sleep for days, with almost no ammunition, scarcely any food and a dearth of water. Communication with our mates in Wanchai had ceased when the Japs severed the southern telephone exchange. There were enemy advance parties in the most strategic Peak mansions overlooking the entire island. Mortar fire rained down at us from far off on that scorching hot December day. All along our lines, rumors abounded about Jap atrocities.

The bastards had massacred a group of Saint John's ambulance stretcher bearers when they surrendered at Happy Valley medical post. They'd bayoneted helpless wounded at the Silesian Mission Hospital at Shaukiwan. They'd gang raped nurses and nuns without mercy at Lyemun Fort. From our perimeter bunkers, we'd looked out with binoculars and seen prisoners shot at point-blank range after they'd laid down their arms. So we knew what we were up against. Regardless of the governor's pronouncements, we weren't in the mood for chatter and empty words.

The remaining fellows in my section, along with the barc guts of the other units left to defend the colony, had holed up around Stanley Fort to wait for the end we knew was coming. There weren't many of us left from the platoon, let alone the regiment. Jake Poirier had died by then, as had the kid from Sept Isles, "Smiley" Gagnon. And the Englishman, Criswell. So many of the old sweats in the Rifles had bought it. But we didn't give up. Stubbornness, I guess. It wasn't anything else. Perhaps we didn't know how to die.

By mid-morning the Japs had allowed a truce so the English could ponder whether or not to surrender, and we'd used up the last of our tobacco and coffee. Pinkie Ward had some Christmas cake he'd winkled out of some toff's home in the retreat from Repulse Bay; we shared the crumbs along with a partial bottle of whiskey.

Our trench was red clay clawed into jungle foliage above a mammoth storm sewer. It had a clear view northward to the one road leading into the village, and provided us with at least the illusion of protection.

And that's about all we had left at the end. Illusions. Like the talk from the governor about putting on a brave last stand. That's all it was, talk for the home fires.

At midday the shelling began again, a creeping barrage that shattered our nerves as it came ever closer. We retreated back to St. Stephen's College and then, as the Japs entered the village in waves, moved still further south past the prison. It looked like it was just about over.

Our sector commander, a captain named Thumper Finnerty, led about forty of us into the surrounding hills away from the onslaught. It was to be a fateful decision.

We hid till nightfall, looking down at the darkened village of Stanley, occasionally hearing the staccato burps of Jap machine guns and the screams of what we knew were our mates below.

Suddenly, out of the darkness by our position, there was a sound of crackling underbrush and the beating back of jungle growth. We tensed. It was a Chinese, Ah Saam, the manservant assigned to the Captain. Ah Saam had been missing for the past few hours of our retreat, but he'd made his way back up from the village to pass on the news that the British garrison had surrendered at 3:15 p.m. He told us what was happening in Stanley. The Japanese were drunk. They were looting, shooting prisoners, ravaging the nurses assigned to the hospital.

For Finnerty, Ah Saam also had a challenging proposal. He hated the Japanese with a passion, had lost relatives in the massacre of Nanking and would do anything he could to get even with them. He had a relative in Aberdeen fishing village who possessed an old junk. He'd convinced the man to help his British friends make the dash along the east coast to Mirs Bay, and there they would strike inland through occupied Japanese territory to the Nationalist capital of Chungking. He was quite blunt about it. He was offering Finnerty and anyone who wanted to risk it a chance at freedom.

Thumper was a fair and open man. He discussed the proposal with us as a group. He'd supply those who wanted to run with weapons and fair rations. For his own, he chose to surrender. I understand he had a local girl among the nursing sisters at Bowen Road. He loved her too much to leave her to the uncertain fates of occupation. He'd cast his fate in the POW camps and wait for her until the inevitable Allied return.

Eleven of us opted to run the gauntlet with Ah Saam. Seven Canucks, a limey cook from Middlesex who'd tagged along the past few days and become one of us, and three Rajputs. Thumper divvied up the food stuffs, then gave us the weaponry: two Thompson guns and the remaining ammunition and workable Lee Enfields.

Near midnight, with the best wishes of all ringing in our ears, we were off. After a half hour's cautious journey northward, we reached Tai Tam main road. Above us we could hear a Jap patrol. They were rollicking drunk. Shouting, carousing, shooting ammo into the sky. The roar of an engine told us there was a tank escorting them. It was no time for bravery. We stuck to the shadows.

We went north two hundred yards to Red Hill and then down some steep rocks to the water's edge and our destination, Turtle Cove Beach. There it was, our passport to freedom: a grimy, tar-trimmed sampan. Ah Saam told us the sampan would take us to the junk, anchored further off the cove in a sheltered part of the bay. And we believed him.

The searchlights that flooded the beach a moment later trapped us like flies on bug paper. A machine gun kicked up flics of sand at our feet. A second one joined in from the far slope. Three of the lads bought it outright, their blood splattering us as we stood frozen in terror.

The Japs came hopping down the hillside skree like monkeys out of caves. They were jabbering away, whether in anger or sheer glee, we couldn't tell. And then they were upon us, maybe forty of them, a captain at their head.

We raised our hands and surrendered. How little did we know of samurai honor! The Rajputs were first to go. Stuck mercilessly, again and again, until the bayonets glinted crimson.

And then it was the Brit cook's turn. Newcombe, the poor sod, made the mistake of kneeling and begging for mercy. They chopped off his head and it rolled across the sand like a soccer ball, spurting jets of blood, its features twitching violently.

Pilon and Geoffrion were next. They panicked when they saw Newcombe's execution, and made a run for freedom. A second later they were dead—shot in their tracks, then hacked apart by the captain's sword. A fitting tribute to his honor.

The rest of us were spared. Not for any reason except maybe because we were too exhausted to react. We just stood there like yellow-bellied scarecrows, cowering, shaking in our boots.

And that bastard Ah Saam—or whatever his name was—was there as well, right next to the Jap captain, getting his shekels, no doubt. I see him even today, standing there motionless, with that stupid walking cane in his hand, gesturing to the Jap as though he was an important man instead of a lowly servant. And when the Toyota half ton pulled up to take the officers back inland to their camp, Ah Saam was invited into it like an honored guest.

It was 1942, late October, that I heard of him again. I was on the escape committee in Sham Shui Po camp. A fat-faced Eurasian captain from the Volunteers came to us with a proposal to run the gauntlet, and try the wire after midnight. To escape to his Kowloon mistress, probably.

In his frenzy for freedom, he tried to curry my favor. He'd heard I was one of the Stanley crowd and he had information that would attest to his credibility. He told me about Ah Saam, that Ah Saam was in reality a Kuo Min Tang agent code named September, a man so important to Chiang Kai Shek's war effort that he was worth a thousand lives. September had been parachuted into Hong Kong at the end to bring back valuable information to the KMT in Chungking, but he'd disappeared into the woodwork, never to be seen again.

Ah Saam was September. But it didn't matter what the fat man said. We didn't trust him and we rejected his escape plan outright. It wasn't worth our necks to save his.

Perhaps what he related was true, about the man named September and his loyalty to the Kuo Ming Tang cause. Maybe he had to sacrifice us to protect his own cover. Maybe it was part of a larger, more necessary plan. But all I know is he had us set up and six of us died, Indians, Chinese and white. I saw him drive away with the Nips and, to my dying day, I swear that man was a traitor. He should be hanged for turning us in.

Ah Saam, September, whatever his bloody name was—I'll never forget what he looked like, and especially that cane he had—a fine mahogany walking stick with a gold and jade phoenix on it. A phoenix for luck, he'd told us.

For luck. Damn him.

A scribbled notation stated simply that Corporal Peter Burdzinski had died in early 1946 at the Royal Canadian Navy hospital at Esquimault, British Columbia, as a result of his war wounds. He was buried with full military honors.

Peng turned the page. There were staple marks on the side of the document, what looked to be tear marks on the sheet. Where was the comment section? Peng knew he'd seen it before. Where was it now?

A hurried call to records. "No, sir. No one has taken the file since—" the sound of pages rustling "—the entry is in your name, sir. On the eleventh of August. Returned by you on the sixteenth. Yes, I'm certain, sir." Peng hung up. Only a few people had access to the report, fewer still would have an interest.

The phone rang. Records again, an apologetic clerk. There had been a mistake. The file had been taken out by someone, quite recently, in fact—only yesterday evening, and returned shortly thereafter. Did the superintendent require the borrower's name?

Peng took a blank piece of paper and scribbled the information onto it. He showed no surprise as he wrote; it was too late for that. Finished, he politely thanked the clerk and hung up, then cursed under his breath. His hands pounded the table. He knew he had been beaten. More frustrating, he began to understand why.

The borrower was none other than Robert Maguire from Special Branch.

Peng swiveled to the typewriter and pounded out a few lines: "Henry Szeto was once a KMT operative. He used the code name 'September' in his professional dealings and is strongly suspected of collaboration with Japanese authorities in World War Two. Source considered reliable. Strongly believed to be involved in present drug transaction. Cannot be corroborated. Proof destroyed. Unknown 'Simon Chan' project coming to an end. Results on the scar-faced suicide forthcoming. Will advise."

Then Peng took a new page and typed all the data on the borrower of the September file.

He placed this second sheet in an envelope and addressed

it to John Cleve, sealed it, and initialed the seams of the letter, just in case. He trusted very few people any more.

Peng took the report and the letter and placed them at the
center of Cleve's desk. "Woodcutter?" He laughed. Let the
chips fall where they may.

Now there remained but one question unanswered.
Returning to his office he dialed the number for Western
police station.

"Is Inspector Andrews in?"

"A moment, sir, he'll be right with you."

Soon the effort spent on Simon Chan would also bear
fruit, and in his heart Peng knew it had everything to do
with an old man nicknamed Woodcutter and a dead
policeman named Williams.

He patiently waited for the phone to be answered. "Hello,
Davie, Jim Peng here. Ready for some more work?"

The phone service was slow. Four rings. Six. Seven. She persisted. Ten rings. Please answer. Someone please answer!

Finally, a voice, irritated, exhausted. "Western Officer's
Mess. Senior Inspector Todd here."

Mei summoned up her strength and asked for David.

"What? Oh, he's not here. He's just stepped out." The
Englishman was young, impatient.

Mei, weak from pain and loss of blood, her face swollen,
found herself unable to speak."Is there any message?" Inspector Todd challenged the silence.

"It's about the death of a policeman named Brendan Williams," Mei whispered weakly. "I think I might have some
evidence. . ."

The faint breathing suddenly ceased. It was strangely quiet
on the line. Quiet for the longest time.

Todd again spoke into the phone, this time anxiously
hoping for a reply. There was none. And then, as he had
been ordered to do, he telephoned Jim Peng.

CHAPTER TWENTY-FOUR

A t 07:00, the first announcement was broadcast on Radio Hong Kong. Many Europeans had been sitting back, sedately observing the disturbance as if it were a matinée on the television. Now they panicked. Full curfews and martial law were in place. The governor directed everyone to stay calm, to ride out the storm, with little effect.

At Ocean Terminal, bold lettering in English, French, Dutch, Chinese and German announced that two ships, the *Rotterdam* and the SS *France,* had canceled their departures indefinitely, without explanation. Marine police were called to expel passengers hiding in the ships' bowels rather than risk confrontation with the "Yellow Peril."

At Kaitak airport, enormous traffic jams choked the morning rush hour and flight counters were besieged with armies of resident Europeans as the expatriate community, laden with satchels, luggage, cameras, handbags, guitars and tape recorders, decided flight was the only alternative.

At 07:33, there was a stabbing at the Philippine Airways counter.

At 08:11, an Indonesian businessman died at Queen Elizabeth Hospital emergency as a result of those wounds.

At 08:18, the Deputy Commissioner of Police/Kowloon closed the airport. Two riot companies were called in, and a tense fifteen minute confrontation ensued as a group of

drunk American executives made a last stand at the Japan
Airlines counter. They faced an equally determined group of
Chinese police constables.

The businessmen backed down.

There were six major explosions in Kowloon—four of
them on Hong Kong Island, all plastique, all professional.
Two were in Kowloon City, on the bus routes to the airport.
Seventeen people were injured, none seriously.

But the rioters, whatever their allegiance, had accom-
plished their goal. In blistering heat and ninety-six percent
humidity, some forty-two thousand vehicles in Kowloon
moved along at the rate of four feet per minute for the next
three and a half hours. The situation on Hong Kong Island
was no better.

Inevitably, flare-ups occurred: on streets, beside cars, on
buses, in business offices, outside banks. A heady mix of
traffic, temper and heat combined with frustration and anger.

Traffic policemen shrewdly stood by and waited for par-
ticipants to spend their anger before interfering. In Happy
Valley, Hong Kong side, an over-eager traffic sergeant made
the mistake of stepping in to settle a dispute. He had both
arms broken and one eye badly gouged before he was
dragged, bleeding, to safety.

The government received an anonymous tip that there was
a bomb planted in the cross-harbor tunnel. The authorities
considered ordering it closed, and called the tunnel master
who halted the traffic while he waited for further instructions. But two lorries at the head of the line at Hung Hom,
Kowloon side, were set ablaze merely because they had
stopped. The tunnel was kept open.

So be it. If people wished to be swept from traffic jam to
traffic jam, there was little that could be done to prevent it.
And the bumper-to-bumper, carbon monoxide dragon went
huffing, puffing blue-gray smoke into the tunnel entrance to
choke on its own fumes, as tunnel staff and police stood in-
differently back. Mass suicide could not have been more effectively planned.

A goods lorry at the Jordan road ferry pier was flung into
the gleaming, green China Sea when its motor stalled and,

blocking the junction, it prevented other vehicles from escaping the snail's pace of Kowloon's urban core. The driver swam to safety.

Bus and streetcar routes were carefully monitored. At the slightest hint of trouble, drivers were instructed to abandon their vehicles. The routes of the Kowloon Motor Bus Company near the poorer resettlement estates were strewn with charred and blackened Austin double deckers, scuttled and left to their doom at the hands of the rampaging mobs. Soon even buses traveled under police escort, or in multiple bus convoys, if they traveled at all. Mini buses jacked their fares one hundred, and sometimes three hundred, percent. By mid-morning, a seventy-five-cent fare from Kennedy Town to North Point was going for twelve dollars, no questions asked.

Police switchboards were jammed with calls of bomb threats and scares as pranksters had a field day. But there were real bombs, too, left in empty lifts, in crowded lobbies and in the garbage cans placed on tram islands. Trained bomb disposal personnel raced from call to call on their Yamaha 450s, their only tools, Scotch tape, pliers, bravado and the grace of God.

By 10:50 there had been more than a hundred threats, nineteen of them real, seven serious. A mother and her child had been killed at Pokfulam Village; a couple of schoolchildren were seriously injured in an elevator at Lai Chi Kok. On Salisbury Road, a young Kiwi inspector lost four fingers when a clock device tripped and detonated before he could clip the mechanism.

At 11:00 the governor closed all schools, and businesses followed suit, padlocking their premises to disgruntled employees. Workers and students joined the milling throngs in the streets where there was a carnival-like atmosphere. Hawkers sold sunhats, Coca-Cola, chicken claws, almond ice creams, Dairy Farm chocolate. The air was electric. In such an atmosphere, one tiny spark could ignite a major conflagration.

Early that day, in the cool, sane hours of morning, John Cleve had wisely ordered out the Police Saracen armored car unit from its coven at Fanling and sent it to its standby points at major urban intersections. And there they stood, just off from the roads, waiting for that spark. And the heat poured down, unabated.

Formaldehyde and cold ice chips. Bare off-white walls with cracks that traced their way downward like the frantic life lines of dying men. Gray, ground pellet floors and row upon row of box-like compartments.

Kennedy Town Morgue was the colony's largest, the Government's only. It was poetic irony that the morgue was located next to the abattoir. The more cynical detectives wondered if the staff practised and perfected their trade in the hog stalls adjacent to Her Majesty's Facility, or if they were rejects from the same.

David Andrews had not been to the morgue for some time. His visit today was urgent and unusual. Andrews was intrigued, by the Blue Cloud mansion, by Henry Szeto, by Simon Chan. What intrigued him most was the call he had made a few minutes earlier, at Peng's behest, to Special Branch, to follow up the scar-face suicide named Simon.

There was no Proctor at SB, the stilted voice had replied impatiently. No one had ever heard of him.

And, if Proctor was not known there, what of Simon Chan?

Andrews had called back Peng, who had been surprisingly calm about the matter. Yes, he'd check the back rooms at Caine House, knock on a few doors, nudge a few elbows to learn who Proctor was. Perhaps he used another name. He'd get back to David, who then agreed it might prove fruitful to do more work on the cadaver known as Simon Chan. Leg work. Alone.

The doors swung open. A portly figure in a sickly green operating gown that fit him like a tent bounded into the room, sweating profusely. He wore gold bifocals on the tip of a hawkish nose and his sparse black hair was matted by brilliantine and combed to one side in a half-hearted attempt at vanity. His skin color, normally Hispanic olive, was wan—his features, puffy and ill-defined like some of his permanent guests. His hands were wet and he wiped them sloppily across his massive chest.

"My name is Emmanual De Silva." He spoke with a slurred voice. "Doctor De Silva." He emphasized the term as if to underline his identity, although it was self-evident. "You can call me Manny."

Emmanual De Silva was Portuguese and proud of it. Educated at the University of Lisbon, then at UCLA on money his father made in the garment trade in far-off Goa, De Silva had made his home in Macau in a political mileu he'd found most suitable to his tastes. Then the political winds had changed and cast him on these shores. The enterprise of the people of Hong Kong easily suited his needs and emotional requirements. Here he made good money doing what he did best. Being a government coroner and forensic pathologist was his way of repaying his debt to the British Crown colony he had adopted as his own. Andrews knew him by reputation as being astute, aspiring and upwardly mobile.

De Silva took Andrews by the arm and led him down the long corridor.

"The receptionist indicated it was urgent, inspector. We've laid out the body for your inspection." De Silva spoke in a half-confiding whisper, a sing-song voice that oozed informality, perhaps overly so. De Silva reminded Andrews of a mortician, a cultured *compradore*.

"No autopsy was ordered, you realize. He's been with us a few days. No next of kin. We're going to have him sent to Queen Mary Hospital for dissection. They have a medical school there, you know."

They entered a long hallway lined with closed doors. By each door was a clipboard on a table, a chromed wash basin with basic utensils: scalpels, knives, mallets. De Silva guided David to the far end of the hall where they stopped outside the room marked #8, the black number stenciled on a silver background.

"Yes, this is the room."

. He handed David a set of plastic gloves and a surgical mask. "I suggest you wear these," he said as he replaced his own. "One never knows with these bodies. . . ." He peered over the glasses as he adjusted one of the gloves. Then he opened the door.

Andrews followed the doctor into a tiny room which was well-lit and functionally tiled in the same pea green as were the walls in the corridors. There was a table and beside it a wash basin and sterilizing equipment. The body lay on a high stretcher covered in starched white cotton.

De Silva flipped the covering off with a majestic swirl. "Is this the man you want to see?" His voice was muffled, distant behind the mask.

Andrews stepped closer. He felt no revulsion this time, just a strange curiosity as he peered down at the remains. The body looked sadly vulnerable, naked, not nearly as horrific as before. "Yes, this is it." He nodded. He considered the cadaver carefully, his fingers touching the dead man's hands in what appeared to be a curious gesture of benediction.

De Silva paid no attention to the policeman. His patience was being strained. He had better things to do with his time than bother with this impertinent and imperious young man. He picked up a chart from the table and began to read from it, mechanically, as he would to a class of wet-eared interns.

"Simon Chan, male Chinese, apparent age is forty-four. Height: 5 feet 5 inches. Weight: 145 pounds. Description: an average bone structure, had a facial scar approximately three inches long from left cheekbone to jaw. No visible birth deformities. Appendix scar. Tonsils removed. Nicotine deposits on fingertips indicate a heavy smoker.

"Apparent cause of death asphyxiation caused by strangulation in the area of the larynx."

De Silva finished the final sentence as if he'd read from a menu, and not one he had a particular taste for.

Andrews turned abruptly to the doctor. "This man is not Simon Chan."

"What?" The bifocals sparkled as they reflected the overhead light.

"I said this man is not Simon Chan."

"Why do you say that?" De Silva's voice was suddenly uneasy. Controversy was the last thing he wanted at this stage of his comfortable career. His government pension was far too near.

"I called the police records bureau just before I came here." Andrews took a notebook from his breast pocket, opened it to a thumb-flapped page, and continued. "There was a Simon Chan reported missing by Mongkok Division on 21 August, and *he* is known to us. Single, with two brothers, forty-four years of age, he has a scar on his face, just like this man." He motioned to the dead body. "Caused by a gang fight."

"So?" The impatient look. De Silva clearly could not see what this fellow was getting at and he didn't like to be toyed with. "Can we get to the point?"

"Certainly, doctor." Andrews forced a smile. "This man seems to be an exact double for Simon Chan." He closed his notebook and put it back in his shirt pocket. "In every way but one."

"And that is?" De Silva could not hide his curiosity.

"Simon Chan had a cross tattooed at the base of his right thumb." Andrews touched the body. "This man has a tattoo, but on his left thumb." He paused. "And it wasn't the best of jobs." He motioned to the hand. The area around the tattoo was raw, infected. "This looks like a recent tattoo, and a poor one at that. In 1968, when Chan was arrested for the first time, his identification chart listed a cross on his right thumb. A bit odd, don't you think, that it would change hands and get infected after all these years? A bit. . . impossible?"

De Silva's eyebrows arched above the surgical mask. "No autopsy was done, you realize," De Silva said uneasily. "Nothing in the report suggested foul play. There were no orders to inspect the body." De Silva was struggling to regain his composure.

"Now, doctor, can you repeat the cause of death?"

De Silva glanced at the clipboard. "The deceased died from asphyxiation of the larynx and tracheal areas."

"Strangulation."

"Yes, that is the popular term for it." The physician wiped his forehead with the back of a gloved hand.

Andrews peered down at the body with practised eyes. "Strangulation?" he uttered in a sharp tone. He glanced back at the doctor with cold, hard eyes. "And these bruises to the neck?" He pointed to several coin-like blotches below the reddened rope burn. "Are they not finger marks, doctor?"

De Silva nosed closer; his eyes shifted nervously. He muttered a cautious yes.

"So it is in the realm of possibility that this man was manually strangled and then roped up to make it look as if he had committed suicide?"

De Silva looked bleakly at David. His tone of voice matched his expression. "Why would anyone do that?"

"Why does anyone murder, doctor? I suggest to you again that someone strangled this male Chinese, roped him up like a slab of beef, and in such a manner that he looked like he had taken his own life. Now, doctor, what do you say to that?"

De Silva pondered the thought. "Possible, Inspector Andrews. Possible. But not probable." An edgy silence. "The evidence points to strangulation by a taut device." He gathered steam. "We have the rope. It is the correct gauge to accomplish this feat. That is the end of the matter as far as this office is concerned, inspector. That is the truth as far as I believe it to be."

"Very well, doctor. As you wish." Andrews leaned against the table and crossed his arms. His voice was curious, in- triguing.

"Doctor De Silva," he said, "let us assume for a moment then that strangulation by manual means is not beyond the realm of possibility." He politely deflected the doctor's attempt at rebuttal.

Andrews was still looking at the body, trying to find more evidence for his theory. He looked at De Silva.

"Can you tell me more about this coolie? Can we get fingernail clippings to determine where he worked? What he did? Is there something on his skin that might give us an idea of what he had contact with before he died?"

De Silva stared at the policeman. He opened his mouth, then closed it again.

"Is there something wrong, doctor?" David asked.

"This man is not a coolie, Inspector Andrews."

"What?"

"He was never a coolie. The police preliminary investigation in front of me makes no mention of it." He adopted the practised tone of the coroner. "The muscle tone is too flabby." He poked at the arms. "Like jelly—no tension. The chest is a small cavity, no built-up lung capacity. No pectoral development in the upper arms. And see here." He gestured to the hands. "Smooth. No calluses." The doctor moved along the body. "The legs are too underdeveloped for the walking one would expect of a laborer. No arterial development. No varicose veins." He moved up the torso again and looked down at the face. "The scar. I know you are interested in it." A pause for thought. "It is hard to say, but I would venture to guess that is was innocently acquired in adult life."

"Why?" David asked.

De Silva, now almost as intrigued as Andrews and no longer impatient, thought about the question carefully. "The stitching around the seams is too professional; a clean neat job. The man may have been in an accident, perhaps. He sought medical attention. Why no plastic surgery? Maybe he thought the scar added an aura of mystery, of covert violence. Who can say?"

"Would you go over the findings again? In detail?"

De Silva took the chart in his hand and commenced the reading once more.

David Andrews listened with renewed interest. He asked questions, about the pectoral development, the lack of dirt in the fingernails, anything that might give him more of a picture of this mysterious corpse and the reason for its curious and violent demise. But there was nothing.

The doctor finished the report and set the chart on the table, then waited patiently. Andrews stood looking down at the body, still searching for a clue. Finally he thanked the doctor and began to leave, turning one last time to look at the dead man, and then over to De Silva.

"Yes, inspector?" The forced politeness.

"What about the ring?" He pointed to the right hand. On the ring finger was a thin gold band.

De Silva began to explain. The man had rigor mortis and arthritis. It was customary to have jewelry removed and kept for safekeeping but, with all the commotion about these days, it hadn't been done yet.

"And the medical dissection scheduled for this man?"

"Really, inspector! We would gather all valuables and return them to the police for referral to next-of-kin prior to that."

"Let me see the ring."

De Silva looked at the policeman incredulously. "It won't come off."

"Then cut it off."

De Silva didn't move.

"I said *cut it off!*"

The shrug, the pettiness in his voice as the Portuguese made to comply. "Very well then, Inspector. But I shall expect a receipt for the item, you know."

"You will have a receipt, doctor. And my signature on as many forms as you wish."

De Silva stared at Andrews for several seconds, then moved to the side table.

The cutting saw buzzed, then gleamed brightly in the bare white light. De Silva placed it over the dead man's finger and began to push down.

The bone was easy to cut through. The job was not at all as messy as Andrews had expected. Little showers of bone and gristle flew up like the filaments of calcium spray at the dentist.

"Just like cutting a chicken bone, eh?" De Silva chuckled.

Andrews said nothing.

De Silva shook the cut-off appendage as he would a salt shaker. The ring plopped into his hand and he gave it to Andrews.

David looked at it carefully. White gold, possibly fourteen karat. The design was simple. He held the ring closer, saw an engraving inside: NPT 1975–1983 HKR Vols.

The man's initials might be NPT. And now Andrews knew

that the man had been in the militia, he'd been a member of the Hong Kong Regiment, the Volunteers.

David glanced up to see the doctor regarding him curiously. "Anything?" The odd smile.

"No. Nothing," he replied stonily as he palmed the ring, put it in his pocket and reached for the hospital receipt De Silva force upon him.

He quickly scribbled his name on the form. "Who signed the police report?" he asked without looking up.

The doctor took the clipboard and leafed through the pages. "Peng," he said. "A police superintendent named James Peng."

David's jaw clenched. "Oh, the last question, doctor, if I may inquire." He caught De Silva's expression. The man's patience was at the breaking point. "Did anyone ask after the body?" He saw the man's indecision and gauged it correctly. "It could save a lengthy public investigation."

Andrews knew when the reply came that he'd measured the man correctly. The last thing De Silva wanted was a homicide investigation, for whatever reason.

The doctor replied slowly, cautiously, perhaps realizing how crucial his words were and how his own fate as a civil servant might depend on it.

"There was one man who asked after the deceased, but he never actually bothered to look in." He paused. "Perhaps you knew him? An unusual chap. His name was Proc. . ." He stumbled over the unfamiliar name.

"Proctor?" Andrews offered.

"That's it." De Silva beamed. "Anthony Proctor. He's one of yours, isn't he?"

"Yes, yes. I suppose in a way he is." Andrews replied to no one in particular as he walked away, leaving De Silva nothing but a swinging door.

Cleve was drawing Chinese characters on his blotter, wondering about September and Henry Szeto, wondering about the syndicate that supplied the wares of people like Elephant Man. If September was dying, he reasoned, a replacement would have to come out of the shadows if the syndicate were to continue. Then Superintendent Dunn arrived to report on the tactical unit's preparations for the day.

After his usual loud greeting, Dunn settled into a chair. He and Cleve began to go through the special security Dunn had worked out for the Hakka boy's funeral procession. But Dunn paused. He could see that his old friend was preoccupied.

"Too bad about the turn things have taken in the streets, John," he began sympathetically. "This personal attack, it's just propaganda, we all know that."

Cleve didn't seem to hear him.

"The governor and the press. Bloody hell. Birds of a feather." He waved his arms about. "Birds of prey."

Cleve smiled grimly, then sighed. "Oh, I suppose it doesn't matter any more. Let the Triads and the syndicates and the Burdens and the Septembers and Hans run the bloody colony. If they make it work as well as they run the drug trade, we can all go home and put up our feet."

"Rather. Make our women happy." Dunn looked questioningly at Cleve.

"Don't ask, my friend, don't ask," Cleve said sadly. "It's enough to say that she and the governor share a common opinion of me at this moment."

Dunn puffed his cheeks, frowned, started to speak, then thought better of it and turned to go. When he left the room, he closed the door softly and Cleve was, for a moment, startled. The first door Digger hasn't slammed in years, he thought.

CHAPTER TWENTY-FIVE

────────

At 07:56 hours, at an undetermined point in one of the fifty-seven exchanges in the Crown colony, a male picked up a telephone owned by the Hong Kong telephone company. A well-manicured index finger moved over the dial with some difficulty. There were liver spots on the fingers, two of which were decorated tastefully with jade and amethyst rings.

The telephone rang quite a few times, but the caller was patient. While he waited, he read a letter that had just been delivered to his private suite by a government courier. It was from His Excellency, the Governor of Hong Kong, and it complimented him obliquely on his persistence and congratulated him on his inclusion in their "collective scheme."

On the tenth ring, a rushed voice answered. "Police. . ."

The male caller whispered unhurriedly into the receiver. "Tse Tsi Fai, the murderer of Yip Lam, if you want him, will be near a divan operated by Dau Pei Kwai in the Walled City, on the second floor of a merchant's shop."

Before the startled constable could ask questions, Lee Shiu Shing hung up. The line was dead.

At police headquarters, amid the insistent cacophony of calls for bomb scares, fires, riotous assemblies, traffic accidents, fights and missing children, the information was put on a card and sent along the recorder's belt to the duty inspector's desk for action. Within moments, it was on the desk of the commissioner of police. Also on the desk was the rather unusual evidence found near a dead prostitute named Mei Ling.

The fate of Tse Tsi Fai was effectively sealed, and that of several other souls was being rapidly, and brutally, determined.

The boy was Hakka, born at Wo Hop Shek, near the ancient tiered cemetery. But his roots were in the honest clay of the New Territories, as were those of his father, who had preceded him in death by three years.

And now, in the heat of the speckled day, the sun shimmering silver on the harsh earth, he was returning home, in a simple casket of cyprus wood.

The body had been washed in water drawn from a well possessed by a guardian spirit, then swathed in cotton cloth. A lucky penny was left at the wellhead in exchange. A pearl was placed in his mouth, hidden so it would not be stolen by evil or covetous spirits, and of sufficient wealth that it would buy him the necessities of the other world. A jade snuff bottle was placed by his side so that he could partake in the carefree happiness and merriment of the gods. And because he would journey through a lonely black void before he reached lasting peace in Western Heaven, his feet were bound with hemp cord so the body would not leap about if it was tormented by demons. The boy's face and body were covered with a veil of silk, which was turned down only when he was viewed by the family for the last time.

Thus the preparations had been completed. Two days of mourning had followed; two solid days of public grief. The coffin was placed on two stools, with the head pointing to the door. A table was set before the casket and five vessels were placed on it: two vases filled with blue-and-white paper flowers; two candlesticks, which illuminated the night; and finally, a pagoda-shaped lamp stand that contained a bowl of sesame seed oil, in which a wick of twisted cotton burned.

Next to the coffin was the spirit table, which bore the name of the deceased and to which one of his souls had passed. On the table, the family placed a small portion of each of their meals for the attendant spirit of the departed one, Lai Chiu Kui. Drinks were also shared.

Visitors knelt at the head of the coffin and were served with a brass wine cup on a tray. An attendant filled this to the brim; the guests poured a portion of it into a bowl set on the floor and in this way shared a last drink with the soul of Lai. Three prostrations followed at which the entire family joined. The guests offered condolences and the family accepted. Gifts were taken to the parlor.

It was a costly funeral, and some callers left money placed in a yellow envelope tastefully wrapped in blue ribbon to indicate proper mourning. Others carried banners and scrolls to be presented to the deceased. The scrolls would be carried in the procession and would be burned after the committal service. Other guests brought gold and silver, paper money, paper cars and paper servants, clothes, fake jewelry and tiny ornaments; all these things were intended to lend splendor and substance to the funeral of a poor child whose chances in the other world were otherwise as pitiful as they had been in this one.

The night before the final cortege, the family had gathered all the paper offerings—the tiny servants with names attached, the motor cars, the clothes, the money—and taken them to an open street corner near the family home on Kui Kiang Street and burned them. In this way, they transmitted the gifts to the dead boy for his subsequent use. An attendant had beaten the ashes with a long pole to prevent the interference of wandering spirits who might steal the boy's belongings, while another had scattered boiling rice and water over the bonfire to distract the attention of hungry ghosts from the newfound property of the deceased.

Little Lai's time for final passing over the threshold had come. Saffron-robed priests, Taoist and Buddhist, chanted the offices of the funeral while the family wept. The silk cloth was lowered to expose the child's face; then the coffin was closed.

Out of the funeral home into the blazing white heat.

A crowd of several thousand had gathered outside on Argyle Street. Subdued, silent, a sea of white shirts, blue trousers, plain cotton dresses. Blue and white lanterns with paper chimneys hung from curved poles and cast a soft, flickering light. The monks chanted while their attendants clashed cymbals and clattered wood ratchets to exorcise evil from the body.

The hearse pulled up, an ancient Packard wagon, laden with white flowers, azaleas, lilies, mountain poppies and silk ribbons. The coffin was placed inside, still visible through the windows that ran along the side of the vehicle. A large framed black-and-white photo of the boy hung from the front of the auto. The smiling face was out of focus, fuzzy.

The procession began.

Street bonfires were lit along the way, with scarlet altars upon which were heaped roast pigs and baked duck and chickens. Toy cars, ships, airplanes and paper money were burned to help the boy in his travels through the gray void. At crossroads, cash bank notes were flung into the air to distract the attention of wandering evil.

A brass band of rag-tag musicians in ill-fitting white tunics played "Colonel Bogey's March" and "Hello Dolly" and "Hail to the Chief."

The procession was calm and orderly. The calm would not be broken until the boy was interred.

The Kowloon Walled City, in Chinese *Sing Ngam*, sits like an unlanced boil in the center of the most densely populated area of Kowloon. A no-man's land, an island of sorrows in a sea of plenty, its perhaps fifty thousand people live within a quarter-mile area in filth and squalor, in grime-ridden hovels piled piggyback. Most have no plumbing and pay to have water brought up from the fetid underground wells that lie beneath the surface of the old town's center. Two dollars buys two tiny plastic buckets of water, but the tenant must pay one dollar extra for each floor the water bearer must climb.

In the height of summer, when the black air simmers, leaving funnels of heat in laneways and hovels and swirling dust envelops the buildings, prices are doubled and sometimes tripled. The same water is used over and over again for cooking, washing and bathing. Anything to obtain value for the precious drops.

Many of the poor cook their meals at street level in the gloomy filth, amid evil, insect-eyed strangers next to open sewers, atop smudge pots or open propane. Fatty pork, gangrenous lamb, roach-infested vegetables—a staple diet for matchstick people, cooked amid the pungent smell of the city's sewers. The neighbors' refuse meanders underfoot in the dungy trickle streams flowing beneath pedestrian gangplanks that enable all to make their way through the narrow streets.

And what streets they are! Scarcely three feet wide, they creep through ramshackle walls of dripping concrete. More like tapering duckwalks than anything else, the streets are made of rotten timber threshed with cut bamboo, a zig-zag labyrinth of impulse and despair. Steep ladder steps, meandering catwalks, concrete-crusted nooks and crannies lead nowhere and everywhere at once.

But somehow business goes on in the Walled City as it does anywhere else in the teeming colony: dentists, their windows filled with stained false teeth; doctors and abortionists without Commonwealth qualification or license; goldsmiths hawking fake gold leaf; butchers and restaurants preparing and serving dogmeat; furniture businesses, hairdressers and whorehouses. Craftsmen some, charlatans many. All without license and regulation, all working in the permanent twilight of a mid-day gloom, mole people seeing daylight only when the sun feebly makes its way through the closely stacked houses to creep down to the darkness below.

The Kowloon Walled City.

There had been walls once, built in the 1800s by Chinese officials of the Ching Dynasty as a precautionary measure, after Hong Kong Island was ceded to the British. The walls were massive, twenty feet high and between six and twelve feet thick. Walls to protect a Chinese hierarchy bent on splendid isolation in the face of the changing realities of the nineteenth century. And isolated it stayed.

The Walled City. A bone of contention claimed by both the British and Chinese for more than a hundred years, yet

somehow wanted by neither. The Walled City, lying below
on the clear weather approach from the Diamond Hill checkerboard to Kaitak's fingerstrip runway.

A city now without walls. They were torn down in 1943
by the Japanese demolition teams who took every possible
pieces of stone for runway improvements. But the Walled
City remains isolated, a haven for the doomed and desperate,
a wall of fear separating it from the twentieth century world.

It was there on a summer morning that Tse Tsi Fai, known
to be the killer of Yip Lam, ventured into the vilest part of
the Walled City, the northwest, where all fugitives and
criminals come to hide or die. It was here he ran, to be hidden where the shadows of night linger long into day. Here,
where he could escape the long-nosed gingers and their
yellow running dogs.

Brown moisture dripped off the dank walls. Roaches and
beetles scurried around. The oily sweet smell of opium,
mixed with the stench of greasy pork and unwashed bodies,
rose from the adjoining divan. Rats, tails swishing, pink eyes
gleaming, scampered underfoot while ticks and fleas seeking
blood flittered about the oppressive air and settled on his
torso. Tse Tsi Fai let them, uncaring.

He cautiously lifted the oily hemp cloth that served as a
curtain and peered out at the street below. He could see the
steps leading down to the town center, with its old temple
and rusting cannons. The hovel he was in had only one
entrance. He eased himself onto the rotting teak floor, peering around in the semi-darkness until his eyes adjusted.

Here, in the womb of his ancestors, Tse felt safe.

It was silent. The street was barren. Nothing moved.

After a time, he began to shake slightly. His eyes rolled
upward and his breathing came in labored gasps. Sweat
poured freely from his pasty skin. He shook off the chills,
once, twice. His spine tingled. He needed more.

He lit the candle with a trembling hand, then pulled a
large foil packet from his pants pocket and feverishly tore it
open.

The coarse-grained white powder was heated in a porcelain

spoon; then Tse took the China Products syringe from its red box and filled it with the hot liquid.

In the flickering glow of the candle, shadows danced around the room. Tse Tsi Fai injected the needle into his arm amid the jagged scars and abscesses, traces of years of piteous self-abuse.

With a rush and a roar, the world whirled around and around and became mellow and serene. And so good.

CHAPTER TWENTY-SIX

W hen he left the bunker at Victoria barracks, David Andrews was much closer to the truth than he wanted to be.

"Simon" was no longer a question mark. A surprisingly accommodating captain in the Volunteers had easily given "Simon" an identity and produced a faded warrant card to confirm it. The corpse in Room #8 at the Kennedy Town Morgue was one Edmond Ng—born Ng Pak Tsi. He had been in the reserves from 1975 until 1983, and was presently inactive, a man who had held the substantive rank of major and was an acknowledged demolitions expert—one of the few locals so trained. His service file indicated that, in civilian life, he was one of the top chartered accountants in the colony, a principal of the firm Farnsworth, Ng and Stedman. Andrews had heard of the firm and knew it had extensive contracts throughout the Asian rim, including some in mainland China.

Andrews started the Mini and pulled angrily out of the car park. He looked south from the garrison, downhill toward the harbor. Huge columns of smoke billowed upward from Tsim Tsa Tsui on the mainland. The wail of sirens filled the leaden air.

In the back of his notebook was an address given to him by the captain, an unpublished address near Hebe Haven on the Mirs Bay side of the New Territories, close to the High

Island dam. It was Ng's home. Andrews hoped to find the information he needed to solve the puzzle, to identify Ng's masters and discover who had destroyed the ship in the harbor.

In the distance, David could see human figures milling around the box-square high-rises of Wanchai. Then he noticed red tongues of flame from ground-floor windows. The situation was worsening by the minute. He passed through the main gate of the barracks, then bore due east toward the waterfront and the Kowloon ferries.

Andrews was convinced that the Blue Cloud mansion and Elephant Man were connected to "Simon." And he feared that James Peng wasn't to be trusted.

David knew he had seen "Simon" at the waterfront the night the ship exploded. Now he knew that "Simon" had rigged the ship, and had been murdered and had his identity disguised in death to protect his masters, members of a mysterious and horribly bloodied syndicate.

He geared down as an army convoy passed him on the right, barreling eastward toward Hennessy Road in the blue prismed wake of a police Land Rover.

He thought of Peng, his mentor and confidant. And, till now, his friend. But Peng had told him not to be concerned about the suicide; Peng had initialed the death report. David began to wonder if Peng were involved in some kind of cover-up.

There was a fine line which governed David Andrews's dealings with the everyday world. On the one side were those trusting individuals trying as best as they could to establish a tolerable life without harming their neighbors. On the other side were the conmen, criminals and low-lifes, predators on the innocents whom he was sworn to protect.

To Andrews, James Peng was entering the gray zone that bordered the two regions. He realized that, as the day's events unfolded, Jim Peng might prove lost to the dark side, yet he also knew in his heart that things had gone too far and he had no alternative but to proceed.

Andrews felt he was slowly losing his mind.

There was only one man left he could turn to, one man he could trust: John Cleve. He hoped he could get the truth and pass it on before it was too late.

He glanced in his rear-view mirror. A ramshackle old Ford sat on his tail, dangerously close. He hadn't noticed it before. He though about his route: east on Hennessy, then turn onto Kings Road, toward the North Point ferry piers.

Traffic was moving slowly, but he hoped he could get through any trouble spots by showing his warrant card. And things might be even worse in Kowloon and the New Territories. He shuddered.

Ahead and to one side he saw a police van, then two, some Mills barriers and some accordian wire. Smoke wafted from a laneway. Policemen in riot gear struggled with youths. Bricks were thrown. The colony seemed to be disintegrating before him.

He looked back. The Ford was still too close! He looked at the driver, a fat, moon-faced man with greasy hair and a miserable expression on his face. His two companions were nondescript in comparison; Andrews thought they were wearing white T-shirts. The traffic poked slowly eastwards and he grew impatient. He spotted a small lane to the left, between an apothecary and an appliance shop and, on an impulse, he turned into it.

The old Ford followed and accelerated. Andrews swerved sharply to the left, fighting to keep control of the steering wheel. In front of him was a jumble of crates, boxes and bamboo, an obstacle course for his little car. The Mini skidded sideways, then stopped, the motor flooded.

Andrews got out of his car and slammed the door, furious at the driver of the Ford that was right behind. The three men were already walking wordlessly toward him.

Andrews was still annoyed. "What are you trying to do, kill me?" he asked angrily. They moved closer, one stepping around to the side.

He took out his police identification and demanded that the moon-faced man produce his license. A grunt of disgust.

Suddenly, the other two lunged at Andrews and pushed him toward the concrete road.

He was falling, surprise catching in his voice, as he grasped onto anything to break his descent. Out of the corner of his eye he caught a sudden movement that, by the time it registered, became a sharp crack as the kick landed on his chest.

He hit the concrete with a solid finality. Wavering between consciousness and blissful darkness, he instinctively lunged at a moving form and caught it off balance with his shoulder.

I'll take the bastard with me! Andrews thought. Tackle him right below the knees! Suddenly, falling directly onto him, a crushing weight reeking of beer. Moon Face, his knees and elbows thrashing wildly as he realized his predicament, attempted to free himself. But Andrews had him in a grip that wasn't about to be broken.

They struggled on the ground, rolling about on the fish heads, spittle and rotten greens. Moon Face's legs were kicking, his knees jabbing Andrews in the face as each man frantically tried to regain his footing. They rolled over and over together, and still Andrews held on to him.

Suddenly, Andrews was on top, but a knee in his jaw snapped his head back. Moon Face blindly tried to wrestle free, but Andrews held him tighter. Andrews arched his revolver, holding on to the bucking body with his right hand. A blow in the side of the face and he'd have this fat pig where he wanted him.

Then, without warning, Moon Face rearranged himself. Andrews felt grasping hands clawing at his, trying to wrench his fingers free from the weapon. And now the others had joined in, holding him down on the pavement.

There were figures above; men, but he couldn't make them out clearly. He felt the presence of another human crouching by his side, saw the gauze lowered down on his face to cover it.

The street, mist-like, began to float before his eyes, gray and formless. There was an eerie silence now. He was passive on a carousel, moving round and round.

At the base of his spine he felt a sharp pain wrenching and tightening. Then the pain stopped, and he heard a humming in his ears. Just before losing consciousness, he saw peering down at him the face of Anthony Proctor.

The Blue Cloud mansion was silent, at rest. It was early and the household staff was scattered about its daily chores, preparing for the day. A cat mewed faintly from a downstairs room.

Lee Shiu Shing swiftly mounted the stairs. The old man came out of his bedroom as Lee approached. Henry Szeto had not slept long or well. His nightclothes were rumpled, his face the color of dusty chalk.

"What are you doing here?" he asked angrily. "Who let you in?"

"Ah Bau," Lee said simply. "He knows me well, Szeto. He knows me very well."

"You have no business here. You are not invited. Leave."

"No business, old man? Oh, but I think we have business," replied Lee coolly. "It is a situation of unavoidable requirements."

"Requirements?" Henry Szeto's face clouded. "I don't know what you mean." Then he recovered. "If you wish to speak of requirements, explain your own actions. What was the requirement of calling in the police? Why did you break your promise? Why did you break our agreement?"

Lee seemed taken aback. "Call the police? I did no such thing."

"Then explain their sudden presence here this past night. Why come here? What are they looking for?"

Lee paused. "I cannot explain it. It's a puzzle. But that doesn't excuse your foolish behavior. You called me to meet with you at the reservoir later today, did you not?"

"I did," Szeto admitted.

"Why?"

Henry Szeto leaned on his cane, his frail body reed thin. "I will not have you exposing my past," he said firmly.

"And so you risked a telephone call? Against all our agreements?"

"I said nothing," Szeto blustered. "You make too much of it."

"Do I?" There was contempt in Lee's eyes. He mounted the final step. Szeto came only to his chest, a tiny, insignificant insect of a human.

"If the police came here, it was because you faltered somewhere, not I." Lee gently rested his hand on Szeto's shoulder. "Somewhere along the way, you have become old, Henry. Old. A useless piece of scar tissue on the face of the earth." He smiled. "And that is why your time is . . . over." There was disdain in his voice, and regret.

Henry Szeto began to shake. "What? What did you say?" His eyes blazed with anger. The cane tapped madly on the marble floor.

Lee pulled the cane from the old man's grasp. Szeto grabbed feebly for it. "No!" he screeched. "No! You cannot do it! You have no right!"

He lost his balance and began to fall backward, teetering at the top of the stairs. Somehow he caught himself, his eyes suddenly opened wide as if he had seen a vision of hell.

A wail rose from his throat. He lunged toward Lee, his shriveled features contorted with hate. But Lee dropped down to one knee, drew back the cane and struck Szeto hard in the ankles. He heard bone crack. The old man crumpled and stumbled toward the edge of the landing. Lee nudged him and he fell, tumbling down the long staircase.

He was dead before he hit bottom, his neck broken, the fine gold brocade of his clothing shimmering in the morning sun. Blood trickled from his mouth onto the cool, frescoed floor.

Lee stood at the top of the stairs and looked at the body. An accidental fall, he reasoned to himself. Certainly what any police investigator would think. An accidental fall from grace.

"I'm sorry, Henry," Lee whispered dryly. "It was only a matter of time for you anyway." He tossed the cane down the staircase. It clattered, end over end, then landed by Henry Szeto's lifeless hands.

At 11:17 hours, two PTU companies stopped on the Ah Chin Wai Road, Kowloon Tong. The white heat of the day glittered and distorted images. Edgy platoon commanders crouched on baked pavement that burned underfoot, intently studying their orders. The blue patrol Bedfords slumped like tired old beetles about the rubble strewn street. The men were hidden in nearby doorways, waiting. There was no movement, not even the hint of a breeze to ease the oppressive oven-like heat that was Kowloon in the unyielding August sun.

At 11:26 hours, the order was given by the superintendent in charge, Steven Tak, who was standing at a mobile command post tucked safely away from the junction of Carpenter Road and Chi Fu Lam Lane, just at the edge of the Walled City. Tak wanted Tse, wanted him alive to erase the painful memories of the previous night's debacle. His pride hurt more than his injuries, though the latter were substantial. Today, through careful planning, revenge would be his.

Around the perimeter, unit logs were carefully placed in canvas satchels, hands were raised as one in silent command and eight tense teams of police moved out of their hideaways in pre-ordained paths to meet their fate. The Walled City, the pauper's citadel, was surrounded.

Patrols crept nearer, house by house, lane by lane, approaching the building from three directions.

The police carried dull silver smoke canisters slung over their shoulders, their firearms at the ready, safety catches off. Slithering, belly down, crab-crawling through the water and brine and mud near building walls where the shadows were the darkest, they rose only when necessary to check each dwelling in turn as they moved along the street. The whole area was cordoned off and all occupants evacuated, but for one.

They were coming at the building from all sides now, their radios on low mute. They spoke in excited, expectant tones as the sphere of their search was narrowed.

Tak moved up with his radio man and knelt in the doorway of the Pik Hop dispensary, less than fifteen feet from the goldsmith shop. He gazed quickly around the street. Uniformed men were hidden everywhere, in doorways, behind packing hampers, under clapboard carriages. Higher up, on the second and third floors of nearby tenements, he could see the glint of polished steel.

Steven Tak waved a red handkerchief over his head so all could see.

Silently, everywhere along the perimeter of 126A Chi Wing Mun Street, occupied for the past twelve years and four months by the Hong Fai goldsmith shop, Chinese police in riot gear took the modern British model A12 E gas masks from their hip satchels and placed them on their faces. And, as they grew accustomed to breathing the rubbery-stale hot air within, they waited.

Tak glanced to his left, to the tear-gas section of number one platoon, the best he had, hidden low behind a series of planks and mortar boards below the goldsmith shop. Their Federals and Webleys were at the shoulder position, pointed up toward the window on the second floor. An old Shanghai sergeant gestured grimly. Thumbs up. Ready.

Tak looked to his right, across the lane, where the man carrying a plastic clearing shield was making his way through an abandoned cooked-food stall. The figure stopped just below the darkened stairwell leading to the second floor of the Hong Fai. The man signaled back for the seven others in the section to follow him. Then the raiding party was in place.

Tak whispered into his radio. The time was logged—11:35 hours. Cordons in the area were checked once more. Secure. There would be no escape.

The superintendent dropped his red handkerchief.

The first tear-gas canister plopped out of the muzzle of a raised Federal. It arched silver and innocent up out of the street below, carommed off the building and bounced off concrete, crumbled brick and shingles before falling back onto the street. There it fizzled and growled about in the dirty water puddles, hissing smoke in harmlessly futile gray sheets.

The second canister was better aimed. It entered the second floor window and disappeared. All was silent for a moment; then the first telltale trailing wisps of smoke curled from the window and floated upward.

Then the third canister, and another, all on target.

Steven Tak peered through the steam-filled visor of his gas

mask. The black rubber, clam-like on his face, his body drenched in sweat.

He gave a final signal, and the constables rushed the stairs.

On the second floor of the Hong Fai goldsmith shop, near the divan operated by Dau Pei Gwai, they found Tse Tsi Fai lying childlike amid the billowing smoke. He had a broken needle in his arm. The police analysis would show that a deadly mixture of strychnine, water and poor quality heroin had coursed through his body. Tak looked at him, then checked his person. He found only a key chain which he carefully buttoned into his pocket. It was for Room 303, the Hotel Lisboa, Macau.

CHAPTER TWENTY-SEVEN

———

Before going home, Mrs. Callicutt had left a thermos of coffee and some sandwiches on his desk. She'd watered the one broad-leafed plant that stood on the window sill and closed the drapes.

Cleve was hot. His body felt itchy and swollen; he removed his Sam Browne and loosened his safari top.

Sitting at his desk with the bow light on in an otherwise dark room, he made a series of slow, deliberate notations on the blotter in front of him.

Elephant Man: dead.

Yip Lam: dead

Tse Tsi Fai: dead.

James Peng and Steven Tak had begun their investigations at the opposite ends of the same road. They had followed that road, step by step, only to meet up with one another in an unillumined light. One held a pack of matches, the other a key for a room at the Hotel Lisboa.

The small color television in the far corner of the room was turned on. Andrew Toombs, the investigative reporter from HKTV, peered out from the screen. Cleve wondered if the blotchy color of the reporter's face was to be blamed on the television or the bottle.

Another checkmark.

One marriage: dead.

The pencil lead broke.

"The streets of this teeming Asian port have been torn asunder by mammoth riots these past few days. . ."

The poetry of the press, Cleve thought. More of this "the British Lion is at the Tiger's Gate" business.

"The major sore spot has been the explosion four days ago of a Communist cargo vessel in Hong Kong harbor, but the riots in Hong Kong are only a reflection of a greater struggle that has engulfed the Chinese mainland for the past week, a struggle that makes last spring's student protests for democratization seem tame by comparison. . ."

The reporter was "on scene." As a consequence, Cleve took note, he was soaking wet.

"The Dadu scandal, as it has come to be known, has brought to the fore a respected member of the Central Committee, an influential friend of Chinese Premier Deng Xiaoping, a man called Yun Jianging. Yun faces allegations of poor workmanship and large-scale corruption in the construction by his firm of a railway bridge over the Dadu River. The recent collapse of that bridge in an incident that took almost three hundred lives, and the attendant innuendo of high-level coverups, has brought the Chinese nation to its feet clamoring for justice.

"Kang Shung, senior official of the *She Hui Pu*, the security branch of the Chinese state, was assigned to investigate the matter. Early this morning, he delivered his verdict. Yun has been found guilty on all counts of corruption and influence peddling. He is to be charged formally and sent before a judicial tribunal as quickly as possible. In the present political climate in Mother China, his sentence will probably be extensive.

"The political crisis in China is a closed book, but its effects will be sweeping. Here in Hong Kong, Governor Thomas Driscoll has been holding round-the-clock meetings with influential Chinese and English businessmen of all political persuasions in the hope of bridging the growing gap between the Colonial regime and the people it rules, which the unsettled situation in China has brought to the fore. . . ."

Cleve got out of his chair.

"Police methods of handling the explosion of the Communist ship and the innocent deaths of eleven Chinese seamen have been a particular sore point, with complaints lodged by all sides."

And what about our side? My side, Cleve heard his own voice.

"Still, assurances have been made by the governor that changes are forthcoming, changes acceptable to the peoples of both China and Hong Kong."

Obviously, Cleve thought, the press has better leads than the police force. Live ones, to boot.

He paged Robert Maguire.

"Wake up, Andrews . . . Wake up." A slap. He felt groggy, drugged. Things were out of focus. Another slap and stinging pain. He sensed shapes, the sound of running water. Above him, he could make out rusty pipes cutting across concrete ceilings. There was mould and dampness. A patch of whiteness floated in the far-off distance. Could it be a door? Sunlight?

"Come on. . ." The voice was impatient, booming like a cannon fired next to his ears. David Andrews blinked, began to feel the nausea. He struggled to form words, squinting his eyes. There was icy dampness all around as well as the continuous dripping of water. He shivered.

"Cold, are we?" He heard a voice, goading, heckling. "Wake up, Andrews. We haven't got all day, you know." Above him loomed the shape of a head, a bright light glowing from behind, shading the face. He thought he knew the voice.

"You remember me, don't you, Andrews?" The voice chiding, needling. "You remember me, Tony Proctor, your old friend from Special Branch."

Andrews tensed. He was tied to a chair, could now feel the rope binding his hands and his chest. His arms ached. He felt the uneven floor with his feet: concrete, stone and dirt. A cave? He could see rusty chairs, a map table, a bayonet sunk in a mound of sand and what appeared to be an old army helmet. On the wall, in flaking paint, the words "Carnaby Street." Perhaps he was in an old cellar. No, it went on for too far. A tunnel? Perhaps. Then he saw light streaming in. Daylight.

How long had he been here? Hours? Days? He was too tired to figure it out.

He felt the splash of water on his face and gasped, struggling for breath. He heard Proctor laughing. Then, ever more insistent as he towered over the captive policeman, Proctor said, "Come on, Andrews. Tell me. You weren't involved in a police investigation when you went to the morgue and then to Vic Barracks this morning. Tell me who you work for. Tell me."

"Work?" Andrews slurred the word.

"Ah, our fine little lad is wakening. Yes, work. We all work for someone." Proctor's voice was sarcastic. "Did you have a nice sleep?"

Andrews blinked, then stared into the Yorkshireman's hatchet face.

"You really are a prize, you know. Do you really think you impress me with this Boy's Brigade bravado?"

Andrews said nothing.

"It isn't going to matter, not in the long run. I'm only trying to let you live."

The realization shocked him like an ice pick to the heart. Live? What the hell was going on? Andrews thought quickly. It began to make sense, all the loose pieces.

"Live? Like you did that scar-faced suicide? Ng the accountant, that's who he was, wasn't he?" For a moment he thought he glimpsed the indecision, the confusion in those eyes. "Yes, Proctor," he continued, "Ng and heaven knows how many others."

Proctor's stare was withering. "I didn't kill the accountant, you simple fool. Not Ng. Or anyone." His voice had taken on the strangest tone.

"Then who did?"

Proctor stood back. Andrews heard him breathing,

hurriedly, as if he had asthma. "The system, perhaps," he said. "But not me."

"The system?" Andrews replied bitterly. "That's a bloody laugh! Seems to me everything gets blamed on the system. Well, it wasn't the system that did Williams in. Not poor Brendan. He didn't have a corrupt bone in his body."

Proctor looked at him sadly.

"You really are a fool, Andrews—a fool or a monk. Brendan Williams was bent, bent as a French sous. And he knew he was going to get caught. That's why he swallowed the poison."

Andrews stared back for the longest time. "Poison? How did you know he took poison? It was never released in the reports."

"Of course it was," Proctor answered quickly. "It was public information."

Andrews noticed that his face was pale, and pushed his advantage.

"Like hell, you bastard! I found the body. We never disclosed the cause of death. There was no inquest at the CP's insistence. It was rumored that Brendan died as the result of a bullet to the brain. Only Williams didn't die from a gunshot. There was no external injury. His weapon was locked in the station armory. It was poison that did him in—lye that rotted out his throat lining and made him die a painful, gurgling death." Now Andrews's eyes bore into Proctor. "But how did you know? Unless you murdered him, too. . . Did you, Proctor? Did you kill Brendan Williams?"

"Tell me who you work for!" Proctor shrieked.

Andrews's stolid silence seemed to enrage him. He raised his hand, as though to strike, but his captive didn't flinch. Proctor dropped his hand, and sighed.

"No, you're not going to tell me, are you?" His tone was once again calm, reasoned. "You should tell me who it is. It won't take me too long to figure out where you fill your pockets, but it would be so much easier for both of us if you'd tell me."

He grabbed a hank of Andrews' hair, pulling it back painfully. David winced. "Whose little errand boy are you, then,

Inspector?" he whispered. "Are you one of Williams' people? Or Maguire's?"

Proctor let him go and then walked around the room for a few moments with a sour leer on his face.

"Maybe you work for Hans, our dear friend Hans, about whom so many know so little." Proctor paused, then started in again. "Or Burden. Perhaps Burden's trying to get a bigger piece of the pie without telling us." He smiled. "Who's your boss, then, Andrews?"

"I haven't any idea what you're talking about," he said stonily.

Proctor's eyebrows shot up. "I think maybe you should cooperate," he said quietly. "It might be to your advantage. For example, do you even know where you are?"

Andrews was silent.

"A tunnel in the Shing Mun Redoubt, in the shadow of Tai Mo Shan. The one we're in is Carnaby Street, and over there—" he pointed down the darkened corridors to a vague change of light "—that's the junction with Regent Street." His voice took on the tone of a tour guide as he talked about the ancient fortifications. "These tunnels go on for miles and miles, and lead nowhere. Part of the British defences in '41. Only they didn't prevent us from being overrun, did they?" The false smile.

"Less than two days to capture the entire peninsula. A few hours to take this redoubt. And you know why, Andrews?" Proctor's speech became suddenly strident. "Because the Royal Scots that held this series of battlements didn't plan for the attack. They never imagined it could break upon them. They sat back and let it happen. They let the little bow-legged slants take them without as much as a fight because they couldn't adapt to the changing situation. To make the best out of what they had and, if necessary, fight dirtier than the Devil to hold on to it.

"There's even the ghost of a Scotsman here in the caves, Andrews. One of your distant relatives." The cruel leer. "He was stubborn like you, too, I should imagine. Didn't know when to stick his nose out and run for daylight. You'll make a handsome pair, the two of you, traipsing around these gloomy corridors, canting in the wind." Proctor laughed.

He suddenly turned serious. "Don't make me angry by ignoring my questions, Andrews. I'm not a criminal or a petty little police inspector. I represent Her Majesty's Government. You don't seem to understand the powers at play here. You never did. None of your provincial groups of people did, and that's why Whitehall gave up trying to deal with you long ago."

David stared at him silently.

"So you won't say who's you are. Well, that's fine. It doesn't really matter a tiddler's twat in the end, not any more. You're too close to it now, Andrews, far too close." Proctor looked away, and took a revolver from his jacket pocket. He opened the cylinder, twirled it, then snapped it shut. The sound clattered through the darkness like wooden ratchets at a funeral.

"Is that why you killed them, Proctor? All of them? Because they were too close?"

Proctor tilted his head to one side. "You really don't know, do you?" The sympathy in his voice was real. "Well, here's a lesson in reality, young Inspector Andrews.

"Brendan Williams was selling himself down the river. He knew some of my people. He had no business getting so deeply into the matter. It was none of his concern. He almost jeopardized some very large, and necessary, political accommodations with his prying."

"And so you killed him?" Andrews interrupted.

Proctor continued. It was as if the question had not been asked.

"Ng, as you no doubt have learned, was a damned fine accountant who, like many of his ancestors, had a certain talent for explosive devices. But Ng liked to dabble in white powder, the stinking stuff, Andrews, the shit these heathens call *bac-fan*. He was useless to us because of it, would have sold his soul to the Devil, and with it our scheme.

"And then there was Hans. Pure and proper Hans. You really wanted him, didn't you, young Davie? And sadly, without realizing it, you came very near to finding him.

"I see the look in your face." Proctor shook his head. "No, the identity of Hans is too important for even a corpse to know about, I'm afraid."

He took the revolver and pointed it at Andrews. "You're on to Ng—it's only a matter of time until you find out about the whole thing. I don't want to kill you, but it's what Her Majesty's Government might term 'a necessity of practice.' You butted into the deal the same way Williams did. And the deal cannot be jeopardized."

He moved the revolver close to Andrews's temple.

A shot rang out.

CHAPTER TWENTY-EIGHT

———

The call from Government House interrupted Cleve in mid-sentence. He was reporting into a dicta-machine on the results of his early morning meeting with Maguire.

"Results" was perhaps the wrong word. He'd talked to Maguire for two hours, but the director of Special Branch had little to say.

What did Maguire know about Henry Szeto?

Practically nothing.

About Hans?

Even less.

Could Special Branch confirm what General Investigations suspected, that Henry Szeto was connected to interests in Peking, and that Peking was somehow aiding illegal business interests in Hong Kong both in the acquisition and sale of land and drugs? Maguire had smugly replied that SB couldn't confirm or deny the suspicions.

Cleve had held himself back. It took all the willpower he had to keep from throttling his director.

Gamesmanship! All they were doing was playing games. He had suspected for a day or so that Maguire was involved in something; and now, finally, when he confronted the man, Maguire was vague and obtuse.

The director had not even seemed to comprehend that while he fenced and parried, the worst was almost upon them. The Hakka boy's funeral would soon be over. The Chinese workers, meeting at the Kowloon Trade Federation, were ready to believe that they'd labored long enough to fill the pockets of the foreign devils. They were ready to fight in the streets for the right to join their brethren in China, and would try to lead the rest of Hong Kong with them. Did Maguire not understand?

But for Maguire the discussion had become all so "unpleasant." Might he not be excused to attend to his duties?

Cleve had asked his last question. Did Maguire not have an archives file in his possession, one personally signed out by him, concerning a Chinese male known only as "September"?

Maguire blanched slightly, then recovered himself. "Perhaps, but it no longer has any relevance."

Silence.

Cleve had then asked for both Maguire's resignation and the file on Henry Szeto, each to be on his desk by one. And that was an order. Disciplinary hearings would commence later.

Cleve ceased reporting into his dicta-machine just as the phone rang.

He listened, then responded that he couldn't come to Government House just now.

An animated voice at the other end of the line then spoke for about a minute.

Cleve rested his forehead in his hand. "I see. Yes, of course."

Ten minutes later he was in a car on his way to the governor. He could see it now for himself: the streets were quieter, businesses opening, the occasional police vehicles stationary.

At Government House, Cleve paced the cool hallway restlessly, the lush velvet carpeting muffling his footsteps. He glanced about the well-appointed ante room, frowning at the calculated formality of the arrangements. Whitehall transplanted, he mused. So elegant it squeaked. French Provincial. Fully in keeping with the taste of Her Majesty's representative in the Crown colony. There were chairs whose velvet seats showed wear only on the front edges, where most of the sitting had been done. In the corner full-length mirror he could see his reflected image. His shoes gleamed and there was still a hint of a press in the wrinkled cotton pants. Etched in his face was the exhaustion of twenty hours without sleep and days without proper food and rest.

At the end of the hall, two huge white doors peaked to a high sculptured ceiling. Behind the doors he could hear four muted voices, two of them familiar.

One of the voices was that of a one-time friend, another belonged to an enemy. He wondered if he had not played his hand well enough. Had he underrated his man? The conversation from behind the double doors continued, although the governor's manservant had reported his arrival fifteen minutes before.

He concentrated on an oak-encased rococo clock on a Louis Napoleon desk. Twenty minutes passed. Cleve played with his pocket flap. He had cooled his heels at Government House before, but never without at least a briefing by his aide-de-camp. But then these were unusual times. He was more needed at the Pol/Mil complex than here catering to the whims of the new governor. Cleve hoped the audience would not be long.

"Mr. Cleve?" The manservant with white gloves had slipped over the carpet as quietly as a cat. "Please come this way."

He led Cleve along a passageway to a small study, next to the room from which the voices came. It was like a doctor's clinic, Cleve thought. One way in, another way out. That encouraged frankness perhaps, and it avoided unnecessary and even embarrassed meetings between interviews.

The servant retreated, leaving the commissioner with four new walls to contemplate. But the voices intruded upon the thoughts he tried to still. They were speaking English, of course. No one expected the governor to understand more than how to greet a visitor in Cantonese. Only one of the voices belonged to an Oriental. Without being able to distinguish what was being said, Cleve recognized a slight Fench accent and Oxbridge accents from the governor and another of his guests. The old-boy network, Cleve thought.

He checked his watch. He had been away too long. "Damn it all," said a half-imprisoned voice somewhere inside him, "I'm going in there."

Four faces looked up, stunned, as Cleve came to attention just inside the door. He clapped his forage cap smartly under the crook of his left arm and brought his hands down to his sides. His eyes were correct, stern, as he punctuated the air with a very correct "Sir."

Three of the figures in the room stiffened. The governor smiled benignly, acknowledging Cleve with a wave of his hand. "Stand easy, Mr. Cleve. This is surely not an occasion for formality." Driscoll underlined this last expression with a touch of irony, to put Cleve in his place, but he hadn't taken color as the others had. "I believe you know Sir Robert Burden, Mr. Cleve."

The nod, perfunctory at best.

"And may I present Lee Shiu Shing of the Bank of China."

Lee turned in his chair and, without flinching, looked him straight in the eye.

"I am called Hans by my friends," he said.

Cleve paused. After a long, thoughtful silence he spoke. "Somehow I thought you would be."

He smiled.

Lee returned the smile and began to say something, but Driscoll interrupted.

"Your timing is excellent, commissioner," he said with deliberate finality. "We have just concluded our business."

The governor opened one of the large white double doors and held out his arm to sweep his visitors away. As Lee stood up, a package of cigarettes fell from the arm of his chair. He bowed slightly in Cleve's direction in what appeared to be a show of diplomatic rather than Oriental deference.

Burden, of course, knew Cleve from the club and asked after Margaret.

Cleve didn't answer. Instead, he kept his eyes on the fourth man.

Robert Maguire did not meet his appraising stare or detect any flicker of irony in his commissioner's, "Hello, Bob. So this is where you've been."

Cleve watched Maguire stoop to retrieve the package of cigarettes with the figure of a skating Dutch boy on its cover. He handed the cigarettes to Lee. Cleve suddenly realized that Maguire would be picking up after his elders quite a lot from now on.

The governor disappeared with his guests for a moment, then returned to the room, audibly changing the tone of this next meeting with a deep breath.

Driscoll closed the door, then took him by the arm.

Cleve knew then. In his heart he knew. Even before the contents of the letter were read to him. And John Cleve, ever the officer and gentleman, walked into the center of the room to meet his fate.

CHAPTER TWENTY-NINE

———

Are you all right?" The words came from the depth of the tunnel. A shadow appeared, then approached him, revolver in hand.

Andrews looked up. The shadow took form in the half-light: Jim Peng. He crouched over Proctor's body, felt the neck for a pulse. "He's dead." He turned toward David, holstering his gun. "Are you all right?" he asked again. He saw the anger in David's face.

"You knew about this, didn't you?" David accused him coldly.

Peng looked away.

"Well, didn't you?" Andrews shouted, his voice echoing in the ancient tombs.

Peng nodded. He began to untie Andrews's bonds.

"And you almost let me die?"

"We didn't know for certain."

"Know what for certain?"

Peng completed his task, then beckoned Andrews to follow him. David stood still, warily eyeing his rescuer.

Peng answered in a slow, carefully measured voice. "We didn't know where you stood until the very end."

"Who's we?"

"The commissioner . . .Me . . ."

Andrews shook his head. "No," he whispered. "I don't believe it."

"Believe it, Davie. It's the truth." There was sadness in his eyes and, somehow, Andrews knew Peng was not lying. "It's a long story."

"I have plenty of time," David replied. His voice was dull, mirthless, drained.

"Yes, you've earned the right to know, haven't you?"

And, quietly, Jim Peng began.

"For the past year or so, the Chinese and British governments have been negotiating a land deal on Kowloon side, the choicest property in Tsim Tsa Tsui, prime land abutting the harbor. The land was to be a kiss-off intended to keep Peking happy until the lease for the colony ran out in 1997.

"The scheme was hush-hush because of its ramifications. If England admitted that she would willingly surrender land without concessions, there would be havoc on the Hong Kong Stock Market. At the same time, Britain and China were negotiating over an airport which China wanted to build near Canton. The airport deal was semi-public. The plan was to sneak the secret deal through while everyone was paying attention to the proposed airport."

Peng took a pack of Royal Crowns from his pocket, lit a cigarette and offered the pack to Andrews, who declined.

"So far, straightforward back-door diplomacy, right?"

David nodded.

"And that's how it should have stayed but for him." He gestured to the body. "Anthony Proctor."

"The second land deal was so secret that only a few parties knew of its existence. Whitehall was to be the donor; the People's Republic of China would be the recipient. That much was clear. When we get to the intermediaries, though, the whole scheme goes for a tumble.

"Proctor was Her Majesty's representative in the negotiations, and a right proper bastard he proved to be. From what I've been able to gather, he was given a nominal position on secondment with Hong Kong SB from MI5; his posting was supposed to be a secret, which explains why he was known to some people and not to others, and why he could prance all over the landscape without appearing out of place.

"We know this much about him. His proper name is Anthony Carmichael Proctor; he's forty-four and an ex-Dragoons officer. He went to the NATO staff college, Imperial War college, the usual sort of saber rattling stuff, but he worked on the intelligence side only.

"When he returned to civvy street he went straight to the Ministry of Foreign Affairs, to a special section whose task was 'Self Determination for Emergent States within the Commonwealth.' We think it was a front for counter-insurgent activity.

"He had postings on secondment to Aden, to Brunei, to Northern Ireland, you name it—wherever there was trouble, he went to sort it out in an unconventional fashion with a minimum of public outcry—and less accountability. His role has always appeared murky. He was a 'negotiator'—a horse trader, one of the types Whitehall got to do its dirty work, with a mandate to get results in any way, shape or form he saw fit.

"But when he got to Hong Kong the picture really muddied." Peng finished his cigarette, ground it into the floor with his foot, then quickly lit a second one.

Andrews shook his head in disbelief and confusion. "How does land on Kowloon tie into a ship explosion at Western, a drug syndicate and the things Proctor said about Williams and Simon and Hans? I don't understand."

"Patience, David, patience. It took us a while to put it together, too. But, as we came closer, it all became ever so logical." He leaned back against the tunnel wall.

"In the late summer of last year," Peng continued, "your friend Brendan Williams was working the drug squad out of Narcotics Bureau. He was assigned to follow a small syndicate, one we knew little about. All we had was the name of one of the street dealers, Lai Man Yi."

"Elephant Man," Andrews whispered.

"Right," Peng said. "Then, shortly after beginning the surveillance, Williams went bent."

David shook his head. "Not Brendan," he said. "There's no way he'd take 'squeeze'"

"I'm afraid so, David," Peng said sadly. "We have the bank records, money orders to England, expense accounts at large

stores in the colony with large overdrafts quickly and mysteriously covered. Everything we needed to prove im-
propriety on Brendan's part."

"But Elephant Man did time after Brendan met him,"
Andrews said. "Maybe it was just coincidence." He sounded
as though he didn't believe it himself.

"Sorry, David, but the payoffs continued even with
Elephant Man behind bars. Someone high up liked Williams,
and put him on the payroll. An envelope of money a week,
no questions asked, delivered by courier to Western. All Williams had to do was leave certain drug dealing locations
alone."

David considered what Peng had said. When he spoke
again, his voice was angry. "If you already knew about
Elephant Man and his part in the syndicate, why did we stay
up all night to find his name?" Even as he asked the question,
David thought he knew the answer.

Peng's reply confirmed his suspicions. "Would you not
have done the same?"

"So you were unsure of me?"

"Let's just say I had some questions that needed answers.
You were an old friend of Brendan's. You were the one to
discover his body. And when the investigation started we had
no way of knowing if you had been helping Williams in the
drug business, or how much you knew of what he was doing,
or if you condoned it. In truth, David, I wasn't even sure if
you weren't involved in the explosion of the ship."

Andrews went white with anger. "Now see here," he began.

Peng interrupted. "You must remember the facts we had
to work with. Before you condemn me, let me explain. A
crooked policeman, sleazy hoods, payoffs, textbook corruption. Nothing out of the ordinary, right?

"But, in this case, there was something different. For some
reason Williams, after being as cunning as a wharf rat in a
cheese factory, seems to have had a change of heart. A limit.

"We think now that Williams was as cautious as he was
corrupt. Hedging his bets, he began clandestine observations
of the very person through which he was collecting tea
money.

"One day in February, the fifteenth, Brendan Williams tailed Elephant Man from their customary rendezvous at the Tai Koo dockyards to another location where he observed a meeting so extraordinary he felt compelled to report it to the commissioner.

"From that point the whole story, including Williams's involvement in it, changed, and he inadvertently chiseled the first letters onto his tomb stone.

"Williams reported seeing a suspected drug dealer, Elephant Man, and a group of wealthy Chinese: an old man with a cane, a man with a scar on his face, and a third fellow, only vaguely described as elegantly dressed. These three were meeting in apparent secrecy with two Europeans. One he indirectly identified—he drove a car that had diplomatic plates. The second was someone he readily knew, a man we've positively identified as Sir Robert Burden, chairman of Burland Group, Windom and Burden Transport, Burden Silver—and on and on. He and his companies run the colony lock, stock and barrel.

"But something you didn't know was that by July of last year, a report on Sir Robert Burden indicated he was in serious financial trouble. He faced the liquidation of much of his assets at ten cents on the dollar to stave off bankruptcy caused by a streak of poor business investments. Commercial Crime felt his track record was so horrid that it would be unlikely for him to get backing from any legitimate commercial interests to stay afloat. But that didn't preclude his going elsewhere for funds.

"The report was snapped up by Special Branch before the ink was dry, on the grounds that its contents were more in the realm of territorial security than commercial data. It was from his time at the Branch that Williams learned of Burden and his predicament."

David considered the prospect. If the Burden empire went for a tumble, the better part of the colony would feel the tremors and many lesser commercial house, and *hongs* would be torn from their foundations. It was unsettling news to say the least. Given Hong Kong's mercurial stock markets, and even more flighty investors, David could appreciate why the item had become a matter for Special Branch monitoring rather than for the bi-speckled, accountant-policemen in the Commercial Crime Squad.

Peng's deep voice intruded on his thoughts. "The CP knew there was something unsavory in the offing when a drug-dealing minion like Elephant Man was seen with someone as financially strapped and lacking in business ethics as Robert Burden. And don't forget—at that time we didn't know the identities of any of the other men Burden was meeting. Cleve gave Williams the green light to continue surveillance—only this time to follow Burden—until we could assign a headquarters unit to the investigation.

"The next day, the sixteenth, Williams was off on his own again, continuing his probe. He tailed Burden from morning to night, and was murdered in the early hours of the very next day. The morning you discovered Williams at Western, I was assigned to the case."

"But I never met you then," David said. He looked almost betrayed.

"No," Peng allowed, almost apologetically. "But you remember that Homicide swore you to secrecy about the cause of death." Andrews nodded. "Because of the sensitive nature of Williams's probe, the commissioner didn't want to divulge too much about the killing or its possible motive."

"So you left me to hang in the wind while you investigated."

"To a degree we did," Peng conceded. "But you have to understand the stakes we were playing for.

"Homicide found little of value on Williams's body: some tissue paper, a stick of chewing gum, a photo spool with the negatives ripped out and a blank notepad.

"We didn't find the negatives on him either—his killer had seen to that. But the notepad had indentations on it. Williams was heavy handed with his pen, and we had our people at forensic examine each leaf. From his notes we know that Williams, as ordered by Cleve, was following Burden and taking photos all along the way. Brendan was a very practical man. He itemized every snapshot with time and location taken.

"He trailed Burden through his daily ritual from his residence at the Peak to breakfast at the Hong Kong Club, the trading offices in Central, a business luncheon at the Peninsula Hotel and shopping for brogues in the Regency arcade—all innocuous events, yet all necessary surveillance profiles.

"Then, in the late afternoon hours, the situation changed. Sir Robert left his offices on Des Voeux Road and walked alone to the coffee shop at the Mandarin Hotel. In the next half hour, four very familiar people—the Chinese with the cane, the Chinese with the scar, the European with the diplomatic plates and the elegantly dressed Chinese—arrived separately at the hotel and passed near Burden's table. Williams watched the elevator lights. All of his visitors got off on the seventeenth floor.

"Then, Burden also went to the seventeenth floor. It wasn't hard to find the room they'd entered, and Williams settled into the stairwell where he could keep an eye on the door. Everyone remained in that room until two o'clock in the morning, at which time all but two of them left.

"Burden stayed till three o'clock. He came out with the elegantly dressed Chinese and they went down to the foyer of the Mandarin, shook hands, and parted. Suspecting that Burden was heading home to bed, Williams decided to follow the elegantly dressed Chinese. He went into the Bank of China and that's where the notes end."

"The Bank of China!" David whispered softly. "Does the CP know?"

"Yes," Peng replied. "Yes, he does, though there was nothing we could do till a few hours ago. For some reason, when Williams died so mysteriously the syndicate put the second land deal, the secret scheme, on ice. We didn't have Brendan's pictures—we know from the notes he shot two rolls—and we couldn't get new pictures because they weren't meeting each other any more.

"We always thought Brendan's killers took both rolls of film. But they didn't. They'd seized only one. And the missing roll?"

There was a gleam in his eye as Peng answered his own

question. "This morning our people found the film. Here," he opened an envelope and took out a contact sheet placing it on a rusting map table. "See if you know these men."

David edged closer. The photographs had been from a distance with a suitcase camera, giving them a curiously candid quality. The camera automatically dated and timed each shot.

The first few were for setting. David easily recognized the Mandarin coffee shop. The broad flaccidness of Robert Burden. The false bonhomie on his features.

In one picture he saw a withered old man, leaning heavily on a cane with a phoenix handle on its end. The man was entering the Mandarin lobby. Henry Szeto.

Then, waiting for the elevator, a shadowed Chinese with a knife-like flaw on his face. Scarface Ng, the accountant turned bomber.

Next, a man brushing past Burden's table, doing his utmost to avoid Burden's looks of recognition. Hair cut rather primly. Suit of conservative trim. A rather short, rather abrasive looking man, a man who might have a chip on his shoulder.

"Proctor," David gasped.

"Yes, it was Proctor," Peng answered. "Anthony Proctor."

And then there was only one, an elderly Oriental, well dressed and sprightly of manner, entering the lobby of the Mandarin. The last of the group.

"And this one," David said simply. "This must be Hans."

"Yes," Peng replied. "This is our friend Hans. We now know he is Lee Shiu Shing, a high official of the Resource Section of the Bank of China and quite the respected little Communist."

David could not hide his excitement. "The drug syndicate," he whispered as he held up the photograph, treasuring it like a precious relic. "The drug syndicate that went after the *Glorious East Wind*." His voice was filled with awe.

"Yes," Peng nodded. "For the most part, with these snaps, paid for by Brendan's blood, I believe you are looking at them."

David shook his head in disbelief. It was all so mind boggling. He thought a moment.

"But what of Proctor's role?" David asked. "Was Proctor involved with the drugs?"

Peng considered the question. "When we first had the data from Williams's notes," he began, "Cleve checked the diplomatic plate discreetly. The CP had begun to distrust Maguire, his aspirations and his agents, so he contacted friends back home without tipping off Special Branch.

"It took a few months to winkle out of Colonial Secretariat's most-secret-of-secret files. Finally, Cleve's mates found the true reason for Anthony Proctor's presence in the colony.

"He represented an attempt by Whitehall to placate the People's Republic of China with a lucrative land deal to smooth the takeover of Hong Kong in 1997.

"The deal was framed to benefit a faithful Tory crony and resident of the Crown colony who was coincidentally a dear friend of the governor's. And to help an old Chinese woodcutter . . ."

"Robert Burden and Henry Szeto!"

"Precisely," Peng said. "As you've seen, up to a short time ago, Burden's empire was barely treading water. Rather than liquidate, he mortgaged to the hilt his most valuable land assets, including lucrative Kowloon waterfront properties.

"Szeto found out and shrewdly took up the mortgages, with first option to buy Burden out should he default. When Tony Proctor came to town with Whitehall's proposal, the governor directed him to Burden and Szeto, with the proviso that, whatever occurred, Burden was not to be excluded from any of the benefits that might accrue from the package. Our friend Hans—Lee Shiu Shing—was the Chinese official Peking assigned to the negotiations.

"Williams interrupted the pivotal meetings for the Kowloon land. Brendan's tragic death put everything on hold. The syndicate was paranoid that the police investigation into his demise would lead to them and disclose their secret.

"The explosion of the *Glorious East Wind*, coming at a comfortable lapse after Williams's passing, gave a tailor-made alibi for the deal's closing. The sale of valuable land on Kowloon was the perfect way for both London and Peking to exhibit to each other their determination to proceed peacefully, rather than with violence, toward the termination of the lease to Hong Kong."

"But was a secret land deal enough to turn Proctor into a murderer?" Andrews asked in bewilderment.

"In itself, no," Peng replied, "but there were some secret considerations involved."

"Kickbacks?" Andrews asked.

"Substantial ones. The kind men die for."

"And murder for," David could not help adding bitterly.

"And murder for." Peng agreed. "Yes, I suspect that none of the principals—Szeto, Burden, Proctor, and even Lee Shiu Shing and the governor—felt that they had to do without. Unfortunately, I also strongly suspect they all neglected to tell their respective governments about any added commissions they'd tacked on to the final negotiated price."

Peng saw David's incredulous look.

He lit a cigarette. "My investigators raided Proctor's flat this morning. We found unaccounted-for monies in his bank books. And a diary with rather foolishly blatant notations about the land deal. None of the money appears to be legitimately obtained."

David thought about that for a while. "But what about the accountant, Ng? How does he fit in?"

"He was a good accountant. He represented Henry Szeto and assisted in the negotiations for the land deal. And he acted as a functionary for the drug syndicate."

"With a big bang," Andrews commented dryly.

"With quite a big bang," Peng replied. There was no mirth in his voice.

"Jim, surely Cleve now knows most of this. We should have them charged. . ."

"Charged, David?" Peng interrupted softly. "And then what would we do? We'll gain nothing by accusing these people openly. They're too powerful for us. And charges?" He shook his head. "They would think you insane!"

"What do you mean? On the basis of what we know, we

could have them arrested right now with conspiracy! With murder!"

Peng butted his cigarette. "Arrest them for murder? There is no evidence, no real evidence these people murdered anyone. It's all conjecture on our part.

"And conspiracy? Conspiracy to do what? Traffic in drugs? Blow up the *East Wind*? Defraud Her Majesty in the land transaction?

"No, Davie. All we have are the diary of a dead policeman, a lifeless Whitehall mole, a body in Kennedy Town Morgue and the half-mad ramblings of two very tired detectives. Scarcely enough to go on, I'm afraid."

"But Brendan Williams was murdered, wasn't he?" Andrews countered sharply.

"Yes," Peng replied. "I've already told you that. We have clear evidence of foul play in his death."

"And you also have evidence of these people entering into his life. They had every motive to kill him, every motive. Be it for land, drugs, or money, he was their meal ticket."

"Yes, David, I agree." Peng's voice was soothing. "You're tired. Overwrought. This has been too much of a strain, an understandable one." Peng moved to lead Andrews away.

Andrews stopped in his tracks: "And you suspected me of involvement in Brendan's death?" He was suddenly very weary.

"Yes," Peng said matter-of-factly. "I'm afraid we did."

"So you didn't trust me throughout."

"Your choice of words," Peng replied. "Let's just say we didn't know. To tell you the truth," he continued, "we didn't know who Williams's killer was until Simon, our friend Scarface Ng, showed up at the waterfront, then on the slab at the morgue. We were able to play our hand with someone the other side thought was Williams's partner, someone who might have been in it with him, who might have had the information Williams had. Someone with a motive for revenge, and that someone was you."

"You set a trap with me as bait?"

"I reiterate, David. What would you have done?"

Andrews was silent. When he spoke next, his manner was

almost resigned. The strain showed on his face. "That explains why you let Ng's murderer go untraced."

"We thought it might be Proctor," Peng said. "Or, if not him, then one of the other principals in the syndicate. The Woodcutter, or Hans and his people. But we weren't sure, and until the photographs were found, we didn't know for certain who Hans and the man with the cane were. They all had a motive of sorts though, didn't they? All of them. Even if we can never prove it."

"And that's why you let him come after me," David motioned to Proctor's corpse. "You wanted to see what would happen when we met." He paused. "A rather risky game to play with someone else's life, don't you think?"

But Peng did not appear alarmed in the least. "Not really, David. We had you followed this morning from the moment you left Western. How else do you think I could find you?"

"And what if they had killed me in the laneway?" Andrews asked. "It was easy enough to do in the circumstances. No one would have been the wiser. Not even you."

Peng shook his head. "No. Not Proctor. He couldn't have done that until he knew for certain who you were serving. By now, he'd become so paranoid that he may have suspected you were on to him from Whitehall—from another section—God only knows. It's only when he found out you were shrewd enough as an adversary to start adding up the missing links that he decided to murder you in these caves."

"Are you sure he didn't kill Ng?" Andrews asked.

"No, David. That seemed beyond his interests and capabilities. Drugs would have been too sordid for his lily-white bureaucratic hands. He was just a weasel.

"But what about Ng's death?" Peng continued. "I suspect that Ng was a victim of his own greed. He dabbled with the syndicate and lost, and he had to be eliminated. He could connect the drug syndicate with the land deal. The other players had to prevent this from happening."

"And they have," David muttered.

"Yes." Peng nodded. "And who knows what they gained. Land, money—they've made several gambles that appear to have worked rather well by any standards."

David was quiet for a moment.

"How did you find the missing film?" he finally asked.

Peng hesitated. "We discovered it this morning."

"How?"

Peng looked away. "Remember Mei Ling's jade brooch? The one she always wore?"

"Mei Ling?" David whispered. "How is she involved?"

"Brendan sent Mei the brooch only hours before he died. An innocent enough looking gift delivered by taxi. Inside was the missing roll of negatives. Williams was shrewd enough to distance himself from the evidence should he be discovered by the syndicate. And brave enough to suffer the consequences."

"So she knew all along," David said.

"No," Peng answered. "Brendan never confided in a soul. That we know for certain." His voice became gentle. "She telephoned you at Western. She knew that if they were looking for her, they were hunting you, too."

"Where is she?"

Peng continued with great difficulty. "We think it was Proctor's people, but we can't be certain. They called me when they found the body. She'd been slashed pretty badly before she died."

A riff of thunder rippled through a far corridor. Or was it the earth settling on the ancient battlements? Tears came slowly to David Andrews's eyes and trickled down his cheeks, tears of weariness, of frustration, of sadness. It had all been too much. Too many people had been hurt; too many people had died. And for what?

For the first time in his life, David Andrews found that he didn't care to know the answer.

CHAPTER THIRTY

━━━━━━

In the early hours of that weary, hot Saturday morning, coordinated raids by plainclothes Special Branch teams, acting on information obtained through a confidential source known only to the new commissioner of police, Robert Maguire, raided six locations in the British Crown colony of Hong Kong and its outlying islands.

Twenty-three Chinese males and four females were arrested and a quantity of offensive weapons and subversive literature was seized.

At the same time in the New Territories, on the old Sai Kung Road near the ancient village of Shek Leung Tsai, three men were arrested and some explosives were recovered, including nitroglycerine, blasting caps and U.S. military surplus ammunition.

The suspects were all taken under heavy escort to Victoria Remand Centre, on an isolated promontory at the west end of Hong Kong Island, for questioning.

At 07:45 hours that morning, after intensive interrogation, six of the Chinsese were charged with killing the crew of the *Glorious East Wind*, despite their protests that the primary evidence against them, the U.S. Army surplus expolsive, type 4BBx263 PAV, some of which had been found near the ship, had been planted on them.

At 10:00 hours, the six appeared at Central Magistracy to face criminal informations of first-degree murder sworn against their persons by constables of Her Sovereign Majesty the Queen.

The others were held incommunicado for further investigation.

The crisis was ended. The file was closed.

The windowless walk-up on the second floor of a nondescript tenement in Central district was empty for the first time in days. The Uher tape recorders were cleared, the master tapes erased, the working copies destroyed. Seven garbage bags of transcripts were burned in the laneway nearby.

At the same time, the telephone intercept and room probe were discreetly, and neatly, removed from the premises of Number 7 Harlech Road, the home of Henry Szeto.

No one knew who was behind the order to pull the plug and terminate the project. And no one would ever find out.

Certainly it hadn't been Superintendent James Peng. He was taken off the case and transferred to the Police Training School at Aberdeen as an administrative officer to feed the paper mill that was the force's internal communications system.

Nor was it Inspector David Andrews. He was returned to Western, without comment on his file, to continue his uniformed duties. Like James Peng, he was sworn to secrecy and held captive by the clauses of the Official Secrets Act "for the good of the colony."

No. No one would ever find out who stopped the probe before it got off the ground. No one. And that was just the way the new commissioner wanted it to be done. In proper SB style. On a hush-hush, need-to-know basis.

John Cleve stayed at his post for four more days to assist the new commissioner, Robert Maguire, in the transition.

He had time to make several calls; all of them he billed to the force.

The first, to his sister-in-law in England, where the brief note had told him his wife and son Matthew would be staying for a time. The call was short. He had nothing to say to his sister-in-law and apparently Margaret wasn't interested in talking to him.

The second, to his daughter Emily in New Zealand, was

that he'd never seen New Zealand and thought maybe he'd like to. She was pleased.

The last call was to mainland China, to a man he'd never met but who he thought might find the topic of converstion informative, to a man named Kang Shung, head of the Security Branch and the appointed hatchetman in the Dadu corruption scandal.

The converstion, too, was short, yet Cleve savored it, every last morsel he passed on. Dates, pick up and delivery points, contacts, cargo, method of carriage and the name of Szeto's Communist partner—Lee Shiu Shing—in a drug syndicate that, with the explosion of the *Glorious East Wind*, had been dismantled by its own leaders.

Lee apparently had no wish to be the front man, so it must have seemed so simple at the time: close shop and leave no evidence behind. Except, Cleve mused, a key for a hotel room in Macau, the name Hans and a package of cigarettes with a skating Dutch boy on the cover. The sacrificial destruction of a "Communist" vessel to precipitate unrest and thereby isolate radical elements in the people's party? A clever ruse to disguise the end of a vile syndicate whose only reason for being was criminal gain.

A slow smile came to John Cleve's face. Not only would Kang be unable to save his wayward friend now, Cleve thought, he might not even want to try. And he took it as a hopeful sign that he still had enough life in him to enjoy a little revenge.

The Kowloon land? Heads would roll for that too, though perhaps not as readily. Initially, the deeds would stay intact; after all, waterfront properties were valuable. Still, the digging into Proctor's background could air the whole stinking mess of Whitehall's involvement, and that in itself was pauper's justice.

Yes, the land deal. Cleve opened his desk drawer for the last time and took out the only remaining file, labeled "Kowloon Project." He looked through the pages. Neat numbered lists, notes, arrows, diagrams, the product of a point-form mind. What would he do when he had no more files to read, reports to sign, memos to write? Would the real regret be in leaving this, the in-baskets, out-baskets, the circulars that did just that, went around and around?

Burden—he underlined the name. Cleve had just about finished the puzzle. Burden, until recently the owner with Henry Szeto of a nice piece of waterfront property. The gift of it, along with Driscoll's assurances of a "new spirit in Government House, in the Police Force and in the colony at large," may well have resigned Peking to Her Majesty's presence for the time being, and given the Chinese the credibility they needed to quiet radicals calling for more forceful action in the light of the explosion of the *East Wind*, and the colony's apparent inability to cope with the ensuing crisis.

Cleve smiled sadly. Yes, he was indeed the old spirit. And Driscoll, Peking, Burden, Lee Shiu Shing, Szeto and Maguire—they had all, for quite different reasons, decided that his time had come. Hand in glove in hand.

A few calls to the papers, the unions, the unwashed mob, and this uneasy alliance had acted to one end. Cleve almost laughed aloud, that he should have been both the problem and the solution.

Maguire? This would be the kind of revenge best tasted cold. Cleve was still quite sure that until the unfortunate scene in the governor's office, Maguire had been able to think his part noble, that he'd "liaised" with Lee for the betterment of all, not to mention himself. Wasn't "all for the good" one of the director's favorite expressions?

But Maguire the "go-for" would surely be haunted by the rewards of his helpfulness. Yes, Cleve guessed, from the governor's point of view, a commissioner in the hand was worth any number of minor inconveniences.

After a last cup of Mrs. Callicutt's coffee, Cleve turned off the desk lamp, picked up his forage cap and the Kowloon file and left the office.

The coconut buns he left behind, for Hong Kong's next Commissioner of Police.

CHAPTER THIRTY-ONE

D avid went back to Western and tried to work, but his heart wasn't in it anymore. The new CP was a far different breed than the last one, and perhaps it was time to move on. Doors once again closed, silences were longer and more damning, as if the rumor mill that had originally condemned him to solitary exile at Western had started up anew. Sworn to secrecy, he had nowhere to turn, nothing to look forward to. He had begun to brood and become sullen.

So it had come almost as a relief when Peng arrived unannounced one Saturday morning at the Mess, the proposal in his pocket. Their conversation was short and stilted. Circumstances had created a gulf between them that even friendship would not bridge.

With Cleve's resignation, David had finally come to realize the immensity of Driscoll's part in the sordid affair. He wasn't naive. He knew that he couldn't just go to the press and air the dirty washing for all to see. It just wasn't done. But still he had asked Peng what he thought could be done to right the wrongs.

"These things aren't so simple," Peng said. "We just can't go and impeach governors like they do presidents, can we? The system can't stand the stress and strain."

"And the commissioner? Maguire?" David asked.

"The same, I'm afraid." Peng looked away from David's

piercing stare. "He's the most acceptable to Peking. He stays."

Then he handed David an envelope. Inside was an airline ticket to England and a check for several thousand dollars with the notation that it was the balance of his earned gratuity. Attached to it was a simple two paragraph document accepting David's resignation forthwith. His contract with Her Majesty's government would be allowed to lapse.

David signed the buff-colored page and handed it back to Peng. A strange sense of relief overwhelmed him as he did so.

"And what will you do, Jim?" he asked.

"I'll stay, what else? I have no other home. They have my silence for as long as I live here. Besides, I'm a Hong Kong belonger. I have no passport to give me freedom. I'm theirs. But you," he said to David, "it's best you leave. The CP doesn't like it; still, it was one of Cleve's parting requirements that when the storm died down a bit, the Force was to give you safe passage from this cesspool. Cleve always did look after his own."

"Yes." Andrews replied slowly, grasping Peng's hand in a parting gesture. "I suppose he did."

They faced each other for the longest time and then Peng turned and wordlessly walked out the door.

The 747 arced over the checkerboard at Diamond Hill and then headed out over the China Sea, its huge silver wings solid and stately like the sails of a deep sea junk. David looked out his window.

The immensity of Kowloon lay below. The chickenwired rooftop dwellings cramped upon thousands of sweat stained high rises, bamboo washpoles jutting everywhere with rainbows of color. The roads thronging with toylike cars, brilliantly painted double deckers, all spouting clouds of smoke and dirt and grit. The people scurrying everywhere like worker ants frenzied in the sun.

And then the jumbo was out over the sparkling, shimmering waters, with the junks bobbing and the ferries chugging dutifully about. And ocean liners and tramps crowding the channel for as far as the eye could see.

David looked over into the distance, toward the island. His island. With more skyscrapers and tenements and clap trap lean-to's.

And majestic above them all were the hills leading up to the Peak, standing purple and green and graceful for all who would try to master her. And yet for none.

And David Andrews knew he would be gazing at this place for the last time.

For a moment he saw them all. Mei Ling. Cleve. Williams and Peng. And the sergeants and the constables. And all his friends. And yes—even Proctor and his enemies and those he had no emotion for at all. And he knew in his heart that a part of him would remain forever on that tiny island he had called home.

The sun was almost overhead in the sky now. It hung fiery red over the China of Marco Polo and Kublai Khan and Mao. Soon the hills of Hong Kong too will be blood stained jade, Andrews thought sadly. As they were meant to be.

And the finality of that truth turned his heart stone cold.